Three Hands in the Fountain

THREE HANDS IN THE FOUNTAIN

Lindsey Davis

CENTURY · LONDON

Published by Century Books in 1997

3 5 7 9 10 8 6 4

Copyright © Lindsey Davis 1996

Lindsey Davis has asserted her right under the Copyright, Designs and
Patents Act, 1988 to be identified as the author of this work.

First published in the United Kingdom in 1997 by
Century Books Limited
Random House UK Limited
20 Vauxhall Bridge Road, London SW1V 2SA

Random House Australia (Pty) Limited
20 Alfred Street, Milsons Point, Sydney,
New South Wales 2061, Australia

Random House New Zealand Limited
18 Poland Road, Glenfield
Auckland 10, New Zealand

Random House South Africa (Pty) Limited
Endulini, 5a Jubilee Rd, Parktown 2193, South Africa

Random House UK Limited Reg. No. 954009

A CIP catalogue record for this book
is available from the British Library.

Papers used by Random House UK Limited
are natural, recyclable products made from wood grown in
sustainable forests. The manufacturing processes conform to
the environmental regulations of the country of origin.

ISBN 0 71 267791 7

Typeset in Bembo by SX Composing DTP, Rayleigh, Essex
Printed and bound in the United Kingdom by
Mackays of Chatham plc, Chatham, Kent

For Heather and Oliver
my wonderful Agent and Editor
(who really deserve a dedication each):
with my thanks for the first ten
— and here's to ten more!

PRINCIPAL CHARACTERS

Friends and Family

Julia Junilla Laeitana	a baby at the centre of attention
M. Didius Falco	a new father, who is said to need a partner
Helena Justina	his partner at home and at work, a new mother
Nux	her own mistress but a good dog
Falco's mother	a landlady; Julia's doting grandmama
Anacrites	her lodger; a troublemaker on the make
L. Petronius Longus	a troubleshooter, but in trouble
Arria Silvia	his wife, who has just shot him down
D. Camillus Verus	Julia's grandfather, the idealistic senator
Julia Justa	Julia's *other* doting grandmama
Camillus Aelianus	who knows he wants to get married
Camillus Justinus	who seems to have no idea what he wants
Claudia Rufina	whose fortune is what Aelianus wants to marry
Gaius	Falco's nephew, a lad about town
Lollius	his absentee father, who has turned up
Marina	a tunic braid twister, allegedly
Rubella	tough but fair tribune of the Fourth Cohort of vigiles
Fusculus	loyal (but hopeful) stand-in for Petronius
Martinus	jealous but relocated rival for Petro's job
Sergius	whose punishments leave his victims half dead
Scythax	the cohort doctor, who likes his patients alive

Lovers, Supervisors, Victims and Suspects:

Balbina Milvia	the cause of Petro's trouble
Cornella Flaccida	her mother; positively awful (and awfully positive)
Florius	Milvia's husband; completely negative
Anon	a registrar of births; dead miserable
Silvius & Brixius	registrars of the dead; happy types
S. Julius Frontinus	yes; *that* Frontinus! a real person
Statius	an engineer; too important to know or do anything
Bolanus	his assistant, who knows it and does it
Cordus	a public slave hoping for a finder's fee
Caius Cicurrus	a corn chandler who has lost his treasure
Asinia	his wife, a good girl, apparently
Pia	her friend, a bad girl indisputably
Mundus	Pia's lover, a ridiculously poor judge of girls
Rosius Gratus	a very old man who lives out of the way
Aurelia Maesia	his daughter, who likes it that way
Damon	a slow driver with a fast reputation
Titus	no; not *that* one; a lad about the country
Thurius	a surly minion

Some Other Suspects:
250,000 people in the Circus Maximus
Everyone else who has a job connected with the Games
All the inhabitants of Tibur, and the nearby countryside
The man in the street

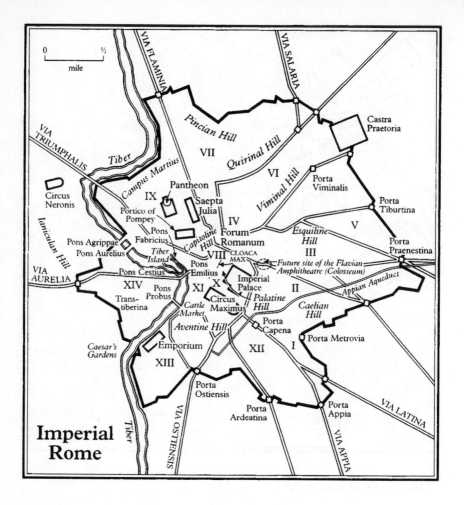

Imperial Rome

Jurisdictions of the Vigiles Cohorts in Rome:

Coh I   Regions VII & VIII (Via Lata, Forum Romanum)
Coh II   Regions III & V (Isis & Serapis, Esquiline)
Coh III   Regions IV & VI (Temple of Peace, Alta Semita)
Coh IV   Regions XII & XIII (Piscina Publica, Aventine)
Coh V   Regions I & II (Porta Capena, Caelimontium)
Coh VI   Regions X & XI (Palatine, Circus Maximus)
Coh VII   Regions IX & XIV (Circus Flaminius, Transtiberina)

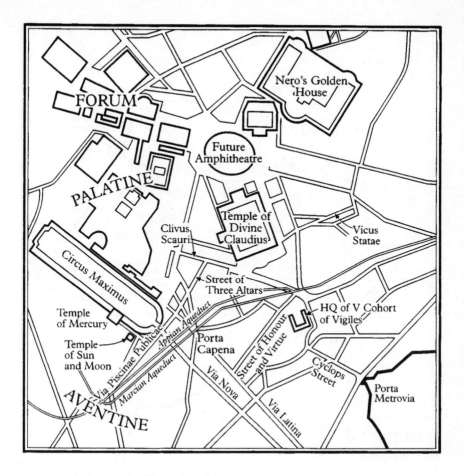

The Circus Maximus Area

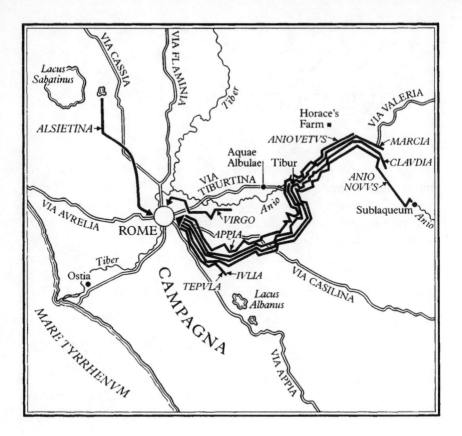

The Roman Campagna

ROME: AUGUST–OCTOBER, AD73

'When [the water pipe] has reached the city, build a reservoir with a distribution tank in three compartments . . . from the central tank pipes will be laid to all the basins as fountains; from the second tank to the baths so they may yield annual income to the state; and from the third, to private houses, so that water for public use will not run short.'

Vitruvius

'I ask you! Just compare with the vast monuments of this vital aqueduct network those useless Pyramids, or the good-for-nothing tourist attractions of the Greeks!'

Frontinus, tr. Trevor Hodge

'Let's have a drink – and leave out the water!'

Petronius Longus of *Falco & Partner*

I

THE FOUNTAIN WAS not working. Nothing unusual in that. This was the Aventine.

It must have been off for some time. The water spout, a crudely moulded cockleshell dangled by a naked but rather uninteresting nymph, was thick with dry pigeon guano. The bowl was cleaner. Two men sharing the bottom of an amphora of badly travelled Spanish wine could lean there without marking their tunics. When Petronius and I sloped back to the party at my apartment, there would be no clues to where we had been.

I had laid the amphora in the empty fountain bowl, point inwards, so we could tilt it on the edge when we wanted to refill the beakers we had sneaked out with us. We had been at it a while now. By the time we ambled home, we would have drunk too much to care what anybody said to us, unless the wigging was very succinctly phrased. As it might be, if Helena Justina had noticed that I had vanished and left her to cope on her own.

We were in Tailors' Lane. We had deliberately turned round the corner from Fountain Court where I lived, so that if any of my brothers-in-law looked down into the street they would not spot us and inflict themselves upon us. None of them had been invited today, but once they heard I was providing a party they had descended on the apartment like flies on fresh meat. Even Lollius the water boatman, who never turned up for anything, had shown his ugly face.

As well as being a discreet distance from home, the fountain in Tailors' Lane was a good place to lean for a heart-to-heart. Fountain Court did not possess its own water supply, any more than Tailors' Lane was home to any garment-sewers. Well, that's the Aventine.

One or two passers-by, seeing us in the wrong street with our heads together, assumed we were conferring about work. They gave us looks that could have been reserved for a pair of squashed rats on the highroad. We were both well-known characters in the

Thirteenth District. Few people approved of either of us. Sometimes we did work together, though the pact between the public and private sector was uneasy. I was an informer and imperial agent, just back from a trip to Baetican Spain for which I had been paid less than originally contracted, although I had made up the deficit with an artistic expenses claim. Petronius Longus lived on a strict salary. He was the enquiry chief of the local cohort of vigiles. Well, he was normally. He had just stunned me by revealing he had been suspended from his job.

Petronius took a hearty swig of wine, then balanced his beaker carefully on the head of the stone wench who was supposed to be delivering water to the neighbourhood. Petro had long arms and she was a small nymph, as well as one with an empty cockleshell. Petro himself was a big, solid, normally calm and competent citizen. Now he stared down the alley with a glum frown.

I paused to slosh more liquor into my own cup. That gave me time to absorb his news while I decided how to react. In the end I said nothing. Exclaiming 'Oh my goodness, old pal!' or 'By Jupiter, my dear Lucius, I cannot believe I heard that correctly' was too much of a cliché. If he wanted to tell me the story he would. If not, he was my closest friend, so if he was playing at guarding his privacy I would appear to go along with it.

I could ask somebody else later. Whatever had happened, he couldn't keep it secret from me for long. Extracting the fine details of scandal was my livelihood.

Tailors' Lane was a typical Aventine scene. Faceless tenement blocks loomed above a filthy, one-cart lane that meandered up here from the Emporium down by the Tiber, trying to find the way to the Temple of Ceres, only to lose itself somewhere on the steep heights above the Probus Bridge. Little near-naked children crouched playing with stones beside a dubious puddle, catching whatever fever was rampant this summer. Somewhere overhead a voice droned endlessly, telling some dreary story to a silent listener who might be driven to run mad with a meat-knife any minute now. We were in deep shade, though aware that wherever the sun could find access the August heat was shimmering. Even here our tunics stuck to our backs.

'Well, I got your letter at last.' Petronius liked to approach a difficult subject by the winding, scenic route.

'What letter?'

'The one telling me you were a father.'

'*What?*'

'Three months to find me – not bad.'

When Helena and I and the new baby sailed back to Rome from Tarraconensis recently it only took eight days at sea and a couple more travelling gently from Ostia. 'That's not possible.'

'You addressed it to me at the station house,' Petronius complained. 'It was passed around the clerks for weeks, then when they decided to hand it over, naturally I wasn't there.' He was laying it on with a mortar trowel – a certain sign of stress.

'I thought it would be safer sent to the vigiles. I didn't know you would have got yourself suspended,' I reminded him. He was not in the mood for logic.

Nobody much was about. For most of the afternoon we had skulked here virtually in private. I was hoping that my sisters and their children, whom Helena and I had invited for lunch in order to introduce them all to our new daughter in one go, would go home. When Petro and I had sneaked out not one of the guests had been showing any sign of leaving. Helena had already looked tired. I should have stayed.

Her own family had had the tact not to come, but had invited us to dinner later in the week. One of her brothers, the one I could tolerate, had brought a message in which his noble parents politely declined our offer of sharing a cold collation with my swarming relatives in our tiny half-furnished apartment. Some of my lot had already tried to sell the illustrious Camilli dud works of art that they couldn't afford and didn't want. Most of my family were offensive and all of them lacked tact. You couldn't hope to find a bigger crowd of loud, self-opinionated, squabbling idiots anywhere. Thanks to my sisters all marrying down I stood no chance of impressing Helena's socially superior crew. In any case, the Camilli didn't want to be impressed.

'You could have written earlier,' Petronius said morosely.

'Too busy. When I did write I'd just ridden eight hundred miles across Spain like a madman, only to be told that Helena was in desperate trouble with the birth. I thought I was going to lose her, and the baby too. The midwife had gone off halfway to Gaul, Helena was exhausted and the girls with us were terrified. I delivered that child myself – and I'll take a long time to get over it!'

Petronius shuddered. Though a devoted father of three himself, his nature was conservative and fastidious. When Arria Silvia was having their daughters she had sent him off somewhere until the screaming was all over. That was his idea of family life. I would receive no credit for my feat.

'So you named her Julia Junilla. After both grandmothers? Falco, you really know how to arrange free nursemaids.'

'Julia Junilla *Laeitana*,' I corrected him.

'You named your daughter after a *wine*?' At last some admiration crept into his tone.

'It's the district where she was born,' I declared proudly.

'You sly bastard.' Now he was envious. We both knew that Arria Silvia would never have let him get away with it.

'So where's Silvia?' I challenged.

Petronius took a long, slow breath and gazed upwards. While he was looking for swallows, I wondered whatever was wrong. The absence of his wife and children from our party was startling. Our families frequently dined together. We had even survived a joint holiday once, though that had been pushing it.

'Where's Silvia?' mused Petro, as if the question intrigued him too.

'This had better be good.'

'Oh, it's hilarious.'

'You do know where she is, then?'

'At home, I believe.'

'She's gone off us?' That would be too much to hope for. Silvia had never liked me. She thought me a bad influence on Petronius. What libel. He had always been perfectly capable of getting into trouble by himself. Still, we all rubbed along, even though neither Helena nor I could stand too much of Silvia.

'She's gone off *me*,' he explained.

A workman was approaching. Typical. He wore a one-sleeved tunic hitched over his belt and was carrying an old bucket. He was coming to clean the fountain, which looked a long job. Naturally he turned up at the end of the working day. He would leave the job unfinished and never come back.

'Lucius, my boy,' I tackled Petro sternly, since we might soon have to abandon our roost if this fellow did persuade the fountain to fill up, 'I can think of various reasons – most of them female – why Silvia would fall out with you. Who is it?'

'Milvia.'

I had been joking. Besides, I thought he had stopped flirting with Balbina Milvia months ago. If he had had any sense he would never

6

have started – though when did that ever stop a man chasing a girl?

'Milvia's very bad news, Petro.'

'So Silvia informs me.'

Balbina Milvia was about twenty. She was astoundingly pretty, dainty as a rosebud with the dew in it, a dark, sweet little piece of trouble whom Petro and I had met in the course of our work. She had an innocence that was begging to be enlightened, and was married to a man who neglected her. She was also the daughter of a vicious gangster – a mobster whom Petronius had convicted and I had helped finally to put away. Her husband Florius was now developing half-hearted plans to move in on the family rackets. Her mother Flaccida was scheming to beat him to the profits, a hard-faced bitch whose idea of a quiet hobby was arranging the deaths of men who crossed her. Sooner or later that was bound to include her son-in-law Florius.

In these circumstances Milvia could be seen as in need of consolation. As an officer of the vigiles Petronius Longus was taking a risk if he provided it. As the husband of Arria Silvia, a violent force to be reckoned with at any time, he was crazy. He should have left the delicious Milvia to struggle with life on her own.

Until today I had been pretending I knew nothing about it. He would never have listened to me anyway. He had never listened when we were in the army and his eye fell on lush Celtic beauties who had large, red-haired, bad-tempered British fathers, and he had never listened since we came home to Rome either.

'You're not in love with Milvia?'

He looked amazed at the question. I had known I was on safe ground suggesting that his fling might not be serious. What was serious to Petronius Longus was being the husband of a girl who had brought him a very handsome dowry (which he would have to repay if she divorced him) and being the father of Petronilla, Silvana and Tadia, who adored him and whom he doted on. We all knew that, though convincing Silvia might be tricky if she had heard about sweet little Milvia. And Silvia had always known how to speak up for herself.

'So what's the situation?'

'Silvia threw me out.'

'What's new?'

'It was a good two months ago.'

I whistled. 'Where are you living, then?' Not with Milvia. Milvia was married to Florius. Florius was so weak even his womenfolk didn't bother to henpeck him, but he was clinging fast to Milvia because *her* dowry – created with the proceeds of organised crime – was enormous.

'I'm at the patrol house.'

'Unless I'm drunker than I think, didn't this whole conversation begin with you being suspended from the vigiles?'

'That,' Petro conceded, 'does make it rather complicated when I want to crawl in for a few hours' kip.'

'Martinus would have loved to take a stand on it.' Martinus had been Petro's deputy. A stickler for the rules – especially when they helped him offend someone else. 'He went on promotion to the Sixth, didn't he?'

Petro grinned a little. 'I put him forward myself.'

'Poor Sixth! So who moved up in the Fourth? Fusculus?'

'Fusculus is a gem.'

'He ignores you curled up in a corner?'

'No. He orders me to leave. Fusculus thinks that taking over Martinus' job means he inherited the attitude as well.'

'Jupiter! So you're stuck for a bed?'

'I wanted to lodge with your mother.' Petronius and Ma had always got on well. They liked to conspire, criticising me.

'Ma would take you in.'

'I can't ask her. She's still putting up Anacrites.'

'Don't mention that bastard!' My mother's lodger was anathema to me. 'My old apartment's empty,' I suggested.

'I was hoping you'd say that.'

'It's yours. Provided,' I put in slyly, 'you explain to me how, if we're talking about a quarrel with your wife, you also end up being suspended by the Fourth. When did Rubella ever have a reason to accuse you of disloyalty?' Rubella was the tribune in charge of the Fourth Cohort, and Petro's immediate superior. He was a pain in the posterior, but otherwise fair.

'Silvia took it upon herself to inform Rubella that I was tangled up with a racketeer's relative.'

Well, he had asked for it, but that was hard. Petronius Longus could not have picked a mistress who compromised him more thoroughly. Once Rubella knew of the affair, he would have had no choice about suspending Petro from duty. Petro would be lucky even to keep his job. Arria Silvia must have understood that. To risk their livelihood she must be very angry indeed. It sounded as if my old friend was losing his wife too.

8

We were too disheartened even to drink. The amphora was down to the grit in the point anyway. But we were not ready to return home in this glum mood. The water board employee had not actually asked us to move out of his way, so we stayed where we were while he leaned around us cleaning the cockleshell spout with a disgusting sponge on a stick. When the plunger failed to work he burrowed in his tool satchel for a piece of wire. He poked and scraped. The fountain made a rude noise. Some sludge plopped out. Slowly water began to trickle through, encouraged by more waggling of the wire.

Petronius and I straightened up reluctantly. In Rome the water pressure is low, but eventually the bowl would fill and then overflow, providing the neighbourhood with not only its domestic supply but an endless trickle down the gutters to carry away muck from the streets. Tailors' Lane badly needed that but, drunk though we were, we didn't want to end up sitting in it.

Petronius applauded the workman sardonically. 'That all the problem was?'

'Seized up while it was off, legate.'

'Why was it off?'

'Empty delivery pipe. Blockage in the outlet at the castellum.'

The man dug his fist into the bucket he had brought with him, like a fisherman pulling out a crab. He came up with a blackened object which he held up by its single clawlike appendage so we could briefly inspect it: something old, and hard to identify, yet disturbingly familiar. He tossed it back in the bucket where it splash-landed surprisingly heavily. We both nearly ignored it. We would have saved ourselves a lot of trouble. Then Petro looked at me askance.

'Wait a moment!' I exclaimed.

The workman tried to reassure us. 'No panic, legate. Happens all the time.'

Petronius and I stepped closer and peered down into the filthy depths of the wooden pail. A nauseous smell rose to greet us. The cause of the blockage at the water tower now reposed in a bed of rubbish and mud.

It was a human hand.

II

NONE OF MY relatives had had the courtesy to leave. More had arrived, in fact. The only good news was, the newcomers did not include my father.

My sisters Allia and Galla made their excuses sniffily the moment I reappeared, though Verontius and bloody Lollius their husbands sat tight. Junia was squeezed into a corner with Gaius Baebius and their deaf son, as usual busy posing as a classic family group so they could avoid talking to anybody else. Mico, Victorina's widower, was grinning inanely and waiting in vain for somebody to tell him how well turned out his horrible offspring were. Famia, the drunk, was drunk. His wife Maia was somewhere in a back room helping Helena clear up. Various children were bored, but doing their best to entertain themselves by kicking dirty boots against my newly painted walls. All present cheered up as they watched me brace myself.

'Hello, Ma. Brought a footman, I see?' If I had been warned in advance I would have hired heavies just to eject this man. A couple of moonlighting gladiators with instructions to turn him away at the door, and break both his arms as an extra hint.

My mother scowled. She was a tiny, black-eyed old bundle who could rampage through a market like a barbarian army. She was holding my new baby daughter, who had begun to bawl her eyes out the moment I appeared. Julia's grief at beholding her father was not why Ma was scowling; I had insulted her favourite.

It was her lodger Anacrites. He looked smooth, but his habits were as savoury as a pigsty after months of neglect. He worked for the Emperor. He was the Chief Spy. He was also pale, silent, and reduced to a wraith after a serious head wound which unfortunately failed to finish him. My mother had saved his life. That meant she now felt obliged to treat him as some special demigod who was worth saving. He accepted the fuss smugly. I ground my teeth.

'Find a friendly greeting for Anacrites, Marcus.' Greet him? He was no friend of mine. He had once arranged to have me killed, though of course that had nothing to do with my loathing him. I could simply find no vacancy in my personal clique for a devious, dangerous manipulator with the morals of a slug.

I grabbed the screaming baby. She stopped crying. No one looked impressed. Against my ear she gurgled in a way I had learned meant she was soon going to be sick down the inside of my tunic. I laid her down in the fine cradle Petronius had made for her, hoping I could pretend any ensuing mess was a surprise to me. Ma began rocking the cradle, and the crisis seemed to pass.

'Hello, Falco.'

'Anacrites! You look terrible,' I told him cheerily. 'Turned back from the Underworld because you'd dirty Charon's punt?' I was determined to floor him before he had a chance to get at me. 'How's espionage these days? All the swallows over the Palatine are cheeping that Claudius Laeta has put a bid in for your job.'

'Oh no; Laeta's skulking in ditches.'

I grinned knowingly. Claudius Laeta was an ambitious adminis-trator at the palace who hoped to incorporate Anacrites and the existing intelligence network in his own section; the two were locked in a struggle for power which I found highly amusing – so long as I could keep myself out of it.

'Poor Laeta!' I sneered. 'He should never have tangled with that Spanish business. I had to make a report to the Emperor which showed him in rather a bad light.'

Anacrites gave me a narrow look. He too had tangled with the Spanish business. He was wondering what I might have reported to Vespasian about *him*. Still convalescent, a film of sweat suddenly shone on his brow. He was worried. I liked that.

'Anacrites isn't fit to return to work yet.' Ma told us some details that had him crawling with embarrassment. I tutted with fake sym-pathy, letting him know that I was delighted he had terrible headaches and trouble with his bowels. I tried asking for further details, but my mother soon twigged what I was playing at. 'He has taken indefinite sick leave, approved by the Emperor.'

'Oho!' I scoffed, as if I thought that was the first step to enforced retirement. 'Some people who get hit very hard on the head have a personality change afterwards.' He seemed to have avoided that; it was a pity, because any change in Anacrites' personality would have been an improvement.

'I brought Anacrites so you and he can have a little chat.' I went cold. 'You'll have to sort out a decent business for yourself now you're a father,' my mother instructed me. 'You need a partner – someone to give you a few tips. Anacrites can help get you on your feet – on days when he feels fit enough.'

Now it was me who felt sick.

Lucius Petronius, my loyal friend, had been surreptitiously showing the dismembered hand from the water tower to my brothers-in-law in a corner. Those ghouls were always eager for anything sensational.

'Pooh!' I heard Lollius boasting. 'That's nothing. We fish worse out of the Tiber every week –'

Some of my sisters' children spotted the grisly item and crowded round to see it. Petro hastily wrapped up the hand in a piece of rag; I hoped it was not one of our new Spanish dinner napkins. It made an intriguing parcel, which caught the eye of Nux, a determined street mongrel who had adopted me. The dog leapt at the parcel. Everyone snatched to save it. The hand fell out of the rag. It landed on the floor, and was captured by Marius, the extremely serious elder son of my sister Maia who just happened to come into the room at that point. When she saw her normally wholesome eight-year-old sniffing at a badly decayed relic, apparently supervised approvingly by Lucius Petronius, my favourite sister used some language I never thought she knew. Much of it described Petronius, and the rest appertained to me.

Maia made sure she snatched up the flagon of fine olive oil which was her present from me from Baetica and then she, Famia, Marius, Ancus, Cloelia and little Rhea all went home.

Well, that cleared some space.

While everyone else was sniggering and looking shifty, Petro threw a heavy arm round my shoulders and greeted my mother with affection. 'Junilla Tacita! How right you are about Falco needing to buckle down. As a matter of fact, he and I have just been outside having a long discussion about that. You know, he seems feckless, but he does recognise his position. He needs to establish his office, take on some lucrative cases and build up a reputation so the work continues to flow in.' That sounded good. I wondered why I had never thought of it. Petronius had not finished his oration. 'We found the ideal solution. While I'm taking a break from the vigiles

I'm going to move into his old apartment – and give him a hand as a partner myself.'

I beamed at Anacrites in a charitable way. 'You're just a fraction too late for the festival. Afraid the job is taken, old fellow. Bad luck!'

III

WHEN WE SLAPPED the parcel on to the clerk's table, Fusculus reached for it eagerly. He had always had a hearty appetite and thought we had brought him in a snack. We let him open it.

For a second he did think it was an interesting new kind of cold sausage, then he recoiled with a yell.

'*Urgh!* Where have you two infantile beggars been playing? Who does this belong to?'

'Who knows?' Petronius had had time to get used to the dismembered hand. While jolly Fusculus still looked pale, Petro could appear blasé. 'No seal ring with a lover's name, no handy Celtic woad tattoo – it's so swollen and misshapen you can't even tell whether it came from a woman or a man.'

'Woman,' guessed Fusculus. He prided himself on his professional expertise. The hand, which had four fingers missing, was so badly swollen from being in water that there were no real grounds for his guess.

'How's work?' Petronius asked him yearningly. I could tell that as a partner in my own business his commitment would be meagre.

'It was all right until you two came in.'

We were at the Fourth Cohort's guard house. Most of it was storage for fire-fighting equipment, reflecting the vigiles' main task. Ropes, ladders, buckets, huge grass mats, mattocks and axes, and the pumping engine, were all ready for action. There was a small bare cell into which cat burglars and arsonists could be flung, and a utilitarian room where those on duty could either play dice or beat all Hades out of the burglars and fire-raisers if that seemed more fun. Both rooms were normally empty at this hour. The holding cell was used at night; in the morning its miserable contents were either released with a caution or marched off to the tribune's office for a formal interrogation. Since most offences occur under cover of darkness only a skeleton staff was on duty by day. They were out searching for suspects – or sitting on a bench in the sun.

Do not be fooled. The vigiles' life was harsh and dangerous. Most of them had been public slaves. They had signed up because eventually, if they survived, they earned honourable discharge as citizens. Their official term of duty was just six years. Soldiers in the legions serve at least twenty. There was a good reason for the short enlistment, and not many vigiles lasted the full term.

Tiberius Fusculus, the best of Petro's hand-picked officers and now standing in for his chief, gazed at us warily. He was a round, cheerful fellow, thin on top, extremely healthy, and sharp as a tenting needle. He was keenly interested in the theory of crime, but we could tell by the way he poked the swollen hand away from him he did not intend to pursue this if he could file it in the 'No Action' pigeonhole.

'So what do you want me to do with it?'

'Find the rest?' I suggested. Fusculus scoffed.

Petronius surveyed the object. 'It has obviously been in the water a long time.' His tone was apologetic. 'We've been told it was found blocking a pipe in a castellum on the Aqua Appia, but it could have got there from somewhere else.'

'Most people are cremated,' Fusculus said. 'You might get some dog digging up a human hand at the crossroads in a village in the provinces, but bodies don't get buried raw in Rome.'

'It smacks of dirty business,' Petro agreed. 'If someone, possibly a woman, has been done in, why hasn't there been an outcry?'

'Probably because women are always being done in,' Fusculus explained helpfully. 'It's their husbands or lovers who do it, and when they wake up sober the men either collapse in remorse and come straight here to confess, or else they find the peace and quiet so welcome that raising an outcry is the last thing they consider.'

'All women have nosy friends,' Petro pointed out. 'A lot have interfering mothers; some are caring for aged aunts who if left on their own would wander out into the highway and frighten the donkeys. And what about the neighbours?'

'The neighbours report it,' said Fusculus. 'So we go to the house and ask the husband; he tells us that the neighbours are poisonous bastards making malicious accusations, then he claims his wife has gone to visit relatives at Antium. We say, when she comes home will he ask her to drop in and confirm it; we file the details; she never comes, but we never have time to pursue it because by then twenty other things are happening. Anyway, the husband will have run off.' He did not add and 'good luck to him', but his tone was eloquent.

'Don't give me the brush-off; I'm not some member of the public.' Petronius was discovering how the public felt when they ventured to his office. He sounded annoyed, probably at himself for not having been prepared for it.

Fusculus was faultlessly polite. He had been putting off the public for the past fifteen years. 'If there has been a crime it could have happened anywhere, sir, and the chances of us picking up the rest of the body are nil.'

'You're not keen on this,' I divined.

'Clever man.'

'The evidence turned up on the Aventine.'

'A lot of filth turns up on the Aventine,' snorted Fusculus sourly, almost as if he included us in that category. 'This isn't evidence, Falco. Evidence is a material object that casts useful light on a known incident, enabling a prosecution. We have no idea where this forlorn fist came from, and I bet we never will. If you ask me,' he went on, evidently thinking he had found an inspired solution, 'it must have been polluting the water supply, so tracing any other body parts is a problem for the water board. I'll report the find. It's up to the Curator of Aqueducts to take action.'

'Don't be stupid,' scoffed Petro. 'When did anyone in the water board ever show any initiative? They're all too busy working fiddles.'

'I'll threaten to expose a few. Any sign of you coming back to work, chief?'

'Ask Rubella,' growled Petro, though I knew the tribune had said my foolish pal was to ditch the gangster's daughter before showing his face around the cohort again. Unless I had missed something, that still left Petro with a goodbye speech to make to Milvia.

'I heard you were in business with Falco nowadays?' For a pleasant man, Fusculus seemed to be in a starchy mood. I was not surprised. Informers have a black name amongst most Romans, but we are particularly reviled by the vigiles. The cohorts keep lists with our names on so they can knock on our doors halfway through dinner and drag us off for questioning about nothing in particular. State servants always hate people who are paid by results.

'I'm just helping him out informally. Why – do you miss me?' Petro asked.

'No, I'm just wondering when I can apply for your post.' It was said in jest, but the fact was, unless Petronius Longus sorted out his private life rather quickly the joke would become fact. Warning him, though, would only make it worse. Petronius had a stubborn side. He had always had a tendency to rebel against authority. It was why we were friends.

The Fourth kept a gruesome museum which they showed to the populace for half a denarius a throw, in order to raise cash for the widows of cohort members. We left the hand for the museum, and told ourselves it was no longer our problem.

Petronius and I then walked via the Circus Maximus to the Forum, where we had an appointment with a wall.

IV

F I HAD had any sense, I would have ended the partnership while
we were standing in front of the wall. I would have told Petro
that although I was grateful for his offer, the best way for us to preserve our friendship would be if I just let him doss at my apartment.
I would work with someone else. Even if that meant pairing up
with Anacrites.

The omens were bad from the very start. My normal method of
advertising my services was to march up to the foot of the Capitol,
quickly clean off someone else's poster from the best position on the
Tabularium, then scrawl up a few swift strokes of chalk, writing whatever jocular message came into my head. Petronius Longus approached
life more seriously. He had written out a text. He had worked up
several versions (I could see the evidence in his note tablets) and he
intended to inscribe his favourite in meticulous lettering, surrounded
by a Greek key border drawn in variously hatched patterns.

'No point making it pretty.'

'Don't be so casual, Falco.'

'The aediles will wash it off again.'

'We need to get it right.'

'No, we need to avoid getting spotted doing it.' Chalking graffiti
on national monuments may not be a crime in the Twelve Tables,
but it can lead to a right thrashing.

'I'll do this.'

'I can write my name and mention divorce and stolen art recovery.'

'We're not dabbling with art.'

'It's my speciality.'

'That's why you never earn anything.'

It could be true. People who had lost their treasures were slow to
pay out more money. Besides, the ones who lost art were often the
mean sort. That was why it had not been protected by decent locks
and alert watchmen in the first place.

'All right, Pythagoras, what's your philosophy? What stunning list of services will you claim we perform?'

'I'm not quoting examples. We need to tantalise. We should hint we cover everything. When the clients come we can weed out the duds and pass them on to some hack at the Saepta Julia. We're going to be *Didius Falco & Partner* —'

'Oh, you're staying anonymous?'

'I have to.'

'So you still want your job back?'

'There was never any suggestion of giving up my job.'

'Just checking. Don't work with me if you despise my life.'

'Shut up a minute. *Falco & Partner: a select service for discerning clients.*'

'Sounds like a cheap brothel.'

'Have faith, lad.'

'Or an overpriced shoemaker. *Falco & Partner: try our triple-stitched calfskin slipperettes. As worn by all decadent layabouts, sheer luxury at the arena and the perfect lounging shoes for orgies* —'

'You're a dog, Falco.'

'Subtlety is fine, but unless you give some delicate hint that we carry out enquiries, and that we rather like to be paid for it, we'll get no work.'

'Listen — *Partners' personal attention may be possible in certain instances.* That implies we are a sound organisation with a large staff who look after the riffraff; we can flatter each punter into believing *he* gets special terms — for which he naturally pays a premium.'

'You have an exotic view of the freelance world.' He was revelling in it. 'Listen, scribe, you still haven't said —'

'Yes I have. It's in my draft. *Specialist enquiries.* Then in small letters at the bottom I'll put *No charge for preliminary consultation.* That lures them in, thinking they'll get something for nothing, but hints at our steep fee for the rest.'

'My fees have always been reasonable.'

'So who's the fool? Half the time you let yourself be bamboozled into doing the work for nothing. You're soft, Falco.'

'Not any longer, apparently.'

'Give me some room here. Don't stand in my way.'

'You're taking charge,' I accused him. 'It's my business, but you're pushing in.'

'That's what a partner is for,' grinned Petro.

I told him I had another appointment somewhere else.

'Push off then,' he murmured, completely absorbed in his task.

V

For my next appointment a formal escort had been provided: my girlfriend, the baby, and Nux the dog.

I was late. They were sitting on the steps of the Temple of Saturn. It was a very public place, at the north end of the Forum on the Palatine side. They were all hot. The baby wanted feeding, the dog was barking at everybody who passed, and Helena Justina had applied her extra-patient face. I was in for it.

'Sorry. I called at the Basilica to put the word around the barristers that I was back in town. It may bring in the odd subpoena delivery.'

Helena thought I had been at a wineshop. 'Don't worry,' she said. 'I realise that registering your firstborn child takes a low priority in your busy life.'

I patted the dog, kissed Helena's warm cheek, and tickled the baby. This overheated, irritable little group was my family. All of them had grasped that my role as the head of their household was to keep them waiting in uncomfortable locations while I pottered around Rome enjoying myself.

Luckily Helena, their tribune of the people, was saving up her comments until she had a complete set to blast me with. She was a tall, well-rounded, dark-haired dream with rich brown eyes whose most tender expression could melt me like a honeycake left on a sunny window sill. Even the scathing glance I was meeting now rattled my calm. A fiery tussle with Helena was the best fun I knew, outside of bedding her.'

The Temple of Saturn lies between the Tabularium and the Basilica Julia. I had guessed Helena Justina would be waiting at the Temple, so when I left Petro I had dodged round the back on the Via Nova to avoid being seen. I hate barristers, but their work might make the difference between survival and going under. Frankly, my financial situation was desperate. I said nothing, so as not to worry Helena; she squinted at me suspiciously.

I tried to climb into my toga in public view, while Nux leapt at the cumbersome folds of woollen cloth, thinking this was a game I had organised just for her. Helena made no attempt to help.

'I do not need to see the child,' sighed the Censor's clerk. He was a government slave, and his lot was gloomy. Faced with a constant stream of the public through his office he had a continual cold. His tunic had first belonged to a much larger man, and he had been dealt a rough throw of the dice by whoever shaved his beard. His eyes had a Parthian squint about them, which in Rome cannot have won him many friends.

'Or the mother, I suppose?' snorted Helena.

'Some like to come.' He could be tactful, if it helped avoid verbal abuse.

I placed Julia Junilla on his desk, where she kicked her legs and gurgled. She knew how to please the crowd. She was three months old now, and in my opinion starting to look pretty cute. She had lost the squashed, shut-eyed, unformed look with which the new-born frighten first-time parents. When she stopped dribbling she was only one stage away from adorable.

'Please remove your baby,' mouthed the clerk. Tactful, but not friendly. He unravelled a scroll of thick parchment, prepared an inferior one (our copy), and applied himself to filling a pen from a well of oakgall ink. He had black and red; we were favoured with black. I wondered what the difference was.

He dipped the pen then touched it to the lip of the well to release unnecessary ink. His gestures were precise and formal. Helena and I cooed over our daughter while he steadily wrote the date for the entry that would confer her civic status and rights. 'Name?'

'Julia Junilla –'

He looked up sharply. 'Your name!'

'Marcus Didius Falco, son of Marcus. Citizen of Rome.' It did not impress him. He must have heard the Didii were a swarm of quarrelsome roughnecks. Our ancestors may have caused trouble for Romulus, but being offensive for centuries doesn't count as a pedigree.

'Rank?'

'Plebeian.' He was already writing it.

'Address?'

'Fountain Court, off the Via Ostiana on the Aventine.'

'The mother's name?' He was still addressing me.

'Helena Justina,' the mother crisply answered for herself.

'Mother's father's name?' The clerk continued to aim his questions at me, so Helena gave in with an audible crunch of teeth. Why waste breath? She let a man do the work.

'Decimus Camillus Verus.' I realised I was going to be stuck if the clerk wanted her father's father's personal name.

Helena realised it too. 'Son of Publius,' she muttered, making it plain she was telling me in private and the clerk could go begging. He wrote it down without a thank you.

'Rank?'

'Patrician.'

The clerk looked up again. This time he let himself scrutinise both of us. The Censor's office was responsible for public morals. 'And where do you live?' he demanded, directly of Helena.

'Fountain Court.'

'Just checking,' he murmured, and resumed his task.

'She lives with me,' I pointed out unnecessarily.

'Apparently so.'

'Want to make something of it?'

Once again the clerk raised his eyes from the document. 'I am sure you are both fully aware of the implications.'

Oh yes. And in a decade or two there would no doubt be tears and tantrums when we tried explaining them to the child.

Helena Justina was a senator's daughter and I was one of the plebs. She had married once, unhappily, at her own level in society, then after her divorce she had had the luck or the misfortune to meet and fall for me. After a few false moves we decided to live together. We intended to make it permanent. That decision made us, by strict legal definitions, married.

In real social terms we were a scandal. If the excellent Camillus Verus had chosen to make trouble over my theft of his noble daughter, my life could have been extremely difficult. Hers too.

Our relationship was our business, but Julia's existence called for a change. People kept asking us when we intended marrying, but there was no need for formality. We were both free to marry and if we both chose to live together that was all the law required. We had considered denying it. In that case our children would take their mother's social rank, although any advantage was theoretical. As long as their father lacked honorific titles to cite on public occasions, they would be stuck in the mud like me.

So when we came home from Spain we had decided to

acknowledge our position publicly. Helena had stepped down to my level. She knew what she was doing: she had seen my style of life, and faced up to the consequences. Our daughters were debarred from good marriages. Our sons stood no chance of holding public office, no matter how much their noble grandfather the senator would like to see them stand for election. The upper class would close against them, while the lower ranks would probably despise them as outsiders too.

For the sake of Helena Justina and our children, I accepted my duty to improve my position. I had tried to achieve the middle rank, which would minimise awkwardness. The attempt had been a disaster. I was not intending to make a fool of myself again. Even so, everyone else was determined that I should.

The Censor's clerk surveyed me as if he were having second thoughts. 'Have you completed the Census?'

'Not yet.' I would be dodging it if possible. The point of Vespasian's new Census was not to count heads out of bureaucratic curiosity, but to assess property for tax. 'I've been abroad.'

He gave me the old *they all say that* expression. 'Military service?'

'Special duties.' Since he did not query it, I added tantalisingly, 'Don't ask me to specify.' He still didn't care.

'So you haven't reported yet? Are you head of a family?'

'Yes.'

'Father dead?'

'No such luck.'

'You are emancipated from your father's authority?'

'Yes,' I lied. Pa would never dream of doing anything so civilised. It made no difference to me, however.

'Didius Falco, are you to your knowledge and belief, and by your own intention, living in a valid state of marriage?'

'Yes.'

'Thanks.' His interest was cursory. He had only asked me to cover his own tracks.

'You should ask me the same question,' Helena sniped.

'Heads of household only,' I said, grinning at her. She regarded her role in our household as at least equal to my own. So did I, since I knew what was good for me.

'Name of the child?' The clerk's indifference suggested that mismatched couples like us turned up every week. Rome was supposed to be a moral sink, so perhaps it was true – though we had never encountered anyone else who took the same risks so openly. For one thing, most women born into luxury cling on to it. And most men who try to lure them away from home get beaten up by troops of very large slaves.

'Julia Junilla Laeitana,' I said proudly.

'Spelling?'

'J-U–'

He looked up in silence.

'L,' said Helena patiently, as if aware that the man she lived with was an idiot, 'A-E-I-T-A-N-A.'

'Three names? This is a girl child?' Most females had two names.

'She needs a good start in life.' Why did I feel I was having to apologise? I had the right to name her as I chose. He scowled. He had had enough of whimsical young parents for one day.

'Birthdate?'

'Seven days before the Kalends of June –'

This time the clerk flung his pen down on the table. I knew what had upset him. 'We accept registrations on the naming day only!'

I was supposed to name a daughter within eight days of her birth. (It was nine days for boys; as Helena said, men need longer for everything.) Custom decreed that a family trip to the Forum for a birth certificate would be made at the same time. Julia Junilla had been born in May; it was August now. The clerk had his standards. He would not permit such a flagrant breach of the rules.

VI

IT TOOK ME an hour to explain why my child had been born in Tarraconensis. I had done nothing wrong and this was nothing unusual. Trade, the army and imperial business take plenty of fathers abroad; strong-minded womenfolk (especially those who regard foreign girls as a walking temptation) go with them. In summer most births in self-respecting families occur at fancy villas outside Rome in any case. Even being born outside Italy is perfectly acceptable; only parental status matters. I did not intend my daughter to lose her civic rights because the inconvenient timing of an investigation for the Palace had forced us to introduce her to the world at a distant port called Barcino.

I had taken all the steps I could. Various freeborn women had been present at the birth and could act as witnesses. I had immediately notified the town council at Barcino (who ignored me as a foreigner) and I had made a formal declaration within the proper time limit at the provincial governor's residence in Tarraco. I had the bastard's seal on a blurred chit to prove it.

There was an obvious cause for our problem today. Public slaves receive no official stipend for their duties. Naturally I had come equipped with the usual ex gratia offering, but the clerk thought that if he made things look difficult he could garner a more spectacular tip than usual. The hour's argument was needed to persuade him that I had no more money.

He started weakening. Julia then remembered she wanted to be fed, so she screwed up her little eyes and screamed as if she were practising for when she grew up and wanted to go to parties that I disapproved of. She received her certificate without further delay.

Rome is a masculine city. Places where a respectable woman can feed her young child modestly are rare. That is because respectable nursing mothers are supposed to stay at home. Helena disapproved of staying at home. Perhaps it was my fault for not providing a more alluring habitat. She also despised suckling the baby at the women's latrines, and seemed in no mood to proffer an as to gain entry to the women's baths. So we ended up hiring a carrying chair, making sure it had window curtains. If there was one thing that grated on me more than paying for a chair, it was paying for it to go nowhere.

'That's all right,' Helena soothed me. 'We can take a trip. You don't have to stand on guard outside feeling embarrassed.'

The child had to be nourished. Besides, I was proud of the fact that Helena was high-mindedly feeding Julia herself. Many women of her status praise the idea but pay a wetnurse instead. 'I'll wait.'

'No, ask the men to carry us to the Atrium of Liberty,' Helena ordered decisively.

'What's at the Atrium?'

'It's where they store the overflow archive of the Censor's records office. Including notices of the dead.' I knew that.

'Who's died?' I had guessed what she was up to, but I hated being shoved into things.

'That's what you have to find out, Marcus.'

'Pardon me?'

'The hand that you and Petro found? I'm not suggesting you will be able to trace its owner, but there must be a clerk who can at least tell you the procedure when a person disappears.'

I said I had had enough of clerks, but we were all carried off to the Atrium of Liberty anyway.

Like funeral directors, the clerks in the death notice section were a chirpy lot, a bright contrast to their surly colleague registering births. I knew a couple of them already, Silvius and Brixius. Informers are often sent to the Atrium archives by heirs or executors of wills. It was the first time I had shuffled into their office with my stately girl-friend, a sleeping baby, and a curious dog, however. They took it well, presuming that Helena was my client – a pushy one who insisted on supervising my every move. Apart from the fact that I would not be sending her an invoice, that was close.

They worked in the same cubicle, swapping bad jokes and scrolls as if they had no idea what they were doing; on the whole I thought they were efficient. Silvius was about forty, slim and neat. Brixius was younger but favoured the same short hairstyle and elaborate tunic belt. It was pretty clear they had a sexual relationship. Brixius was the soppy one who wanted to dandle Julia. Silvius, putting on a show of tart annoyance, dealt with me.

'I'm seeking general information, Silvius.' I explained about the discovery of the hand, and that Petronius and I were now curious. 'Looks like a blind alley. If a person goes missing, and it's reported to the vigiles, they keep a note, but I wouldn't like to speculate how long the scroll stays active. Whether they pursue the issue depends on a lot of things. But that's not the problem. This relic is in no condition to be identified. It may be ages old, too.'

'So how can we help?' asked Silvius, suspiciously. He was a public slave. He spent his life trying to think up novel ways of referring requests for information to a different department. 'Our records relate to whole personalities, not unpleasant portions of their anatomy.'

'Suppose we had found a whole body, then. If it was nameless, and stayed so, would it be recorded here?'

'No. It could be a foreigner or a slave. Why would anyone want to know about them? We only register the extinction of known Roman citizens.'

'All right; consider it from the other end. What if somebody goes missing? A citizen, one of the three ranks? When their anguished relatives reach the point where they are forced to assume the person is dead, do they come to you?'

'They might. It's up to them.'

'How?'

'If they want a formal record of their loss, they can ask for a certificate.'

'It's not needed for any official purpose, though?'

Silvius consulted Brixius with a glance. 'If the missing person was a head of household, the certificate would confirm to the Treasury that he had ceased to be liable for taxation, by virtue of paying his debts in Hades. Death is the only acknowledged let-off.'

'Very droll.'

'A formal certificate is not relevant for the will?' Helena put in.

I shook my head. 'Executors can decide to open the will whenever it seems reasonable.'

'What if they make a mistake, Marcus?'

'If a false report of a death is made to the censors deliberately,' I said, 'or if a will is knowingly opened before time, that's a serious offence: theft and probably conspiracy, in the case of the will. A genuine mistake would be viewed leniently, I imagine. What would you do, lads, if a person you had listed as dead turned up unexpectedly after all?'

Silvius and Brixius shrugged, saying it would be a matter for their superiors. They regarded their superiors as idiots, of course.

I was not interested in mistakes. 'When people come to register, they don't have to prove the death?'

'Nobody has to *prove* it, Falco. They make a solemn declaration; it's their duty to tell the truth.'

'Oh honesty's a *duty!*'

Silvius and Brixius tutted at my irony.

'There doesn't have to be a body?' Helena was particularly curious because her father's younger brother, who was certainly dead but had been given no funeral as his body had disappeared.

Trying not to remember that I personally had dropped the rotting cadaver of Helena's treacherous uncle down a sewer to avoid complications for the Emperor, I said, 'There could be many reasons for not having a body. War, loss at sea –' That was what had been given out by the family about Helena's Uncle Publius.

'Vanishing among the barbarians,' trilled Silvius.

'Running off with the baker,' supplied Brixius, who was more cynical.

'Well, that's the kind of case I'm talking about,' I said. 'Someone who disappears for no known reason. They *may* be an eloping adulterer – or they may have been abducted and murdered.'

'Sometimes people deliberately choose to vanish,' said Brixius. 'The pressure of their lives becomes intolerable, and they flit. They may come home one day – or never.'

'So what if a relative actually admits to you that someone is not stiffening on a bier but only missing?'

'If they really believe the person is dead they should just report that.'

'Why? What do you do to them otherwise?' smiled Helena.

He grinned. 'We have ways of making life extremely difficult! But if the circumstances seem reasonable, we issue a certificate in the normal way.'

'Normal?' I queried. 'What – no little stars in the margin? No funny-coloured ink? No listing in a special scroll?'

'Ooh!' shrieked Silvius. 'Falco wants a squint at our special scroll!'

Brixius leaned back on one elbow, surveying me playfully. 'What special scroll would that be, Falco?'

'The one where you list dubious reports that may pop up as trouble later.'

'Why, that's a good idea. I might put that forward as a staff suggestion and get the Censors to instigate the system by edict.'

'We have enough systems,' groaned Silvius.

'Exactly. Listen, Falco,' Brixius explained cheerfully, 'if something looks stinky, any clerk with all his acorns just writes it up as if he hadn't noticed. That way, if there ever are nasty repercussions he can always claim it smelt perfectly sweet at the time.'

'What I'm trying to ascertain,' I ploughed on, realising it was hopeless, 'is whether if anyone goes missing in Rome, you might hold any useful information here?'

'No,' said Brixius.

'No,' agreed Silvius.

'The register of deaths is a revered tradition,' Brixius went on. 'There has never been any suggestion that it might actually serve useful purposes.'

'Fair enough.' I was getting nowhere. Well, I was used to that.

Helena asked Brixius to hand the baby back, and we went home.

VII

I KNEW HELENA was remembering her dead uncle. I needed to avoid awkward questions in view of what I had done with him. I produced the excuse that I ought to check up on Petronius Longus. Since I would only be across the street it sounded harmless and she agreed.

My old apartment, the one I was now lending to Petro, was on the sixth floor of a truly unpleasant tenement. This block of gloomy rentals jutted like a bad tooth over Fountain Court, blotting out the light as effectively as it was blotting out its tenants' hope of happiness. The ground-level space was taken up by a laundry run by Lenia, who had married the landlord Smaractus. We had all warned her not to do it, and sure enough within a week she had been asking me whether I thought she should divorce him.

Most of that week she had been sleeping alone. Her unsavoury beloved had been accused of arson and incarcerated by the vigiles following an accident with the wedding torches, which had set ablaze the nuptial bed. Everyone thought it was hilarious – except Smaractus, who had been badly singed. Once the vigiles released him he turned nasty, a facet of his character which Lenia claimed had come as a complete surprise to her. Those of us who had been paying him rent for years knew differently.

They were still married. It had taken Lenia years to decide to share her fortune with him, and it was likely to be just as long before she gave him the shove. Until then her old friends were stuck with having to listen to endless debates on the subject.

Ropes of damp linen hung across the entrance, allowing me to skip lightly past and up the stairs before Lenia noticed me. But Nux, that frowsty bundle, scampered straight in, barking madly. There were outraged yells from the tub-treaders and carding girls, then Nux raced back out again, trailing somebody's toga and pursued by Lenia herself.

She was a wild-eyed, snaggle-haired fury who carried too much

weight but was otherwise pretty muscular from her trade. Her hands
and feet were swollen and red from being in warm water all day; her
hair made a flamboyant pretence of being red too. Gasping a little,
she roared obscenities after my hound, who hared off across the road.

Lenia picked up the toga. She shook it lethargically, trying not to
notice the dirt it had just acquired. 'Oh, you're back, Falco.'

'Hello, you old bag of malice. How's the dirty clothes business?'

'Stinking as usual.' She had a voice that could have carried
halfway to the Palatine, with all the sweetness of a one-note trum-
pet giving the orders in a legionary parade. 'Did you tell that bastard
Petronius he could doss upstairs?'

'I said he could. We're working together now.'

'Your mother was here with that pet snake of hers. According to
her you'll be working for him.'

'Lenia, I haven't done what my mother told me for at least
twenty years.'

'Big talk, Falco!'

'I work *for* myself – and *with* persons I select on the basis of their
skill, application, and amiable habits.'

'Your ma says Anacrites will keep you up to the mark.'

'And I say he can wind himself on to a catapult and wang himself
over the Tiber.'

Lenia laughed. Her mirth contained a mocking note. She knew
the hold Ma had over me – or thought she did.

I arrived upstairs out of breath, out of practice for the climb.
Petronius seemed surprised it was only me. For some reason he supposed that having drawn up a strikingly attractive advertisement in
the Forum he would be inundated with sophisticated clients all seeking his help with intriguing legal claims. Of course none had come.

'Did you put our address?'

'Don't make me weep, Falco.'

'Well, did you?'

'Yes.' A vague look crossed his face.

The apartment looked smaller and shabbier than ever. There were
two rooms, one for sleep and one for everything else, plus a balcony.
That had what Smaractus described as a river view. It was true, if
you were prepared to sit in a permanent twist on its wonky ledge.
There was room to perch on a bench out there with a girlfriend, but
it was wise not to wriggle about too much in case the brackets
holding up the balcony sheared off.

The only things I had thought worth taking away when Helena and I moved across the street were my bed, an antique tripod table Helena had once bought for me, and our collection of kitchenware (not exactly imperial equipment). That meant there was now nothing to sleep on, but Petro had created a neat floor-level nest for himself with some sort of bedding roll he had probably kept from our army days. A few clothes were hung on the hooks I had knocked in when I lived there. A stool was set pedantically with his personal toilet things: comb, toothpick, and strigil and oilflask for the baths.

In the outer room nothing much had altered. There was a table, a bench, a small brick cooking range, a couple of lamps, and a bucket for slops. On the griddle sat an extremely well-scoured mess tin that I failed to recognise. On the table were ranged a redware bowl with matching beaker, a spoon and a knife. More organised than I had ever been, Petronius had already bought in a loaf, eggs, dried beans, salt, pine nuts, olives, a lettuce, and a small collection of sesame cakes. He had a sweet tooth.

'Come in. Well, Marcus, my boy; this is like old times.' My heart sank. Of course I was nostalgic for the old days of freedom, of women, drink, and careless irresponsibility . . . Nostalgia was pleasant, but that was all. People move on. If Petronius wanted to regress to being a lad again, he was on his own. I had learned to enjoy clean bedding and regular meals.

'You know how to camp out.' I wondered how soon the novelty would fade.

'It's not necessary to live in squalor as you did.'

'My way of life as a bachelor was perfectly respectable.' It had had to be. I had spent much of the time trying to lure women into the apartment with fake tales of its fantastic amenities. They all knew I was lying, but the spell I spun made them expect certain standards. Anyway, they had all heard that even after I left home my mother took care of me. 'Ma put the fear of all Hades into the roaches. And Helena kept us very smart once she moved in.'

'I had to sweep under the cooking bench.'

'Don't be an old biddy. Nobody sweeps under there.'

Petronius Longus stretched his tall frame. He hit the ceiling and swore briefly. I warned him that if he had been in the bedroom he would have gone through the roof tiles, possibly dislodging some and killing people in the street, causing their relatives to sue him. Before he could start criticising my choice of apartment, I said, 'I can see one startling omission from the bijou housekeeping: no amphorae.'

A black look darkened Petro's face. I realised all his wine must be back at the house Silvia still occupied. She would know what depriving him of it meant to him. If their dispute remained acrimonious Petronius could have seen the last of his wonderful ten-year collection. He looked sick.

Luckily there was still an old half-amphora of mine hidden under the floorboards. I pulled it out quickly and sat him out on the balcony in the evening sun to apply himself to forgetting his tragedy.

I was still intending to go home to dine with Helena, but somehow bolstering Petro took longer than I expected. He was deeply depressed. He was missing his children. He was missing the vigiles even more. He was furious with his wife, but unable to rant at her since she wouldn't speak to him. He already harboured suspicions about working with me. Uncertainty about his future had started to gnaw at him, so instead of being full of anticipation about his new life he was beginning to grow truculent.

I let him take the lead with the wine, a role he assumed with panache.

Soon we had both drunk enough to start arguing once more about the dismembered hand. Then there was nothing for it but to brood on the condition of society, the brutality of the city, the harshness of life, and the cruelty of women.

'How did the cruelty of women creep in there?' I pondered. 'Fusculus says that hand is almost certainly a woman's – so it was probably hacked off by an angry man.'

'Don't be pernickety.' Petro had plenty of theories about how brutal women were, and was liable to relate them for hours if I allowed it.

I sidetracked him with my abortive enquiries at the Atrium of Liberty. 'So that's it, Petro. Some poor bitch is dead. Dead and unburied. Jointed like a roast, then flung into the water supply.'

'We ought to do something.' It was the violent declamation of a man who had forgotten to eat, although he remembered what a wine cup was for.

'What, for instance?'

'Find out more about this corpse – like where the rest of it is.'

'Oh, who knows?' My head was swimming more than my conscience liked. I felt none too keen on tripping down six flights of stairs then up a few more on the opposite side of the street to reach Helena and home.

'Somebody knows. Somebody did it. He's laughing. He thinks he's got away with it.'

'He has, too.'

'Falco, you're a miserable pessimist.'

'A realist.'

'We're going to find him.'

It was now clear we were going to get very drunk indeed.

'You can find him.' I tried to rise. 'I have to go and see my wife and baby.'

'Yes.' Petro was magnanimous, with all the despairing self-sacrifice of the newly bereaved and the heavily drunk. 'Never mind me. Life has to go on. Go and see little Julia and Helena, my boy. Lovely baby. Lovely lady. You're a lucky man, a lovely man –'

I couldn't leave him. I sat down again.

Thoughts persisted in my old friend's head, spinning round and round like off-balance planets. 'That hand was given to us because we are the lads who can sort this.'

'It was given to us because we stupidly asked what it was, Petro.'

'But that's it exactly. We asked the question. That's what this is all about, Marcus Didius: being in the right place and asking the apt question. Wanting answers, too. Here are some more questions: how many more bits of body are there floating like shrimps in the city water supply?'

I joined in: 'How many bodies?'

'How long have they been there?'

'Who will co-ordinate finding even the other parts of this one?'

'Nobody.'

'So we start from the opposite end of the puzzle. How do you track down a missing person in a city that never devised a procedure for finding lost souls?'

'Where all the administrative units remain strictly pigeonholed?'

'If the person was killed, and if it happened in a different part of the city from where the severed hand turned up, who ought to be responsible for investigating the crime?'

'Only us – if we're stupid enough to take the job.'

'Who will bother to ask us?' I demanded.

'Only a friend or relative of the deceased.'

'They may not have any friends – or any who care where they are.'

34

'A prostitute.'

'Or a runaway slave.'

'A gladiator?'

'No – they have trainers who want to protect their investment. Those bastards keep track of any missing men. An actor or actress, perhaps.'

'A foreigner visiting Rome.'

'There may be any number of people looking for lost relatives,' I said sadly. 'But in a city of a million people, what are the chances they will hear we found an ancient mitt? And even if they do, how can we ever identify something like that?'

'We'll advertise,' Petronius decided. He thought that was the answer to everything.

'Dear gods, no. We would get thousands of useless replies. What would we be advertising for, anyway?'

'Other parts of the puzzle.'

'Other parts of the body?'

'Maybe the rest is still alive, Falco.'

'So we're looking for someone one-handed?'

'If they're alive. A corpse won't answer an advertisement.'

'Neither will a killer. You're drunk.'

'So are you.'

'Then I'd better stagger across the road.'

He tried to convince me that I ought to stay there and get sober first. I had been on enough bouts to know the folly of that one.

It felt extremely odd, finding Petronius Longus acting like a reprobate bachelor who wanted an all-night party, while I was the sober head of household seeking an excuse to scuttle off home.

VIII

===

THE ACTIVITY OF running down six flights of stairs ought to be enough to clear a tipsy head, but it just leads to bruises when you fail to negotiate the corners. Cursing the damage can attract unwanted attention.

'Falco! Come here! Tell me I ought to leave Smaractus.'

'Lenia, don't just leave him. He's a household pest; knock him down and jump on him until he stops squeaking.'

'But what about my dowry?'

'I told you: divorce him, and you can keep it.'

'That's not what he says.'

'Him? He told you if you got married you would have prosperity, peace, and a life of uncloying happiness. That was a lie, wasn't it?'

'It's a lie even he never tried on me, Falco.'

Maybe I should have stayed in the laundry and tried to console my old friend Lenia. In the old days I had spent half my time in the cubbyhole she used as an office, drinking bad wine with her and moaning about injustice and lack of denarii. Now, since she was still married to Smaractus, there was every chance he would roll in to join us so I tended to avoid the risk. Besides, I had a home of my own to go to, when other people stopped distracting me.

What I didn't know was that my home had been invaded by another pest: Anacrites.

'Hello, Falco.'

'Help! Fetch me a broomstick, Helena; someone's let a disgusting roach in here.' Anacrites was giving me a quiet tolerant smile. It really wound up my rope to straining point.

Helena Justina scrutinised me sharply. 'How was your friend?' She had obviously decided that having Petronius camping out in our spare apartment could threaten our domestic life.

'He'll be all right.'

Helena deduced that meant he was in a bad way. 'There's a pine nut omelette and rocket salad.' She had eaten hers already. My dinner was set out in a dish. There was slightly less than I would have served for myself, the omelette had gone cold, and it was accompanied rather pointedly by water.

Anacrites cast a few yearning glances, but it was made clear he was excluded. Helena was ignoring him. She disliked him as much as I did, although she had no strong views on his efficiency or character. Helena simply loathed him for trying to kill me. I like a girl with principles. I like one who thinks I'm worth keeping alive.

'Any chance of Petronius Longus going back to his job?' Anacrites had come straight to the point of his visit. Before his head wound he would never have been so obvious. He had lost his social guile and his sleek, seditious confidence. But his eyes were as untrustworthy as ever.

I shrugged. 'Balbina Milvia's a very pretty girl.'

'You think the infatuation is serious?'

'I think Petronius Longus doesn't take kindly to being told what to do.'

'I hoped there was a chance you and I could work together, Falco.'

'Anyone would think you were afraid of my mother.'

He grinned. 'Isn't everyone? I'm serious about this.' So was I, about avoiding it.

I continued eating my dinner. I wasn't going to joke about Ma with him. Helena deposited herself on a second stool alongside me. She linked her hands on the edge of the table and glared at Anacrites. 'Your question seems to be answered. Is that all you came here for?'

He looked flustered in the face of her hostility. His pale grey eyes wandered uncertainly. Since he'd been clouted on the head he seemed to have shrunk slightly, both physically and mentally. It was odd to have him sitting here with us. There was a time when I only ever saw Anacrites at his office on the Palatine. Until Ma brought him to our party he had never met Helena formally, so he must be wondering how to deal with her. As for Helena, even before he came to our house she had heard a great deal about the troubles Anacrites had caused me; she had no doubt how to react to him.

Ignoring Helena, he appealed to me again. 'We could be a good partnership, Falco.'

'I'm working with Petro. Apart from the fact that he needs to keep occupied, we're old team-mates.'

'This could be the end of your friendship.'

'You're a pessimistic oracle.'

'I know how the world works.'

'You don't know us.'

He bit back any rejoinder. I then kept my head down over my food bowl, making no attempt at conversation, until the spy took the hint and went home.

Helena Justina turned to face me. 'What's he up to, do you think?'

'I made my feelings clear the other day. He's behaving impulsively coming here again; I put it down to his crack on the head.'

'According to your mother he keeps forgetting things. And he looked very worried by the noise at our party. He's not right.'

'All the more reason not to work with him. I can't afford to carry a dud. Whatever Ma says, he's not up to it.'

Helena was still perusing me critically. I enjoyed the attention. 'So Petro is coping. And how are you, Marcus Didius?'

'Not as drunk as I could have been, and not as hungry as I was.' I wiped round my bowl neatly with the last of a bread roll, then laid my knife at an exact angle in the bowl. I drained my beaker of water like a man who was really enjoying her choice of drink. 'Thank you.'

Helena inclined her head quietly. 'You could have brought Petronius over,' she conceded.

'Another day maybe.' I lifted her hand and kissed it. 'As for me, I'm where I want to be,' I said to her. 'With the people I belong to. Everything is wonderful.'

'You say that as if it were the truth,' scoffed Helena. But she smiled at me.

IX

THE NEXT TIME I ate dinner the surroundings were more luxurious, though the ambience was less comfortable: we were being
formally entertained by Helena's parents.

The Camilli owned a pair of houses near the Capena Gate. They
had all the amenities of the nearby busy area around the Via Appia,
but were ensconced in a private insula off a back street where only
the upper classes were welcome. I could never have lived there. The
neighbours were all too nosy about everyone else's business. And
someone was always having an aedile or a praetor to dinner, so
people had to keep the pavements clean lest their highly superior
enclave be officially criticised.

Helena and I had walked there over the Aventine. Her parents
were bound to insist on sending us home in their beaten-up litter,
with its just-about-adequate slave bearers, so we enjoyed a stroll
through the early evening stir of suburban Rome. I was carrying
the baby. Helena had volunteered to lug the large basket of Julia's
impedimenta: rattles, spare loincloths, clean tunics, sponges,
towels, flasks of rosewater, blankets and the rag doll she liked to try
to eat.

As we came under the Porta Capena, which carries the Appian
and Marcian aqueducts, we were splashed by the famous water leaks.
The August evening was so warm we were dry again by the time we
arrived at the Camillus house and I worked up a temper rousing the
porter from his game of dice. He was a dope with no future, a lanky
lout with a flat head who made it his life's work to annoy me. The
daughter of the house was mine now. It was time to give up, but he
was too dumb to have noticed.

The whole family had assembled for the ceremonial meeting with
our new daughter. Considering the household boasted two sons in
their early twenties, this was quite a coup. Aelianus and Justinus
were ignoring the call of theatres and the races, dancers and musicians, poetry parties and dinners with drunken friends in order to

greet their firstborn niece. It made me wonder what threats to their allowances must have been issued.

We handed over Julia to be admired, then beat a retreat to the garden.

'You two look exhausted!' Decimus Camillus, Helena's father, had sneaked out to join us. Tall, slightly stooped, and with short, straight, upstanding hair, he had his problems. He was a friend of the Emperor, but still laboured under the shadow of a brother who had tried to hijack the currency and disrupt the state; Decimus could not expect to be awarded any senior post. His coffers were light too. In August a senatorial family ought to be sunning themselves at some elegant villa on the spa coast at Neapolis or on the slopes of a quiet lake; the Camilli owned farms inland, but no proper summer haven. They passed the million sesterces qualification for the Curia, yet their cash in hand was insufficient to build on, either financially or socially.

He had found us sitting side by side on a bench in a colonnade, heads together and motionless, in a state of collapse.

'Having a baby's hard work,' I grinned. 'Were you allowed a glimpse of our treasure before she was mobbed by cooing women?'

'She seems skilled at handling an audience.'

'She is,' confirmed Helena, finding the energy to kiss her papa as he squashed informally on to our seat. 'Then when the flatterers finish, she's good at being sick on them.'

'Sounds like someone I knew once,' the senator mused.

Helena, his eldest child, was his favourite; and unless I had lost my intuitive powers, Julia would be next in line. Beaming, he leaned across Helena and clapped me on the arm. He ought to view me as an interloper; instead I was an ally. I had taken a difficult daughter off his hands, and proved I intended to stick with her. I had no money myself, yet unlike a conventional patrician son-in-law I did not come round once a month whining for loans.

'So, Marcus and Helena, you are back from Baetica – in good repute as usual, say those in the know on the Palatine. Marcus, your resolution of the olive oil cartel greatly pleased the Emperor. What are your plans now?'

I told him about working with Petronius, and Helena described our skirmishes with the Censors' clerk yesterday.

Decimus groaned. 'Have you done the Census yourself yet? I hope you have better luck than I did.'

'In what way, sir?'

'Up I marched, full of self-righteousness for reporting promptly, and my estimate of my worth was disbelieved. I had reckoned my story was foolproof too.'

I sucked my teeth. I thought him an honest man, for a senator. Besides, after the business with his treasonous brother, Camillus Verus had to prove his loyalty every time he stepped into the Forum. It was unjust, since he was that political rarity: a selfless public man. The condition was so rare, nobody believed in it. 'That's hard. Do you have any right of appeal?'

'Officially, there's no audit. The Censors can overrule anybody on the spot. Then they impose their own tax calculation.'

Helena's dry sense of humour was inherited from her father. She laughed and said: 'Vespasian declared he needed four hundred million sesterces to refill the Treasury after Nero's excesses. This is how he intends to do it.'

'Squeezing me?'

'You're good-natured and you love Rome.'

'What an appalling responsibility.'

'So did you accept the Censors' ruling?' I asked, chuckling slightly.

'Not entirely. The first option was to protest – which meant I would have to put in a lot of effort and expense producing receipts and leases for the Censors to laugh at. The second option was to pay up quietly; then they would meet me halfway.'

'A bribe!' cried Helena.

Her father looked shocked; anyway, he made a pretence of it. 'Helena Justina, nobody bribes the Emperor.'

'Oh, a *compromise*,' she snorted angrily.

Feeling cramped with three on the bench, I stood up and went to investigate the garden fountain on a nearby wall: a spluttery drunken Silenus pouring feebly from a wineskin. The poor old god had never been up to much; today his flow was being additionally obstructed by a fig which had dropped from a tree trained to grow against the sunny wall. I fished out the fruit. The gurgle resumed slightly more strongly.

'Thanks.' The senator tended to put up with things that failed to work. I strolled to a fancy border, where last year's pot lilies had been planted out. They were struggling against beetle, their leaves bitten and badly stained with rust. They weren't flowering, and

41

would be seriously ailing next season. Lily beetles are bright red and easily outwitted, so I was able to knock some off on to the palm of my hand, then drop them on to the paving where I flattened them under my boot.

Checking the result of my work on the fountain, I told the senator about the dismembered hand. I knew he had paid for private access to one of the aqueducts. 'Our supply seems pretty clean,' he said. 'It comes from the Aqua Appia.'

'Same as the Aventine fountains,' I warned.

'I know. They receive priority. I pay a huge premium, but the rules are strict for private householders.'

'The water board regulates your quantity?'

'The board gives me an officially approved calix let into the base of a water tower.'

'Can't you bend it a bit and increase the flow?'

'All private access pipes are made from bronze to prevent their being illegally enlarged – though I believe people do try.'

'How big is your pipe?'

'Only a quinaria.' Just over a digit in diameter. The smallest, but given an uninterrupted flow day and night sufficient for a reasonable household. Camillus had no spare cash. He was the kind of millionaire who seriously needed to economise.

'Too small for objects to come floating down,' Helena commented.

'Yes, thank goodness. We get a lot of sand, but the thought of receiving body parts is decidedly unpleasant.' He warmed to his theme. 'If there were loose debris in the aqueduct my calix could become blocked inside the water tower. I might not complain immediately; private houses are always the first to be cut off if there's a problem. I suppose that's fair.' Camillus was always tolerant. 'I can't see the water board admitting that they'd found something unhygienic inside the castellum. I imagine I'm being supplied with sparkling water straight from the Caerulean Spring – but is the stuff from the aqueducts really safe to drink?'

'Stick to wine,' I advised him. Which reminded us to go indoors to dine.

When we passed through the folding doors to the dining room we found a more formal spread than was usual here, so fatherhood brought some benefits. There were seven adults dining. I kissed the cheek of Julia Justa, Helena's mother, a proud, polite woman who managed not to flinch. I greeted her arrogant elder son Aelianus with a mock sincerity that I knew would annoy him, then gave an unfeigned grin to the tall, more slightly built figure of his brother Justinus.

As well as the entire Camillus family and myself, there was Claudia Rufina, a smart but rather solemn young girl Helena and I had brought over from Spain who was staying here because we had no guest bed to offer her. She was of provincial birth but good family, and would be welcome in all but the snobbiest homes, since she was of marriageable age and sole heiress to a large fortune. Helena and I greeted her kindly. We had introduced Claudia to the Camilli in the flagrant hope that this could be their route to a villa at Neapolis at last.

So it might prove: we heard that she had already agreed to a betrothal. The Camilii must possess a ruthless streak. Less than a week after Helena and I had delivered this reserved young woman to their house, they had offered her Aelianus. Claudia, who knew him from the time he had spent in Spain, had been brought up to be a good-mannered guest – and Julia Justa had not let her meet any other young men – so she had meekly agreed. A letter had been despatched to her grandparents inviting them to Rome to seal the arrangements straight away. Things had happened so fast it was the first we had heard of it.

'Olympus!' cried Helena.

'I'm sure you will both be extraordinarily happy,' I managed to croak. Claudia looked sweetly pleased by this concept, as if nobody had led her to think her well-being came into it.

They would be as miserable together as most couples, but were rich enough to have a large house where they could avoid one another. Claudia, a quiet girl with a rather big nose, was dressed in white in mourning for her brother, the intended heir, who had been killed in an accident; she probably welcomed something new to think about. Aelianus wanted to enter the Senate, for which he needed money; he would go along with anything. Besides, he was crowing over Justinus, his better-looking and more popular younger brother.

Justinus himself only smiled, shrugged, and looked mildly curious, like a sweet-tempered lad who wondered what the fuss was all about. I had once worked closely with him abroad. His vague air was masking a broken heart; he had fallen heavily for a blonde visionary prophetess in the forests of barbarian Germany (though once back in Rome he had swiftly consoled himself by starting an even more impossible liaison with an actress). Quintus Camillus Justinus always looked as if he didn't know the way to the Forum – but he had hidden depths.

The evening passed off so peacefully that when we were dawdling home in the litter, ignoring the grumblings of the bearers who had expected me to walk alongside, Helena felt drawn to comment: 'I hope you noticed the transformation, now we have produced a child?'

'How's that?'

Her great brown eyes danced with complicity. 'Nobody takes the slightest notice of you and me. Not one person asked us when we were going to find somewhere better to live –'

'Or when I would be starting a decent job –'

'Or when the formal wedding was to be –'

'If I'd have known all it took was a baby I would have borrowed one long ago.'

Helena surveyed Julia. Worn out by several hours of accepting adulation, she was sleeping deeply. In about another hour, just as I nodded off in bed, all that would change. Most informers stay unmarried. This was one of the reasons. On the other hand, a night-time surveillance in some street away from home – even if it contained a tannery and an illegal fish-pickle still and was infested with garlic-eating prostitutes whose pimps carried butcher's knives – was starting to offer unexpected attractions. A man who knows how to prop himself up can doze quite refreshingly in a shop portico.

'What about Aelianus and Claudia?' asked my beloved.

'Your mild-mannered parents have the knack of taking prompt action.'

'I hope it works.' She sounded neutral; that meant she felt concerned.

'Well, she said yes. Your father is a fair man, and your mother wouldn't let Aelianus be trapped if it was likely to go wrong.' They needed Claudia's money badly, however. After a moment I asked quietly, 'When you were married to that bastard Pertinax, what did your mother have to say?'

'Not much.'

Helena's mother had never liked me – which proved there was nothing wrong with her judgement. Helena Justina's first marriage had been suggested for his own sticky reasons by her uncle (the one

I shoved in the sewer later), and at the time even Julia Justa would have found the match hard to oppose. Helena herself had tolerated Pertinax as long as she could, then without consultation had issued a notice of divorce. The husband's family tried to arrange a reconciliation. By then she had met me. That was the end of it.

'Before her grandparents arrive, we'd better talk to Claudia,' I said. Since we had brought the girl here, we were both feeling responsible.

'I had a few words while you were hiding with my father in his study. And by the way,' demanded Helena warmly, 'what exactly were you two up to?'

'Nothing, my darling. I was just letting him complain some more about the Census.'

In fact, I had been testing an idea on Camillus Verus. His mentioning the Census had suggested a way that I might earn some money. I won't say I was exerting my authority by not telling Helena about it, but it would amuse me to see how long it took her to winkle out the details from her father or me. Helena and I had no secrets. But some schemes are men's work. Or so we like to tell ourselves.

X

GLAUCUS, MY TRAINER, was as sharp as a kitten's claw. A short, wide-shouldered Cilician freedman, he ran a bath-house two streets behind the Temple of Castor. It had a select gymnasium attached for people like me who had life-and-death reasons for keeping their bodies in trim. A library and pastry shop amused other clients – the discreet middle class who could afford to pay for his overheads and whose moderate habits never disrupted the hushed atmosphere. Glaucus only offered membership by personal introduction.

He knew his regulars better than they knew themselves. Probably none of us were at all close to him. After twenty years of listening to other people revealing their secrets while he worked on their muscle tone, he knew how to avoid that trap. But he could tease out embarrassing information as smoothly as a thrush emptying a snail shell.

I had his measure. When he started the extraction process, I grinned and told him, 'Just stick with asking if I'm planning any holidays this year.'

'You're overweight and ridiculously tanned; you're so relaxed I'm surprised you don't fall over; I can tell you've been lying around on a farm somewhere, Falco.'

'Yes, it was hideously rural. All work, I assure you.'

'I hear you're a father now.'

'True.'

'I gather you've finally been forced to rethink your slack attitude to work. You've taken a big leap forward and you're in business with Petronius Longus.'

'You do keep your ears open.'

'I stay in touch. And before you ask,' Glaucus told me crisply, 'the water in this bath-house is drawn from the Aqua Marcia. It has the best reputation for coldness and quality – I don't want to hear any ugly rumours that you two schemers might be looking into nasty things in the reservoir!'

'Just a hobby. I'm surprised even you knew anything about it. Petro and I are advertising for divorce and inheritance jobs.'

'Don't try to bluff me, Falco. I'm the man who knows your left leg's weak from when you broke it three years ago. Your old fractured ribs still ache if the wind is northwesterly, you like to fight with a dagger but your wrestling's adequate, your feet are good, your right shoulder's vulnerable, you can throw a punch but you aim too low and you have absolutely no conscience about kicking your opponent in the balls —'

'I sound a complete wreck. Any other tantalising personal details?'

'You eat too many street-caupona rissoles and you hate redheads.'

'Spare me the canny Cilician peasant act.'

'Just let's say, I know what you and Petronius are up to.'

'Petro and I are merely harmless eccentrics. Are you suspicious of us?'

'Does a donkey shit? I've heard exactly what you're advertising,' Glaucus informed me sourly. 'Every client today has been full of it: Falco & Partner are offering a fat reward for any information relating to dismembered body parts found in the aqueducts.'

The word 'reward' acted on me faster than a laxative. Weak left leg or not, I was out of his discreet establishment in the time it took to fling on my clothes. But when I raced up to the apartment in Fountain Court intent on ordering Petronius to retract his dangerous new poster, it was too late. Somebody was there before me, proffering another corpse's hand.

===============

XI

'LISTEN, YOU IDIOT, – if you're doling out rewards in the name of my business, you'd better put up your own collateral!'

'Settle down, Falco.'

'Show me the colour of your denarii.'

'Just shut up, will you? I'm interviewing a visitor.'

His visitor was exactly the kind of unprepossessing lowlife I would expect to come crawling up here looking for a bribe. Petronius had no idea. For a man who had spent seven years apprehending villains he remained curiously innocent. Unless I stopped him, he would ruin me.

'What's this then?' demanded the interviewee. 'What's gone wrong about the money?'

'Nothing,' said Petro.

'Everything,' said I.

'I heard you was giving rewards,' he complained accusingly.

'Depends what for.' I was hopping mad, yet experience had taught me to stand by any promise that had lured a hopeful here. Nobody climbs six flights of stairs to see an informer unless they are either in desperate trouble or believe that what they know is worth hard cash.

I glared at Petro's catch. He was a foot shorter than average, malnourished and filthy. His tunic was threadbare, a mucky brown garment that hung on his shoulders by a few rags of wool. His eyebrows met in the middle. Wiry black stubble ran from his jutting chin right up his cheekbones to the bags under his eyes. His ancestors may have been high kings of Cappadocia, but without doubt this man was a public slave.

On his feet, which looked as flat as bread-shovels, he was wearing rough clogs. They had thick soles but they had not kept him dry; his felt leggings were black and had oozed water everywhere. A trail of puddles marked his path through our door, and a dark little pond was slowly gathering around the spot where he had come to rest.

'What's your name?' asked Petronius haughtily, trying to reassert his authority. I leant on the table with my thumbs in my belt. I was annoyed. The informant didn't need to be told about it, but Petronius would pick it up from my stance.

'I said, what's your name?'

'Why do you need to know?'

Petro scowled. 'Why do you need to keep it a secret?'

'I've nothing to hide.'

'That's commendable! I'm Petronius Longus; he's Falco.'

'Cordus,' admitted the applicant grudgingly.

'And you're a public slave, working for the Curator of Aqueducts?'

'How did you know that?'

I saw Petro control himself. 'Given what you brought me, it fits.' We all looked at the new hand. We looked away again rapidly. 'What family do you work in?' asked Petro, to avoid discussing the relic.

'The state.' The water board used two groups of public slaves, one derived from the original organisation set up by Agrippa and now in full state control, the other established by Claudius and still part of the household of the Emperor. There was no rationale in perpetuating these two 'families'. They ought to be part of the same workforce. It was a classic bureaucratic mess with the usual openings for corruption. The inefficiency was worsened by the fact that nowadays major work programmes were carried out by private contractors instead of direct slave labour anyway. No wonder the Aqua Appia always leaked.

'What's your job, Cordus?'

'Masonry. Vennus is my foreman. He doesn't know I found that . . .'

We all reluctantly looked at the hand again.

This one was a dark, pungent, rotted nightmare, recognisable only because we were in the mood to see what it was. It was in desperate condition, only half there. Like the first, the fingers were missing but the thumb remained, attached by a thread of leathery skin though its main joint had parted. Maybe the fingers had been gnawed off by rats. Maybe something even worse had happened to them.

The relic now lay on a dish – my old supper dish, I was annoyed to notice – which had been placed on a stool between Petronius and his interviewee, as far as possible from both of them. In the small room that was still too close. I edged further along the table, in the opposite direction. A fly buzzed in to have a look, then flew off fast in alarm. Gazing at this object changed the atmosphere for all of us.

'Where did you find it?' Petronius enquired in a low voice.

'In the Aqua Marcia.' Tough luck, Glaucus. So much for crystal-clear bathing. 'I went in through a top hatch with a surveyor to check if we needed to scrape the walls.'

'Scrape them?'

'Full-time job. They get coated with lime, legate. Thick as your leg, if we leave it. We have to keep chipping it away or the whole works would clog up.'

'So was there water in the aqueduct at the time?'

'Oh, yes. Shutting the Marcia's next to impossible. So much depends on it, and if we send inferior water because we're running a diversion, nobs start jumping up and down.'

'How did you find the hand then?'

'It just came floating along and said hello.'

Petronius stopped asking questions. He looked as if he would be happy for once if I interrupted him, but there was nothing I was burning to interject. Like him, I felt slightly ill.

'When it knocked my knee I jumped a mile, I can tell you. Do you know who it belongs to?' asked the water board slave curiously. He seemed to think we had answers to the impossible.

'Not yet.'

'I expect you'll find out.' The slave was consoling himself. He wanted to believe something proper would come out of this.

'We'll try.' Petro sounded depressed. He and I both knew it was hopeless.

'So what's this about the money then? Cordus was looking embarrassed. No doubt if we did produce any payment, he would overcome his reserve. 'To tell you the truth, it wasn't for the reward that I come here, you know.' Petronius and I listened with an air of decent concern. 'I heard you was asking questions so I thought you ought to have it . . . but I wouldn't want the bosses to hear –'

Petronius surveyed the slave with his friendly look. 'I suppose,' he suggested, 'if you find anything of this nature, the rule is you have to keep it quiet to avoid upsetting public confidence?'

'That's it!' agreed Cordus excitedly.

'How many castoff bits of corpse have you found before?' I asked. Now a second person was starting to take an interest he cheered up.

Maybe we liked his offering after all. It might increase what we paid him.

'Well, not me myself, legate. But you'd be surprised. All sorts of things turn up in the water, and I've heard of plenty.'

'Any handless bodies?'

'Arms and legs, legate.' It was hearsay, I reckoned. I could tell Petro agreed.

'Ever seen any of them?'

'No, but a mate of mine has.' Everyone in Rome has a mate whose life is much more interesting than his own. Funny; you never get to meet the mate.

'The hand is your own first big discovery?' I made it sound like something to be proud of.

'Yes, sir.'

I glanced openly at Petronius. He folded his arms. So did I. We pretended to be holding a silent conference. Really we were both as gloomy as sin.

'Cordus,' I ventured, 'do you know if the waters of the Aqua Appia and the Aqua Marcia originate in the same place?'

'Not me, legate. Don't ask me nothing about the aqueducts. I'm just a mutt who works in the wet, chipping off clink. I don't know nothing technical.'

I grinned at him. 'That's a pity! I was hoping you could spare us having to talk to some long-winded hydraulic surveyor.'

He looked crestfallen.

He was probably a villain but he had convinced us he meant well. We knew how hard life was for public slaves so Petro and I both dug in our pockets and arm-purses. Between us we managed to find him three quarters of a denarius, all in smalls. Cordus seemed delighted. Half an hour in our den above Fountain Court had warned him that the best he could expect from a pair of duds like us might be a kick on the backside and an empty-handed trudge down-stairs. A few coppers was better than that, and he could see he had cleaned us out.

After he had gone, Petronius pulled on his outdoor boots and vanished: running off to remove his reward poster. I carefully lifted the stool with the hand on it on to the balcony, but a pigeon flew down for a nibble almost straight away. I brought it back in and used Petro's smart mess tin upside-down over the hand as a lid.

He would curse me, but by then I would be across the road peacefully closeted with Helena. The good thing about having a work partner was that I could leave him to fret all night over any new evidence. As senior executive I could forget it then stroll in tomorrow, refreshed and full of unworkable ideas, to ask in an annoying tone what solutions my minion had come up with.

Some of us are born to be managers.

XII

THE CURATOR OF Aqueducts was an imperial freedman. He was probably a slick and cultured Greek. He probably carried out his work with dedicated efficiency. I say 'probably' because Petro and I never actually saw him. This exalted official was too busy being slick and cultured to find time for an interview with us.

Petronius and I wasted a morning at his office in the Forum. We watched a long procession of foremen from the gangs of public slaves march in to receive their orders for the day, then march out again without a word for us. We tackled various members of an ever-changing secretariat, who all handled us with diplomacy, and some were even polite. It became clear that members of the public were not likely to be granted an audience with the lord of the waters – not even when they wanted to suggest how he might keep the flow free of mouldering bits of dead people. The fact we had said we were informers did not help. Probably.

We were allowed to write a petition stating our concern, though a frank scribe who had glanced at it told us the Curator would not want to know. That at least was not just probable but definite.

The only way around this would be pulling rank on the Curator. I disapproved of such low tactics; well, I rarely knew anyone important enough to pull rank for me. So that was out.

Still, I did consider possibilities. Petro started getting angry and treated the whole business as if it smelt; he just wanted to go for a drink. But I always like to take the historical view: the water supply was a vital state concern, and had been for centuries. Its bureaucracy was an elaborate mycellum whose black tentacles crept right to the top. As with everything else in Rome that he could possibly stick his nose into, the Emperor Augustus had devised extra procedures – ostensibly to provide clear supervision, but mainly to keep him informed.

I knew there was a Board of Commission for the aqueducts which comprised three senators of consular rank. While carrying out his duties each was entitled to be preceded by two lictors. Each was also accompanied by an impressive train containing three slaves to carry his handkerchief, a secretary, and an architect, plus a large staff of more nebulous officials. Rations and pay for the staff were provided from public funds, and the commissioners could draw stationery and other useful supplies, a proportion of which they no doubt took home for their private use in the traditional manner.

These worthy old codgers clearly held seniority over the Curator. Luring just one of them into taking an interest in our story could have acted as a fulcrum under the Curator's arse. Unfortunately for us, the three consular commissioners simultaneously held other interesting public posts, such as governorships of foreign provinces. The practice was feasible because the Commission only met formally to inspect the aqueducts for three months of the year – and August was not one of them.

We were stuck. That was not unusual. I agreed that Petronius had been right all along. We consoled our injured feelings in the traditional way: having lunch in a bar.

Reeling slightly, Petronius Longus later led me to the best place he knew for sleeping it off, his old patrol house. There was no sign of Fusculus today.

'Time off to visit his auntie, chief,' said Sergius.

Sergius was the Fourth Cohort's punishment officer – tall, perfectly built, permanently flexed for action, and stupendously handsome. Flicking the whip gently, he was sitting on the bench outside, killing ants. His aim was murderous. Muscles rippled aggressively through gaps in his brown tunic. A wide belt was buckled tightly on a flat stomach, emphasising his narrow waist and well-formed chest. Sergius looked after himself. He could look after trouble too. No neighbourhood troublemaker whom Sergius looked after bothered to repeat his crime. At least his long tanned face, dagger-straight nose and flashing teeth made an aesthetic memory for villains as they fainted under the caress of his whip. To be beaten up by Sergius was to partake in a high-class art form.

'What auntie?' scoffed Petro.

'The one he goes to see when he needs a day off.' The vigiles were all experts in acquiring a maddening toothache or having to attend the funeral of a close relative they had doted on. Their work was hard, ill paid and dangerous. Inventing excuses to bunk off was a necessary relief.

'He'll be sorry he was out.' Unwrapping it with a flourish, I flipped the new hand on to the bench alongside Sergius. 'We brought him another piece of black pudding.'

'Urgh! Sliced a bit thick, isn't it?' Sergius didn't move. My theory was that he lacked any emotion. Still, he understood what stirred the rest of us. 'After the last treat you brought him, Fusculus took a religious vow never to touch meat; he only eats cabbage and rosehip custard now. What caupona served this up to you?' Somehow Sergius could tell we had just been at lunch. 'You ought to report the place to the aediles as a danger to health.'

'A public slave pulled the hand out of the Aqua Marcia.'

'Probably a ploy by the guild of wine producers,' Sergius chortled. 'Trying to convince everyone to stop drinking water.'

'They've convinced us,' I warbled.

'That's obvious, Falco.'

'Where's the last hand?' demanded Petro. 'We want to see if we've got a pair.'

Sergius sent a clerk to fetch the hand from the museum, where it had apparently been a great attraction. When it came, he himself placed it on the bench side by side with the new one, as if laying out a pair of new cold-weather mittens. He had to fiddle with the loose thumb on the second one, making sure it was the correct way round. 'Two rights.'

'Hard to tell.' Petronius kept well away. He was conscious that the new one was in a poor state. After all, he had spent a night in the same apartment with it; the experience was bothering him.

'There's a lot missing, but this is how the thumb goes, and they're both palm up. I tell you, these are both rights.' Sergius stuck by his point, but he never warmed up in an argument. Mostly he never needed to. People eyed up his whip and then gave him the benefit.

Petronius accepted it gloomily. 'So there are two different bodies.'

'Same killer?'

'Might be coincidence.'

'Fleas might drop off before they bite,' scoffed Sergius. He decided to shout in for Scythax to supply a professional opinion.

Scythax, the troop's doctor, was a dour Oriental freedman; his hair lay in a perfectly straight line on his eyebrows as if he had trimmed it himself using a cupping vessel on his head as a straight-edge. The previous year his brother had been murdered, since when he had become even more taciturn. When he did speak his manner was suspicious and his tone depressing. That didn't rule out medical jokes. 'I can't do anything for this patient.'

'Oh, give it a try, Hippocrates! He might be very rich. They're always desperate to go on for ever, and they pay well for a hint of extra life.'

'You're a clown, Falco.'

'Well, we didn't expect you to sew these back on.'

'Who lost them?'

'We don't know.'

'What can you tell us about them?' asked Petro.

Sergius expounded his theory that the hands had come from different people. Scythax said nothing for long enough to cast doubt on the idea, but then confirmed it. He was a true medical man; he knew just how to aggravate people with his superior, scientific air.

'Are they male corpses?' Petro muttered.

'Could be.' The doctor was as definite as the route through a marsh in a thick mist. 'Probably not. Too small. More likely women, children, or slaves.'

'What about how they came to be separated from their arms?' I enquired. 'Could they have been dug up from a grave by dogs or foxes?' Before it was made illegal to bury bodies within the city boundary there had been a graveyard on the Esquiline Hill. The area still gave out a stink. It had been turned into gardens, but I would not fancy double-digging an asparagus patch there.

Scythax peered at the hands again, unwilling to touch them. Sergius picked one up fearlessly and held it so the doctor could inspect the wrist. Scythax jumped backwards. He pursed his lips fastidiously and said: 'I can't see any identifiable animal teeth-marks. It looks to me as if the wristbone has been severed with a blade.'

'That's murder, then!' crowed Sergius. He brought the hand right up in front of his face and peered at it, like someone inspecting a small turtle.

'What kind of blade?' demanded Petro of Scythax.

'I have no idea.'

'Was it a neat job?'

'The hand is too decomposed to tell.'

'Look at the other one too,' I commanded. Sergius dropped the first and eagerly offered the second relic to Scythax, who went even paler as its thumb finally dropped off.

'Impossible to say what happened.'

'There's about the same amount of wrist attached.'

'That's true, Falco. There is some arm bone. This is not a natural separation at the joint, such as might occur through decay.'

Sergius laid the second hand back on the bench again, carefully aligning the loose thumb in what he deemed to be its natural position.

'Thanks, Scythax,' said Petro gloomily.

'Don't mention it,' muttered the doctor. 'If you find any more pieces of these people, consult another physician if you please.' He glared at Sergius: 'And you – wash your hands!' Not much point, if all the available water came from contaminated aqueducts.

'Take a headache powder and have a lie down for a while,' Sergius advised humorously as the doctor fled. Scythax was notorious for his reluctance to prescribe this remedy to people who needed it; his normal routine was to tell badly wounded vigiles to get straight back on duty and take plenty of exercise. He was a hard man, with the living. Apparently we had found his weakness with our sad sections of the dead.

Ours too, in fact.

XIII

BY NEXT DAY it was clear that the water board's public slaves had been talking among themselves. They had devised a competition to see who could produce the most revolting 'evidence' and persuade us to let them hand it over. They trotted up Fountain Court looking meek and innocent, and furtively carrying parcels. They were bastards. Their offerings were useless. They smelt too. Sometimes we could tell what the ghastly item was; mostly we preferred not to know. We had to go along with the joke in case one day they brought us something real.

'Well, you asked for it,' Helena said.

'No, my darling. Lucius Petronius Longus, my wonderful new partner, was the idiot who made the request.'

'And how are you getting on with Petro?' she asked me demurely.

'You know I've just answered that.'

Once the public slaves inveigled their foremen into joining the game, Petro and I locked up the office and withdrew to my new apartment. Helena saw her chance. In two ticks she had dressed up in a smart red gown, glass beads chinking in her earlobes, and was tying on a sunhat. She was off to visit a school for orphans of which she was the patron. I made her take Nux for protection; Julia would take care of me.

The baby caused some friction.

'I don't believe you're allowing this!' Petronius growled.

'I tend not to use the word "allow" in connection with Helena.'

'You're a fool, Falco. How can you do your job while you're acting as a children's nurse?'

'I'm used to it. Marina was always parking Marcia on me.' Marina was my late brother's girlfriend, a woman who knew how to leech. I was particularly fond of little Marcia, a fact Marina exploited with skill. After Festus died she had wrung me dry of sympathy, guilt and (her unashamed preference) cash.

'There have to be rules,' Petro continued darkly. He was sitting on my front porch with his big feet up on the rotted handrail, blocking the stairs. In the absence of action he was eating a bowl of damsons. 'I'm not having us appear unprofessional.'

I pointed out that the main reason we looked like stray dogs in a market was that we spent our time lounging around winebars because we had failed to acquire any paying clients. 'Julia's no bother. All she does is sleep.'

'And cry! How can you impress visitors with a newborn bawling on a blanket on the table? How can you interrogate a suspect while you're wiping her backside? In the name of the gods, Falco, how can you go out on discreet surveillance with a crib strapped on your back?'

'I'll cope.'

'The first time you're in a scrimmage and some thug grabs the babe as a hostage, it will be a different tale.'

I said nothing. He had got me there.

He had not yet finished, however. 'How can you even enjoy a flagon and a quiet discussion at a caupona –' When my old friend started devising a list of grievances, he made it a ten scroll encyclopaedia.

To shut him up I suggested we went for lunch. This aspect of the freelance life cheered him up as usual and out we went, of necessity taking Julia. When it was nearly time for her to be fed we had to go home again, in order to hand her over to Helena, but a short meal – like taking water with our wine jug for once – could only be healthy, as I pointed out to Petro. He told me what I could do with my praise for the abstemious life.

Helena was not home yet, so we settled back on the porch as if we had been there ever since she left. To reinforce the fraud, we resumed the same argument too.

We could easily have continued wrangling for hours. It was like being eighteen-year-old legionaries again. On our posting to Britain we had wasted days debating pointless issues, our only entertainment in the compulsory periods of guard duty that intruded between drinking Celtic beer until we were sick and convincing ourselves tonight would be the night we gave up our virginities to one of the cheap camp prostitutes. (We could never afford it; our pay was always in hock for the beer.)

But our doorstep symposium was to be disturbed. We watched the approaching trouble with interest.

'Look at this bunch of idiots.'

'Seem to be lost.'

'Lost and daft.'

'It must be you they want, then.'

'No, I'd say it's you.'

There were three deadweights and a dozy lout who seemed to be their leader. They were dressed in worn tunics that even my frugal mother would have refused to use as floorcloths. Rope belts, bum-starver skirts, ragged necklines, unstitched seams, missing sleeves. When we first spotted them they were wandering around Fountain Court like stray sheep. They looked as if they had come here for something, but had forgotten what. Somebody must have sent them; this group didn't have enough gumption to have devised a plan themselves. Whoever it was may have given full directions, but he had wasted his breath.

After a time they converged on the laundry opposite. We watched them discussing whether to venture inside until Lenia bounced out; she must have thought they were bent on stealing clothes from her drying lines so she had emerged to help them pick out something good. Well, she could see that they needed it. Their present attire was deplorable.

They all held a long conversation, after which the four dummies wandered off up the stone stairs that would lead – if they persisted – to my old apartment at the top. Lenia turned towards Petro and me with a rude mime that said it was us these inept persons were seeking. We also guessed she had told them that if they failed to find us up there they would not have missed much. Typically, she had made no attempt to point out that we were both lounging over here in full view.

Much later the four dopey characters ambled aimlessly back down again. They all hung around in the street for a while. Vague discussions took place. Then one spotted Cassius, the baker whose shop had been burned down during Lenia's ill-fated marriage rites. He now hired ovens somewhere else, but ran a stall here for his old regulars. The hungry dummy begged a roll, and must have asked after us at the same time. Cassius presumably owned up. The dummy wandered back to his companions and told them the story. They all turned round slowly and looked up at us.

Petro and I did not move. He was still on a stool with his feet up; I was lodged against the frame of the front door filing my nails.

Surprisingly, there was more talking. Then the four dimwits decided to come our way. We waited for them patiently.

'You Falco and Petronius?'

'Who's asking?'

'We're telling you to answer.'

'Our answer is: who we are is our business.'

A typical chat between strangers, the kind that happened frequently on the Aventine. For one of the parties the outcome was usually short, sharp, and painful.

The four, none of whom had been taught by their mothers to keep their mouths closed properly or to stop scratching their privates, wondered what they could do now.

'We're looking for two bastards called Petronius and Falco.' The leader thought that if he repeated himself often enough we would cave in and confess. Maybe nobody had told him we had been in the army once. We knew how to obey orders – and how to ignore them.

'This is a good game.' Petronius grinned at me.

'I could play it all day.'

There was a pause. Over the ranks of dark apartments rose the ferocious noonday sun. Shadows had shrunk to nothing. Balcony plants lay down fainting with hollow stems. Peace had descended on the dirty streets as everyone crept indoors and braced themselves for several hours of unbearable summer heat. It was time for sleep and unstrenuous fornication. Only the ants still laboured. The swallows still circled, sometimes letting out their faint high-pitched cries as they swooped endlessly over the Aventine and Capitol against the breathtaking blue of a Roman sky. Even the endless clack of an abacus from a high-up room where somebody's landlord usually sat counting his money seemed to falter a little.

It was too hot for causing trouble, and certainly too hot for receiving it. Even so, one of the dummies had the bright idea of grabbing me.

XIV

I HIT HIM hard in the stomach before he made contact. At the same time Petro swung to his feet in one easy movement. Neither of us wasted time shrieking, 'Oh dear, what's happening?' We knew — and we knew what we would be doing about it.

I grabbed the first man by the hair, since there was not enough cloth in his tunic to allow a grip. These fellows were stunted and sleepy. None had any will to resist. With one arm round his waist I was soon using him as a sweeper to shoo the others back down the steps. Petro still thought he was seventeen; he had shown off by clambering over the handrail and dropping to the street. Wincing ruefully, he was then in position to field the crowd as they rushed down. Rounding them up in a pincer movement we were able to give them a thrashing without too much loss of breath. Then we piled them up in a heap.

Holding them down with his boot on the top one, Petro shook my hand formally. He had hardly raised a sweat. 'Two each: nice odds.'

We looked at them. 'Pitiful opposition,' I decided regretfully.

We stood back and let them pull themselves upright. In a few seconds a surprising crowd had gathered to watch. Lenia must have warned everyone in the laundry; all her washer-girls and tub-boys had come out. Somebody cheered us. Fountain Court has its sophisticated side; I detected a hint of irony. Anyone would think Petronius and I were a pair of octogenarian gladiators who had jumped out of retirement to capture a group of six-year-old apple thieves.

'Now you tell us,' Petro commanded, in the voice of an officer of the vigiles, 'who you are, who sent you, and what you want.'

'Never mind that,' dared the leader, so we grabbed him and threw him between us like a beanbag until he grasped our importance in these streets.

'Hold off, the melon's getting squashed!'

'I'll pulp him if he doesn't stop acting up —'

'Going to be a good boy now?'

He was gasping too much to answer but we stood him up again

anyway. Petronius, who was really enjoying himself, pointed to Lenia's girls. They were sweethearts as singletons, but together they turned into a hooting, foul-mouthed, obscene little clutch. If you saw them coming you wouldn't just cross to the other pavement, you'd dive into a different street. Even if it meant getting mugged and your money pinched. 'Any more trouble and you're all tossed to those lovelies. Believe me, you don't want to be dragged off into their steam room. The last man the washtub Harpies got hold of was missing for three weeks. We found him hung up on a pole with his privates dangling and he's been gibbering in a corner ever since.'

The girls made lewd gestures and waggled their skirts offensively. They were a cheerful and appreciative audience.

Petro had done the threats so the interrogation was mine. These pieces of flotsam would faint if I tried sophisticated rhetoric so I kept it simple. 'What's the story?'

The leader hung his head. 'You've got to stop making a fuss about blockages in the fountains.'

'Who gave out that dramatic edict?'

'Never mind.'

'We do mind. Is that it?'

'Yes.'

'You could have said it without starting a scrum.'

'You jumped one of my boys.'

'Your wormy sidekick threatened me.'

'You've hurt his neck!'

'He's lucky I haven't wrung it. Don't come around this part of the Aventine again.'

I glanced at Petro. They had no more to tell us, and we might get legal complaints if we bruised them too badly, so we told the leader to stop moaning, then dusted off his trio of backers and ordered them all off our patch.

We allowed a few moments for them to mutter about us in a huddle once they had turned the corner. Then we set off unobtrusively to tail them home.

We should have worked out for ourselves where they were going. Still, it was a good practical exercise. Since they had no idea of keeping watch, it was simple to stroll along after them. Petronius even turned off once to buy a stuffed pancake, then he caught me up. We went down the Aventine, around the Circus and into the Forum. Somehow this was no surprise.

As soon as they reached the office of the Curator of Aqueducts Petro threw what was left of his snack into a gutter and we speeded up. We marched in; the four goons had vanished. I approached a scribe. 'Where are the officers who just came in? They told us to follow them.' He nodded to a door. Petro whipped it open; we both strode through.

Just in time. The four dummies had started complaining to a superior; he had realised we would have followed them, and was on his feet to throw a bolt across the door. Seeing it was too late, he suavely pretended he had jumped up to greet us, then ordered his pitiful group of enforcers to leave. There was no need for introductions. We knew this fellow: it was Anacrites.

'Well, well,' said he.

'Well, well!' we retorted.

I turned to Petro. 'It's our long-lost shipwrecked brother.'

'Oh I thought it was your father's missing heir?'

'No, I made sure I had him exposed on a really reliable mountainside. He's bound to have been eaten by a bear.'

'So who's this?'

'I think it must be the unpopular moneylender we're going to hide in a blanket chest before we lose the key —'

For some reason Anacrites was failing to appreciate our banter. Still, no one expects a spy to be civilised. Taking pity on his head wound, we pretended to stop ganging up on him, though the sheen on his brow and the wary look in those half-closed grey eyes told us he still thought we were looking for a chance to hold him upside-down in a bucket of water until we stopped hearing choking sounds.

We took possession of his room, tossing scrolls to one side and shoving the furniture about. He decided not to make a fuss. There were two of us, one large and both very angry. Anyway, he was supposed to be sick.

'So why are you threatening us about our innocent curiosity?' demanded Petronius.

'You're scaremongering.'

'What we've discovered is cause for alarm!'

'There's no reason for disquiet.'

'Every time I hear that,' I said, 'it turns out to be some devious official telling me lies.'

'The Curator of Aqueducts takes the situation seriously.'

'That's why you're skulking here in his office?'

'I've been co-opted on special assignment.'

'To clean out the fountains with a nice little sponge?'

He looked hurt. 'I'm advising the Curator, Falco.'

'Don't waste your time. When we came to report that there were corpses blocking the current, the bastard didn't want to know.'

Anacrites regained his confidence. He assumed the gentle, self-righteous air of a man who had stolen our job. 'That is how it works in public service, friend. When they decide to hold an investigation they never use the man who first alerted them to the problem. They distrust him; he tends to thinks he's the expert and to hold crackpot theories. Instead they bring in a professional.'

'You mean an incompetent novice who has no real interest?'

He smirked triumphantly.

Petronius and I exchanged one frigid look, then we leapt to our feet and were out of there.

We had lost our enquiry to the Chief Spy. Even on sick leave Anacrites carried more clout than the pair of us. Well, that was the end of our interest in assisting the state. We could busy ourselves with private clients instead.

Besides, I had just remembered something terrible: I had come out without Julia. Dear gods, I had left my three-month-old daughter completely alone in a rough area of the Aventine, in an empty house.

'Well, that's one way to avoid carrying a baby and looking unprofessional,' Petro said.

'She'll be all right – I hope. What's worrying me is that Helena will probably be back by now and she'll know what I've done –'

It was too hot to run. Still, we made it back home at the fastest possible gentle trot.

When we took the stairs, it soon became clear that Julia was safe and now had plenty of company. Women's voices conversed indoors at what seemed a normal pace. We exchanged a glance that can only be called thoughtful, then we sauntered in looking as if in our honest opinion nothing untoward had happened.

One of the women was Helena Justina, who was now feeding the baby. She said nothing. But her eyes met mine with the degree of scorching heat that must have melted the wings off Icarus when he flew too near the sun.

The other was an even fiercer proposition: Petro's estranged wife Arria Silvia.

XV

'**D**ON'T BOTHER LOOKING. I haven't brought the children.' Silvia wasted no time. She was a tiny spark, as neat as a doll. Petronius used to laugh at her as if she just had a vigorous character; I thought her completely unreasonable. Gripping her hands together tightly she mouthed, 'In an area like this you don't know what types they might meet.' Silvia had never minded being rude.

'They are my children too.' Petronius was the paterfamilias. Since he had acknowledged the three girls at birth they belonged to him legally; if he wanted to be difficult he could insist they lived with him. Still, we were plebs. He had no means of looking after them, as Silvia knew.

'That's why you abandoned them?'

'I left because you ordered me to.'

Petro's very quietness was working Silvia into a rage. He knew exactly how to drive her wild with restraint. 'And is that a surprise, you bastard?'

Silvia's rage was increasing his stubbornness. He folded his arms. 'We'll sort it out.'

'That's your answer to everything!'

Helena and I had carefully stayed neutral. I would have kept it that way, but since there was a lull Helena inserted sombrely, 'I'm sorry to see you two like this.'

Silvia tossed her head. She went in for the untamed mare attitude. Unfortunately for Petro it took more than a handful of carrots to calm her down. 'Don't interfere, Helena.'

Helena assumed her reasonable expression, which meant she wanted to hurl a bowl of fruit at Silvia. 'I'm just stating a fact. Marcus and I always used to envy your loving family life.'

Arria Silvia stood up. She had a secretive smile that Petronius had probably once thought enthralling; today she was using it as a bitter weapon. 'Well, now you see what a fraud it was.' The fight died in her, in a manner I found worrying. She was leaving. Petronius

66

happened to be standing in her way. 'Excuse me.'

'I would like to see my daughters.'

'Your daughters would like to see a father who doesn't pick up every broken blossom that drops in his path.'

Petronius did not trouble to argue. He stepped aside and let her pass.

Petro hung around just long enough to be sure he would not run into Arria Silvia when he went back out to the street. Then he too left, with nothing more said.

Helena finished patting up Julia's wind. A new toy, which Silvia must have brought as a gift for the baby, lay on the table. We ignored it, knowing both of us would always find its presence uncomfortable now. Helena laid the baby down in her cradle. Sometimes I was allowed that privilege, but not today.

'It won't happen again,' I promised, not needing to specify what.

'It won't,' she agreed.

'I'm not making excuses.'

'No doubt you were called away to something extremely important.'

'Nothing is more important than her safety.'

'That's what I think.'

We stood on opposite sides of the room. We were talking in low voices, as if to avoid waking the baby. The tone was strangely light, cautious, with neither Helena's warning nor my apology stressed as they might have been. The searing quarrel between our two old friends had affected us too heavily for us to want or to risk a fight ourselves.

'We shall have to have a nurse,' Helena said.

The reasonable statement involved major consequences. Either I had to give in and borrow a woman from the Camilli (already offered by them, and proudly refused by me), or I had to purchase a slave myself. That would be an innovation for which I was hardly prepared – having no money to buy, feed or clothe her, no inclination to expand my household while we lived in such cramped conditions, and no hope of improving those conditions in the near future.

'Of course,' I replied.

Helena made no response. The soft material of her dark red dress clung slightly to the rocker of the cradle at her feet. I could not see the baby, yet I knew exactly how she would look and smell and snuffle and squint if I went over and peered in at her. Just as I knew the lift of Helena's own breathing, the surge of her annoyance that I had left the child unprotected, and the tightening muscle at the corner of her sweet mouth as she fought her conflicting feelings about me. Maybe I could win her round with a cheeky grin. But she mattered too much for me to try it.

Presumably Petro had once felt about his wife and family as I did about mine. Neither he nor Silvia had changed fundamentally. Yet it seemed that somehow he had stopped caring whether his indiscretions were apparent, while she had stopped believing he was perfect. They had lost the domestic toleration that makes life with another person possible.

Helena must have been wondering whether one day the same thing would happen to us. Yet perhaps she read the sadness in my face because when I held out my hands she came to me. I wrapped her in my arms and just held her. She was warm and her hair smelt of rosemary. As always our bodies seemed to come together in a perfect fit. 'Oh, fruit, I'm sorry. I'm a disaster. What made you choose me?'

'Error of judgement. What made you choose me?'

'I thought you were beautiful.'

'A trick of the light.'

I pulled back slightly, studying her face. Pale, tired perhaps, and yet still calm and capable. She could handle me. Still holding her hip to hip, I dropped a light kiss on her forehead, a greeting after being apart. I believed in daily ceremonial.

I asked after her orphans' school, and she reported her day to me, speaking formally but without wrangling. Then she asked what had been so important as to drag me from home, and I told her about Anacrites. 'So he's pinched our puzzle from under our noses. It's a dead end anyway, so I suppose we should be glad to let him take over.'

'You're not going to give up, Marcus?'

'You think I should go on?'

'You were waiting for me to say it,' she smiled. After a moment she added, watching me, 'What does Petro want to do?'

'Haven't asked him.' I too waited a moment then said wryly, 'When I'm brooding I talk to you. That won't ever change, you know.'

'You and he have a partnership.'

'In work. You're my partner in life.' I had noticed that even

68

though Petro and I were now in harness I still wanted to chew over debatable issues with Helena. 'It's part of the definition, my love. When a man takes a wife it's to share his confidence. However close a friend may be, there remains one last modicum of reserve. Especially if the friend himself is behaving in ways that seem senseless.'

'You'll support Petronius absolutely –'

'Oh, yes. Then I'll come home and tell you what a fool he is.'

Helena looked as if she was about to kiss me in a more than fleeting manner, but to my annoyance she was interrupted. Our front door was being repeatedly kicked by a pair of small feet in large boots. When I strode out to remonstrate it was, as I expected, the surly, antisocial figure of my nephew Gaius. I knew his vandalism of old.

He was thirteen, rising fourteen. One of Galla's brood. A shaved head, an armful of self-inflicted tattoos of sphinxes, half his teeth missing, a huge tunic belted in folds by a three-inch-wide belt with a 'Stuff you' buckle and murderous studs. Hung about with scabbards, pouches, gourds and amulets. A small boy making a big man's fashion statement – and, being Gaius, getting away with it. He was a roamer. Driven on to the streets by an unbearable homelife and his own scavenging nature, he lived in his own world. If we could get him to adulthood without his meeting some dreadful disaster we would do well.

'Stop kicking my door, Gaius.'

'I wasn't.'

'I'm not deaf, and those new footprints are your size.'

'Hello, Uncle Marcus.'

'Hello, Gaius,' I answered patiently. Helena had come out behind me; she reckoned Gaius needed sympathetic conversation and cosseting instead of the belt round the ear which the rest of my family regarded as traditional.

'I've brought you something.'

'Will I like it?' I could guess.

'Of *course*! It's a smashing present –' Gaius possessed a developed sense of humour. 'Well, it's another disgusting thing you want for your enquiry. A friend of mine found it in a drain in the street.'

'Do you often play in the drains?' asked Helena anxiously.

'Oh no,' he lied, alert to her reforming mood.

He fumbled in one of his pouches and brought out the gift. It was small, about the size of a draughts token. He showed me, then quickly whipped it out of sight. 'How much will you pay?' I should have known the rascal would have heard about the reward Petro had advertised. This sharp little operator had probably prevailed upon half the urchins in Rome to scour unsavoury spots for treasures that I could be bribed to buy.

'Who told you I wanted any more foul finds, Gaius?'

'Everyone's talking about what you and Petro are collecting. Father's at home again,' he said, so I knew who was sounding off most wildly.

'That's nice.' I disapproved of telling a thirteen-year-old boy I thought his father was an unreliable pervert. Gaius was clever enough to work it out for himself.

'Father says he's always fishing pieces of corpses out of the river –'

'Lollius always has to cap everyone else's stories. Has he been telling you wild tales about dismembered bodies?'

'He knows all about them! Have you still got that hand? Can I see it?'

'No, and no.'

'This is the most exciting case you've had, Uncle Marcus,' Gaius informed me seriously. 'If you have to go down the sewers to look for more bits, can I come and hold your lantern?'

'I'm not going down any sewers, Gaius. The pieces that have been found were in the aqueducts; you ought to know the difference. Anyway, it's all been taken care of now. An official is investigating the matter for the Curator of the Aqueducts, and Petronius and I are going back to our ordinary work.'

'Will the water board pay us for bones and stuff?'

'No, they'll arrest you for causing a riot. The Curator wants to keep this quiet. Anyway, what you've found may be nothing.'

'Oh yes it is,' Gaius corrected me hotly. 'It's somebody's big toe!'

At my shoulder Helena shuddered. Keen to impress her, the wretch brought out the knob of dark matter again, then once more demanded how much I would pay for it. I looked at it. 'Come off it, Gaius. Stop annoying me by trying to palm me off with an old dog's bone.'

Gaius scrutinised the item himself, then sadly agreed he was trying it on. 'I'll still hold the lamp for you if you go down the sewers.'

'The aqueducts, I told you. Anyway, I'd rather you held the baby so I don't get told off for abandoning her.'

'Gaius hasn't even seen Julia yet,' suggested Helena. My nephew had bunked off from our introduction party. He hated family gatherings: a lad with hidden sense.

Rather to my surprise he asked for a viewing now. Helena took him indoors and even lifted the baby out of the cradle so he could hold her. After one appalled glance he accepted the sleeping bundle (for some reason Gaius had always been fairly polite to Helena), and then we watched the famous tough being overcome by our tiny tot until he was positively eulogising her miniature fingers and toes. We tried not to show our distaste for this sentimentality.

'I thought you had little brothers and sisters of your own,' said Helena.

'Oh, I don't have anything to do with *them*!' returned Gaius scornfully. He looked thoughtful. 'If I did look after her, would there be a fee?'

'Of course,' said Helena at once.

'If you did it properly,' I added weakly. I would sooner leave Gaius in charge of a cage of rats, but the situation was desperate. Besides, I never thought he would want to do it.

'How much?' He was a true member of the Didii.

I named a price, Gaius made me double it, then he handed Julia very carefully back to Helena and decided to go home.

Helena called him back to be given a cinnamon pastry (to my annoyance, since I had already spotted it on the table and had been looking forward to devouring it myself). Then she kissed his cheek formally; Gaius screwed up his face, but failed to avoid the salute.

'Jupiter! I hope he's clean. I haven't dragged him to the baths since we went to Spain.'

We watched him go. I still held his little treasure from the drains. I was pleased with myself for rebuffing his attempt at bribery, though I had mixed feelings all the same.

'Why's that?' asked Helena dubiously, already suspecting the worst.

'Mainly because I rather think it really is a human toe.'

Helena touched my cheek gently, with the same air of taming a wild creature that she had shown when kissing Gaius. 'Well there you are,' she murmured. 'Anacrites can do what he likes – but you're obviously still taking an interest!'

XVI

LENIA LET PETRO and me put up a notice on the laundry advising that all samples of body parts from the waterways were now
required By Order to be handed in to Anacrites. That helped.

We had become so notorious that even our flow of regular clients
improved. Mostly they brought in work we could do with our eyes
closed. There were the usual barristers wanting witness statements
from people who lived out of Rome. I sent Petro to do those. It was
a good way to take his mind off missing his children – and to make
sure he could not disgrace himself again by visiting Balbina Milvia.
Besides, he had not yet realised that the reason the barristers wanted
to employ us for this work was that it was tedious as all Hades riding a mule to Lavinium and back just to hear some crone describe
how her old brother had lost his temper with a wheelwright and
bopped him on the nob with half an amphora (bearing in mind that
the wheelwright would probably get cold feet about suing the
brother and withdraw the case anyway).

I busied myself tracing debtors and carrying out moral health
checks on prospective bridegrooms for cautious families (a good
double bind, because I could sneakily ask the bridegrooms if they
wanted to pay for financial profiles of the families). For several days
I was a dedicated private informer. When that palled I retrieved the
big toe from an empty vase on a high shelf out of Nux's reach, and
went down to the Forum to see if I could irritate Anacrites.

He had had so many revolting finds handed in by people who
assumed the reward still applied that a separate room and two dedicated scribes had had to be assigned to the enquiry. A quick glance
told me most of the horrid deposits should have been rejected, but
the officials were receiving and logging everything. Anacrites had
progressed only as far as devising a form to be filled in laboriously by
his scribes. I tossed in the toe Gaius had found, refused to supply the
prescribed half a scroll of details, leered round the door of Anacrites'
strictly private office, then disappeared again.

I had had my fun. I could have left it at that. Instead, gnawed at by something Gaius had said and what I had overheard myself at Julia's party, I decided I would go and visit Lollius.

My sister Galla struggled to exist with an uncertain number of children and no support from her husband. She rented a doss down by the Trigeminal Gate. It could have been described as a fine river-bank property with fabulous views and a sun terrace, but not to anyone who had seen it. Here my favourite nephew Larius had grown up, before he had the sense to elope and become a wall painter in the luxurious villas on the Bay of Neapolis. Here in theory lived Gaius, though he rarely put in an appearance, preferring to steal sausages from street sellers and curl up at night in a temple portico. Here, on extremely infrequent occasions, one could encounter the Tiber water boatman Lollius.

He was lazy, deceitful, and brutal – quite civilised by my brothers-in-law's standards. I despised him more than any of the others except Gaius Baebius the puffed-up customs clerk. Lollius was ugly, too, yet so cocky that he somehow convinced women he was vitally attractive. Galla fell for it – every time he came back to her from the others. His success with tavern trollops was just unbelievable. Galla and he regularly tried to make an effort with their marriage, saying they were embarking on that defeatist course for the children's sake. Most of the children ran away to my mother's house when it happened. Almost as soon as the pitiful pair were supposedly together again Lollius would be playing pop the bunny down the hole with some new fifteen-year-old flower-seller; inevitably Galla would hear the news from a kind neighbour, and he would stagger home one night in the small hours to find the door locked. This always seemed to surprise him.

'Where's Gaius?' shouted Galla as I entered their sordid home and tried to clean my boot where I had stepped in a bowl of puppies' gruel left in the hall.

'How should I know? Your unwashed, undisciplined little rag-picker isn't my affair.'

'He was coming to see you.'

'That must have been two days ago.'

'Oh, was it?' No wonder young Gaius ran wild. Galla was a hopeless mother. 'What are you going to do about Larius?'

'Nothing, Galla. Don't keep asking me. Larius is doing what he wants, and if that happens to be painting walls miles from Rome I don't blame him. Where's Lollius?' I roared, since I had not actually encountered Galla face to face and was still uncertain which room she was bawling from.

'Who cares? He's asleep.' At least he was in.

I tracked down the unprepossessing blackguard and dragged him out from under a grimy bolster where he was snoring with his arm round an empty flagon. This was the boatman's idea of uxorious devotion. Galla sounded off at him as soon as she heard him grumbling, so Lollius winked at me and we sauntered from the house without calling out that we were going. Galla would be used to it.

I walked my brother-in-law towards the Forum Boarium. He was probably drunk, but always had a serious limp that made him walk with a lurch, so I had the distasteful task of holding him upright. He looked as if he smelt, though I tried to avoid snuggling up close enough to find out.

We were on the stone-clad side of the Tiber, what they call the Marbled Bank, a good way past the wharves that surround the Emporium but before the elegant theatres and porticoes and the great bend in the river that encompasses the Campus Martius. After the Sublician Bridge we steered round the Arch of Lentulus, and the Market Inspector's office, and ended up looking out over the water near the ancient Temple of Portunus, immediately above the exit arch of the Great Sewer. A nice smelly place if I had thrown Lollius off the embankment. Something I should have done. Rome, and Galla's children, deserved it.

'What do you want, young Marcus?'

'It's Falco to you. Show some respect for the head of the family.' He took it that I was joking. Being head of our family was an unenforceable honour. Unendurable, too; a punishment I had been give by the Fates out of malice. My father, the auctioneer and fillollicking finangler Didius Geminus, ought to carry out the prescribed duties, but he had fled from home many years back. He was callous, but shrewd.

Lollius and I stared gloomily towards the Aemilian Bridge. 'Tell me about what you find in the river, Lollius.'

'Shit.'

'Is that a considered answer, or a general curse?'

'Both.'

'I want to hear about dismembered bodies.'

'More fool you.'

I fixed him sternly. It did no good.

When I forced myself to survey him I was looking at a miserable specimen. Lollius appeared to be about fifty, though he could have been any age. He was shorter and stouter than me, in such bad condition that things looked cheerful for his heirs. His face had been ugly even before he lost most of his teeth and had one of his eyes permanently closed by Galla's hitting him with a solid-bottomed pancake pan. His eyes had been too close together to start with, his ears were lopsided, his nose had a twist that made him snuffle and he had no neck. A traditional waterman's woollen cap covered his lank hair. Several layers of tunics completed the dreary ensemble; when he had spilt enough wine down himself he just pulled a new one on top.

So was there nothing to recommend him? Well, he could row a skiff. He could swim. He could curse, fight and fornicate. He was a potent husband, though a disloyal father. He made regular earnings, then persistently lied about them to my sister, and never handed over anything for the upkeep of his family: a classic. True metal from the traditional Roman mould. Surely overdue to be elected to a priesthood or a tribunate.

I looked back at the river again. It wasn't much. Brown and gurgling fitfully as usual. Sometimes it floods; the rest of the time the fabled Tiber is a mediocre stream. I had stayed in smaller cities whose waterways were more impressive. But Rome had been built on this spot not just because of the fabled Seven Hills. This was the prime position in central Italy. To our right at Tiber Island had been the first bridgeable position above the sea, a decent one-day stage from the coast. It had probably seemed a sensible location to the kind of slow-witted shepherds who thought they were clever fortifying a floodplain and placing their Forum in a stagnant marsh.

Nowadays the narrow, silting river was a grave disadvantage. Rome was importing fabulous quantities of goods from all over the world. Every amphora and bale had to be dragged along the highroad in carts or on muleback, or carried up by barges to the Emporium. The new harbour at Ostia had had to be rebuilt but was still unsatisfactory. So as well as the barges there was plenty of small boat traffic, and that enabled the existence of parasites like Lollius.

He was the last person I wanted to see credited with assisting any enquiry I took part in. However, Petro and I were stuck for useful information. If we were to vie with Anacrites even my brother-in-law had to be tackled. 'Lollius, either shut your trap about finding things, or tell me what in the name of the gods they are.'

He gave me his most unreliable squint, bleary and sly. 'Oh, you mean the festival fancies!'

I knew at once that the bastard had just told me something significant.

XVII

'WE CALL THEM that,' he gloated. Slow to grasp a point himself, he assumed I was just as dim. 'Festival fancies . . .' he repeated lovingly.

'What exactly are we talking about, Lollius?'

He drew two lines on his own body with his index fingers, one across his filthy neck and one at the top of his fat legs. 'You know –'

'Torsos? Limbless?'

'Yes.'

I was no longer feeling chatty, but my brother-in-law looked eager. To forestall more horrible details I asked: 'I suppose the heads are missing too?'

'Of course. Anything that can be chopped off.' Lollius flashed what remained of his stumpy teeth in an evil grin. 'Including the melons.' He drew circles on his chest then sliced down with the flat of his hand as if cutting off breasts. At the same time he made a revolting squelching sound through his gums.

'I gather they are women?' His mime had been graphic, but I had learned to make sure of everything.

'Well, they were once. Slaves or flighty-girls presumably.'

'What makes you think that?'

'Nobody ever comes looking for them. Who else could they be? All right, slaves might be valuable. So they're all good-time girls – ones who had a really bad time.' He shrugged off-handedly. I deplored his attitude, though he was probably right.

'I've never heard anything about these limbless lasses.'

'You must move in the wrong circles, Falco.'

I made no plans to alter my social life. 'Have you fished any out?'

'No, but I know someone who did.' Again.

'You saw it yourself?'

'Right.' Remembering, even he went quiet.

'How many are we talking about?'

'Well, not so many,' Lollius conceded. 'Just enough for us to think *"He's still at it!"* when one floats to the top or gets tangled in an oar. They all look pretty much the same,' he explained, as if I was too dumb to work out how the boatmen made the connection.

'With the same mutilations? You talk as if pulling these beauties out of the river is a traditional perk of your job. How long has it been going on?'

'Oh, years!' He sounded quite definite.

'Years? How many years?'

'As long as I've been a waterman. Well, most of the time anyway.' I should have known better than to hope Lollius would be definite, even about something as sensational as this.

'So we're looking for a mature murderer?'

'Or an inherited family business,' Lollius cackled.

'When was the last one discovered?'

'The last *I* heard about' − Lollius paused, letting me absorb the implication that he was at the centre of life on the river so bound to know everything important − 'would have been about last April. Sometimes we find them in July, though, and sometimes in the autumn.'

'And what did you call them?'

'Festival fancies.' Still proud of the definition, he didn't mind repeating it once more. 'Like those special Cretan cakes, you know −'

'Yes, yes, I get it. They turn up at public holidays.'

'Neat, eh? Somebody must have spotted that it's always when there's a big set of Games, or a Triumph.'

'The calendar's so crammed with public holidays I'm surprised anyone noticed.'

'The joke is, it's always when we roll back to work with a really vile headache and can't face anything too raw.' That happened frequently too; the water boatmen all had a notorious capacity for drink.

'When they get fished out, what do you do with the bodies?'

Lollius glared at me. 'What do you think we do? We shove in a spike to let the gas out, tow them downstream out of trouble, then sink them if we can.'

'Oh, the humane touch.'

His scorn was justifiable. 'We're certainly not daft enough to hand them in to the authorities!'

'Fair enough.' Public spirit is at best a waste of time, at worst positively asking for ten months rotting in the Lautumiae jail without a trial.

'So what are you suggesting?' Lollius jibed. 'That we should dig a dirty great hole in a public garden and bury the lumps when nobody's looking – or when we hope they're not? Or we could all club together and arrange something through our guild's funeral club, maybe? Oh, yes. You try arranging a polite cremation for someone you don't know who has had all their extremities hacked off by a pervert. Anyway, Falco, if I had found one of the fancies, and even if I was prepared to do something about it, can you imagine how I'd explain it to Galla?'

I smiled drily. 'I expect you'd tell my wonderful trusting big sister some complicated lies, Lollius – just as you normally do!'

XVIII

PETRONIUS WAS FURIOUS. When he returned from his trip out of town, the tale I reported from Lollius brought out his worst side as a member of the vigiles. He wanted to storm down to the Tiber and arrest anyone who carried an oar.

'Back off, Petro. We don't know any names, and we won't be told any either. I poked around a bit but the boatmen have clammed up. They don't want trouble. Who can blame them? Anyway, without an actual torso what can you do? We now know that the rivermen find these things; it's no real surprise, because if there are dismembered hands floating about then the other body parts had to be somewhere. I let it be known along the embankments that next time we'll take delivery of what they trawl up. Let's not annoy the bastards. Lollius only coughed to me because he was yearning to play the big prawn.'

'He's a rotten old bloater.'

'Don't tell me.'

'I'm sick of messing about, Falco.' Petronius seemed tetchy. Maybe when I sent him to Lavinium I had made him miss an assignation with Milvia. 'The way you do things is incredible. You tiptoe all around the facts, sidling up to suspects with a silly smile on your face, when what's needed is to hand out a few beltings with a cudgel –'

'That's the vigiles' trick for encouraging public trust, eh?'

'It's how to run a systematic enquiry.'

'I prefer to woo the truth out of them.'

'Don't fib. You just bribe them.'

'Wrong. I'm too short of cash.'

'So what's your method, Falco?'

'Subtlety.'

'Bulls' bollocks! It's time we had some routine around here,' Petro declared.

To impose this fine concept, he rushed off, despite the hot

weather, and took himself to the river where he would try working on the boatmen although I had told him not to. I knew he would get nowhere. Clearly the harsh lessons I had absorbed in seven years as an informer would have to be learned all over again by him before Lucius Petronius carried weight as my partner. He was used to relying on simple authority to generate something even simpler: fear. Now he would find he lacked that. All he would inspire in the private sector was scorn and contempt. Anyway, for private citizens putting the boot in was not a legal option. (It was probably illegal for the vigiles too, but that was a theory nobody would ever test.)

While Petro was exhausting himself among the water bugs, I applied myself to earning some petty cash. First I cheered myself up extracting payment for various jobs I had done months ago, before Petro joined up with me; the denarii went straight into my bankbox in the Forum, minus the price of a couple of shark steaks for Helena and me.

Then, thanks to our recent notoriety, we had a few tasty tasks. A landlord wanted us to investigate one of his female tenants who had been claiming hard luck; he suspected she was harbouring a live-in boyfriend who should be coughing up a share of the rent. A glance at the lady had already revealed that this was likely; she was a peach and in my carefree youth I would have strung out the job for weeks. The landlord himself had tried unsuccessfully to waylay the boyfriend; my method only took an hour of surveillance. I settled in at midday. As I expected, promptly at lunchtime a runt in a patched tunic turned up looking furtive. He couldn't bear to miss his snack. A word with the tenement's water-carrier confirmed that he lived there; I marched in, confronted the culprits as they shared their eggs and olives, and clinched the case.

A well-to-do papyrus-seller thought his wife was two-timing him with his best friend. We had been watching the set-up; I decided the friend was innocent, though the dame was almost certainly being screwed on a regular basis by the family steward. The client was overjoyed when I cleared his friend, didn't want to hear about the cheating slave, and paid up on the spot. That went in the honesty dish Petro and I were sharing, even the large gratuity.

On the way back to Fountain Court I dropped in at the baths, scraped myself down, listened to some unimportant gossip, and bantered with Glaucus. He was working with another client and I didn't stay. Back at base Petronius Longus had failed to reappear. I was in for a hard time worrying over his whereabouts; it was like being in charge of a love-lorn adolescent. I hoped his absence meant he had gone to attempt a reconciliation with his wife. I knew it was more likely the dog had sneaked off to see Balbina Milvia.

Pleased with my own efforts I shut up the office, exchanged a few words with Lenia, then strolled across the street. I was the cook here, so long as we lacked a troop of whining slaves. Helena had been marinading the fish steaks in olive oil with a few herbs. I pan-fried them simply over the embers in our cooking bench and we ate them on a green salad dressed with vinegar, more oil and a dash of fish sauce. We had plenty of oil and sauce after our Spanish adventure, though I applied them sparingly. A good shark steak should stand alone.

'Did you rinse them well?'

'Of course,' retorted Helena. 'I could see they had been salted. Mind you, I was wondering what had been in the washing water . . .'

'Don't think about it. You'll never know.'

She sighed. 'Well, if Lollius was right and people have been murdered, cut up, and dumped over several years, I suppose we're all used to it.'

'The torsos must have been put straight into the river.'

'How reassuring,' muttered Helena. 'I'm worried about the baby's health. I'll ask Lenia if we can draw our water from the laundry well.'

She wanted the horror stopped. So did I. She wanted me to stop it; I was not so sure I could.

We left a decent period so it didn't look as if we were hoping to be given dinner, then walked over the Aventine to her parents' house. I thought we were just enjoying a cheap night out, but I soon realised Helena Justina had more precise plans. For one thing she wanted a closer inspection of the situation regarding Claudia Rufina. Claudia and both Helena's brothers were there, moping because their parents were holding a dinner party for friends of their own generation, so the house was full of tantalising food scents while the youngsters had to make do with leftovers. We sat around with them until Aelianus grew bored and decided he was off out to hear a concert.

'You could take Claudia,' Helena prompted.

'Of course,' said Aelianus at once, since he came from a sharp-witted family and had been brought up well. But Claudia was frightened of Rome at night and decided to opt out of this invitation from her betrothed.

'Don't worry; we'll look after her,' his brother told the prospective bridegroom. The comment was quiet and non-judgmental; Justinus had always known how to niggle in an underhand way. There was no love lost between these lads; born barely two years apart they were too close. They had no habit of sharing anything, least of all responsibility.

'Thanks,' Aelianus responded laconically. Perhaps he looked as if he were having second thoughts about going. And perhaps not.

He did leave us. Claudia carried on discussing the orphans' school with Helena, which suited both of them. Claudia was nursing our baby, being the kind of girl who grabs them and shows off how sentimental she can be. It may not have been the way to her betrothed's heart. Aelianus could only just stomach the thought of getting married; it was tactless of Claudia to let him see she expected him to play his part in filling a nursery.

I enjoyed a long talk with Justinus. He and I had shared an adventure once, rampaging like heroes all over northern Germany, and I had thought highly of him ever since. If I had been of his own class I would have offered him patronage, but as an informer I had no help to give.

He was now in his early twenties, a tall, spare figure whose good looks and easy nature could have wreaked havoc among the bored women of the senatorial classes if it had ever struck him he was cut out to be a heartbreaker. Part of his charm was that he appeared to have no idea of either his talents or his seductive potential. Those big brown eyes with their intriguing hint of sadness probably noticed more than he showed, however; Quintus Camillus Justinus was a shrewd little soldier. According to rumour he was chasing after an actress, but I wondered if the rumour had been carefully cultivated so that people would leave him alone while he chose his own path. Actresses were death to senators' sons. Quintus was too clever for social suicide.

Vespasian had hauled him back to Rome from a military tribunate in Germany, apparently in great favour. As so often happens, once Justinus arrived home the promise of an upward push evaporated; other heroes were catching attention. Justinus himself, always diffident, showed neither surprise nor resentment. I was angry for him, and I knew that Helena was too.

'I thought there was talk of you trying for the Senate at the same

83

time as your brother? Didn't the Emperor hint that accelerated entry might be possible?'

'The impetus died.' His smile was wry. Any barmaid would have given him a free refill on the spot. 'You know how it is, Marcus. So I suppose I'll now stand for election at the normal age. It spreads the financial burden for Papa.' He paused. 'I'm not sure that's what I want, in any case.'

'Going through a tricky phase, eh?' I grinned at him. He wanted to do well – and to beat Aelianus at it. That was understood.

'Being difficult,' he agreed.

Helena looked up. She must have been paying attention even though she had appeared deep in conversation with Claudia. 'I suppose you scratch yourself in front of Father's illustrious friends and refuse to change your tunic more than once a month, and you're surly at breakfast time?'

He beamed at his sister fondly. 'I don't turn up at breakfast at all, dearest. In the middle of the morning when all the slaves are busy washing floors I emerge from bed – walking straight through the clean bit in last night's dirty shoes – then I demand a fresh sardine and a five-egg omelette cooked *exactly* right. When it comes, I leave most of it.'

I laughed. 'You'll go far – but don't expect an invitation to stay with us!'

Looking over her large nose, Claudia Rufina gazed at the three of us with troubled solemnity. Maybe it was just as well she had been linked to Aelianus. He was proper and conventional. He never indulged in ludicrous fantasies.

Helena patted the young girl's heavily bangled arm, for no obvious reason. Also for no reason her eyes met mine; I winked at her. Shameless, she winked back without a second thought. Then we held each other's gaze as established lovers sometimes do even when it is socially inconvenient, shutting out the other two.

Helena was looking well. Clear-skinned, good-humoured, alert and intelligent. More formal than she would be at home, since you never quite know what to expect when visiting a senator's house: a pristine white gown with a shimmering golden stole, an amber necklace and light earrings, her face defined with hints of colour, her hair tucked into several fancy combs. Seeing her confident and content reassured me. I had done Helena no wrong luring her from her father's house. She had the knack of being able to return temporarily to this upper-class world without embarrassment, taking me with her. But although she must miss the comforts, she showed no trace of regret.

'Well, Marcus!' Her eyes were smiling in a way that made me take and kiss her hand. The gesture was acceptable in public, but must have spoken of far deeper intimacy.

'You have such great affection,' exclaimed Claudia impulsively. Alarmed by her mood our baby awoke, whimpering. Helena reached to take the child.

Justinus rose from his couch and came round behind his sister, to hug her and kiss her too. 'Claudia Rufina, we are a loving family,' he said wickedly. 'And now you are to join us – aren't you glad?'

'Be a pet,' Helena reproved him. 'While you're jumping about and making silly remarks, pop into Father's study and bring me his annual calendar.'

'Planning another party?'

'No. Showing Marcus that his best partner is the one who lives with him.'

'Marcus knows that,' I said.

The senator had an expensive set of the Official Year in Rome: all the dates of all the months, marked with a C for when the Comitia could be in session, F for days when general public business was allowed and N for public holidays. Bad luck days had their black marks. All the fixed festivals, and all the Games, were named. Decimus had sweetly added to the almanac his wife's and children's birthdays, his own, and those of his favourite sister and a couple of well-off ones (who might remember him in their wills if he kept in with them). The latest addition in the blackest ink, which Helena pointed out to me, was the day when Julia Junilla had been born.

Helena Justina read all the way through in silence. Then she looked up and surveyed me with a stern gaze. 'You know why I'm doing this?'

I looked meek, but made sure I demonstrated I could think too. 'You're wondering about what Lollius said.'

Naturally Claudia and Justinus wanted to know who Lollius was and what he had pronounced upon. I told them, keeping it as tasteful as possible. Then while Claudia shuddered and Justinus looked grave Helena gave her opinion. 'There must be well over a hundred public holidays annually, and a good fifty formal festivals. But the festivals are spread throughout the year whereas your brother-in-law said there were special times for finding these women's remains. I think the connection is the Games. Lollius said they find bodies in April – well, there are the Megalensis Games for Cybele, the Games of Ceres, and then the Floral Games, all in that month. The next big concentration is in July –'

'Which he also mentioned.'

'Quite. That's when we have the Apolline Games starting the day before the Nones, and later the Games for the Victories of Caesar which last for a whole ten days.'

'It all fits. Lollius maintains there is another bad time in the autumn.'

'Well, September has the great Roman Games lasting fifteen days, and then at the beginning of next month are the Games in memory of Augustus followed at the *end* of October by the Games for the Victories of Sulla –'

'And the Plebeian Games in November,' I reminded her. I had spotted them earlier when squinting over her shoulder.

'Trust a republican!'

'Trust a plebeian,' I said.

'But what does this mean?' demanded Claudia excitedly. She thought we had solved the whole case.

Justinus threw back his neatly shorn head and regarded the smoke-stained moulded plaster of the ceiling. 'It means that Marcus Didius has found himself an excellent excuse to spend much of the next two months enjoying himself in the sporting arenas of our great city – all the while calling it work.'

But I shook my head sadly. 'I only work when somebody pays me, Quintus.'

Helena shared my mood. 'Besides, there would be no point in Marcus hanging around the Circus when he still has no idea who or what he should be looking for.'

That sounded like most of the surveillance work I ever did.

XIX

Petronius Longus was in an organising mood. His session
with the Tiber boatmen had been as useless as I had prophesied,
and he declared that we should abandon the pointless effort of wondering who was polluting the water supply. Petronius was going to
sort out our business. (He was going to sort out *me*.) He would
impose order. He would attract new work; he would plan our case-
load; he would show me just how to generate wealth through blistering efficiency.

He spent a lot of time composing charts, while I plodded around
the city delivering court summonses. I brought in the meagre
denarii, then Petro wrote them up in elaborate accounts systems. I
was pleased to see him keeping out of trouble.

Petronius seemed to be happy, though I was beginning to suspect
he was covering something up even before I happened to pass by
the vigiles' patrol house and was hailed by Fusculus. 'Here, Falco;
can't you keep that chief of ours occupied? He keeps moping
around here getting in the way.'

'I thought he was either in our office causing havoc among my
clients or out flirting.'

'Oh, he does that too – he pops in to see his honeycake when he
finally leaves us in peace.'

'You're depressing me, Fusculus. No hope that he's dropped
Milvia?'

'Well, if he had done,' Fusculus told me cheerfully, 'your clients
would be safe; we'd have him back here permanently.'

'Don't flatter yourselves. Petronius loves the freelance life.'

'Oh, sure!' Fusculus laughed at me. 'That's why he's constantly
nagging Rubella for a reprieve.

'He doesn't get it, though. So how does Rubella know that
Milvia is still live bait?'

'How does Rubella know anything?' Fusculus had a theory, of
course. He always did. 'Our trusty tribune stays in his lair and

information flows through the atmosphere straight to him. He's supernatural.'

'No, he's human,' I said despondently. I knew how Rubella worked, and it was strictly professional. He wanted to make his name as a vigiles officer then move up to the refined ranks of the Urban Cohorts, maybe even go on to serve in the Praetorian Guard. His priorities never changed; he was after the big criminals, whose capture would cause a flutter and win him promotion. 'I bet he's keeping a full-time watcher on Milvia and her exciting husband in case they revive the old gangs. Every time Petronius goes to the house he'll be logged.'

Fusculus agreed in his usual comfortable way: 'You're right. It's no secret, though the surveillance is concentrating on the old hag. Rubella reckons if the gangs do get reconvened, it will be by Flaccida.'

Milvia's mother. Still, Petro was no better off, because Cornella Flaccida lived with her daughter and son-in-law. She had been forced to move in with them when Petronius convicted her gangster husband, whose property had then been confiscated. One more reason to avoid tangling with the dainty piece, if Petro had had any sense. Milvia's father had been a nasty piece of work, but her mother was even more dangerous.

'So when,' demanded Fusculus in his cheery way, 'can we expect you to have a quiet word with Balbina Milvia, pretty floret of the underworld, and persuade her to leave our cherished chief alone?'

I groaned. 'Why do I always have to do the dirty work?'

'Why did you become an informer, Falco?'

'Petronius is my oldest friend. I couldn't possibly go behind his back.'

'Of course not.' Fusculus grinned.

An hour later I was rapping on the huge bronze antelope knocker that summoned the door porter at the lavish home of Milvia and Florius.

XX

IF I EVER acquire slaves of my own, they will definitely *not* include a door porter. Who wants a lazy, bristle-chinned, rat-arsed piece of insolence littering up the hall and insulting polite visitors – assuming he can bring himself to let them in at all? In the quest for suspects an informer spends more time than most people testing out that despicable race, and I had learned to expect to lose my temper before I was admitted to any house of status.

Milvia's establishment was worse than most, in fact. She kept not merely the usual snide youth who only wanted to get back to the game of Soldiers he was playing against the underchef, but a midget ex-gangster called Little Icarus whom I had last seen being pulverised by the vigiles in a battle royal in a notorious brothel, during which his close crony the Miller had had both feet cut off at the ankles by a rampaging magistrate's lictor who didn't care what he did with his ceremonial axe. Little Icarus and the Miller were murderous thugs. If Milvia and Florius were pretending to be nice middle-class people they ought to employ different staff. Apparently they were no longer even pretending.

Little Icarus was rude to me before he remembered who I was. Afterwards he looked outraged, and as if he was planning to butt me in the privates (as far up as he could reach). When he was installed as Milvia's Janus someone had stripped him of his weapons; maybe that was her mother's notion of house-training. The fact that a gangster's enforcer was the doorstop here said everything about what kind of house this was. The place looked pretty. There were standard roses in stone tubs flanking the door and good copies of Greek statues dotted around the interior atrium. But every time I came here the skin on the back of my neck crawled. I wished I had told somebody – anybody – that I was coming. By then it was too late; I had barged my way inside.

★

Milvia seemed wildly excited to see me. It was not because of my charm.

Not for the first time I found myself wondering whatever possessed Petro to involve himself with miniature puppets like this: all big trusting eyes and piping little voices, and probably just as deceitful under the heartfelt innocence as the bold, bad girls I once fell for myself. Balbina Milvia was a priceless specimen. She had a coronet of dark ringlets held up by indecent wreaths of gold, a tightly trussed bosom peeking from swathes of rich gauze, tiny feet in sparkly sandals – and an anklet, needless to say. Snake bracelets with real rubies for eyes gripped the pale skin of her delicate arms. Whole racks of filigree rings weighed down her minute fingers. Everything about her was so petite and glittery I felt like a blundering brute. But the truth was, the glitter covered dirt. Milvia could no longer pretend not to know that her finery was financed by theft, extortion, and organised gang violence. I knew it too. She gave me a bad, metallic taste in the mouth.

The provocative bundle simpering so sweetly had been spawned by parents from Hades, too. Her father had been Balbinus Pius, a widescale, wholesale villain who had terrorised the Aventine for years. I wondered if chittery-chattery Milvia realised – as she ordered mint tea and honeyed dates – that I was the man who had stabbed a sword into her father then left his dead body to be consumed in a raging house fire. Her mother must know. Cornella Flaccida knew everything. That was how she had managed to take over the criminal empire her husband had left behind. And don't suppose she wept too long after he vanished from society. The only surprise was that she never sent me a huge reward for killing him and putting her in charge.

'How is your darling mama?' I asked Milvia.

'As well as can be expected. She has been widowed, you know.'

'That's tragic.'

'She's heartbroken. I tell her the best way to endure it is to keep herself occupied.'

'Oh, I'm sure she does that.' She would have to. Running criminal gangs efficiently demands time and boundless energy. 'You must be a great consolation to her, Milvia.'

Milvia looked smug, and then slightly anxious as she noticed that my words and tone were not a matching set.

I ignored the refreshments spread before me. When Milvia waved airily to dismiss her slaves I pretended to be nervous and shocked. I was neither. 'How is Florius?' The girl became vague. 'Still attending the races whenever he can? And I hear your devoted husband has an expanding business portfolio?' Florius (whose devotion was insipid) also fancied dipping his grubby equestrian toe into the murky pool of rack-rents, extortion and organised theft. In fact Milvia was surrounded by relatives with creative financial interests.

'I am not sure what you mean, Marcus Didius?'

'It's Falco. And I think you understand me very well.'

That brought on a fine performance. The little lips pouted. The brows knit. The eyes were downcast petulantly. The skirts were smoothed, the bracelets adjusted, and the over-ornamented silver tisane bowls rearranged on their natty dolphin-handled tray. I watched the whole repertoire approvingly. 'I like a girl who gives her all.'

'Pardon?'

'The acting's good. You know how to rebuke a sucker until he feels he's a brute.'

'What are you talking about, Falco?'

Letting her wait for my answer, I leant back and surveyed her at long distance. Then I said coldly, 'I gather you have become very friendly with my friend Lucius Petronius?'

'Oh!' She perked up, clearly thinking I was an intermediary. 'Has he sent you to see me?'

'No – and if you know what's good for you you'll not mention to him that I came.'

Balbina Milvia wrapped her glinting stole round her narrow shoulders protectively. She had perfected the attitude of the frightened fawn. 'Everyone shouts at me, and I'm sure I don't deserve it.'

'Oh, you do, lady. You deserve to be upended over that ivory couch and spanked until you choke. There is a wronged wife on the Aventine who should be allowed to tear your eyes out, and three little girls who should be cheering while she does it.'

'That's a horrid thing to say!' cried Milvia.

'Don't worry about it. Just you enjoy the attention, and being bedded by a man who knows how, instead of by your limp radish of a husband, and don't you distress yourself with the consequences. You can afford to keep Petronius in the luxury he would like to discover – after he loses his job, and his wife, and his children, and most of his outraged and disappointed friends. Though do remember,' I concluded, 'that if you should be the cause of his losing everyone he treasures, it may be you he ends up cursing.'

She was speechless. Milvia had been a spoiled child and an unsupervised wife. She commanded gross wealth and her father had governed the most feared street gangs in Rome. Nobody crossed her. Even her mother, who was a ferocious witch, treated Milvia with diffidence – perhaps scenting that this doe-eyed moppet was so spoiled she could turn truly filthy one day. Appalling behaviour was the one luxury Milvia had not yet indulged herself with. It was bound to come.

'I don't blame you,' I said. 'I can see the attraction. It will take a strong will to close the door on him. But you're a very clever girl, and Petronius is an innocent when it comes to emotions. You are the one with the intelligence to see that in the end it's going nowhere. Let's hope you are the one with the courage to put things right.'

She drew herself up. Like all Petro's women, she was not tall. He used to shelter them against his powerful chest like little lost lambs; for some reason the darlings accepted the refuge as promptly as he made it available.

I wondered whether to tell Milvia about all the others, but that would only give her an opening to assume she was the one who was different. As they all did. And as none of them ever were, except Arria Silvia who had spiked him with a dowry (and a personality) that made sure of it.

I watched the damsel work herself up to insult me. I was too calm. She was finding it hard work having a one-person quarrel. Some of the women I knew could have given her lessons, but under the finery this one was a dull girl of twenty who had been brought up away from the world. She owned everything she wanted, yet she knew nothing. Being rich, even now that she was married she was still kept indoors most of the time. Of course that explained Petronius: when women are locked up, trouble soon comes to them. In the good old Roman tradition Milvia's only source of excitement was her secret lover's visits.

'You have no right to invade my house upsetting me! You can leave now, and don't come again!' The gold granulations in her hairdressing flashed as she tossed her head angrily.

I raised one eyebrow. I must have looked weary, instead of impressed. She tossed her head again – a sure sign of her immaturity. An expert would have brought out some devious alternative effect.

'Dazzling!' I mocked. 'I will leave – but only because I was intending to anyway.' And so I did. Then, of course, Milvia looked sorry that her drama was over.

I had been lying when I had suggested she ought to be the one who ended the affair. If he wanted to do it, Petronius could easily crack down the fortress gates in her face. He had had enough practice.

The only problem was that so many people were telling him to do it that they kept reviving his interest. My old friend Lucius Petronius Longus had always hated being told what to do.

XXI

O F COURSE SOMEBODY told him I had been there. My bet was Milvia herself. For some reason the spectacle of his loyal friend selflessly trying to protect him from disaster did not fill Lucius Petronius with warmth towards the loyal friend. We had a blistering row.

This made working together uncomfortable, though we persisted, since neither of us would concede that he was to blame and should withdraw from the partnership. I knew the quarrel wouldn't last. We were both too annoyed by people reminding us that they had told us it wouldn't work. Sooner or later we would make it up, to prove the doubters wrong.

Anyway, Petro and I had been friends since we were eighteen. It would take more than a silly young woman to drive us apart.

'You sound like his wife,' Helena scoffed.

'No, I don't. His wife has told him to take a long hike to Mesopotamia, and then jump in the Euphrates with a sack over his head.'

'Yes, I heard they had another amiable chat this week.'

'Silvia brought him a notice of divorce.'

'Maia told me Petro threw it back at her.'

'It's not essential she delivers it.' Informing the other party by notice was a polite gesture. Bitter women could always turn it into a drama. Especially women with hefty dowries to be reclaimed. 'She drove him out and refuses to let him go home; that's enough evidence of her intention to separate. If they live apart much longer a notice will be superfluous.'

Petronius and Silvia had left each other before. It normally lasted a day or two and ended when whoever had stayed away from the house went home to feed the cat. This time the split had begun months ago. They were well dug in now. They had in effect positioned palisades and surrounded themselves with triple ditches filled with stakes. Making a truce was going to be difficult.

94

Undaunted by one failure, I forced myself to visit Arria Silvia. She too had heard that I had been to plead with Milvia. She sent me packing in double time.

It was another wasted effort that just made the situation worse. At least since Petro refused to speak to me I was spared hearing what he thought of my taking a peace mission to his wife.

It was now September. In fact Petro and I had had our quarrel on the first day of the month, the Kalends, which as Helena pointed out wryly was the festival of Jupiter the Thunderer. Apparently passers-by in Fountain Court who overheard Petro and me exchanging opinions had believed the god had come to stay on the Aventine.

Three days later, also in honour of Jupiter Tonans, began the Roman Games.

The two young Camillus brothers used their aristocratic influence – which meant they found a lot of sesterces – to acquire good tickets for the first day. There were always debenture-holders with reserved seats who passed them on to touts. Descendants of military heroes, who sold off their hereditary seats. Descendants of heroes tend to be mercenary – unlike the heroes *of course*. So Helena's brothers acquired seats, and they obligingly took us. For me, sitting down with a decent view made a change from squashing into the unreserved terraces.

Young Claudia Rufina was being formally introduced to the Circus in Rome; watching scores of gladiators being sliced up while the Emperor snored discreetly in his gilded box and the best pick-pockets in the world worked the crowds would show her what a civilised city her intended marriage had brought her to. A sweet girl, she tried her best to look overwhelmed by it all.

Smuggling in cushions and large handkerchiefs which we could use as hats (illegal measures once, though tolerated now if you kept them discreet), we sat through the parade and the chariot race, then bunked off for lunch while the inferior gladiators were being booed, and returned to stay until dark. Helena remained at home with Julia after lunch, but rejoined us for the final hour or two. Being pleasant became too much of a strain for Aelianus and he left in the late afternoon, but his shy betrothed stuck it out to the finish with Helena, Justinus and me. We slipped away during the final fight, to avoid the traffic jams and the pimps who mobbed the gates at the close.

Aelianus looked perturbed that his Spanish bride was so keen on circuses. He must have feared that he would find it hard to disappear from home for the traditional masculine debauch on public holidays if his noble lady always wanted to come too. While you're holding a parasol and passing the salted nuts it's hard even to get drunk and tell filthy stories; coarser male behaviour would be quite ruled out. Claudia Rufina did enjoy herself, and not just because Justinus and I encouraged Aelianus to slink away early. She was eager to be part of my enquiry. I was not simply relaxing at the Circus; I was looking out for something suspicious in connection with the aqueduct murders. Nothing happened, of course.

The Roman Games last for fifteen days, four of them comprising theatrical performances. Aelianus never regained interest. For one thing he had treated us to the tickets for the opening ceremony (playing the generous bridegroom), so his purse was now rather light. Having to ask his brother or me to stand him his mulsum every time he wanted a beaker from a passing drinks-seller was bound to pall. By the third day it had become routine for Aelianus to escape with Helena when she went home to feed the baby. From time to time I would leave Claudia bantering with Justinus while I moved around the Circus looking for anything untoward. With a daily changing audience of a quarter of a million people, the chances of spotting an abduction in process were slim.

It did happen. I missed it. At some point early in the Games a woman was lured to an ugly fate. Then on the fourth day a new victim's hand was discovered in the Aqua Claudia and the news caused a riot.

As I returned to rejoin Claudia Rufina and Justinus after having lunch at home with Helena, I noticed large numbers of people rushing in one direction. I had come down from the Aventine on the Clivus Publicus. I was expecting to meet crowds, but these were clearly not heading into the Circus Maximus. No one could be bothered to tell me where they were going. It was either a very good dog fight, an executor's sale with astonishing bargains, or a public riot. So naturally I raced along with them. I ignore snapping dogs, but I always jump at a chance to acquire a cheap set of stockpots, or to watch the public throwing rocks at a magistrate's house.

From the starting-gate end of the Circus the throng pushed and shoved through the Cattle Market Forum, past the Porta Carmentalis, around the curve of the Capitol, and into the main Forum, which lay strangely peaceful because of the Games. Yet even on public holidays the Forum of the Romans was never entirely empty. Tourists, killjoys, workhogs, latecomers heading back to the show and slaves who had no tickets or no time off were always passing to and fro. Those who did not realise they were in the middle of an incident had their feet trampled, then were buffeted again as they stood around complaining. Suddenly panic exploded. Litters tumbled over. Off-duty lawyers (with their keen noses) hid in the Basilica Julia, which was untenanted and echoing. The money-lenders, who never closed their stalls, slammed their chests shut so fast some of them nipped their fat fingers in the lids.

By now a certain element had turned themselves into an audience, sitting on the steps of monuments watching the fun. Others co-ordinated their efforts, raising chants of denigration against the Curator of the Aqueducts. Nothing too politically abstruse. Just sophisticated insults like 'He's a useless bastard!' and 'The man must go!'

I jumped up into the portico of the Temple of Castor, a favourite watching post of mine. This gave me a fine view of the mob who were listening to orations under the Arch of Augustus; there various hotheads waved their arms as if they were trying to lose a few pounds while they declaimed against the government in a manner the could land them in jail being beaten up by unwashed guards – another offence against their liberty to roar about. Some of them wanted to be philosophers – all long hair, bare feet and hairy blankets – which in Rome was a sure way to be regarded as dangerous. But I also noticed cautious souls who had taken care to come out girded with water gourds and satchels of lunch.

Meanwhile groups of pale, sad women in mourning garments solemnly laid floral offerings at the Basin of Juturna – the sacred spring where Castor and Pollux were supposed to have watered their horses. Invalids rashly taking the nasty-tasting liquor for their ailments fell back nervously as these middle-class matrons deposited their wilting blooms, amid much wailing, then took hands and circled in a dreamy fashion. They weaved their way over to the House of the Vestals. Most of the Virgins would be in their seats of honour at the Circus, but there was bound to be one on duty to attend the sacred flame. She would be used to receiving deputations of well-meaning dames who brought tasteful gifts and earnest prayers but not too much sense.

On the opposite side of the Sacred Way, near the old Rostrum and the Temple of Janus, is the ancient Shrine of Venus Claocina, the Purifier. This too had its posse of clamouring protesters. Venus definitely needed to gird her beauteous thighs for action.

From a fellow observer I heard that the new hand had been found yesterday in the Claudian Aqueduct, one of the newest, which poured into a collection system near the great Temple of Claudius opposite the end of the Palatine. That explained these scenes in the Forum. The citizens of Rome had finally realised that their water contained suspicious fragments that might be poisoning them. Physicians and apothecaries were being besieged by patients with as many kinds of nausea as a sick Nile crocodile.

The crowd was more noisy than violent. That would not stop the authorities cracking down heavily. The vigiles would have known how to move people on with a few shoves and curses, but some idiot had called up the Urban Cohorts. These happy fellows assisted the Urban Prefect. Their job description is 'keeping down the servile element, and curbing insolence'; to do it they are armed with a sword and a knife each, and they don't mind where they stick them.

Barracked with the Praetorian Guard, the Urbans are equally arrogant. They love any peaceful demonstration they can mishandle until it turns into a bloody riot. It justifies their existence. As soon as I glimpsed them marching up in ugly phalanxes, I hopped down the back of the Temple on to the Via Nova and strolled off up the Vicus Tuscus. I managed to leave the troublespot without having my head split open. Others cannot have been so fortunate.

Since I was near to Glaucus' baths, I swerved inside and stayed there in the deserted gymnasium shifting weights and battering a practice sword against a post until the danger had passed. It would take more than the Urbans to get past Glaucus; when he said 'Entry by invitation only' it stuck.

The streets were quiet again when I emerged. There was not too much blood on the pavements.

Abandoning the Games, I headed back to the office in the faint hope of finding Petronius. As I sauntered along Fountain Court I could see something was up. This was too much excitement for one day. I backtracked immediately to the barber's; it was illegally open, since men like to look smart on public holidays in the hope that some floozy will fall for them, and anyway the barber in our street usually had no idea of the calendar. I ordered myself a leisurely trim, and surveyed the scene cautiously.

'We're having a visitation,' sneered the barber, who harboured little respect for authority. His name was Apius. He was fat, florid, and had the worst head of hair between here and Rhegium. Thin, greasy strands were strung over a flaking scalp. He hardly ever shaved himself either.

He too had noticed the highly unusual presence of some tired lictors. Desperate for shade, they were flopping under the portico outside Lenia's laundry. Women brazenly stopped to stare at them, probably making coarse jokes. Children crept up giggling, then dared one another to risk their little fingers against the ceremonial axe blades that lurked in the bundles of rods that the lictors had let fall. Lictors are freed slaves or destitute citizens: rough, but willing to rehabilitate themselves through work.

'Who rates six?' I asked Apius. The barber always talked as if he knew everything, though I had yet to hear him answer a straight question accurately.

'Someone who wants to be announced a long way ahead of himself.' Lictors traditionally walk in single file in front of the personage they escort.

Six was an unusual number. Two was a praetor or other high official. Twelve meant the Emperor, though he would be escorted by the Praetorians too. I knew Vespasian would be chained to his box at the Circus today.

'A consul,' decided Apius. He knew nothing. Consuls also had twelve.

'Why would a consul be visiting Lenia?'

'To complain about dirty marks when she returned his smalls?'

'Or a dull finish to the nap of his best toga? Jupiter, Apius – it's the Ludi Romani and the laundry's closed! You're useless. I'll pay you tomorrow for the haircut. It offends me to part with money during a festival. I'm off to see what's going on.'

Everyone believes a barber is the source of all gossip. Not ours. And Apius was typical. The myth about barbers being up to date with scandal has as much truth as that tale foreigners are always being spun about Romans socialising in the public latrines. Excuse me! When you're straining your heart out after last night's rather runny rabbit-in-its-own-gravy, the last thing you want is some friendly fellow with an inane grin popping up to ask your opinion of this week's Senate decree about freemen co-habiting with slaves. If anyone tried it with me, I'd ram him somewhere tender with a well-used gutter sponge.

These elevated thoughts entertained me as I walked along Fountain Court. At the laundry the lictors told me they were escorting an ex-consul, one who had served earlier in the year but had stood down to give some other big bean a chance. He was over the road visiting someone called Falco, apparently.

That put me in a happy mood. If there's one thing I hate more than high officials burdened with office, it's officials who have just shed the burden and who are looking for trouble they can cause. I bounced indoors, all set to try to insult him, bearing in mind that if he was still in his named year as consul I was about to be rude to the most revered and highest ranking ex-magistrate in Rome.

XXII

THERE ARE WOMEN who would panic when presented with a consul. One benefit of importing a senator's daughter to be my unpaid secretary was that instead of shrieking with horror, Helena Justina was more likely to greet the prestigious one as an honorary uncle and calmly ask after his haemorrhoids.

The fellow had been supplied with a bowl of refreshing hot cinnamon, which I happened to know Helena could brew up with honey and a hint of wine until it tasted like ambrosia. He already looked impressed by her suave hospitality and crisp common sense. So when I marched in, hooking my thumbs in my festival belt like an irritated Cyclops, I was presented with an ex-consul who was already tame.

'Afternoon. My name's Falco.'

'My husband,' smiled Helena, being especially respectable.

'Her devoted slave,' I returned, honouring her courteously with this blithe romantic note. Well, it was a public holiday.

'Julius Frontinus,' said the eminent man, in a plain tone.

I nodded. He shadowed the gesture.

I took a seat at the table and was handed my personal bowl by the elegant hostess. Helena was striking in white, the proper colour for the Circus; although she wore no jewellery because of the marauding pickpockets, she was bound up in braided ribbons which made her frivolously neat. To emphasise how things were in this house, I pulled up another bowl and poured her a drink too. Then we both raised our cups solemnly to the Consul, while I took a good look at him.

If he was the usual age for a consul he was forty three; forty four if he had had this year's birthday by now. Clean-shaven and close-shorn. A Vespasian appointment, so bound to be competent, confident and shrewd. Undeterred by my scrutiny and unfazed by his poor surroundings. He was a man with a solid career behind him, yet the energy to carry him through several more top-notch roles before he went senile. Physically spare, a trim weight, undebauched. Someone to respect – or walking trouble: primed to stir things up.

He was assessing me too. Fresh from the gym and in festive clothes, but with militaristic boots. I lived in a squalid area, with a girl who had high social standards: a sophisticated mix. He knew he was facing plebeian aggression, yet he had been soothed with expensive cinnamon from the luxurious east. He was being bombarded by the peppery scent from late summer lilies in a Campanian bronze vase. And his drink came in a high-gloss redware bowl, decorated with exquisite running antelopes. We had taste. We had interesting trade connections – or were travellers ourselves – or could win friends who gave us handsome gifts.

'I'm looking for someone to work with me, Falco. Camillus Verus recommended you.'

Any commission sent via Helena's papa had to be welcomed politely. 'What's the job and what's your role in it? What would *my* role be?'

'First I need to know your background.'

'Surely Camillus briefed you?'

'I'd like to hear it from you.'

I shrugged. I never complain if a client is particular. 'I'm a private informer: court work, acting for executors, financial assessments, tracing stolen art. At present I have a partner who is ex-vigiles. From time to time the Palace employs me in an official capacity for work I can't discuss, usually abroad. I have been doing this for the past eight years. I served in the Second Augustan legion in Britain before that.'

'Britain!' Frontinus jerked. 'What did you think of Britain?'

'Not enough to want to go back.'

'Thanks,' he commented drily. 'I've just been appointed to the next governorship.'

I grinned. 'I'm sure you'll find it a fascinating province, sir. I've been twice; my first mission for Vespasian also took me there.'

'We liked Britain more than Marcus Didius admits,' put in Helena diplomatically. 'I think if informers are ever barred from Rome we might even retire there; Marcus dreams of a quiet farm in a fertile green valley –' The girl was wicked. She knew I loathed the place.

'It's a new country with everything to do,' I said, sounding like any pompous forum orator. I was trying not to meet Helena's dancing eyes. 'If you like work, and a challenge, you should enjoy your term there, sir.'

He seemed to relax. 'I'd like to talk further – but there's

something more urgent first. Before I leave for Britain I have been asked to supervise a commission of enquiry. I would like to see it completed as swiftly as possible.'

'So this is not about a private investigation?' Helena enquired innocently.

'No.'

She fished the cinnamon stick from her bowl, squeezing it slightly against the rim. Nobody was rushing the formalities. Well, I could rely on Helena's finely probing curiosity. 'Is the commission for the Senate?' she asked.

'The Emperor.'

'Did he suggest Marcus to assist you?'

'Vespasian suggested your father could put me in touch with someone reliable.'

'To do what?' she insisted sweetly.

Frontinus turned to me. 'Do you have to be given approval?' He sounded amused.

'I don't even sneeze without permission.'

'You never listen to me,' Helena corrected.

'Always, lady!'

'Accept the job, then.'

'I don't know that it is.'

'Papa wants you to do it, and so does the Emperor. You need their goodwill.' Ignoring Frontinus, she leaned towards me, beating my wrist lightly with the long slim fingers of her left hand. On one was the silver ring I had given her as a love token. I looked at the ring, then at her, playing moody. She flushed. I clapped my fist to one shoulder and hung my head: the gladiator's submission. Helena clucked reprovingly. 'Too much of the Circus! Stop playing. Julius Frontinus will think you're a clown.'

'He won't. If an ex-consul demeans himself by a hike up the Aventine, it's because he has already read my immaculate record and been impressed.'

Frontinus pursed his lips.

Helena was still urgent: 'Listen; I can guess what you are being asked to do. There was a public disturbance today in the Forum –'

'I was there.'

She looked surprised, then suspicious. 'Did you cause it?'

'Thanks for the faith, sweetheart! I'm not a delinquent. But maybe the public anxiety did originate with me and Lucius Petronius.'

'Your discoveries are the talk of the town. You stirred it up; you ought to sort it out,' Helena said sternly.

'Not me. There is already an enquiry into the aqueduct murders. It's under the auspices of the Curator, and he's using that bastard Anacrites.'

'But now Vespasian must have ordered a superior commission,' said Helena.

We both stared at Julius Frontinus. He had put down his bowl. He opened his hands in a gesture of acknowledgement, though slightly baffled at the way we had talked around him and pre-empted his request.

Once more I grinned. 'All I need to hear from you, sir, is that your commission takes precedence over anything being carried out by the Curator of Aqueducts – so your assistants take precedence over his.'

'Count my lictors,' responded Frontinus rather tetchily.

'Six.' He must have been awarded a special pack to match the special task.

'The Curator of Aqueducts is only entitled to two.' So Frontinus outranked him – and I would outrank Anacrites.

'It's a pleasure to do business, Consul,' I said. Then we swept aside the pretty drinking cups and settled down for a practical review of what needed to be done.

'I'd like to borrow a dish,' Frontinus requested calmly. 'One you don't use very much, I suggest.'

Helena's eyes met mine, dark with concern. We both realised what he probably wanted it for.

XXIII

THE THIRD HAND was swollen, but undamaged. Julius Frontinus unwrapped and presented it without drama, placing it in our dish like an organ removed by a surgeon. The first two relics had been dark with decay. This hand was black because its owner had been black. She must have come from Mauretania or Africa. The fine skin on the back of her hand was ebony, the palm and finger-tips much lighter. The cuticles had been kept manicured, the nails neatly trimmed.

It looked a young hand. The fingers, all still present, would recently have been as fine and slender as those of Helena's which had just now so urgently tapped my wrist. This was a left hand. Trapped in the swollen flesh of the fourth finger was a plain gold wedding ring.

Julius Frontinus stayed fastidiously silent. I felt depressed.

Helena Justina had reached out abruptly and covered the severed remains with her own much paler hand, fingers splayed and straight, thankfully not quite touching the other. It was an involuntary sign of tenderness for the dead girl. Helena's expression held the same absorption as when she made that gesture above our sleeping child.

Perhaps my recognition of it struck a chord; without a word Helena rose, and we heard her walk into the next room where Julia Junilla was safe in her cradle. After a short pause as if she was check-ing on the baby Helena came back and resumed her seat, frowning. Her mood was dark, but she said nothing so Frontinus and I began discussing our work.

'This was found during the cleaning of the Aqua Claudia reservoir in the Arch of Dolabella.' Frontinus' manner and tone were busi-nesslike. 'It came up in the sand in one of the dredging buckets. The work gang who discovered it were badly supervised; instead of reporting the find officially they displayed it in public for money.' He spoke as if he disapproved, yet didn't blame them.

'That caused today's riot?'

'Apparently. The Curator of Aqueducts was at the Circus, fortunately for him. One of his assistants was not so lucky; he was identified in the street and beaten up. There has been damage to property. And of course there is an outcry for hygienic supplies to be restored. The panic has caused all kinds of difficulties. An epidemic started overnight –'

'Naturally,' I said. 'The minute I heard the city's water might be contaminated, I started feeling dicky myself.'

'Hysteria,' stated the consul tersely. 'But whoever is doing this must now be found.'

Helena had heard enough. 'So inconsiderate!' She spoke too sweetly. We were about to be blasted. 'Some silly girl gets herself killed by a madman, and disrupts Rome. Women really will have to be deterred from putting themselves in this position. Dear Juno, we cannot have females being responsible for fevers, let alone damage to property –'

'It's the man who needs deterring.' I tried to ride out the tempest. Frontinus shot me a helpless glance and left me to cope. 'Whether his victims fall into his clutches through their own folly or whether he grabs them from behind in a dark street, nobody suggests they deserve it, love. And I don't suppose the public have even started to think about what he does to these women before he kills them – let alone the way he treats them afterwards.'

To my surprise Helena subsided quietly. She had had a sheltered upbringing, but she paid attention to the world and had no lack of imagination. 'These women are being subjected to terrible ordeals.'

'Not much doubt of it.'

Her face clouded with compassion again. 'The owner of this hand was warm and young. Only a day or two ago she was sewing perhaps, or spinning. This hand was caressing her husband or their child. It was preparing their food, combing her hair, laying wheatcakes before the gods –'

'And she was only one in a long line, snatched away to end up hideously like this. All with lives ahead of them once.'

'I was hoping this was a recent phenomenon,' Frontinus said.

'No, it has been happening for years, sir,' Helena explained angrily. 'Our-brother-in-law works on the river and says mutilated bodies have been discovered for as long as he can remember. For years the disappearance of women has been going unreported – or uninvestigated, anyway. Their corpses have been hidden away in

silence. It's only when people begin to think the aqueducts are contaminated that anybody cares!'

'It has initiated an enquiry at last.' Frontinus was a braver man
than me to suggest it. 'Of course it's a scandal, and of course this
enquiry is too late; nobody denies that.'

'You're being disingenuous,' she chided him mildly.

'Practical,' he said.

'Whoever they were,' I assured Helena, 'these women will have
the investigation they deserve.'

'Yes, I think they will now.' She trusted me. It was a serious
responsibility.

I reached for the dish and held it. 'One thing I shall have to do –
even though its seems disrespectful – is remove this poor soul's
wedding ring.' It would be best done unobserved. The ring was
embedded in waterlogged flesh and would be ghastly to extricate.
'The only way we stand any chance of solving this is to identify at
least one of the victims and work out exactly what happened to her.'

'How likely is that?' Frontinus asked.

'Well, it will be the first time the killer has to dispose of remains
while somebody is actually looking out for him. The girl's torso is
likely to be dumped soon in the Tiber, as Helena said.' The consul
looked up quickly, already responding and considering logistics. 'In
the next few days,' I told him. 'At the latest just after the Games finish. If you have any men at your disposal they could be watching the
bridges and embankments.'

'A day and night watch calls for more resources than I have.'

'Which are?'

'A modest allocation of public slaves.' His expression told me he
realised he was heading an investigation on the cheap.

'Do your best, sir. Nothing too obvious, or the killer will be
scared off. I'll put the word among the water boatmen, and my partner may be able to get some help from the vigiles.'

Helena's great brown eyes were still sorrowful, but I could see she
was thinking. 'Marcus, I keep wondering how these smaller remains
are being put into the water system in the first place. Surely most of
the aqueducts are either deep underground or high on arches and
inaccessible?'

I passed on the query to Frontinus. 'Good point,' he agreed. 'We
must consult with officials about how unauthorised entry is possible.'

'If we can find where it's happening we may trap the bastard in
action.' I was interested in how our intervention would affect

Anacrites. 'But won't speaking to water board officials cut across the Curator's own investigation?'

Frontinus shrugged. 'He knows I have been asked to provide an overview. I will ask for an engineer to be made available for consultation tomorrow. The Curator will have to accept it.'

'He won't encourage his staff to help. We'll have to win them over with guile,' I said.

'Use your charm,' smirked Helena.

'What do you recommend, love? Approachability and the dimpled grin?'

'No, I meant slip them some coinage.'

'Vespasian won't approve of that!' I pulled my face straight for Frontinus. He was listening to our banter rather cautiously. 'Consul, we should be able to extract something useful from the engineers. Will you want to be in on this part of the enquiry, sir?'

'Certainly.'

Oh dear. 'Oh good!'

I wondered how Petro and I would manage, sharing our hunches with an ex-magistrate. Cosying up to a consul was not our style.

The question was about to be addressed; Petronius had shambled up to visit us. He must have spotted the lictors wilting in Lenia's entrance. In theory he and I were still not speaking, but curiosity is a wonderful thing. He hovered in the doorway briefly, a tall, wide-shouldered figure looking diffident at interrupting.

'Falco! What have you done to acquire six rod-and-axe men in your train?'

'Belated recognition of my value to the state . . . Come in, you bastard. This is Julius Frontinus.' I saw that Petro was receiving the message in my glance. 'He's this year's Consul – and our latest client.' As Petronius nodded pleasantly, pretending to be unaffected by rank, I explained about the commission of enquiry and how our expertise was needed for the legwork. I managed to slide in a warning hint that our client intended to impose himself on our interviews.

Sextus Julius Frontinus was of course the man who in our lifetime would achieve an unrivalled reputation for his talents as lawyer, statesman, general, and city administrator, not to mention his skilled authorship of major works on military strategy, surveying and water provision (an interest which I would like to think he acquired while working with us). His career structure would be the illustrious ideal. At the time, though, the only question that concerned Petro and me was whether we could endure him as a supervisor – and whether the mighty Frontinus would be prepared to bunch up his purple-bordered toga on his knobbly knees and stand his round like an honest trooper in the seedy winebars where we liked to hold our debates about evidence.

Petronius found himself a seat and installed himself comfortably in our group. He took the dish containing the most recent hand, stared at it with a suitably depressed sigh, listened while I pointed out some apparent axe-marks on the wrist bones, then placed it carefully on the table. He did not waste his breath on hysterical exclamations; nor did he demand a tiresome review of the conversation he had missed. He simply asked the question which he reckoned took priority, 'This is an enquiry of major importance. I presume the fee will be appropriate?'

I had trained him well. Lucius Petronius Longus was a real informer now.

XXIV

WITH THE WEDDING ring we had our first useful clue. Removing it sickened me. Don't ask me how I managed it. I had to slide off to another room alone. Petronius assessed the job then pulled a face and left me to it, but I relied on him to keep Helena and the Consul out of the way.

I was glad I persevered: inside were engraved the names 'Asinia' and 'Caius'. There were thousands of men called Caius in Rome, but finding one who had recently lost a wife called Asinia might prove feasible.

Our new colleague said he would ask the City Prefect to make enquiries of all the vigiles cohorts under his command. We let Frontinus take this initiative, in case his rank speeded up the response. Knowing how the vigiles tended to react to rank, however, Petronius also made a private approach to the Sixth, who patrolled the Circus Maximus and were now the hapless hosts of his old second in command Martinus. Since the murders seemed to be connected with the Games, the Circus might be where the victim had met her assailant. The Sixth were the most likely candidates to receive her husband's plea to find her. Martinus, in his unreliable-sounding way, promised to tell us at once if it happened. Well, he wasn't entirely hopeless; he might eventually get round to it.

While we waited to hear something, we tackled the aqueduct issue. Petro and I presented ourselves at Frontinus' house early the next morning. We wore neat tunics, combed-down hair, and the solemnity of efficient operatives. We looked like the men for the business. We folded our arms a lot and wore thoughtful frowns. Any ex-consul would be happy to have two such sparks on his staff.

Although we were allowed to interrogate an engineer, the Curator of Aqueducts had had the choice of which to send. The man he imposed on us was called Statius, and we could tell he would be a nincompoop by the size of his back-up team: he brought a couple of slaves with note tablets (to record what he said so he could check it minutely afterwards and send us corrections if he had inadvertently been too frank), a satchel-carrier, an assistant, and the assistant's chubby clerk. Not to mention the litter-bearers and the armed guard with cudgels he had left outside. In theory he was here to contribute expert knowledge, but he behaved as if he had been summonsed on a full-blown corruption charge.

Frontinus asked the first question, and it was typically direct: 'Do you have a map of the water system?'

'I believe a locational diagram of the substrata and superstrata conduits may exist.'

Petronius caught my eye. His favourite: a man who called a spade a soil redistribution implement.

'Can you supply a copy?'

'Such classified information is not generally available –'

'I see!' Frontinus glared. If he ever assumed a position administering water, we could tell who would be the first bad nut tossed out of the window.

'Perhaps, then,' suggested Petro, playing the sympathetic fraternal type (well, a big brother with a hard stick in his fist), 'you could just tell us something about how things work?'

Statius had recourse to his satchel, wherein he had secreted a linen handkerchief to mop his brow. He was overweight and red in the face. His tunic crumpled around him in grubby-looking folds, even though it had probably been clean on that day. 'Well, it is complicated to explain to lay persons. What you are requesting is highly technical . . .'

'Try me. How many aqueducts are there?'

'Eight,' admitted Statius, after a horrified pause.

'Nine, surely?' I ventured quietly.

He looked annoyed. 'Well, if you're going to include the Alsietina –'

'Is there any reason why I should not?'

'It's on the Transtiberina side.'

'I realise that.'

'The Aqua Alsietina is only used for the naumachia and for watering Caesar's Gardens –'

'Or for the Transtiberina paupers to drink when the other aqueducts are dry.' I was annoyed. 'We know the quality is filthy. It was only ever intended to fill the basin for mock trireme fights. That's not the point, Statius. Have any women's hands, or other parts of human corpses, been found in the Alsietina?'

'I have no precise information on that.'

'Then you concede remains *may* be there?'

'It could be a statistical possibility.'

'It's statistically certain that a watercourse somewhere is awash with heads, legs and arms too. Where there are hands the rest of the set tends to exist – and we haven't found any of them yet.'

Petronius weighed in again, still complementing me by playing the kind-hearted reasonable type: 'Well, shall we call the tally nine? With luck some can be eliminated fairly quickly, but we must start by considering the whole system. We have to decide how a man, and his accomplices if he has any, are taking advantage of the aqueducts to flush away the relics of their hideous crimes.'

Statius was still bound up in irrelevance. 'The water board accepts no responsibility for that. You cannot be suggesting that the notoriously unpleasant quality of the Aqua Alsietina is accounted for by illegal impurities of human origin?'

'Of course not,' said Petro grimly.

'Of course not,' I agreed. 'The Alsietina is full of perfectly natural crap.'

The engineer's eyes, which were too close together, fluttered nervously between us. He knew Julius Frontinus was too important to despise, but he saw us as unpleasant insects he would like to swat if he dared. 'You are trying to trace how a few – a relatively few – undesirable remains have been introduced to the channels. Well, I sympathise with the initiative –' He was lying. 'But we have to appreciate the magnitude of scale impeding us –' At least he was talking. We listened in silence. He had somehow gained confidence; maybe refusing requests made him feel big. 'The freshwater installation comprises between two and three hundred miles of channel –' That seemed a very vague calculation. Somebody must have measured more accurately, at the very least when the aqueducts were built. 'I am given to understand that these extraordinary pollutants –'

'Limbs,' stated Petronius.

'Have been manifesting themselves in the water towers – of which the system is provided with a daunting multitude –'

Frontinus demanded immediately, 'How many?'

Statius consulted his assistant, who readily informed us, 'The Aqua Claudia and Anio Novus together have nearly a hundred castelli, and for the whole system you could more than double that –'

I noticed that Frontinus was jotting down the figures. He did it himself, not using a scribe though he must own plenty. 'What's the daily water discharge?' he barked. Statius blenched. 'Roughly,' Frontinus added helpfully.

Again Statius needed the assistant, who said matter-of-factly: 'It's difficult to measure because the currents are constantly flowing and also there are seasonal variations. I roughed up some statistics once for the Aqua Claudia, one of the big four from the Sabine Hills. It was mind-boggling, sir. We managed to do some technical measurements, and when I extrapolated the figures I reckoned on a daily delivery of something over seven million cubic feet. Call it, in everyday terms, going on for seven million standard amphorae – or by the culleus, if you prefer, over sixty thousand.'

Since a culleus is one great mountain of a cartload, sixty thousand rolling up full of water was indeed hard to imagine. And that was only the quantity delivered to Rome by a single aqueduct in one day.

'Is it relevant?' asked Statius. Far from being grateful, he seemed annoyed at being shown up by a subordinate.

Frontinus looked up, still round-eyed from the figures. 'I have no idea, yet. But it's fascinating.'

'What nobody knows,' continued the assistant, who was rather enjoying himself, 'is whether any human remains are lying undiscovered in the settling tanks along the route.'

'How many tanks are there?' asked Petro, jumping in before the intrigued Consul could beat him to it.

'Innumerable.' Statius supplied the put-down crisply for himself. The assistant looked as if he knew the real answer, but he kept quiet.

'You can take a census and count them now,' growled Frontinus to the senior engineer. 'I understand this revolting contamination has been happening for years. I am astonished the water board has not investigated long ago.'

He paused, obviously expecting an explanation, but Statius failed to take the hint. Petro and I were watching a head-on clash between intelligence and stodge. The ex-Consul had all the flair and quickness that shines in the best administrators; the engineer had floated up through a corrupt agency by virtue of just sitting back and putting the seal on whatever his underlings passed to him. Neither man could quite believe the other specimen existed.

Frontinus saw he had to be firm. 'Vespasian intends this dreadful business to be stopped. I shall instruct the Curator to have all the castelli searched immediately – then you must start working through all the settling tanks as quickly as possible. The victims need to be found, identified and given reverent funerals.'

'I understood they were assumed only to be slaves,' Statius, still resisting, said feebly.

There was a pause.

'They probably are,' agreed Petronius. His tone was dry. 'So this is all a waste of resources as well as a risk to public health.'

The engineer wisely made no reply. We could hear echoing in his silence all the mockery and obscenity that must have greeted each new ghastly discovery by the aqueduct workers over the years, and the groans of their superiors as they planned how to cover it up. Helena had been right: these deaths were seen as an inconvenience. Even the formal commission that might stop them was an irritation imposed unfairly from above.

Julius Frontinus glanced at Petro and me. 'Any further questions?' He was making it no secret that he had had enough of Statius and his noncommittal verbiage. We shook our heads.

As the engineer's party was leaving, I collared the assistant's chubby clerk. I had brought out a note-tablet and a stylus, and asked him for his name as if I had been deputed to take minutes of the meeting and needed to concoct the normal list of persons present to fill up my scroll. He confided his cognomen as if it were a state secret. 'And who's the assistant?'

'Bolanus.'

'Just in case I need to check that I've got his statistics correctly, where can I find Bolanus?'

The clerk reluctantly gave me directions. He must have been warned to be unhelpful, but clearly thought that if I did approach the assistant, Bolanus would put me off. Well, that was fine.

I went back and told Frontinus that I reckoned Bolanus might be a goer. I would seek him out in private and request his help. Petronius meanwhile would visit the City Prefect's office and our own contacts in the vigiles, to see if anything new had turned up on the latest dead girl. Looking rueful because neither of us seemed to need him, Frontinus could only spend his day busying himself with whatever ex-consuls do at home.

Presumably they potter about the same as the rest of us. But with more slaves to tidy up their half-eaten apple cores and to look for the tools and scrolls they put down somewhere and then can't find again.

XXV

T HE ENGINEER, STATIUS, almost certainly lorded it over a neat
spacious office full of charts he never consulted, comfortable
folding chairs for visitors, and wine-warming apparatus for reviving
his circulation if ever he was forced to climb up an aqueduct on a
slightly chilly day. I could guess how often that happened.

Bolanus had a hutch. It was close to the Temple of Claudius, hard
to find because it was crammed in a corner, against the Aqua
Claudia's terminal reservoir. There was a reason for that: Bolanus
had to be near his work. Bolanus, of course, was the person who *did*
the work. I was pleased I had spotted it. I would be saving us a lot
of pain.

I knew he would talk. He had so much to do he couldn't afford
to fluff about. We were going to be imposing extra tasks whatever
he did, so it was best to respond practically.

His tiny lean-to site hut was a haven from the summer heat. A
rope on a couple of bollards protected the occupant from unofficial
sightseers. A mere gesture: anyone could step over it. Outside, ladders, lamps and wind-breaks were piled up, looking well used. The
inside was also crammed with equipment: those special levels called
chorobates, sighting rods, dioptra, gromas, a hodometer, a portable
sundial, plumb bobs, pre-stretched and waxed measuring cords, set
squares, dividers, compasses. A half-eaten bread roll stuffed with
sliced meat perched on an unfurled skin that I could see was one of
the charts which the lofty Statius had suggested were too confidential
for us. Bolanus kept his openly on his table, ready to be consulted.

When I turned up he must have just arrived back himself.
Workmen who had been waiting for his return were queuing outside patiently to present him with chits and variation orders. He
asked me to wait while he dealt swiftly with those he could, promis-
ing others a site visit shortly. They went away looking as if they
knew he would follow up. The queue was cleared well before I
grew bored.

He was a short, wide, solid, shaven-headed man with stubby fingers and no neck. He wore a dark cerise tunic, the shade that always grows streaky in the wash, under a twisted leather belt that he should have thrown out five years ago. When he sat down he hoiked himself on to the stool awkwardly, as if his back troubled him. One of his brown eyes looked misty, but both were intelligent.

'I'm Falco.'

'Yes.' He remembered me. I like to think I make an impression, but plenty of people can talk to you for an hour, then if they see you in a different context they can't recollect you.

'I don't want to be a nuisance, Bolanus.'

'We all have our jobs to do.'

'Mind if I try to take this morning's conversation further?'

Bolanus shrugged. 'Pull up a seat.'

I squatted on a spare stool while he took advantage of the occasion to finish his half-eaten salami roll. First he dug out a basket from under the table, flipped open a pristine cloth, and offered me a bite from a substantial picnic. That worried me. People who are polite to informers are usually hiding something. However, the tastiness of his snack convinced me to stop being cynical.

'Look, you know what the problem is . . .' I paused to signal that the welcome bite was top quality. 'We have to find a maniac. One thing that's puzzling us is how he gets his relics into the water in the first place? Aren't the conduits mostly underground?'

'They do have access shafts for maintenance.'

'Like the sewers.' I knew all about those. I had disposed of a body down there myself. Helena's Uncle Publius.

'The sewers at least have an exit to the river, Falco. Anything in the aqueducts is bound to end up startling the public in a bath-house or a fountain. Does he *want* the things to be discovered?'

'Maybe he doesn't put the remains there deliberately. Maybe they arrive in the aqueducts by accident?'

'Seems more likely.' Bolanus bit off a huge mouthful with a hearty appetite. I waited while he chewed it. I felt he was a man I did not need to push. 'I've been thinking about this, Falco.'

I knew he would have done. He was practical, a problem-solver. Mysteries of all kinds would prey on his mind. His solution, if he proposed one, was liable to work. He was the kind of fellow I could use as a brother-in-law, instead of the deadbeats my sisters had actually wed. A man you could build a sun terrace with. A man who would drop in and mend your broken shutter if you were away on holiday.

'The aqueducts that run up on arcades have vaulted roofs, or occasionally slabs. It's to stop evaporation mainly. So you can't just throw up rubbish and hope it lands inside, Falco. There are access shafts, at two-hundred-and-forty-foot intervals. Anyone can find them, certainly; they are marked by the cippi –'

'The "gravestones"?'

'Right. Augustus had the bright idea of numbering all the shafts. We don't use his system, actually; it's easier to go by the nearest milestone on the road. That's how a work gang will be approaching the site, after all.'

'I don't expect Caesar Augustus worked in many gangs.'

Bolanus grimaced. 'Things might run a bit more smoothly if a few weeks in a labour force was part of the Senate career ladder.'

'Agreed. Give me a man who's had to get his hands dirty.'

'Anyway, finding the access points isn't difficult – but they're all stoppered with mighty plugs of stone that only a crane can lift. We don't need access as often as the sewer gangs – and we have a running battle trying to stop the public fixing their own pipes and stealing water. So getting in hardly seems a possibility for this maniac of yours.'

Actually this was good news. 'All right. What's the scenario? We're not talking about unpremeditated domestic murder. This is some bastard who regularly, over a long period of time, has taken women with the intention of abusing them both alive and dead. Then he has to get rid of the evidence, in some way that doesn't point straight back to him. So when he kills a woman he chops her up to make the corpse easier to dispose of.'

'Or because he likes doing it.' Bolanus was a cheery soul.

'Both, probably. Men who repeatedly kill can detach their minds. He must be obsessive – and he's calculating. So why has he chosen to use the aqueduct channels, and if they are so inaccessible, how?'

Bolanus took a deep breath. 'Maybe they aren't inaccessible. Maybe he works in them. Maybe he is one of us.'

I had wondered about that, of course.

I gave Bolanus a sober stare. 'That's a possibility.' He seemed relieved to have it out in the open. Although he was being frank with me, it must feel like disloyalty to his colleagues. 'I don't much like it, Bolanus. As the public slaves all work in gangs, unless a whole gang knows about the murders and has been covering up for one of their members for years, just think of the problems. Could this killer really have disposed of numerous corpses without any of his mates ever noticing? And if he had been noticed, then by now something would have been said.'

Bolanus frowned. 'It's horrible to imagine someone going into a conduit with a human hand or foot in his pocket –'

'Foot?'

'One turned up here once.' I wondered how many other grim discoveries we were going to hear about. 'Then he would have to wait until he was certain none of his workmates was looking when he threw it in.'

'Stupidity. Would it be worth the risk?'

'Taking the risk might be part of the thrill,' Bolanus suggested.

I wondered whether he was revealing too much understanding of the killer's mind. After all, he worked on the aqueducts himself and as an engineer's assistant he could make inspections alone if he wanted to. He would also be well placed to hear about any enquiry, and attach himself to it so he could check what was going on.

Unlikely. Yes, he was a loner, because of his specialist knowledge. But this was a man who made things work, not one who destroyed and hacked up women out of some dark inhuman motive. Bolanus was one of the skilled world-movers who built the Empire and kept it in trim. Still, the killer too, with years of undetected crime behind him, must have his own efficiency. If we ever identified him, I knew clues to his madness would be there – and yet he would be somebody who had lived in society without arousing qualms in those he met. The real terror in such men is how closely they resemble the rest of us.

'You may be right,' I said, deciding to test Bolanus anyway. I didn't want to end up as the dumb informer who let himself be led all round the problem by some helpful volunteer, only to find after weeks of frustration that the volunteer was the real quarry. It's been done often enough. Too often. 'His main thrill will be in assuming power over his victims. When we find him, he'll be somebody who hates women.'

'The odd man out in the crowd!' Bolanus jeered.

'He finds them awkward to approach; when he tries it they probably laugh at him. The more he resents them for their rejection, the more they sense trouble and shrink from him.'

'Sounds like every boy's nightmare.'

'But it's out of all proportion, Bolanus. And unlike most of us, he never learns to take a chance. He's more than just an awkward character. He has an inbuilt flaw so he doesn't *want* to win anybody over, and they know it. This man is locked in his refusal to communicate properly, whereas the rest of us make a lot of mistakes along the way but if we're lucky we do manage a few winning throws too.'

Suddenly Bolanus grinned, looking nostalgic. 'And when we do, it's magic!'

That seemed all right.

Of course addictive killers are usually also cunning liars who can act well. This man could be one of those, a manipulating fraud who knew just what I wanted to hear. So pervertedly clever he could counterfeit normality and outwit me at every move.

'It could be me or you,' suggested Bolanus, as if he knew what I was thinking. He was still munching his snack. 'He's not going to stand out like some mad-eyed monster, or he would have been apprehended years ago.'

I nodded. 'Oh yes, he probably looks very ordinary.'

Again, he gave me a narrow look, as if he read my mind.

We went back to discussing how the killer was disposing of the bodies.

'You know the water boatmen find torsos in the river as well?'

'Makes sense, Falco. He might have found a way to float the hands down the aqueducts, but the torsos are too large. They would stick. The killer is presumably trying to disperse the pieces over a wide area to avoid being traced, so he certainly doesn't want a regular blockage half a mile from where he lives.'

'Right.'

Bolanus offered me his picnic again, but I had gone off the idea. 'How long have you known about the finds in the aqueducts, Bolanus?'

'It goes back beyond my time.'

'How long's your career?'

'Fifteen years. I learned my stuff originally abroad in the legions, got invalided out, then came home just at the right time to work on the dams Nero built at his big villa at Sublaqueum. That's on the River Anio, you know – which is also the source of the four Sabine aqueducts.'

'Is this relevant?'

'I think it might be. As far as I know, the body parts only turn up in certain places in our system. I'm starting to have a little theory about this.' I perked up. A theory from Bolanus might be one to respect. 'I became something of a specialist in all the aqueducts that come from the Anio.'

'These are the long ones built by Caligula and Claudius?'

'And the old monster, the Anio Vetus.'

'I've seen them marching across the Campagna, of course.'

'A grand sight. That's when you know why Rome rules the world. They pick up good cold water from the river and the springs in the Sabine Hills, take a detour around the gracious homes at Tibur, and travel for miles to get here. It's a staggering engineering feat. But let me tell this my own way –'

'Sorry.' His theories might be sound, but I felt a sudden terror of his rhetoric. I had talked to engineers before. For hours and hours. 'Do go on, friend.'

'Let's jump back a bit. You had a spat this morning with Statius about the Aqua Alsietina.'

'He wanted us to ignore it. Have there been any grisly finds there?'

'No. In my opinion it can safely be ignored. It comes from Etruria – west of us – and I don't reckon the killer goes anywhere near it. Nor the Aqua Virgo either.'

'Isn't that the one Agrippa built specially for his baths near the Saepta Julia?' I knew the Saepta well. Apart from being a traditional haunt of informers, which I had to avoid to ensure I never encountered my low-class colleagues, the Saepta was full of antique dealers and jewellers – including my father, who had an office there. I liked to avoid Pa too.

'Yes. The Virgo is drawn from a marsh near the Via Collatina, and it's almost entirely underground. I'd also rule out the Aqua Julia and the Tepula.'

'Why them?' I asked.

'I've never heard of anything that relates to these killings being discovered in either. The Julia has its source in a reservoir only seven miles outside Rome on the Via Latina. The Tepula isn't far from it.'

'Near the Alban Lake?'

'Yes. The Julia and Tepula come into Rome carried on the same arcades as the old Aqua Marcia – and that's where my theory might creak a bit, because the Marcia *has* had finds in it.'

'Where does the Marcia come from?'

Bolanus opened his hand in a triumphant gesture. 'It's one of the big four from the Sabine Hills!'

I tried to look as if I understood the significance. 'Are all these various conduits linked at all? Can water be transferred between them?'

'They are indeed!' Bolanus seemed to think he was teaching me logic. 'There are places throughout the network where water from one aqueduct can be diverted into another if we need extra supplies, or if we want to close part of the system to work on it. The only constraint is that you have to divert downwards from a high aqueduct to a lower one. You can't lift water up. Anyway, once they get here the Claudia, Julia and Tepula share one reservoir. That might be of interest. What could also be relevant is that the Marcia has a major link with the Claudia. The Claudia arrives in Rome with the Anio Novus; they are both carried on arcades which join on one set of arches near the city.'

'In one channel?'

'No, two. The Claudia was built first. It's coupled underneath.' He paused. 'Look, I don't want to confuse you with technicalities.'

'Now you're sounding like bloody Statius.' He was right though; I had had enough of this.

'All I mean to say is that I wouldn't be surprised if the human hands that turn up in Rome had been put into the water well outside the city.'

'You're saying they enter the system way back – before the channels are covered or go underground?'

'More than that,' said Bolanus. 'I bet they are slung in right at source.'

'At source? Up in the hills, you mean? Surely nothing as large as a hand could float down all the way to Rome?'

'We've done tests with gourds. The current would bring it. We extract mounds of pebbles that have escaped the settling tanks. They arrive perfectly round, from the friction.'

'Wouldn't that friction destroy a hand?'

'It might just bob along safely. Otherwise, there may still be pieces of body out there in the settling tanks – or more remains than we know about might have arrived in Rome so pulverised nobody realised what they were.'

'So if something floated, and if it survived, how long might the journey here take?'

'You'd be surprised. Even the Aqua Marcia, which is sixty miles long after it's meandered over the countryside to maintain a gradient, only takes a day to bring water to Rome. In the shorter ones it can be as little as a couple of hours before it arrives. Of course, friction would slow a floating object down slightly. Not much, I'd say.'

'So you're trying to convince me this maniac may be operating right out in the country at somewhere like Tibur?'

'I'll be specific. I bet he dumps the severed pieces into the River Anio.'

'I can't believe it.'

'Well, I'm just making the suggestion.'

I was talking to a man who was used to putting forward good ideas that incompetent superiors simply ignored. He had gone past caring. I could take it or leave it. The proposal sounded too far-fetched yet somehow ludicrously feasible.

I did not know what to think.

XXVI

I WAS ABLE to put off making a judgement. Something more urgent needed investigation first.

I had arranged to meet Petronius back at Fountain Court. Arriving in the early afternoon I found, first, that I had missed having lunch with Helena; she had eaten hers, assuming I must be having mine elsewhere. My second discovery was that since Petronius had dropped in to see if I was home yet, he had been given my food.

'Nice to have you in the family,' I commented.

'Thanks,' he grinned. 'If we'd known you were on your way we would have waited, of course.'

'There are some olives left,' Helena reported soothingly.

'Nuts to that!' I said.

Once we settled down, I went over what Bolanus had told me. Petronius was even more scathing than me about the idea that the killer lived in the countryside. He did not take much interest in my newly acquired aqueduct lore either. In fact, as a partner he was jealous as Hades. All he wanted was to pass on what he himself had discovered.

At first I wasn't having it. 'We've got trouble if Bolanus is right and the murders take place on the Campagna or up in the hills.'

'Don't think about it.' Petro's vigiles experience was speaking. 'The jurisdiction problems are a nightmare if you have to go outside Rome.'

'Julius Frontinus may be able to override the normal bureaucratic rigmaroles.'

'He'll need several legions to do it. Trying to take an investigation past the city gates is unspeakable. Local politics, semi-comatose local magistrates, dimwit posses of horse-thief catchers, antique old retired generals who think they know it all because they once heard Julius Caesar clear his throat –'

'All right. We'll follow up every feasible clue in Rome first.'

'Thanks for seeing sense. While I shall always be an admirer of your intuitive approach, Marcus Didius –'

'You mean you think my method stinks.'

'I can prove it, too. Legitimate policing procedures are the ones that bring results.'

'Oh yes?'

'I've traced the girl.'

Apparently his method did have something to recommend it: that mystical ingredient called success.

Helena and I played him up by refusing to ask further questions even though he was bursting to tell us. We stayed cool, aggravating him by debating whether his one identification would be more useful than my obtaining background which could spark ideas that could lead to eventual solutions . . .

'Either you two stop goading me,' snapped Petro, 'or I'm going out by myself to interview the man.'

'What man, dear Lucius?' asked Helena gently.

'The man called Caius Cicurrus, who this morning reported to the Sixth Cohort that he has lost his beloved wife Asinia.'

I gazed at him benignly.

'Falco, this is a damned sight more useful than wasting the best hours of your shift finding out that if you pee at Tibur in the morning you can be poisoning people at a snackshop outside the Baths of Agrippa by breakfast next day.'

'Petro, you haven't been listening. The Baths of Agrippa are supplied by the Aqua Virgo, which has its source on the Via Collatina, not at Tibur. The Virgo is also only about fifteen miles long, compared with the Marcia and the Anio Novus at four or five times that, so if you pee in the marsh in the morning, allowing for how slowly the local water-carrier waddles to and from the fountain for your hypothetical snackshop, your noxious residue will actually be poured from his bucket into winecups about mid-afternoon –'

'Dear gods, you're a self-satisfied bastard. Do you want to hear my story, or just mess about all day?'

'I'd love to hear your story, please.'

'Wipe off that stupid grin then.'

Perhaps fortunately, just then Julius Frontinus knocked and came straight in. He was not the type to sit around waiting for us to report back when we fancied it.

Thanks be to Jupiter, Juno and Minerva we did have news to relay.

'Falco's been absorbing some fascinating facts and figures about water supply.' Petronius Longus said it straight-faced. What a hypocritical Janus. 'Meanwhile I learned from my personal contact in the Sixth Cohort of vigiles that a man called Caius Cicurrus has reported his wife missing; the wife's name is Asinia. It matches the ring on the hand you brought us, sir.'

'I haven't been told this by the City Prefect.' Frontinus was put out. Senior channels had failed him. We low dogs had anticipated his illustrious peer network, apparently without exerting ourselves.

'I'm sure the news is winging its way to you.' Petro knew how to make it sound as if he reckoned the City Prefect would never catch up. 'Excuse me for pre-empting official channels: I wanted to be in a position to interview the man before those idiots on the Curator's enquiry interfere.'

'We had better do it now, then.'

'It's going to be delicate,' I said, hoping to deter the Consul.

'Caius has not yet been told his wife is dead,' Petro explained. 'My old subordinate Martinus managed to avoid revealing that her fate is already known.' Martinus in fact was so slow he probably only made the connection after Caius Cicurrus had gone.

'Should he not have put the poor man out of his misery?' Frontinus asked.

'Better for us to explain. We know the details of the find and we're engaged on the main enquiry.' Petro rarely showed his disapproval of Martinus.

'We want to see the husband's reaction when he first hears the news,' I added.

'Yes, I'd like to see that myself.' Nothing put off Frontinus. He was determined to accompany us. Petronius had the bright idea of saying the Consul's formal purple-striped robes might overawe the bereaved husband – so Frontinus whipped off his toga, rolled it in a ball, and asked to borrow a plain tunic.

I was the closest to him in size. Helena quietly went and fetched one of my least mended plain white pull-ons. The ex-Consul stripped and dived into it without a blush.

'Better let us do the talking, sir,' Petro insisted.

I found our new friend Frontinus rather endearing, but if there's one thing Petronius Longus hates more than high-flown birds who stand aloof, it's high-flown birds who try to join in like one of the boys.

★

As we all trooped outside, Petro checked abruptly on the porch.

Opposite, a smart litter was pulling up outside the laundry. A small figure jumped out. All I could see was flimsy swathes of light violet, with heavy gold hems dragging at the fancy cloth, and a glimpse of anklet on a slim leg. The wearer of this flimflam spoke briefly to Lenia, then nipped up the stairs to my old apartment.

Immediately she was out of sight Petronius hopped down to ground level and made off with a long easy stride. Frontinus had noticed nothing, but I followed feeling curious. It rather looked as if Petro's sweet little turtledove had become somebody he was trying to avoid.

I glanced back to my own door. Helena Justina was waving us off, standing on the porch holding Julia. She too was looking thoughtfully across the street. I caught her eye. She smiled at me. I knew that expression. When little Milvia came down again she was going to be treated to a stern conversation with the daughter of the illustrious Camillus. I would be very surprised if Milvia ever showed her dainty ankle in Fountain Court again.

By the way he was sneaking off round the corner into Tailors' Lane, that suited Petronius.

XXVII

A S WE WERE walking to the address Martinus had passed on to Petro, we heard a muffled roar from the Circus. The fifteen-day Ludi Romani were still in progress. The president of the Games must have dropped his white handkerchief, and the chariots had set off around the long arena. Two hundred thousand people had just exclaimed in excitement at some spill or piece of dramatic driving. Their massed exhalation whomphed through the valley between the Aventine and the Palatine, causing doves to rise and circle before they dropped back on to heated roofs and balconies. A lower hum continued as the race went on.

Somewhere in the Circus Maximus would be the young Camillus brothers and Claudia Rufina (well, Justinus and Claudia anyway). Somewhere there too might be the killer who chopped up women, the man whose latest dreadful deed we now had to explain to an unwitting husband. And unless Caius Cicurrus could tell us something useful, then somewhere at the Circus Maximus might be the next woman who was destined to end up in pieces in the aqueducts.

Caius Cicurrus was a chandler. With his wife but no children he lived in a typical third-floor apartment in a tenement full of identical small lets. His living space was cramped, but well kept. Even before we had knocked at his gleaming bronze lion-head knocker, the respectable flower tubs and rag mat on the landing had warned us of one thing: his Asinia had probably not been a prostitute. A young female slave let us in. She was clean and neat, shy though not cowed. Careful housekeeping was evident. Ledges looked dusted. There was an attractive scent of dried herbs. The slave girl automatically invited us to remove our outdoor shoes.

We found Caius just sitting by himself, staring into space, with Asinia's spinning in a basket at his feet. He was holding what must have been her jewel box, running skeins of glass and rock crystal beads through his hands. He looked obsessively troubled and drowsy with grief. Whatever was making him miserable, it was not the purely financial loss of a deserted pimp.

Caius was swarthy, but plainly Italian. He had the hairiest arms I had ever seen, though his head was nearly bald. In his mid-thirties, he was just a perfectly harmless, perfectly ordinary man who still had to learn of his loss and its terrible circumstances.

Petronius introduced us, explained that we were conducting a special enquiry, and asked if we could talk about Asinia. Caius actually looked pleased. He liked talking about her. He was missing her badly and needed to console himself by telling anyone who would listen how sweet and gentle she had been. The daughter of his father's freedwoman, Asinia had been loved by Caius since she was thirteen. That explained why her wedding ring had grown so tight. The girl grew up wearing it. She would have been – she was, said Caius – only twenty now.

'You reported her missing this morning?' Petronius continued to lead the interview. Through his job with the vigiles he had had considerable experience of breaking bad news to the bereaved, even more than me.

'Yes, sir.'

'But had she been missing for longer?'

Caius looked perturbed by the question.

'When did you last see her?' Petro probed gently.

'A week ago.'

'Have you been away from home?'

'Visiting my farm in the country,' said Caius; Petro had guessed something of the sort. 'Asinia remained at home. I have a small business, a chandlery. She looks after it for me. I trust her entirely with my affairs. She is a wonderful partner –'

'Wasn't your business closed for the public holiday?'

'Yes. So when the Games began, Asinia went to stay with a friend who lives much closer to the Circus: then Asinia would not have to make her way home late at night. I am very particular about her being out in Rome alone.'

I saw Petronius breathe heavily, embarrassed by the man's innocence. To relieve him I weighed in quietly, 'When exactly did you realise that Asinia was missing?'

'Yesterday evening when I returned. My slave told me Asinia was at her friend's house, but when I went there the friend said Asinia had gone home three days ago.'

'Was she sure?'

'Oh, she brought her here in a litter and left her right at the door. She knew I expected it.' I glanced at Petronius; we would need to speak to this friend.

'Excuse me for asking this,' Petro said. 'We have to do it; you'll understand. Is there any possibility Asinia was seeing another man in your absence?'

'No.'

'Your marriage was perfectly happy, and she was a quiet girl?'

'Yes.'

Petronius was treading very carefully. Since we had begun our enquiry with the assumption that the victims were good-time girls (who could vanish without attracting too much notice), there was always the possibility that Asinia had led a double life, unknown to her anxious mate. But we knew it was more likely the maniac who carved her up was a stranger; that Asinia had just had the bad luck to put herself where she caught his eye and he was able to abduct her. The mutilations Lollius had described to me pretty well stamped a seal on it. Men who carve up women in that way have never been emotionally close to them.

Now we were being told that this victim was a respectable girl. Where had she been after she was dropped at her door? What adventure had she set out for? Did even her girlfriend know about it?

Petronius, who had been carrying the ring, now brought it out. He took his time. His movements were slow, his expression grave. Caius was supposed to have started guessing the truth, though I could see no signal that he had let himself be warned. 'I'd like you to look at something, Caius. Do you recognise that?'

'Of course! It's Asinia's ring. You've found her, then?'

Helpless, we watched as the husband's face lit with delight.

Slowly he realised that the three men sharing his tiny room had remained sombre. Slowly he saw that we were waiting for him to reach the real, tragic conclusion. Slowly he grew pale.

'There is no way I can make this easy for you,' Petronius said, 'Caius Cicurrus, I am afraid we are assuming that your poor wife is dead.' The stricken husband said nothing. 'There really can be very little doubt about it.' Petronius was trying to tell Cicurrus that there was no actual body.

'You have found her?'

'No – and the worst part is that we perhaps never will find her.'

'Then how can you say –'

Petronius sighed. 'Have you heard about the dismembered human remains that have been found from time to time in the water supply? Women have been murdered, over a long period, by a killer who cuts up his victims and deposits them in the aqueducts. My colleagues and I are investigating that.'

Cicurrus still refused to understand. 'What can this have to do with Asinia?'

'We have to believe that this killer has abducted her. Asinia's ring was found in the terminal reservoir of the Aqua Claudia. I'm sorry to have to tell you, one of her hands was with it.'

'Only her hand? She could still be alive!' The man was desperate. He sprang at any shred of hope.

'You mustn't believe that!' Petro rasped. He was finding this almost unbearable. 'Tell yourself she is dead, man. Tell yourself she died quickly, when she was first abducted three days ago. Believe she knew as little as possible. Tell yourself what was done to the corpse afterwards does not matter because Asinia did not feel it. Then tell *us* anything you can that will help us catch the man who killed your wife before he robs any other citizens of their womenfolk.'

Caius Cicurrus stared at him. He could not go so fast. 'Asinia is dead?'

'Yes, I'm afraid she must be.'

'But she was beautiful.' He was grappling with the truth now. His voice rose. 'Asinia was unlike other women – so sweet-natured, and our domestic life was so affectionate – Oh, I cannot believe this. I feel she is going to come home any minute –' Tears began streaming down his face. He had accepted the truth at last. Now he had to learn to endure it: that might take him for ever. 'Only her hand has been found? What will happen to the rest of her? What am I to do? How can I bury her?' He became wilder. 'Where is her poor hand now?'

It was Frontinus who said, 'Asinia's hand is being embalmed. It will be returned to you in a locked casket. I beg of you, don't break the lock.'

We were all crushed by the thought that if other remains did appear, we would have to decide whether to return them to this devastated man piecemeal. Was he then to hold funerals for each limb separately, or collect them for one final burial? At what point was he supposed to decide that enough of his darling had been returned to him to justify a ceremony? When we found her torso, with her heart? Or her head? What philosopher would tell him where the girl's sweet soul resided? When should his agony end?

There was no doubt his devotion to Asinia was genuine. The next few weeks were likely to drive him into insanity. Nothing we could do would protect him from brooding over the horror of her last hours. We would say very little to him, but like us he would soon be imagining how the killer probably treated his victims.

Petronius left the room as if he were going to fetch the slave to attend to her master. First I could hear him speaking to her in a low voice. I knew he was discreetly checking the story of Asinia's last known movements, and probably taking the name and address of the female friend with whom she had stayed. He brought the girl in, and we took our leave.

Outside the apartment we paused for a moment in a group. The encounter had demoralised us all.

'*A perfect housewife,*' said Frontinus, grimly quoting the conventional memorials. '*Modest, chaste and unquarrelsome. The best of women, she kept indoors and worked in wool.*'

'*Twenty years old,*' growled Petronius in despair.

'*May the earth lie lightly upon her.*' I completed the formula. Since we had yet to find what was left of Asinia, perhaps it never would.

XXVIII

NONE OF US could face doing any more that evening. Petro and I escorted the Consul to his house, where he returned my tunic after divesting himself on the doorstep. You could tell he was upper class. A plebeian would shy off such eccentricity. I've known wrestlers who turned their backs to strip, even in the suitable surroundings of the baths. Frontinus' own door porter looked alarmed, and he presumably was used to his master. We handed over the Consul into safe keeping, and the porter winked to thank us for keeping straight faces.

Then Petro and I walked slowly back to Fountain Court. A few shops were reopening to catch the evening trade as the Circus emptied. All the streets seemed to contain men with sly expressions, drunks, hustlers, slaves up to no good, and girls on the make. People talked too loudly. People barged us off the pavement, then when we took to the roadway others knocked us into open drains. It was probably by accident, but anyway they didn't care. Instinctively we started shoving too.

This was the city at its worst. Maybe it was always like this, and I was just noticing it more tonight. Maybe the Games had brought out extra dross.

Upset by the interview with Cicurrus, we did not even pop into a winebar for a pre-dinner relaxer. Perhaps for once we should have done. We might have missed a very unpleasant experience in Fountain Court. We were walking along glumly with our heads down, which gave us no time to make good our escape. Instead I laid a warning hand on Petro's arm, and he groaned loudly. The litter we had seen outside the laundry when we left earlier was still there. Its occupant had clearly been watching for our return.

She jumped out and publicly accosted us. However, this was not little light-footed, violet-clad Balbina Milvia. The litter must be a shared one, used by all the women of the Florius household. It had brought us a much more terrifying visitor than Petro's pert piece of dalliance: this was Milvia's mama.

Even before she flew at Petronius and started bawling, we could tell she was furious.

XXIX

CORNELLA FLACCIDA HAD all the grace of a flying rhinoceros: big hands, fat feet, an irretrievably immodest mien. She was nicely decked out, though. On the features of a bitter hag had been painted a mask of a fresh-faced maiden, newly risen from the foam of Paphos in a rainbow of scintillating spray. On a body that had indulged in long evenings of gorging wine-soaked heron wings were hung translucent silks from Cos and fabulous collars of granular gold filigree, all so light they fluttered and tinkled and assaulted the startled senses of tired men. The feet that stumped towards us wore pretty tinselled bootees. A devastating waft of balsam punched us in the throat.

Considering that when Balbinus Pius had been put away by Petronius all the gangster's property had been transferred to the state, it was amazing so much money could still be spent on his ferocious relict. On the other hand, Balbinus was a hard nut. He had made sure a good proportion of his worldly effects had been cunningly dumped out of official reach. Much of it had been placed in trust for Flaccida by calling it part of the dowry of her nifty offspring Milvia.

Mama was living with her daughter now: her own mansions had all been confiscated, so the two were thrust together in the far-from-dowdy abode of Milvia's husband Florius. All the vigiles cohorts were running books on how long the three could put up with each other. So far they were clasping hands as stickily as bee-keepers in the honeycomb season: it was the only way they could hang on to the cash. An accountant from the Treasury of Saturn checked the health of Milvia's marriage daily, because if she divorced Florius and her dowry reverted to her family, then the Emperor wanted it. This was one case where the encouragement-of-matrimony laws did not apply.

Since our new Emperor Vespasian had made a platform of supporting the quaint old-fashioned virtues of family life, it will be seen that if the amount of money he stood to grab on Milvia's divorce could persuade him to muffle his quaint old-fashioned conscience, then it must be very large indeed. Well, that's the joy of organised crime for you. It's astonishing more people don't take it up.

No; actually, there was a reason why other people stayed honest: setting up as a rival to Cornella Flaccida was just too frightening. Who wants to be parboiled, roasted, skewered through every orifice, and served up trussed in a three-cheese glaze with their internal organs lightly sautéed as a separate piquant relish?

Of course I made that up. Flaccida would have said that as a punishment it was far too refined.

'Don't you damn well run away from me!' she yelled.

Petro and I were not running anywhere; we had not been given time even to think of it.

'Madam!' I exclaimed. Neutrality was a dubious refuge.

'Don't play about with me!' she snarled.

'What a repulsive suggestion.'

'Shut up, Falco.' Petro thought I wasn't helping. I shut up. Normally he was big enough to look after himself. The hard-bitten Flaccida might be more than he could deal with, though, so I stuck around loyally. Anyway, I wanted to see the fun.

I noticed Helena coming out on to our porch. My dog Nux nosed eagerly after her, sensing the master's return. Helena bent and clutched her collar nervously. She must be able to tell that our visitor was a woman who probably bit off watchdogs' heads as a party piece.

'Haven't I met you two grimeballs before?' Milvia's mother cannot have forgotten Petronius Longus, the enquiry chief who convicted her husband. Meeting her again face to face, I decided I preferred that she should not realise I was the hero with the social conscience who had actually widowed her.

'Charming that our vibrant personalities made such an impression,' I gurgled.

'Tell your clown to keep out of it,' Flaccida ordered Petro. He just smiled and let her run.

The dame tilted back her fading blonde coiffure, and surveyed him as if he were a flea she had caught in her underwear. He gazed back, completely calm as usual. Big, solid, full of understated presence: any mother should have envied her daughter's choice of him for a lover. Petronius Longus reeked of the controlled assurance women go for. The gods know, I had seen enough of them rush at him. What he lacked in looks he made up in size and obvious character, and these days he wore wicked haircuts too.

'You've got a nerve!'

'Spare me, Flaccida. You're embarrassing yourself.'

'I'll embarrass you! After everything you've done to my family –'

'After everything your family has done to Rome – and is probably doing still – I'm surprised you haven't felt obliged to move to one of the remote provinces.'

'You destroyed us, then you had to seduce my little daughter too.'

'Your daughter's not so little.' And she doesn't take much seducing, Petronius implied. He was too courteous to insult her, though, even in his own defence.

'Leave Milvia alone!' It came out in a low hard growl, like the raw noise of a lioness threatening her prey. 'Your superiors in the vigiles would like to hear about you visiting my Milvia.'

'My superiors know.' His superiors, however, would not take kindly to angry visits to the tribune's office by the termagant Cornella Flaccida. This stinging hornet could cause Petro's dismissal.

'Florius hasn't heard about it yet.'

'Oh, I'm terrified.'

'You'd better be!' yelled Flaccida. 'I've still got friends. I don't want you showing your face at our house – and I promise you, Milvia's not coming to see you either!'

She turned away. At that moment Helena Justina lost her hold on Nux, who tore down from our apartment, a shaggy bundle of grey and brown fur, with her ears back and her sharp teeth bared. Nux was small and smelly, with a canine distaste for domestic upsets. As Flaccida stepped back into her litter, the dog raced straight for her, seized the embroidered hem of her expensive gown, and then backed away on her strong legs. There seemed to be diggers and boar-hunters somewhere in Nux's lineage. Flaccida slammed the litter door for her own safety. We heard a satisfying wrench of expensive material. Shrieking abuse, the dame ordered her bearers to be off, while my stubborn hound gripped her skirt hem until it tore free.

'Good dog!' cried Petronius and I. Nux wagged her tail proudly as she worried half a yard of Coan gown as if it were a dead rat.

Petro and I exchanged a private glance, not quite looking up at Helena. Then we gave each other a grave public salute. He went up to the old apartment, bouncing on his heels like a chirpy dissident. I went home, looking like a good boy.

My darling's eyes were warm and friendly, and richly brown as the meat sauces at Imperial banquets. Her smile was dangerous. I kissed her anyway. A man should not be intimidated on his own doorstep. The kiss, though, was formally on the cheek.

'Marcus! What was all that about?'

'Just a homecomer's greeting –'

'Fool! The fright who left her flounce behind? Didn't I recognise Cornella Flaccida?' Helena had once helped me interview the woman.

'At a guess, somebody has upset Balbina Milvia, and she's gone crying home to Mother. Mother came dashing to scold the delinquent lover. Poor Mother must be very alarmed indeed to discover that a member of the vigiles has easy access to her household. She must be wetting herself at the thought of him winding his way into Milvia's confidence.'

'Do you think she spanked Milvia?'

'It would be the first time. Milvia was brought up a spoiled princess.'

'Yes, I gathered that,' replied Helena, rather laconically.

'Oh?' I asked, feigning mild curiosity. 'Can it be that the princess has just had a hard time from more than her scraggy bag of a parent?'

'It is a possibility,' Helena conceded.

'I wonder who that might be?'

'Someone she met when she was out riding in her nice litter maybe?' Helena returned my formal kiss on the cheek, greeting me like a demure matron after my afternoon away. She smelt of rosemary hairwash and attar of roses. Everything about her was soft and clean and begging to be intimately fondled. I could feel myself going twittery. 'Maybe that will teach Milvia to stay at home plying her loom,' she said.

'As you do?' I walked her indoors, getting both arms round her. Nux scampered after us, alert to canoodling she could bark at.

'As I do, Marcus Didius.'

Helena Justina did not possess a loom. Our apartment was so tiny we did not have much room for it. If she had asked she could have had one. Obviously I would encourage traditional virtuous pursuits. But Helena Justina hated long, repetitive tasks.

She stayed indoors and worked in wool? Like most Romans I was forced to admit, no; not my devoted turtledove.

At least I knew how mine behaved, even when I was away from home. Well, so I told myself.

XXX

ETRONIUS CAME OVER to fetch me the next morning. He
looked like a man who had failed to supply himself with breakfast. Since I was the cook in our household, I was able to let him
have some of our bread rolls, while Helena ate hers in silence. She
had fetched them, running down barefoot that morning to buy them
fresh from Cassius, then I had arranged them in a neat pattern in the
bowl.

'You're in charge, I see, Falco.'

'Yes, I'm a stern Roman paternalist. I speak; my women veil their
heads and scurry to obey.'

Petronius snorted, while Helena wiped honey from her lips fastidiously.

'What was all that fuss yesterday?' she asked him outright, to
show how subservient she was.

'The old battering ram's terrified that I'll infiltrate too far and put
the screw on the gangs again by acquiring inside knowledge. She
thinks Milvia is daft enough to tell me anything I ask.'

'Whereas the rest of us know you don't go there to talk . . .
Interesting situation,' I mulled, teasing him. Then I told Helena,
'Apparently Milvia is now chasing Lucius Petronius, while her formally ardent lover has actually been witnessed trying to dodge out of
the way.'

'Oh? Why can that be?' Helena queried, subjecting him to a
bright look.

'Frightened of her ma,' I grinned.

Petro scowled. 'Milvia has suddenly acquired some very peculiar
notions.'

I raised an eyebrow. 'You mean she finally noticed you're no
good?'

'No. She wants to leave Florius.' He had the grace to blush
slightly.

'Oh dear!'

'And live with you?' asked Helena.

'And *marry* me!'

Helena took it more stalwartly than I did. 'Not a good idea?'

'Helena Justina, I am married to Arria Silvia.' Helena restrained herself from commenting on his bold claim. 'I concede,' Petro went on, 'Silvia may dispute that. It just shows how little Silvia knows about anything.'

Helena passed him the honey. I was expecting her to throw it at him. We kept our honey in a Celtic face-pot we had acquired when travelling through Gaul. Petro eyed it askance. Then he held it up, rudely comparing the round-eyed cartoon features with my own.

'So you were never serious about Milvia?' Helena grilled him.

'Not in that way. I'm sorry.'

'When men need to apologise, why can they only say it to the wrong person? And now she wants to be more important to you?'

'She thinks she is. She'll figure it out.'

'Poor Milvia,' murmured Helena.

Petronius made an attempt to look responsible. 'She's tougher than she looks. She's tougher even than she thinks she is.'

Helena was wearing an expression that said she thought Milvia might turn out to be tougher – and much more trouble – than Petro himself yet realised. 'I'll be going to see your wife today, Lucius Petronius. Maia's coming with me. I haven't seen the girls for ages, and I have some things for them that we brought from Spain. Are there any messages?'

'Tell Silvia I promised to take Petronilla to the Games. She's old enough now. If Silvia leaves her at her mother's tomorrow, I'll pick her up and return her there.'

'Her mother's? You're trying to avoid seeing Silvia?'

'I'm trying to avoid being battered and browbeaten. Anyway, if I go to the house, it upsets the cat.'

'This won't get you all back together again.'

'We'll sort it out,' snapped Petronius. Helena took a deep breath, then once again said nothing. 'All right,' he told her, capitulating. 'As Silvia would remark, that's what I always say.'

'Oh, I'll keep quiet then,' Helena returned, not unkindly. 'Why don't you two men talk about your work?'

There was no need. Things had taken off at last. Today we knew what we had to do, and what we hoped to learn.

Not long afterwards I kissed the baby, kissed Helena, burped, scratched myself, counted my small change and took a vow to earn more, combed my hair roughly, and set out with Petronius. We had avoided telling Frontinus our plans. In his place we had Nux. Helena would not be taking her visiting as our dog was deadly enemies with Petro's famous cat. I didn't mind in the least if Nux savaged the flea-ridden creature, but Petronius would turn nasty. Besides, Helena did not need a guard dog if she was with my sister Maia. Maia was more aggressive than anything they might meet on a short walk over the Aventine.

Petro and I were going the other way. We were off to Cyclops Street on the Caelian. We had to interview Asinia's friend.

Her name was Pia, but the scruffy building she lived in convinced us in advance that her lofty name would be inappropriate. Hard to tell how she had ever become friendly with anyone who gloried in Asinia's good reputation, though we had heard the relationship went back years. I was too old to worry about how girls chose their friends.

We climbed several flights of stinking stairs. A janitor with a goitre let us in, but he declined to come up with us. We passed dark doorways, barely lit by slits in the blackened walls. Dirt marked our tunics where we brushed against the render as we turned corners. Where shafts of light intruded, they were thick with motes of dust. Petronius coughed. The sound echoed hollowly, as if the building was deserted. Maybe some tycoon was hoping to drive out his remaining tenants so he could redevelop at a profit. While the place waited to be torn down, the air had filled with the dank smell of despair.

Pia was hoping for visitors. She looked even more interested when she saw that there were two of us. We let her know we weren't buying, and she relapsed into a less friendly mood.

She was lounging on a reading couch, though apparently not for mental improvement. There was nothing to read. I doubted if she could. I didn't ask. She had long hair in a strange shade of vermilion, which she probably called auburn. Her eyes were almost invisible amongst dark circles of charcoal and coloured lead. She looked flushed. It wasn't good health. She wore a short undertunic in yellow and a longer, flimsier outer one in a nasty burnt turquoise; the outer garment had holes in it, but she had not stopped wearing it. Gauzes don't come cheap. Every finger was horribly ringed, seven greenish chains choked her scrawny neck, she had bracelets, she had base metal charms on fragile ankle chains, she had jingling ornaments in her tresses. Pia overdid everything except taste.

Still, she could be a warm-hearted honest poppet for all that.

'We want to talk about Asinia.'

'Sod off the pair of you,' she said.

XXXI

'YOU LIKE A challenge; you can start,' I told Petronius.
'No; you're the expert with unpleasant hags,' he courteously replied.

'Well, you choose,' I invited Pia. 'Which of us?'

'Stuff you both.' She stretched her legs, letting us see them. It would have been better if they had been cleaner and not so sturdy in the knee.

'Nice pins!' Petronius lied in his light, admiring tone. The one they believed for about three seconds before they noticed it came with a sneer.

'Get lost.'

'Play us a new tune, darling.'

'How long did you know Asinia?' I threw in. Petronius and I would share the questioning between us and it was my turn now.

'Years and years.' Despite her bluster she could not resist answering.

'How did you first meet?'

'When she was serving in the shop.'

'The chandlery? Were you sent there shopping?' I had guessed, though refrained from saying, that Pia was a slave at the time. She must be independent now, though hardly in funds.

'We liked a chat.'

'And to go to the Games together?'

'No harm in that.'

'No harm at all – if you really went.'

'We did!' It came out fast and indignant. So far the tale was true.

'Did Asinia have a boyfriend?' Petronius took over.

'Not her.'

'Not one she hadn't told even you about?'

'I'd like to see her try. She couldn't keep a secret, that one. Not that she ever wanted to.'

'She loved her husband?'

'More fool her. Have you met him? He's a weed.'

'His wife is missing. It's understandable.' Wasting his breath, Petronius reproved the girl, while she just wound her grubby fingers annoyingly in her tousled hair. 'So nobody came with you, and Asinia didn't meet anyone afterwards? Then you'd better talk about what happened when you came out from the Circus.'

'Nothing happened.'

'Something happened to Asinia,' I said, taking over again.

'Nothing's happened to her.'

'She's dead, Pia.'

'You're fooling me.'

'Somebody killed her and cut her up in bits. Don't worry; we'll find her gradually, though it may take a few years.'

She had gone pale. She looked far away. Obviously Pia was thinking *It could have been me!*

Petronius resumed harshly: 'Who did she meet, Pia?'

'Nobody.'

'Don't lie. And don't be afraid we'll tell Caius Cicurrus. We can be discreet, if need be. We want the true story. Whoever Asinia took off with is a dangerous killer; only you can get him stopped.'

'Asinia was a good girl.' We said nothing. 'She really was,' Pia insisted. 'She didn't go off with anyone; I did. I met someone. Asinia said she'd go home.'

'Here?'

'No. I needed to bring my man back here, stupid! She was going back to her own place.'

'How was she getting there?'

'Walking. She said she didn't mind.'

'I thought the pair of you hired a litter? Cicurrus thinks that's what happened. You told him you came with Asinia all the way to her own door.'

'We'd spent our cash. Anyway, it was late. The Circus was turning out. All the hired chairs were gone.'

'So you left her alone,' I barked. 'This good girl who was such an old friend of yours, knowing that she had to find her way through crowds of raucous revellers and walk halfway to the Pincian?'

'She wanted to,' the girl insisted. 'Asinia was like that. She would do anything for anyone. She saw I was set up, so she got out of the way.'

'Did she help you chat up your fellow?' asked Petro.

'No.'

'Was she used to talking to men?'

'No. She was useless.'

'But pretty?'

'Oh yes! She drew the looks. She never noticed them looking, though.'

'Was she too trusting?'

'She knew enough.'

'Apparently not!' Petro rasped angrily. He made a disgusted movement and handed the interrogation back to me.

'Who was the man you met, Pia?'

'How should I know? He could have been from anywhere. I'd never seen him before. He was drunk, and he didn't have any money. I'm stupid that way. If I meet him again I'll have his balls.'

'Young love, eh? I'm a sucker for a sentimental story. Would you know him?'

'No.'

'Sure of it?'

'I'd had plenty of wine myself. Believe me, he wasn't worth remembering.'

'So where exactly was the last place you saw Asinia?'

'At the Circus Max.'

'*Where?* Which exit did you use?'

Pia threw back her shoulders and addressed me distinctly as if I was deaf. 'I last saw Asinia by the Temple of the Sun and Moon.' That was clear enough. Then she spoilt it with a rethink. 'Tell a lie – she was walking down the Street of the Three Altars.'

The Street of the Three Altars runs from the apsidal end of the Circus, near the Temple of Sol and Luna which Pia had mentioned, up to the Clivus Scaurus. The Clivus Scaurus goes past the Temple of the Divine Claudius as far as the ancient Arch of Dolabella, now used as a reservoir for the Aqua Claudia. That was where Asinia's hand had been found.

I wondered if it was significant, or just some terrible poignant coincidence, that the missing woman was last seen so near where her dismembered hand later ended up. How far had she travelled in between? I wondered drearily if we would ever know.

I gazed at Pia sourly. 'So Asinia turned off on her long trek north-wards and you came here. How many people were in the Street of the Three Altars?'

'Hundreds, of course. It was turning out time . . . Well, quite a lot.'

'No litters, you said? Any other vehicles?'

144

'Only private stuff.'

'Stuff?'

'You know – loads of big bollocks in their sharp carriages. It was well after curfew.'

'How many carriages?'

'Oh, hardly any.' Self-contradiction was her speciality. 'It's the wrong end. The nobs like to be picked up at the starting gate or near the Imperial box. You know.'

'Afraid we don't,' Petro commented. 'The apsidal end of the Circus, after curfew, is far too rough for us.'

Pia gave him a withering look. It took more than the screwed-up face of a painted girl to diminish Petronius.

'Did you see Asinia speak to anyone?' I asked.

'No I didn't. Asinia wouldn't.'

'Anyone try to speak to her?'

'I just told you!'

'Somebody could have catcalled. It doesn't mean she answered them.'

'No,' said Pia.

'You're not being much help.' Petro decided it was time to be openly rude to her. 'What happened to her could have happened to you. It still could.'

'No chance. I'm not going to the Games again.'

'That's wise. But will you come with us one evening, about the time you left with Asinia, and see if we can spot anyone you recognise?'

'I'm not going near the place again.'

'Not even to help find your friend's killer?'

'It won't do any good.'

'How can you be certain?'

'I've lived in the world.'

Petro looked at me. If we let ourselves be as pessimistic as this cheap piece, we would give up. Perhaps we would never have started. Perhaps we never should have done – but we were in it now. Without his saying anything I guessed he intended to have Pia interviewed again by the vigiles in the hope they could put the frighteners on her. Cyclops Street where she lived must be in the First or Second districts; I wasn't sure offhand, but the boundary ran somewhere near the Porta Metrovia at the end of the street: all this territory belonged to the Fifth Cohort. If they hadn't heard that Petro had been suspended by Rubella he could probably get away with making the request 'officially'.

There was no incentive for us to carry on. The girl was painful to deal with.

Only as we were leaving did she become tearful and terrified. 'You didn't mean it, what you said about Asinia being dead?'

Petronius leaned in the doorway, thumbs in his belt. 'Unfortunately it's true. Want to tell us any more?'

'I don't know nothing else,' Pia retorted defiantly.

We went out, closing the door quietly. Petronius Longus walked steadily down half a flight of the stinking stairs. Then he stopped briefly. I looked at him. He chewed a finger reflectively.

'The silly bitch is lying,' he said.

XXXII

OUTSIDE PIA'S TENEMENT Petro and I parted company. As I had expected, he was off for a word with the Fifth Cohort. Their headquarters was right at the end of this street – and also pretty well adjacent to the reservoir in the Arch of Dolabella. I suggested he ask them to be particularly watchful every night after the Games ended, in case our maniac killer was polluting the water supply right under their noses.

'All right, I don't need you to write my speech for me.'

'Just a few rhetorical points, partner.'

'You're an interfering bastard.' He was looking thoughtful again. Then he said, even more defiantly, 'Pia's lying about something, Falco, or I'm the Colossus of Rhodes.'

'You're just a colossal bighead,' I grinned, and since we were almost at the Fifth's station house I left him, so he could sustain the myth of representing his own cohort. Turning up with an informer would be a dead giveaway that he was freelancing.

Cyclops Street is only two away from the Street of Honour and Virtue, another run-down and ineptly named sanctuary for drabs with appalling histories: including Marina, the flaky pastry who had been my late brother's girlfriend and brought my niece Marcia into the world. I took responsibility for Marina, since she had made it clear she had no intention of ever being responsible herself. Since I was so close that it seemed unavoidable, I forced myself to go to see her and the child.

Useless. I should have known it would be while the Games were on. Marina had gone to the Circus. Trust her to home in on a place that contained two hundred thousand men. She must have dumped Marcia somewhere. I could find hardly anyone to ask, and no one I did roust out could tell me. I left a message to warn Marina there was a bad character abducting females in her locality. She wouldn't care about that. But if she thought I was prowling about nearby on surveillance it might scare her into looking after my niece more carefully.

Marcia was nearly six now. She seemed a happy, well-adjusted, vibrant child. That was just as well. Helena and I were not in a position to rescue her.

A handful. My brother Festus had died in Judaea without knowing he had fathered Marcia. For various reasons, a few of them noble, I tried to take his place.

The day had heated up to scorching, but a chill ran over me. I hoped the aqueduct killer was not tempted to turn to paedophilia. Marcia was too friendly with everyone. I dreaded the thought of my favourite little niece scampering around these streets with her innocent gregarious smile while a perverted butcher was roaming the same neighbourhood looking for unprotected female flesh.

Nobody was safe. When we found the first badly decayed hand its anonymous owner had seemed so remote that Petro and I could stay neutral. We were never going to identify that one – or the next. Now we were getting closer. This was where the nightmares started. I had learned enough about a victim to feel I knew her. I had seen how her death was affecting her family and friends. Asinia, wife of Caius Cicurrus, aged twenty, had a name and a personality. Soon it would be all too easy to wake in the night sweating in case the next person was somebody close to me.

I walked back again to the Fifth Cohort's billet; Petronius had already left. Being so close I went to see Bolanus at his hut, but he was somewhere out on site. I wrote him a message to say the snatched women might be disappearing in his immediate vicinity so I would like to talk to him about it. I was wondering whether there was any feasible access to the Appia Claudia or any other water system nearby.

Having failed to find three different people I followed up my bad fortune with an old informers' trick: I went home for lunch.

I did not see Petronius again until late that evening. When the swallows were at their busiest before the light started dimming, I went across to the office, where he was just clearing up his dinner. Like me he was dressed to go out. We wore white tunics and togas to look like regular idlers at the Games, but underneath we had working boots that were good for kicking scoundrels. He took a thick stick twisted through his belt under the toga. I relied on the knife in my boot.

We strolled down to the Temple of the Sun and Moon, hardly talking. Petro parked himself on the steps of the Temple. I went back a bit and took the Street of the Three Altars. By day it was a business quarter, with a fairly open aspect despite the proximity of the Circus Maximus. The valley between the Aventine and the Palatine is broad and flat-bottomed, with not much through trade since people try to avoid having to walk all the way round the Circus to get anywhere else. It may be quick in a quadriga drawn by snorting steeds with the roar of the crowd to spur them on, but it's murder on foot.

At dusk the atmosphere deteriorated. Foodshops that had seemed smarter than you expected at midday suddenly looked dingy again. Beggars – runaway slaves, probably – came out to annoy the departing crowds. Old graffiti became more obvious on buildings that seemed worse kept. As the Circus vomitaria disgorged the tired hordes, for a time the noise was atrocious; this was why it could never be a select domestic area. People shouting their loud farewells after having a good time are a deep annoyance to others who have not been entertained. And who wants racegoers who have had too much sun and too many snacks being sick on their front doormat fifteen nights in a row?

The first to exit were simply large groups going home. Friends or family parties, or workmates on an outing, they came out briskly, sometimes pushing a bit if the crush was bad, then rapidly dispersed. The dawdlers were more varied, and more raucous too. Some were drunk; forbidding wine in an arena had no effect anywhere in the Empire, and those who smuggled it in always took enough to swamp themselves. Gambling was illegal too, yet it was the whole point of the Circus. Those who had won liked to celebrate around the Temple of the Sun and Moon where Petro was stationed, or the nearby Temple of Mercury, before they reeled off through the streets dangerously happy, thieves flitting hopefully after them in the shadows. Those who had lost their stakes were either maudlin or aggressive. They hung about looking for heads to bash. Finally, when the gates of the Circus were about to close, out sauntered the silly girls wanting to ruin their reputations and the show-off males they were hoping to attract.

Most of the girls were in pairs or little groups. They usually are. It gives them confidence, which in my experience they don't need. Sooner or later they home in on a set of layabouts, planning to sort out one target each, though there is sometimes a plain, clumsy wench whose traditional role is to tell the others she thinks they are asking for trouble, then stomp off alone while her brazen friends fling themselves into it.

I watched a few of the plain ones, and even followed them discreetly for a short distance, to see if they were tailed by anyone sinister. I soon gave it up. For one thing I had no wish to frighten them. Worse, someone I knew might have noticed me dogging unattractive women; it could have ruined my good name.

The transport situation interested me. At the start of the debouchment commercial chairs seemed to be everywhere, but the prudent who came straight out in search of transport home soon snapped them up. Only a few chairs returned for second fares and by then anyone still waiting was desperate so they quickly vanished again. There were a few private conveyances; they of course had instructions to park up waiting for their specific owners, so they were theoretically unavailable – though the slaves in charge of them seemed to receive plenty of requests to moonlight, and I saw some accept.

The fashion was for either sit-up-and-beg chairs with two carriers or shoulder-high litters with four or even eight hefty men on the corners. Carriages were rare. In the city they were so much less versatile. Wheeled vehicles are barred from Rome in the daytime, apart from builders' carts working on public monuments and the Vestal Virgins' ceremonial carpentaria.

As far as I knew no Vestal had ever in living memory offered a stray kitten a lift. A woman could be giving birth in a gutter and the Virgins would loftily ignore her. So with no money, once she left Pia that fatal night, Asinia would almost certainly have stayed on foot. This was no place for a lone woman. I imagined how it must have been: a black girl, very pretty but endearingly unaware of it, looking nervous perhaps, shyly pulling her stole close and staring at the pavement. Even if she walked quickly she would be easily marked as vulnerable. The quick walk might actually attract attention. Maybe whoever stalked her had already been gawping at Pia, but had been beaten to it; then when Asinia demurely set off on her own, so much more respectable than the friend she had rashly abandoned, he cannot have believed his luck.

All around the arena tonight prostitutes were plying their trade with gusto. The working girls looked vicious, but once they gathered that my business was nothing which involved them they left me alone. They had too much to do. These long hot nights meant there were good denarii to be made under the shadow of the Circus. Being obnoxious to me would be a bad advertisement – and, more important, a waste of earning time.

What struck me about the other young women, and the not-so-young ones too, was that many were more threatening than the bands of youths. A row of sauntering, swearing maidens swinging their yellow parasols, all white-lead eyelids and looking for action, scared even me. At their approach, any sexual inadequate who found women difficult would jump behind a pillar and wet himself.

I saw nobody who fitted that description. But down there in the Street of the Three Altars, I began to feel certain someone like that must be habitually drawn to this spot. I could imagine him being scorned and insulted. And I could understand how his brooding spirit might savagely foment thoughts of revenge.

XXXIII

PETRONIUS AND I planned to spend every evening of the remaining Ludi Romani outside the Circus Maximus. We might have been near the killer all the time. He could have passed so close his clothes brushed ours, and we would not have known.

We needed to find out more. We were working with too little information. It was beginning to look as though only when another woman was murdered would we stand any chance of uncovering more clues. We could not wish that on anyone. It remained unspoken, but both Petro and I wanted Asinia — whose name and sweet nature we had learned — to be the last to suffer.

The day after we started the surveillance, the young Camilli were all struck down with the after-effects of an underdone grilled chicken; unable to visit the Circus they sent a slave to offer their tickets to Helena and me. Somehow, even at short notice, she fixed up young Gaius to sit with the baby for a few hours. It was a welcome chance to go out together on our own. Well, on our own apart from a quarter of a million noisy companions.

Helena Justina was not the world's keenest chariot race follower. I was happy, because the Blues were doing well that day. While I squirmed in my seat, yelled at their drivers' incompetence or screamed at their successes, and munched too many figs during the tense moments, Helena sat patiently letting her mind roam elsewhere. When I leapt to my feet cheering, she picked up my cushion and placed it ready for when my backside hit the bench again. Nice girl. You could take her anywhere. She knew how to let you know that only an idiot would be enjoying this, but she did not openly complain.

While I relaxed, she attempted to solve the case for me. Helena understood that we were looking for somebody about whom we could only put together the sketchiest of details. During a quiet interval she produced a summary:

'The nature of the crime, especially what Lollius told you about the mutilations that are carried out, indicates you are looking for a man.

'The killer could be anyone, senator or slave. The one thing about him that you can safely deduce is that he does not look suspicious. If he did, the dead women would never have gone with him.

'You know something about his age: these deaths go back years. Unless he started in his cradle, he must be middle-aged or older.

'You and Petro both think he's a loner. If he was working with someone else, then after all this time one or other would either have made a mistake or let slip part of the story. That's human nature. The more people involved, the greater the chance of one getting drunk, or being spied on by his wife, or attracting notice from the vigiles on an unrelated charge. Shared knowledge spills out more easily. So you reckon it's one person.

'You think he finds it hard to make social contact. The nature of the crime suggests its motive is sexual gratification, excitement through revenge.

'If Bolanus is right that he lives outside Rome – which you are still considering – then he is someone with access to transport. So women like Asinia are being abducted near the Circus then taken elsewhere – whether they are still alive or already dead by then we don't know.

'He can use a knife. He must be fit. Overpowering people, butchering them, and carrying their bodies, takes physical strength.

'He lives somewhere he can be secretive. Or at least he has access to a bolthole. He has privacy for killing, and whatever else he does. He can store bodies while he starts disposing of them. He can wash himself and his bloodstained clothes without being noticed.

'It does *sound* quite detailed,' Helena mused as she completed the picture for me. 'But it isn't enough, Marcus. Most urgently you need to know what he looks like. Someone must be able to describe him, though they obviously don't realise who he is. He can't be successful every time. He must sometimes have approached women who ignored him or told him to get lost. There may even be a girl somewhere he has tried to grab, who got away from him.'

I shook my head. 'No one has come forward. Even Petro's famous advertisement in the Forum failed to produce any witnesses.'

'Too scared?'

'More likely it's never even occurred to them that the pest they escaped from might be the aqueduct killer.'

153

'She would report him,' Helena decided. 'Men who shoo away muggers just snort and say *"Ha! Let him give someone else a shock!"* but women worry about leaving dangers for others like themselves.'

'Women have a lot of imagination,' I said darkly. For some reason she smiled.

I found myself glancing round the Circus at the audience nearby. I didn't see an obvious killer. But I did notice my old tentmate, Lucius Petronius. He was only a few rows behind us, talking gravely to his female companion about the race that was about to start. If I knew him, he was explaining that the Greens were disasters who couldn't steer a chariot straight even if they had the whole Field of Mars to do it in, whereas the Blues were a stylish, streamlined out-fit who would wipe the floor with everybody else.

I nudged Helena, and we smiled together. But we were saddened too. We were watching what was likely to become a much rarer spectacle: Petronius enjoying the company of his seven-year-old daughter.

At his side Petronilla listened gravely. Since I last saw her she had stopped looking babyish and become a real little girl. She seemed quieter than I remembered her; I found that worrying. She had brown hair, neatly tied in a topknot, and solemn, almost sad brown eyes.

They were both eating pancakes. Petronilla had managed quite nicely, for she had inherited her mother's daintiness. Her father had a sticky chin and honey sauce down his tunic front. Petronilla noticed this. She soon cleaned him up with her handkerchief.

Petronius submitted like a hero. When his daughter sat back he slung an arm around her while she snuggled up against him. He was staring at the arena with a set expression; I was no longer sure he was watching the race.

XXXIV

NEXT DAY JULIUS Frontinus summoned us to a case conference. It was the kind of formality I hate. Petronius was in his element.

'I'm sorry to have to press you, but I am being urged to produce results.' The Consul was being poked from on high, so he was passing down the aggravation to us. 'It's now the eighth day of the Games –'

'We already have a much better picture of what's been happening than when you commissioned us,' I assured him. It seemed unwise to argue that we had only been on his enquiry for four days. Always look ahead, or it sounds as if you're wriggling.

'I expect that's how you normally lull your clients into a sense of security.' Frontinus seemed to be joking. But we did not bank on it.

'Identifying Asinia gave us a good start,' declared Petro. More lulling. Frontinus remained unimpressed.

'It has been suggested to me that we ought to aim to solve the problem by the end of the Games.'

Petronius and I exchanged a glance. We were both used to impossible deadlines. Sometimes we met them. But we both knew never to admit they might be feasible.

'We have had graphic evidence that this killer carries out his work during festivals,' Petro answered levelly. 'He snatched Asinia on the first day of the Ludi Romani. However, I am wary about assuming too readily that he is still here. Maybe he visited Rome for the opening ceremony only. Grabbed a girl, had his thrill, then left. Maybe once he had carved up Asinia, his bloodlust subsided until some future time. Besides, there is a theory that he does the carving up and dumping outside the city.'

That was rich. It was Petronius who had insisted we should ignore that possibility on logistical grounds. When I had discussed it with Helena, she inclined to the theory that we were searching for a man who travelled to and fro, and I had a feeling she would be right.

155

Given what I had heard about such men, I also thought privately: the corpse is only a week old yet. He has cut off one hand, but he could still be snuggling up to the rest of her in some lair . . . No. September was a very hot month.

Frontinus was grumbling at us. 'I cannot have my enquiry put into limbo until the start of the next Games. If we do that, we lose impetus and the whole thing stagnates. I have seen it happen too often. Besides, what would it entail? That we allow the man an opportunity to kill some other girl during the Augustales opening ceremony?'

'Too great a risk,' Petro agreed. We might have no choice.

'That's the worst scenario,' I suggested, rousing myself to take part. 'But we don't plan to sit on goosedown cushions until October, just because our quarry *might* have left Rome.'

'If he has, you ought to go after him,' said Frontinus.

'Oh, we would, sir, but we don't know where to look. Now is the time to follow leads – and we do have some.'

'Can we go through them?' The Consul's manner as always was brisk. He managed not to suggest he was calling us incompetent, although his presumption that professionals would be eager to supply exactly what he wanted did impose a strain. We would need to be sharp with this one. His standards were sky high.

To start, I plied him with Helena Justina's summary of what we knew about the killer's personality. He looked pleased. This was well thought out. He liked its clarity and sense. Petronius assumed I was extemporising; he let me know by a frozen expression that he preferred not to have an imaginative orator for a partner. Still, he too recognised good stuff. He was only annoyed he had not thought of it first.

Petro then did some fly work of his own. 'We know, sir, that Asinia disappeared somewhere between the apsidal end of the Circus Maximus, where she was last seen, and her home. She had set off heading north. She may have been abducted in the press around the Circus, or later when she reached quieter streets. It depends whether this man works by tricking his victims, or if he just jumps on them. Falco and I will continue our nightly surveillance. Solid routine may throw up something.'

'Solid routine,' repeated Frontinus.

'Exactly,' said Petronius in a firm voice. 'What I want to pursue as well is whether any of the commercial chair and litter hire men saw anything on opening night.'

'You think it's one of the commercial transporters doing this?' We could see Frontinus immediately deciding to hammer the aedile who had responsibility for managing the streets.

'It's an ideal cover.' Petro clearly had a ruse. Trust the vigiles; they have to invent a single hypothesis then prove it, whereas informers can cope with several ideas at once. When real life throws up something that departs from the vigiles' scenario, they come unstuck. Being Petro, however, his theory did sound apt. 'The chairmen can pick up the women without looking at all suspicious – and afterwards they have the means of conveying the corpses about.'

'They tend to work in pairs, though,' I demurred.

Petro went on levelly, 'Maybe we'll find in the end that a couple of them work as a pair for more than carrying. Julius Frontinus, I'll be making my own enquiries, but there are plenty of these characters. It would help, sir, if you could ask the Prefect of Vigiles to order an official survey.'

'Certainly.' Frontinus made a swift note on a waxed tablet.

'He needs to get the Fifth and the Sixth Cohorts on to it so we can cover both ends of the Circus. The killer may stick to a favourite route, but we cannot rely on that. The vigiles should also make enquiries among the night moths.'

'Who?'

'The prostitutes.'

'Ah!'

'If this man approaches women regularly, one of the moths who flit around near the Circus must have encountered him.'

'Yes, of course.'

'He may in fact hate the professionals; he may prefer respectable women because they are cleaner, or less adept at escaping from trouble. Who knows? But if he hangs about a lot, then the night girls may know he exists.'

It was my turn to make suggestions. Like Petro I adopted a pious manner. 'I want to look further into the water systems, sir. The engineer's assistant who came here, Bolanus, had some good ideas. He's willing to examine the aqueducts out in the country too, just in case our man's not a city boy. That's another reason we aren't rushing outside Rome ourselves; Bolanus may turn up something specific.'

'Pursue it with him,' Frontinus commanded. 'I will give instructions to the Curator that Bolanus is to assist as we require.'

'What about the magnificent Statius?' Petro enquired wickedly.

Frontinus looked over the rim of his note-tablet. 'Suppose I say we have asked for Bolanus so as not to remove his superior from his more vital managerial work. What else?'

'Make contact with the Prefect of Vigiles —'

He nodded, though he looked as if he realised we were giving him the boring jobs while we escaped on our own. Still, we were confident the two contacts would be made. He would do it this very morning, then he would keep chasing the Curator and the Prefect for results. He had not minded us telling him his duties either; he accepted as much chivying himself as he handed out to us. For a man of his rank that was rare.

We had hoped the enquiry was just taking off. The new evidence connected with Asinia seemed to give us a boost. It was temporary, though. We left the conference with Frontinus already aware we were bluffing, and as the next few days passed depression overtook both of us.

Petronius wore himself out interviewing chairmen, which was dreary enough, and trying to interview streetwalkers, which was positively dangerous. He learned precious little from any of them. Meanwhile I eventually managed to make contact with Bolanus, who seemed to be always out on site now. When I did catch him, he appeared curiously deflated. He said he had been conducting searches of the castelli and other parts of the aqueducts out across the Campagna; as yet he had found nothing. I feared he might have been warned to be obstructive. Ready to bring in the full might of the Consul to lean on his superiors, I asked him straight, but Bolanus denied it. I had to leave him to it.

We had hit a low point. It was one both Petro and I recognised. Unless we had some luck, this was as far as we would ever go. The Ludi Romani were trundling through their final days. The damned Greens were going to come out ahead of the Blues overall in the chariot racing. Several prized gladiators had suffered unexpected defeats and gone to Hades, breaking women's hearts and bankrupting their trainers. The dramatic performances were dire as usual. As usual nobody but me dared say so.

And the case was slipping away from us.

XXXV

WE WERE NOT going to complete the enquiry by the end of the Ludi Romani.

I expected that Julius Frontinus would pay us off. Instead, he accepted that without further clues we were stuck. He cut our retainer. He gave us stern talks. Without a solution to offer the Emperor, he was deprived of glory too, so he must have felt he needed us.

Our only advance was that Petro's enquiries drew out a few names of women who had gone missing in the past. Most had been prostitutes. Others in the same profession named them to us, and when we berated them for not reporting the disappearances to the vigiles, half the time they insisted that it had been done. (Sometimes there were children to care for; sometimes the women's pimps had noticed they had lost part of their livelihood.) Nobody had ever made a connection between the incidents; nobody had bothered much at all, frankly. It was difficult to put together a reliably complete file on the old cases, but Petro and I both felt there had been increasing numbers recently.

'He's bolder now,' said Petro. 'Common pattern. He's almost defying discovery. He knows he can get away with it. He's addicted; increasingly he needs his thrills.'

'He thinks he's invincible?'

'Yes. But he's wrong.'

'Oh? And if we can't find the crucial clue to his identity?'

'Don't think about it, Falco.'

It was impossible to link either of the first two hands we had found to any of the missing women. To show willing, we did regularly copy our list of victims to Anacrites in case he could make a connection with anything reported to the Curator. He never responded. Knowing him, he never read what we sent.

We had hoped the previous cases would throw up more information. It was hopeless. The abductions were too old. The dates were vague. The ethics of the profession discouraged the women's friends from helping. Seeing a whore approached by a man had hardly aroused other people's curiosity. All the women had apparently vanished off the streets without any witnesses.

At least we had some progress to report to the Consul. At our next conference Petronius suggested to Frontinus that we should call on the vigiles to help us watch during the final night of the Games; he wanted to smother the area around the Circus with plainclothes observers keeping a special eye on the prostitutes.

'The killer does not confine his attentions to prostitutes,' Frontinus reminded Petro. 'Asinia was perfectly respectable.'

'Yes, sir. It's possible that Asinia was a mistake. She was alone, late at night, so he may have jumped to the wrong conclusions. Alternatively, he is now widening his interests. But the night moths working the colonnades are still the most vulnerable girls.'

'How many registered prostitutes are there in Rome?' the Consul asked, ever keen on figures.

'Thirty-two thousand at the last count.' Petronius made the statement in a typically calm manner; he left Frontinus to reach his own conclusions about the impossibility of protecting them.

'And what is being done to discover whether any other respectable women have been similarly taken?'

'My old second in command, Martinus, is now assigned to enquiries in the Sixth Cohort. He has been reviewing unsolved missing person reports and in likely cases the family is being re-interviewed. He thinks he has found one or two that may be aqueduct killings, but so far there is nothing definite.'

'Should this have been spotted by the vigiles before?'

Petronius shrugged. 'Maybe. You certainly can't blame Martinus because he was with me then up on the Aventine. Different officers took the reports, and over a long period. Besides, if a woman disappears during a public holiday, we first assume that she has run off with her lover. In one or two cases, Martinus has found out that was true; the woman is now definitely living with a boyfriend. One has even returned to her husband because she and the boyfriend fell out.'

'At least Martinus can close those files now,' I said.

My own area of investigation was still the water supply.

Bolanus grew tired of my nagging him. He was certain that there was no easy access to the aqueducts in Rome itself. Those which did not come in underground were carried on immense arcades which thrust across the Campagna on arches a hundred feet high. Once they reached the city they stayed high, to take them above the streets and to supply the citadels.

Bolanus had been asking workmen he trusted whether our man might actually be employed by the water board and have gained admittance that way. If anyone had had doubts about a fellow slave Bolanus would probably have been tipped a wink. Corruption was rife on the aqueducts, that was understood. The willingness of water board officials to take bribes was legendary – and they knew how to be obstructive if the bribes were not forthcoming. But perverted killing is a special crime. Anyone with real suspicions about a colleague would have turned him in.

Julius Frontinus began to show an interest in Bolanus. He was intrigued by the system, and drew up his own sketch plans. One day Bolanus took the two of us to see the crossover of the Aqua Claudia and Aqua Marcia, to demonstrate his theory that severed limbs might start out in one channel but be transferred later to another, confusing us about their real source.

Bolanus took us into the channel of a branch of the Marcia. It was about twice the height of a man, flat-roofed, and lined with smooth, continuous waterproof cement.

'Lime and sand, or lime and crushed brick,' Bolanus told us, while we were reaching our destination through a manhole above. 'Watch your step, Consul – It's laid in layers. Takes three months to set. The last lot is polished to mirror brightness, as we call it.'

'Seems a lot of effort,' I remarked. 'Why is the water board such a keen housekeeper?'

'A smooth surface inhibits the formation of sediment. It helps the flow too, if you reduce friction.'

'So if a foreign body got in, would it be damaged much as it tumbled along?' asked Frontinus.

'Falco and I discussed that. There'd probably be some friction effect, but if the severed hands look badly damaged I'd be more inclined to put it down to decay, given that we do keep the walls so smooth. But one major tumble could batter them badly. If any foreign body ends up just here while we're switching, I reckon not much would survive –'

We had arrived at the point that he wanted us to see. The Aqua Claudia was passing the Marcia directly overhead – not a thought for anyone who hated confined spaces. Bolanus told us there was a shaft let into the side of the Claudia's channel above us, controlled by a sluice-gate. He was showing us the shaft, about a yard square. Frontinus and I were peering up obediently into the gloom. We had lamps with us, but we couldn't see much at the top of the dark, narrow chimney.

'As you can see, down in the Marcia the flow is very feeble at present. We need to replenish it quickly because the Marcia supplies the Capitol. Ideally the channel ought to be at least a third full –'

It was a set up, of course. As we listened politely someone had been primed to pull up the sluice. We heard it creak faintly high above us. Then without warning a huge quantity of water was released from the Aqua Claudia and thundered straight down the shaft through the Marcia's roof. It poured towards us, falling over thirty feet and hitting bottom with a tremendous noise. The water in the Marcia surged with furious force, and its level rose alarmingly. Waves went careering down the channel. Spray soaked us and we were deafened.

We were in no danger. We were standing on a platform out of reach. Bolanus grabbed Frontinus in case the shock made him topple in. I stood my ground, having met jokers before, though I felt my legs quake. The tumbling water made a fantastic sight. Bolanus mouthed something that looked like 'In the Caerulean Spring only this morning!' though it was pointless even to try to speak.

As Bolanus said, any foreign bodies from the Aqua Claudia that dropped down in that cascade would probably be pulverised. On the other hand, they just might go bobbing away in the current of the replenished Aqua Marcia, to be found eventually in its reservoir, like the second hand which was produced by the public slave Cordus when he replied to Petro's Forum advertisement.

Frontinus was thrilled by this sightseeing. I would not have missed it myself, come to that. We learned nothing specific, so strictly it was a wasted day. But there seemed little to be discovered in Rome either.

'Tell me when you want a guided trip out to Tibur!' Bolanus offered with a grin as we were leaving.

I do like a man who can stick with a theory.

There had been no further grim discoveries. Many people now bathed, drank water, and cooked their food with hardly a thought for the consequences.

Though the absence of limbs in the aqueducts was a relief in some ways, it did mean that a man called Caius Cicurrus was left suspended in misery. Just before the Games ended, I walked out to see him. I took Helena, in case a woman's presence was consoling. Anyway, I wanted to know what she thought of him. When a wife is murdered the husband is inevitably the first suspect. Even if there have been scores of similar deaths before, it is wiser to consider that the man may have deliberately copied them.

We went at midday in case Cicurrus was now back running his chandlery. We did find him at home, though it looked as if he was spending most of his time there now and letting the shop remain closed. The same slave as before let us in.

'I'm sorry, Cicurrus, I have very little to tell you. This visit is just to let you know we are still looking, and we will look until we find something. But I cannot pretend we have achieved much yet.'

He sat meekly listening. He still seemed dreamy. When I asked if he wanted to know anything, or if Frontinus could do anything to help him officially, he shook his head. Sudden death causes anger and recriminations usually; they would come. At some inconvenient time, when he had too much to do, poor Caius would find himself demanding endlessly: why her? Why had Asinia walked by the route she chose that night? Why had Pia left her alone? Why Asinia and not Pia, who courted trouble so openly? Why Cicurrus himself gone to the country that week? Why had Asinia been so beautiful? Why did the gods hate him?

Not yet. So far he had been granted no formal end to the nightmare. He was caught between knowing and not knowing the exact, horrendous details of his young wife's fate.

Cicurrus indicated a brown marble casket which he said contained her embalmed hand. Thank the gods he did not offer to open it. It looked too small, more like a pen case than a reliquary. Even to us it seemed an unreal symbol of the lost Asinia.

'We are still watching the Circus Maximus every night,' I said. 'On the last night of the Games there will be saturation coverage –'

'She was a perfect wife,' he interrupted quietly. 'I cannot believe she has gone.'

He did not want to hear what we were doing. All the man really needed was to be given his wife's body so that he could hold a funeral and grieve for her. I could not help him.

After we left his house Helena Justina said nothing immediately. Then she reached her decision. 'He's not involved. I think if he had killed her he would rail against the supposed murderer more dramatically. He would issue threats, or offer ostentatious rewards. When he says Asinia was perfect, his protestations would be louder and longer. But he just sits there, hoping his visitors will soon leave him alone. He's still in shock, Marcus.' I thought she had finished, but then Helena murmured, 'Did you see the rock crystal necklace that the slave girl was wearing? I imagine it's one which belonged to his wife.'

I was shocked. 'Has she stolen it?'

'No, she was wearing it openly.'

I was even more shocked. 'Are you telling me after all that Cicurrus had a reason to dispose of Asinia?'

'No.' Helena shook her head and smiled at me gently. 'He's heartbroken; that's genuine. I'm telling you he's just a typical man.'

XXXVI

As THE DAYS passed and the clues diminished, we were gearing ourselves for a last night on surveillance outside the Circus Maximus when the Games ended. Frontinus and the Prefect of the Vigiles were making it an official exercise. Every spare man was to be drawn from the watch cohorts.

I spent some time at home during that day. Helena needed rest, and I needed to be with her. Working night shifts all week helped me avoid being wakened when the baby cried, but it left Helena with all the duties when she was already exhausted. I knew she was feeling demoralised. Julia had discovered that she could rack our nerves to breaking point by wailing for long periods, though if either of her grandmothers came over to see Helena the dear child stopped as soon as they picked her up. Helena was tired of being glared at as if she were either not trying or plainly incompetent.

Helena had slept all afternoon. I kept Julia quiet by a method Petro had revealed to me. It involved the baby and me snoozing in the porch together with a cup of honeyed wine, not all of which went into Papa.

The only real interruption was a visit from that latrine-wall lizard Anacrites.

'What do you want? And keep your voice down. If you wake the baby she'll wake Helena, and if you cause that to happen I'll wring your grimy neck.'

There was no reason to suggest he failed to wash; Anacrites had always looked almost too sleek. His clothes were faintly dandified. His haircuts were suspiciously neat. He fancied himself as a looker. The only truly filthy thing about him was his character.

'How did you get yourself hitched up to a consul, Falco?'

'A good reputation and impeccable contacts.'

'That must have cost a lot to fix. Can I sit down?'

'Still poorly? Have a step.'

I myself had carried out a wicker chair, in which I was sprawled with one arm around the sleeping baby. Nux, lying at my feet, filled up the rest of the tiny landing outside my apartment. Anacrites could neither step round me to go indoors and fetch out a stool, nor even reach the shade. He had to drape himself in the baking heat on the dusty stone stairs. I'm not a complete bastard. I was not trying to give the invalid another headache, just turning him into a sun-dried raisin to encourage him to leave.

I tipped my cup at him and drained it. As there was only one, he could only nod in response. Even this hint failed to work.

'Your game of draughts with Frontinus is getting in my way, Falco.'

'Oh, I am sorry!'

'There's no need to pretend.'

'Irony, dear fellow.'

'Crap, Falco! Why don't we join forces?'

I knew what that meant. He was as thoroughly stuck as Petronius and me. 'You want to link up, pinch any ideas we have, and claim all the credit yourself?'

'Don't be harsh.'

'I've seen you at work before.'

'I just think we are duplicating our efforts.'

'Well, maybe that gives us twice as much chance of success.' I too could sound so reasonable it made the other party squirm.

Anacrites darted to a new subject. 'So what's this rumble you've got going on tonight?' His ears were well pricked, apparently. Though with all the vigiles cohorts being stretched to breaking point in order to supply us with our troops at the Circus, word was bound to filter out to any half-trained spy.

'Just some anti-vandalism measure Frontinus dreamed up.'

'How's that? He's ex-officio, apart from the water deaths enquiry.'

'Oh, is he? I wouldn't know; I don't take much interest in politics – too murky for a simple Aventine lad. I leave all that unscrupulous stuff to suave types with Palace upbringings.' He knew I was being disingenuous – and insulting him with his inferior social status. I had never bothered to find out, but Anacrites was bound to be an ex-Imperial slave; all Palace officials were nowadays.

Unable to settle, he changed tack. 'Your mother's been complaining that you never come and visit her.'

'Tell her to get a new lodger then.'

'She wants to see more of the baby,' he lied.

166

'Don't tell me what my mother wants.' When Ma wanted to see the baby she did what she had always done. She swanned over to my apartment, walked in as if she owned it, and made a nuisance of herself.

'You ought to look after her,' claimed Anacrites, who knew how to throw a low punch.

'Oh, go away, Anacrites.'

He left. I rearranged the baby and myself more comfortably. Nux looked up with one eye open, then thumped her tail.

My afternoon was now ruined. I spent the rest of it wondering what the bastard was up to. I told myself he was only jealous, but that made it worse. Being envied by Anacrites meant I was a man in jeopardy.

Petro came over to our apartment for a light meal in the early evening. I winked and thanked him for his childcare tip, then we pecked at a meat pie bought from Cassius. He always oversalted them, but we were too keyed up to be hungry in any case.

'What's up?' demanded Petro, noticing that Helena seemed especially quiet. I had not needed to ask her.

'I worry when Marcus goes out on the trail of a murderer.'

'I thought it was because we were off observing prostitutes.'

'Marcus has better taste.'

Petronius looked as if he was planning to recite scurrilous stories; then he decided not to upset my domestic harmony. 'It's not only the prostitutes we have to watch,' he commented gloomily. It was like him to have been brooding on the coming night's events. 'I've been thinking about how many different people could be involved if these killings are linked to festivals.'

'Anyone involved with transport, you mean?' said Helena, who still stuck with the theory that the killer drove in from outside Rome.

'Yes; or the ticket-sellers on the gates –'

'Programme-sellers.' I joined in the game. 'Garland girls, gambling agents, ticket touts, food and drink pedlars.'

'Parasol and souvenir stallholders,' Petro contributed.

'Aediles and ushers.'

'Arena sweepers.'

'All the charioteers and gladiators, their stable hands and trainers, the actors, the clowns, the musicians,' chimed in Helena. 'The Circus employees who open the starting gates and turn the markers for the laps. The slaves who manoeuvre the water organ.'

'The snobby chamberlain who opens the gate at the back of the Imperial box when the Emperor wants to slip out for a pee —'

'Thank you, Marcus! All the audience from the Emperor down, not forgetting the Praetorian Guard —'

'Stop, stop!' cried Petronius. 'I know it's true, but you jolly pair are depressing me.'

'That's the trouble with the vigiles,' I told Helena ruefully. 'No staying power.'

'It was your idea,' she reminded him. 'Some of us think the deaths only occur at festivals because the murderer is a visitor from elsewhere.'

Nevertheless, when it was time for us to leave for our evening patrol Petro had the tact to walk off ahead of me so I could hold Helena tight for a moment. I kissed her tenderly while she begged me to take care.

It was another warm night. The area around the Circus Maximus was dreary with litter and bad smells. After two weeks of festivity the street-cleaners had given up. The audience must have been played out too, because some were starting to leave almost as soon as we arrived, which was well before the trumpets that signalled the closing ceremonial

Petronius was taking the Street of the Three Altars tonight. We reckoned that swapping kept us fresh. I clapped his shoulder and walked on, towards the Temple of Sol and Luna. At the end of the street I glanced back; it took me a moment to find him. Despite his size Petro could blend in. His brown-clad, brown-headed figure merged into the crowds as he sauntered nonchalantly under a portico looking like a man who had every right to be there, doing nothing much and paying attention to nobody.

I knew he would have noticed all the female passers-by, filing the lookers in his 'noteworthy' pigeonhole, yet remembering the discards too. He would spot the lurkers and loungers. He would wince because there were too many children out so late, scowl at the yobbish louts, groan at the senseless girls. If an unprotected woman or a pervert came near Petro, he would mark them. If anyone was too closely watched, or shadowed, or bothered, let alone openly assaulted, the heavy hand of Petronius Longus would descend out of nowhere and collar the criminal.

I passed members of the vigiles both obvious and well disguised.

Their Prefect had given Frontinus a good response and the district had been decently packed with men. But, like us, they had no idea who they were really looking for.

I turned into the Street of the Public Fishpond. My heart was pounding. This was the night. I was suddenly sure he would be here.

By now there was a slow but constant exodus from the stadium. People were walking lazily, tired out by fifteen days of Games, tired of excitement and yelling themselves hoarse, tired of commercial food and cheap sticky wine, ready for normal daily life again. Mid-September. The weather would become cooler soon. The long hot summer must be reaching its end. Two weeks would see the traditional finish of the fighting season. October brought the end of the school holidays; after three and a half months, it would be a relief to some (including schoolteachers, by now desperate to earn new fees). October would also bring fresh festivals, but we were not there yet. There was still tonight, one last chance to make these Games memorable, a few final hours left for simple pleasure or outright debauchery.

Inside the Circus I could hear the *cornu* band going at it now: the huge, almost circular brass horns, supported on the players' shoulders by cross-bars, their different notes blown with sheer puff. Or missed, frequently. Especially after a long day of events.

I decided there was one class of suspect we could discount: no *cornu* player would have the strength to overpower a woman after blowing his heart out with the band.

Limp applause down the length of the valley finally ended the Ludi Romani for another year.

By that time those of the audience who had been glad to see the Games over were long gone. The remainder were now shuffling from the Circus, chivvied by the ushers who wanted to close the gates, yet reluctant to depart. Outside, groups were standing about. Young people were hoping for more excitement. Visitors were saying farewell to friends they only saw during festivals. Youths cat-called after giggling girls. Musicians stood around in case somebody offered to buy them a drink. Snack-sellers slowly packed up. Gypsy-eyed pedlars from the Transtiberina drifted from group to group still trying to force last-minute sales of shoddy trinkets. A dwarf, hung all around his waist with cheap cushions, waddled off towards the Temple of Mercury.

Deep in the shadow of the stadium hovered the working women.

Skirts hitched, legs flashing, tottering on high cork heels, goggling through soot-rimmed lashes, they showed themselves in ones or twos. False hair, or real hair endlessly mistreated until it looked false, towered above their chalked faces, each mask-like visage slashed with lips dyed the colour of pig's liver. Men regularly went up to them. They exchanged a few words then quietly disappeared into the darker gloom, reconvening not long afterwards for another businesslike encounter.

Behind me, up in the darkness of the Temple entrance, I could hear noises that suggested commerce went on there too. Or perhaps the fun was not being paid for, and some youth had struck lucky with one of the bad, loud girls marauding among their sassy friends hours after their mothers had told them to be home. I might have cheered it once. I was a father now.

The whole scene was sordid. From the drunks lolling against closed shops offering horrible overtures to scared passers-by, to the squashed melon pieces in the gutter, their innards as red as bright fresh blood. From the sneak thieves skulking off home looking pleased with themselves to the smell of urine in the alleys, where antisocial deadbeats couldn't wait. It was growing worse. The few lamps that were now hung outside open lock-ups or in overhead apartment windows only made the spaces between them even darker and more dangerous. A couple of chairs lurched by, their horn lanterns swinging on hooks. Someone was singing an obscene song that I remembered from the legions.

Two men clung together on the back of one donkey, both so drunk they hardly knew where they were; their grey-coated mount was trotting off down the Via Piscinae Publicae with them, choosing the route for himself. Perhaps he knew of a jolly winebar under the Servian Walls, down by the Raudusculana Gate. I was in two minds to follow him.

There were so many people who looked up to no good it was difficult to choose which to watch. In every direction women were being brazenly foolish while sinister men eyed them hopefully. I hated having to stand here looking like part of all this. My nerves were so wound up I almost felt anyone who put themselves amidst this ghastly scene deserved all they got.

The exodus continued for a couple of hours. In the end my mind was so benumbed it started wandering. I suddenly came to; I realised that for the past ten minutes I had been staring fixedly in front of me, perfecting my plan to hire a hall and give a public recital of my poetry. (This was a dream I had been nurturing for some time now; so far I had been gently dissuaded by the good advice of my close friends, especially those who had read my odes and eclogues.) I returned to real life with a guilty start.

Outside the nearby gate of the Circus a young girl was standing all by herself. She was dressed in white, with a glint of gold embroidery on the hem of her stole. Her skin was delicate, her hair neatly dressed. Jewellery that only an heiress could afford was innocently on display. She was gazing around as if she was part of an untouchable procession of Vestals in broad daylight. She had been brought up to believe she would always be treated with respect – yet some idiot had dumped her here. Even if you didn't know her she looked glaringly out of place. And I did know her. She was Claudia Rufina, the shy young creature Helena and I had brought from Spain. As she stood there alone, all kinds of bad characters were poised to move in on her.

XXXVII

'CLAUDIA RUFINA!' I managed to appear at her side before any of the would-be muggers, rapists, or kidnappers. Various seedy types edged back a bit, though they hustled still within earshot, hoping I myself was a chancer Claudia would reject, leaving the booty for them.

'How nice to see you, Marcus Didius!'

Claudia was docile and well-meaning. I tried to moderate my voice. 'May I ask what are you doing alone in a rough street at this time of night?'

'Oh, I don't mind,' the silly girl assured me sweetly. 'I'm waiting for Aelianus and Justinus to come back with our litter. Their mother insists we have it sent to collect me, but in the crush it's so very hard to find.'

'This is not the place to hang about, lady.'

'No, it's not nice, but this exit is nearest to the Capena Gate. We could walk home from here, but Julia Justa won't hear of it.'

Walking home as a brisk threesome would be a damned sight safer than having the lads bunk off searching for the family chair while Claudia was positioned here like live bait.

Justinus turned up while I was fuming. 'Oh, Claudia, I warned you not to talk to any strange men.'

I lost my temper. 'Don't ever do this again! Don't you realise this is the area where the last known victim of the aqueduct killer disappeared? I am standing here watching for some stupid female to get herself followed by a maniac — and I really would rather it isn't someone I myself introduced to Rome, one who is my future sister-in-law!'

He had not known about the location. But he had a fine sense of danger once the character of the district had been pointed out. 'We've been fools. I apologise.'

'Think nothing of it,' I returned harshly. 'So long as you and your brother are prepared to be the ones who explain your stupidity to Helena! Not to mention your noble mother, your illustrious father, and Claudia's loving grandparents —'

Claudia turned solemn eyes on Justinus. He was one of the few people tall enough to meet her gaze directly despite her habit of leaning back and looking at the world down her large nose. 'Oh, Quintus,' she murmured. 'I do believe Marcus Didius is a little bit cross with you!'

'Oh, goodness! Am I in trouble, Falco?' It was the first time I had seen Claudia teasing anyone. That rascal Quintus seemed suspiciously used to it. 'Don't worry; if anything is said at home, we'll just blame Aelianus!' This seemed to be some old shared joke; amid a clatter of bracelets Claudia hid a smile in her beringed hand.

Aelianus himself arrived just then from a different direction, bringing the litter for his betrothed. As well as the bearers, three lads with staves acted as bodyguard, but they were puny and vague-looking. I instructed the two Camilli to clear off fast. 'Stick together, keep your eyes open, and get yourselves home as quick as possible.'

The Capena Gate was very close or I would have felt obliged to go with them.

Aelianus looked as if he wanted to argue on principle, but his brother had grasped the point. When Claudia tried to soothe me with a goodbye kiss on the cheek, Justinus shooed her into the litter. I noticed he now parked himself at the open half-door, shielding the girl from onlookers and keeping himself between her and trouble. He muttered a few words in an undertone to his brother, who glanced about as if confirming that we were surrounded by misfits. Aelianus then had the grace to close ranks with Justinus, marching close to the chair as it moved off.

Justinus bade me farewell with a crisp military salute; it was a reminder of our time in Germany, and meant to let me know he was now taking care. Aelianus must have been in the army too, though I had no idea which province he had served in. Knowing him, some place where the hunting was good and the locals had forgotten how to revolt. If his younger brother seemed more mature and responsible in a tricky situation, that was because Justinus had been taught how to survive in barbarian territory – and taught by me. I would have passed on techniques for handling women too, but at the time he had not seemed to need it. I was not sure he needed any teaching nowadays.

Grimly I returned to my post at the Temple of Sol and Luna. I felt shaken. There were enough young people out looking for trouble without ones I knew worrying me.

The next woman I saw being ridiculous was another one I

recognised: Pia, the dead Asinia's friend. The hussy in turquoise who had assured Petro and me she would not go anywhere near the Circus again after what had happened to Asinia. It was no surprise that this trembling blossom had emerged from the stadium tonight, having clearly attended the Games just the same as usual. What was more she had a man in tow.

I strode up to her. She was annoyed at seeing me. I was annoyed too, that she had lied to us and that she so blatantly lacked any loyalty to her murdered friend. But it did give me a faint hope of exposing her lies.

The fellow with sickly taste who was crawling over Pia was a greasy tyke with patches on his clothing and a yellowing black eye. He was playing the part of an old friend, so maybe Pia herself had whacked him with the shiner. She, however, was trying to make out to me that she hardly knew this dreamboat.

I weighed straight in. 'Is this the weasel you were screwing the night you parted from Asinia?'

She wanted to deny it, but he failed to notice she was trying to disown him so he owned up straight away. Pia had clearly picked him for his intelligence. Don't ask me why he went for her.

They must already have discussed the night in question. Clearly he knew all about Asinia's grim fate, and I guessed he knew even more than that.

'What's your name, friend?'

'I'd rather not say.'

'That's all right.' Sometimes it pays to allow them their secrecy. I wanted to know what he had seen, never mind who he was. 'Did you hear the bad news about poor Asinia?'

'Terrible!'

'I'd be interested in your side of the story. Pia said you both left her about here – but you saw her again in the Street of the Three Altars?'

'Yes, we must of caught up with her. She didn't see us.'

'Was she all right at that point?'

He glanced at Pia. 'Didn't you tell him about that fellow, then?'

'Oh,' lied Pia, utterly shamelessly. 'I think I must have forgot.'

'What fellow was this then?' I wished Petro was here with me. Less scrupulous than I was, he would have dragged her arm up her back in a vigiles' bodyhold, while encouraging free speech with his spare fist around her throat.

'Oh,' mouthed Pia, as if it was unimportant and anyway she had only just remembered it. 'I think we saw some man talking to Asinia.'

XXXVIII

I WAS SO furious I could cheerfully have thrown both of them to the public torturer and had them scarified with hooks. I think Pia realised the atmosphere was stickier than she liked. Even now she had no intention of telling me herself, but when her lousy bed companion coughed up freely she scowled and let him speak. Whatever she did to him afterwards would be between the two of them.

'We saw this fellow,' he told me, with a helpful demeanour. I would have admired him more for it if I had not suspected Pia had told him to keep his mouth shut. I was livid. He had held on to this vital information for over a week, even though he knew it could help catch a pervert and save other women's lives.

'You say you saw this fellow?'

'He was talking to Asinia'

'Harrying her?'

'No, it looked all right. We noticed because Asinia never had anything to do with men. But he seemed cheery enough. We would of gone up to them otherwise, of course.'

'Of course.' The way he was winding himself around Pia even now suggested this charmer did not readily abandon a grope. 'So what happened?'

'She answered him and he went off.'

'Is that it?'

'That's all, legate.'

'You're sure you saw Asinia walk on by herself?'

'Oh yes.'

'What was the man like?'

'Nothing much. We only saw him from behind.'

'Tall?'

'No, short.'

'Build?'

'Ordinary.'

'Age?'

'Couldn't say.'

'A youth or older?'

'Older. Probably.'

'Much older?'

'Probably not.'

'Any national characteristics?'

'What?'

'Did he look Roman?'

'How do you mean?'

'Forget it. Hair?'

'Don't know.'

'Hat?'

'Don't think so.'

'What was he wearing?'

'Tunic and belt.'

'What colour tunic?'

'Nothing particular.'

'White?'

'Could have been.'

'Nothing you noticed?'

'No, legate.'

'Boots or shoes?'

'Couldn't say, legate.'

'Couldn't care less either, eh?'

'We just never noticed him much. He was ordinary.'

'So ordinary he may be a bestial killer. Why did neither of you come forward with this information before?'

'I never thought it was important,' the man assured me earnestly. Pia made no attempt to bluff. I understood her problem; she was frightened that Caius Cicurrus would blame her for letting his wife get into trouble while she herself was preoccupied with bedding this worm.

'Right. I want you to come with me to the Street of the Three Altars and point out exactly where this exchange with Asinia took place.'

'We've got things in mind!' protested the greaseball. Pia, still pretending she hardly knew him, just looked surly.

'That's all right,' I replied in a pleasant tone. 'I've got something in mind too: I'm planning to haul you both in front of a judge tonight on charges of obstructing a consular enquiry, perverting justice, and putting free citizens in danger of abduction, disfigurement

176

and death.'

'Oh well; make it quick then,' muttered Pia's friend. She said nothing, but she dawdled along with us, just in case he said something she wanted to hit him for afterwards.

The rancid pair stood at the junction of the Street of the Public Fishpond, at the far end, after we had passed by the Circus Maximus. To the left a roadway ran along the north side of the Circus towards the Forum Boarium and the river. To the right was the incoming Via Latina. Ahead of us, across the junction, the road we had come on changed its name. A left-hand fork went to the Forum, coming out opposite the Colossus and the new Flavian Amphitheatre site. The right-hand fork was the Street of the Three Altars.

'So when you got here, you two were going hard right down the Via Latina, to pass the end of the Street of Honour and Virtue, and then wend your way into Cyclops Street?' They nodded. Not knowing my brother's girlfriend lived in the Street of Honour and Virtue they seemed subdued by the extent of my local knowledge. 'Then up ahead of you was Asinia?'

The man nodded again. 'She must have just walked into the Street of the Three Altars.'

'Wouldn't it have been quicker for her to go the other way?'

'She didn't like going through the Forum on her own,' volunteered Pia.

'Jupiter! She preferred a route that was quieter, so that if she got picked up by a pervert no one would hear her scream?'

'Asinia was shy.'

'You mean, she was scared stiff of being out alone, and you knew it!' The worldly Pia should also have known that a nervous woman alone on the streets is begging to be noticed by the kind of man who for all the wrong reasons likes his women terrified. From the moment the two friends parted, Asinia would have been a target for harassment. Perhaps she had discovered it on previous occasions. Perhaps that was why she liked to scuttle along away from the crowds.

'How many people were about that night?'

'Not many. A bit more than now.'

'The shows had finished? Most people had gone home?'

'Unless they had things to do.' Pia's swain giggled and groped her, in anticipation of a sweaty coupling. I ignored it.

I had not noticed Petro but he must have spotted us, for suddenly he materialised and listened in. I introduced Pia's lovelife, as best I could.

'Oh, I know him,' Petronius sneered. 'His name's Mundus.' He did not mention what Mundus had done to attract notice from the vigiles. His expression gave me a few clues, though.

I told Petro the tale. He went over it all again with Mundus, then tried the same with Pia. She still clammed up, but we had the impression it was now bad temper rather than deceit.

'What I don't see is why you broke up with Asinia by the Temple of Sol and Luna, yet you were following her again by the time she reached here?'

'At first we were going into the Temple for a smooch,' explained Mundus, as if it ought to be obvious. 'We thought we would have a quick fiddle around at the Temple, then buy some food and take it to Pia's house before we really got stuck in. But when we got up the steps the portico was full of old men screwing pretty boys, so we missed out the first part.'

Petronius winced with disgust.

It seemed there was probably no more useful information to squeeze from this sordid pair. We were ready to let them go. 'Just one more thing,' I said sternly, attempting to grab Mundus' attention before he lost himself completely inside Pia's grubby garments. 'Are you absolutely certain that the man you saw accosting Asinia was on foot?'

'Yes, legate.'

'No litter?' demanded Petro. 'No carriage? No cart in sight?'

'He told you.' Pia wanted to be shot of us now. 'There was nothing.'

If she was right there could be various explanations. The encounter they saw may have had nothing at all to do with Asinia's later abduction. Or maybe the killer harassed the girl then pretended to leave her, but followed – unnoticed by Pia and Mundus – to grab her when she was alone and get her to his transport later. Or else he made initial contact – had a look at her, decided if she met his requirements – then went off for transport he was keeping nearby, and trapped her in a quieter street. If the first conversation was amiable, it might make the girl an easier target the second time he caught up with her.

'It was him,' I decided.

'Most likely,' Petro agreed.

We told the dewy-eyed lovers to go. They vanished down the Via Latina, Mundus slobbering all over Pia while she coarsely insulted him.

'She still wants to lie to us – on principle.' It was my turn to announce the verdict. 'If she could get away with it she would. But the radish is telling the truth.'

'Oh, he's a darling,' Petronius agreed glumly. 'Pure and true. And his lack of remorse for Asinia is almost as heartwarming as Pia's. Where would we be without such upright citizens to assist our work?'

The crowds had mainly dispersed by now. Only dawdlers who would be out carousing until they fell down in the gutters were still here. Petro was intending to stay out all night on surveillance. My stamina was up to it, but my liking for the task had spoiled. I said I would walk the route Asinia might have taken, then work back for a look along the river before going home. Since I had a woman and child waiting for me, Petro accepted that. He did not need his hand held. He had always been a loner when it came to work. So had I. Maybe this was the best way for us to continue our partnership.

I went all the way to Caius Cicurrus' house. I saw nothing unusual. The house was shuttered and in darkness. Cypress trees framed the doorway as a sign of mourning. I wondered how long they would have to be kept there before Cicurrus was able to hold a funeral.

I strolled back towards the Forum by a slightly different route. I still saw nothing, except cat burglars and the kind of pavement-creeping women who had men waiting up alleys to rob their hapless clients. I considered asking if they had ever noticed a handsome black woman being snatched off the street. But approaching them was asking to get my head cracked open. I know when to chicken out.

I hit the Forum just north of the Temple of Venus and Rome. I started walking down the Sacred Way, keeping my ears and eyes peeled, like a prowling animal watching every shadow for movement. I kept to the centre of the road, treading the uneven old slabs as quietly as possible.

By the Temple of Vesta a girl was bent double being noisily sick. Another woman was holding on to her. As I approached warily a casual vehicle clattered from a sidestreet: unladen and no passenger, a one-horse country trap. The wench who was more or less upright called out brazenly to the driver. He ducked his head, apparently terrified of being hassled, and hurried on the horse, quickly turning away from the Forum again somewhere up by the Basilica Julia.

I sighed gently. Then, although it would normally have been against my principles to go anywhere near such a couple of tipsy witches, I strode straight across to them. The one who had called out was Marina, the mother of my little niece Marcia. I had recognised her voice.

XXXIX

THERE WERE PROBABLY more people here with us than we realised, but they were lurking around the Regia, flitting among temple columns, or hovering in the deep shadow under the Arch of Augustus. Nobody I could actually see was within earshot. Just as well. The tall girl flopping over Marina's left arm had just been sick against the stately Corinthian columns of the Temple of Vesta. This was supposed to resemble an ancient hut built of wood and straw though the mock antique construction appeared pretty crisp. It was less than a decade old, having been burnt down in Nero's great fire then hastily rebuilt 'to ensure the continued existence of Rome'. Marina's friend was making a stout job of imparting a more weathered look to the new colonnade.

The girl being ill with such gusto was also very thin, like a long puppet who had lost her stuffing, hooked around the waist by Marina. Marina herself only came halfway up my chest even when she was upright – a feat she achieved rather unsteadily at the moment. I was accosting a seriously disgraceful pair of women, and I felt ten years too old for it.

'Hello, Marcus. Something for the sacred housekeepers to clean up!'

Marina may have lacked stature but what there was of her had a well-packed allure that turned heads at all levels. She was dressed to show it off, and gorgeously painted. With her free right hand she made a mannered obscene gesture. 'Bitches!' she yelled at the House of the Vestals, rather more loudly than was wise when addressing the guardians of the Sacred Flame. Her friend threw up again. 'Stuff that up your Palladium!' Marina growled at the hallowed hut.

'Now look here,' I began weakly. 'What's happening to –'

'Marcia's at home, idiot. She's safely tucked up in her own little bed, and my neighbour's daughter's looking after her. Clean, sensible girl, thirteen years old, not interested in boys yet, thank the gods – Anything else your nosiness wants to know?'

'Have you been at the Games?'

'Certainly not. Too full of low characters. Is that where you've been, Falco?' The gorgeous vision cackled with abominable laughter.

A lamp stood on the ground, placed there while Marina attended to her companion. By its wavering light I could see my brother's exotic girlfriend: translucent skin, breathtakingly regular features, and the remote beauty of a temple statue. Only when she spoke did the mystique fade; she had the voice of a winkle-seller. Even then, she had just to roll those huge eyes a few times and I remembered all too clearly the jealous throb that used to drive me wild when Festus was bedding her. Then Festus died and I had to pay Marina's bills. That helped keep me chaste.

'If you weren't at the Games, what coven have you witches been casting spells at?'

'We ladies,' Marina enunciated pompously, although she did seem a great deal more sober than whoever was vomiting against the Temple, 'have been at the monthly reunion of the Braidmakers' Old Girls.'

There had once been a rumour that Marina worked in the field of tunic decoration, though she was doing her best to disprove it. The only thing she reckoned to twist nowadays was me. 'Isn't this late to be leaving a party, girl?'

'No, it's quite early for the Braidmakers.' She let out a disreputable giggle. An answering hiccup came faintly from the bent beanpole.

'Dawn daisies, eh? I suppose when you finished disporting yourself among the pensioned-off tassel-knotters, you came home by way of a tipple at the Four Fish?'

'As I recollect, it was the Old Grey Dove, Marcus Didius.'

'And the Oystershell?'

'Then probably the Venus of Cos. It was bloody Venus who did for this one –'

Marina applied more tender nurture to her friend – an act which consisted of jerking her upright and forcing her head back with a dangerous click of the neck. 'Well, keep your voice lower,' I muttered. 'You'll have the Vestals scampering out here in their nightclothes to investigate.'

'Forget it! They're too busy screwing the Pontifex Maximus around the sacred hearth.'

If I was to be hauled before a judge on a treason trial, I would rather choose the infamy for myself. It seemed high time to leave. 'Can you get home all right?'

'Course we can.'

'What about this petal?'

'I'll drop her off. Don't worry about us,' Marina soothed me kindly. 'We're used to it.'

I could believe that.

Supporting one another, they tottered off down the Sacred Way. I had warned Marina again to take care because the aqueduct snatcher might be working her neighbourhood. She, quite reasonably, had then enquired whether I really thought any pervert would pluck up the courage to attack two of the Braidmakers' Old Girls after their monthly night out? A ridiculous idea, of course.

I could still hear them singing and laughing all the way to the end of the Forum. I myself walked unobtrusively down towards the Tabularium, veering left round the Capitol and out through the River Gate near the Theatre of Marcellus, opposite the end of Tiber Island. I took myself along the embankment past the Aemilian and Sublician bridges. In the Forum Boarium I met a patrol of vigiles, headed by Martinus, Petro's old deputy. They were looking out for whoever I was looking out for. None of us thought we would find him. We exchanged a few quiet words, then I pressed on to the Aventine.

Only as I climbed up towards the Temple of Ceres did I remember that I had meant to ask Marina whatever she thought she was doing when she called out to a strange driver. It was an odd reversal of the scene I presumed might have happened with Asinia: the woman's brash approach and the man's nervousness; then her mockery as he quickly skulked away. I dismissed it as unimportant. For the encounter to connect with my enquiry would be too much of a coincidence.

Even so, something had happened down there in the Forum. Something all too relevant.

XL

I T BEGAN AS an ordinary, bright Roman morning. I woke late, alone in bed, sluggish. Sunlight streaked the wall opposite the closed shutter. I could hear Helena's voice, talking to someone, male, unfamiliar.

Before she called me I struggled into a clean tunic and rinsed my teeth, groaning. This was why informers liked to be solitary men. I had gone to bed sober, yet today I felt like death.

I had a dim recollection of returning in the dark last night. I had heard Julia crying fretfully. Either Helena was too exhausted to waken, or she was trying out a plan we had half-heartedly discussed of leaving the baby sometimes to cry herself back to sleep. Helena had certainly moved the cradle out of our bedroom. Trust me to disrupt the plan: at Julia's heartrending wail I forgot what was agreed and went to her; I managed to walk about with her quietly, avoiding disturbing Helena, until eventually the baby dozed off. I put her back down in the cradle successfully. Then Helena burst in, woken up and terrified by the silence . . . Ah, well.

After that it was obviously necessary for lamps to be filled and lit, drinks to be made, the story of my night's surveillance to be told, the lamps to be doused again, and bed to be sought amid various snugglings, foot-warmings, kissings, and other things that are nobody's business which left me unconscious until way past breakfast time.

Breakfast would not be featuring in my routine today.

The man whose voice I had heard was waiting downstairs outside. Glancing over the porch rail, I saw thin curly black hair in a polished brown scalp. A rough red tunic and the tops of stout thonged boots. A member of the vigiles.

'From Martinus,' Helena told me. 'There is something you have to see on the embankment.'

Our eyes met. It was not the moment to speculate.

I kissed her, holding her closer than normal, remembering and making her remember how she had welcomed home her late-night hero. Homelife and work met, yet remained indefinably separate. Helena's faint smile belonged to our private life. So did the rush of blood I felt answering it.

She ran her fingers through my hair, tugging at the curls and attempting to tidy them so I was fit to be seen. I let her do it, though I realised the appointment to which I was being summoned would not require a neat coiffure.

We assembled up on the embankment just below the Aemilian Bridge. In charge was Martinus, the ponderous, big-buttocked new enquiry agent of the Sixth Cohort. He had a straight-cut fringe and a mole on one cheek, with large eyes that could look thoughtful for hours as a cover for not bothering to think. He told me he had decided against sending for Petro because his situation with the vigiles was so 'delicate'. I said nothing. If Petronius had stayed out on watch last night as long as I suspected, he would be needing his sleep. Anyway, the good thing about having a partner was that we could share the unpleasant tasks. This did not call for both of us. All we needed to do in person was note the discovery and record our interest.

With Martinus were a couple of his men and some water boatmen, not including my brother-in-law Lollius, I was pleased to see. Well, it was before midday. Lollius would still be asleep in some little barmaid's lap.

Lying on the edge of the embankment were a dark lump and a piece of cloth. Around them the stone paving was damp for a large area. Water dribbled from both. The items, as Martinus called them when he took down details slowly on his note-tablet, had been retrieved from the Tiber that morning, after tangling in the mooring rope of a barge. The barge had come upriver only yesterday so had been here just one night.

'Anyone see anything?'

'What do you think, Falco?'

'I think somebody must have.'

'And you know we'll have a hard time finding them.'

The material was perhaps old curtaining, for it was fringed at one end. It must have been heavily bloodstained before it went into the water, the blood sufficiently coagulated to survive a short immersion. The cloth had been wrapped around the slender, youthful trunk of a woman who must have had fine, dark skin. Now her once-supple body was discoloured by bruising and decay, its texture altered to something inhuman. Time, the summer heat, and finally the water, had all worked terrible changes. But worse had been done to her first by whoever robbed her of life.

We assumed this was the torso of Asinia. Nobody would be suggesting that her husband be asked to identify her. Her head and limbs had been removed. So had other parts. I looked, because it seemed obligatory. Then it was hard not to throw up. By now Asinia had been dead nearly two weeks. She had been lying somewhere else for most of that time. Martinus and the water boatmen all gave as their opinion that the decomposing torso had only been in the water for a few hours. We would have to think about its history before that because the details could help us trace the killer. But it was hard to force our minds to the task.

A member of the vigiles pulled the curtain over the remains. Relieved, we all stood back, trying to forget the sight.

We were still discussing the possibilities when a messenger came for Martinus. He was wanted in the Forum. A human head had been discovered in the Cloaca Maxima.

XLI

WHEN THEY FLUNG open the access hole we could hear water in the darkness some distance below. There was no ladder. There were not enough wading boots and torches either. We had to wait for these to be fetched from a depot, while curious crowds gathered. People could tell something was happening.

'Why aren't these bastards ever around when the killer comes to dump remains? Why don't they ever catch him at it?'

Swearing, Martinus got his men to organise a cordon. It failed to stop the ghouls from clogging up the west end of the Forum.

We were still waiting for our boots when to my disgust Anacrites appeared. The Curator's office was near here. Some clown had been to notify him.

'Sod off, Anacrites. Your chief is only responsible for aqueducts. Mine has a total remit.'

'I'm coming with you, Falco.'

'You'll terrify the rats.'

'*Rats*, Falco?' Martinus became eager to stand back and let Anacrites represent him in this unpleasant enterprise.

I glanced at the sky, aware that if it rained the Cloaca would become a raging torrent and impossibly dangerous. Cloudless blue reassured me, just.

'Why didn't they just bring the remains to the surface?' Martinus really did not want to go down there. Where I merely lacked enthusiasm, he was openly panicking.

'Julius Frontinus has given instructions that anything found in the system must be left in situ for us to inspect. I'll go. If there are any clues I'll bring them back. You can take my description of the layout. I'm a good witness in court.'

'I reckon I'll send for Petronius.'

'There's too many of you already,' put in the gang leader of the sewer men. 'I don't like taking strangers down.'

'Don't worry me,' I muttered. If he was nervous, what chance for the rest of us? 'Listen, when Marcus Agrippa was in charge of the waterways, I thought he toured the entire sewer system by boat?'

'Bloody madman!' scoffed the gang leader. Well, that cheered me up.

Leather waders had arrived: thick clumsy soles and flapping thigh-high tops. A wooden ladder was produced but when they slung it over the edge, we could see it reached only halfway to the water; how deep that was at this point even the sewer men seemed not to know. We were being taken in near where the head was found; they themselves must have approached originally by some underground route, one that was reckoned too difficult for soft stylus-pushers like us.

A new length of ladder soon arrived, which was lashed on to the first with cords. The whole cockeyed artefact was dangled down the dark hole. It just reached the bottom, leaving no spare at the top. It looked almost vertical. Anyone who deals with ladders will tell you that's fatal. A large man was posted up top to hang on with a piece of ragged rope. He seemed happy; he knew he had the best job.

It was settled that I would go down, with Anacrites and one of Martinus' lads who was keen for anything. There was no point forcing Martinus to venture into the burrow if he was nervous; we told him he was our watchman. If we were too long below he was to fetch help. The gang leader accepted this rather too readily, as if he thought something might well go wrong. He told us to cover our heads with hoods. We wrapped our faces in pieces of cloth; muffled hearing and heavy feet made everything worse.

We went one at a time. We had to launch ourselves into thin air above the manhole to find treads on the ladder. Once on, the whole thing bowed disturbingly and looked completely unsafe. The gang leader had gone first; as he was descending we saw the top part swing away from where it was lodged and he had to be pulled back by main force applied to the rope. He went a bit white, as he looked up anxiously from the dark shaft, but the fellow on the rope called out something encouraging and he carried on.

'You don't want to fall in,' Martinus counselled.

'Thanks,' I said.

It was my turn next. I managed not to disgrace myself, though the treads were tiny rungs, too far apart to be comfortable. As soon as I started I could feel my thigh muscles protesting. With every step the whole flimsy ladder moved.

Anacrites hopped down after me, looking as if he had spent half his life on a wobbly ladder. A knock on the head had robbed him of both sensitivity and sense. Martinus' lad followed, and we stood carefully in the pitch dark, waiting for the torches to be lowered down to us. I suppose I could have shoved Anacrites in the water. I was too preoccupied to think of it.

The air was chilly. Water – or water and other substances – rushed past our feet and ankles, feeling cold and giving a false sensation that our boots leaked. There was a tolerable, yet distinct, smell of sewage. We asked the gang leader whether bare-flamed pitch torches were safe if there might be gas down here; he replied cheerfully that there were not often accidents. Then he told us about one the week before.

When the torches came down we could see we were in a long, vaulted tunnel, over twice as high as us. It was lined with cement and at the point where we had entered it the water out in the channel was easily shin-deep. In the centre the current raced, a fine tribute to gradient. In the shallows along the edges we could see brown weed, wavering all in one direction as it was pulled by slower currents. Underfoot was paved with slabs like a road but there was a great deal of detritus, sometimes rubble and rocks, sometimes sandy areas. The torchlight was not strong enough to let us see our feet properly. The gang leader told us to be careful how we trod. Immediately afterwards I stepped into a hole.

We waded along towards a bend in the tunnel. The water grew deeper and more worrying. We passed an inlet from a feeder channel, dry at present. We were deep under the Forum of the Romans. All this area had once been marsh, and was still natural wetland. The fine monuments above us raised their pediments to baking sun but had damp basements. Mosquitoes plagued the Senate; foreign visitors, lacking immunity, succumbed to virulent fevers. Seven hundred years ago Etruscan engineers had shown our primitive ancestors how to drain the swamp between the Capitol and the Palatine – and here their work still stood. The Cloaca Maxima and its brother under the Circus kept the centre of Rome habitable and its institutions working. The Great Drain sucked down standing and surface water, the overflow from fountains and aqueducts, sewage and rainwater.

Then last night some bastard had dragged up an access cover and chucked down a human head.

It was probably Asinia. Her skull had lodged on a sandbank, where a low beach of fine brown silt jutted into the shallow current.

The condition was too poor for even somebody who had known her to be certain, though some hair and facial flesh survived. Rats had been here in the night. I was prepared to make an identification despite that. There were other black women in Rome, but as far as I knew only one had disappeared a couple of weeks ago.

We could be fairly accurate about the timing: this skull was put into the Cloaca last night. We were told the public slaves with their baskets had worked their way downstream cleaning out the channel yesterday, and they saw nothing then. She must have been dumped just before or just after her torso was disposed of. There was not enough depth of water in the Cloaca to have carried the torso down this way to the Tiber. Anyway, I remembered that it was found upstream of the outlet. It must have been thrown into the river direct, off the embankment or over the parapet of a bridge, the Aemilian probably.

So the head and body had been dumped separately. A distinct pattern was emerging: the killer disposed of body parts in several different locations, even though it meant there was more chance of his being spotted doing it. He had wheels; last night he started out carrying at least the head and the body, plus maybe limbs we had not found yet. He could drop a parcel and run. On to another location, then quickly heave the next piece down a manhole or over a parapet. For year after year he had been doing this, learning to look so casual that any chance witnesses thought nothing of it.

Water tumbled past Asinia's head so the sand ran away from beneath her in rivulets, to be replaced by more. Left alone, she might bury herself on the bank or she might suddenly break free and roll along the channel to the great arch of peperino stone that gave on to the river.

'Have you ever found heads before?'

'Occasional skulls. You can't tell where they come from or how old they are – not normally. This is more . . .' The gang leader faded out politely.

'Fresh?' Not quite the word, Anacrites. I gave him a disapproving look.

The gang leader breathed, deeply uncomfortable. He made no reply.

He reckoned there was another sandbank like this further down. He said we could wait while he took a look. We could hear Martinus shouting in the distance, so his lad went back to the ladder to confirm we were all right. That left Anacrites and me together in the tunnel.

It was quiet, smelly, safe only to the point where hairs curled on your neck. The cold water continually raced past our boots as they sank slightly into the fine mud while we stood still. Around us was silence, broken by infrequent quiet drips. Asinia's skull, a parody of humanity, still lay in the silt at our feet. Ahead, lit from behind by wavering torchlight, the black figure of the gang leader walked away towards a bend in the tunnel through deeper and deeper water, eerily diminishing. He was alone. If he walked round the turn in the tunnel we would have to follow him. Going out of sight alone in a sewer was unsafe.

He stopped. He was leaning against the side wall with one hand, bending over as if inspecting the area. Suddenly I knew; 'Too much for him. He's throwing up.' We stopped watching.

There was a task waiting for us. I handed my torch to Anacrites. Regretting that I had put on a clean overtunic that morning, I stripped off a layer. I planted one boot right against the head to steady it, then bent and tried to ease the tunic underneath. I was trying not to touch the thing. A mistake. It rolled. Anacrites scuffled up his own foot, making a wedge with mine. We trapped the head, and I captured it as if we were playing some ghastly game of ball. Unwilling even to hold the weight directly with a supporting hand underneath, I held on to the four corners of my garment, letting the water stream off as I stood up. I kept the tunic and its contents at arm's length.

'Dear gods, how does he manage it? I thought I was tough. How can the killer bring himself to handle the body parts once, let alone repeatedly?'

'This is a filthy job.' For once Anacrites and I spoke the same language. We were talking in low voices while he held the lights and with his free hand helped me knot the corners of my tunic to make a secure bundle.

I agreed with him. 'I have nightmares that just by being involved in scenes like this some of the filth might rub off on me.'

'You could leave it to the vigiles.'

'The vigiles have been ducking out of things for years. It's time someone stopped this man.' I gave Anacrites a rueful grin. 'I could have left it to you!'

Holding up the torches, he returned the wry look. 'That wouldn't be you, Falco. You do have to interfere.'

For once the comment was dispassionate. Then I felt horrified. If we shared many more foul tasks and philosophical interludes, we might end up on friendly terms.

We waded back to the ladder. There we waited for the gang leader.

Martinus' lad was sent up first with the torches. I went next. I had threaded my belt through the knots on the bundle and made the belt into a shoulder loop, in order to leave me two free hands. On a bowing ladder with narrow treads, in wet footwear, going up was even worse than coming down.

When I climbed out like a mole into the glare of the sunlight Martinus dragged me upright. I was telling him what had happened while Anacrites came clambering out behind me. I moved to give him room. That was when I realised the Chief Spy was quite professional; as he emerged in his turn he looked round rapidly at the faces in the ogling crowds. I knew why; I had done it myself. He was wondering whether the killer was there: whether the man had dumped remains in different places specifically in order to taunt us, and whether he was hanging about now to watch their discovery. Seeing Anacrites checking like that was a curious relevation.

Shortly afterwards I discovered something else. When you have walked through a sewer, you have to pull off your own boots.

XLII

MARTINUS TOOK CHARGE of the head. It would be reunited with the torso at the station house. Then the formalities would be set in motion so Cicurrus could hold a funeral for his wife.

For the first and probably the only time ever, Anacrites and I went to a bath-house together. We were both extremely thorough with the strigil. Nevertheless, I did not offer to help him scrape his back.

I had taken him as my guest to the baths attached to Glaucus' gym, only a few steps from the Forum. A mistake. Soon Anacrites was glancing around as if he were thinking how civilised it was here and that he might apply for a subscription. I let him leave by himself to go back to whatever he wasted his time on at the Curator's office, while I stayed behind to warn Glaucus that the Chief Spy was not the type he wanted to patronise his esteemed premises.

'I could see that,' sniffed Glaucus. When I admitted whom exactly I had brought today, he gave me a disgusted look. Glaucus liked to avoid trouble. His way of doing it was to bar people who habitually caused it. He only let me in because he viewed me as a harmless amateur. Professionals are paid for their work; he knew I rarely was.

I enquired if Glaucus had a free period for a spot of wrestling practice. He snorted. I took it as a negative, and I knew why too.

I strolled out down the steps, between the pastry shop and the small library which were provided for patrons' extra delight. Glaucus ran a luxurious establishment. You could not only exercise and bathe, but borrow some odes to rekindle a flagging love affair and then stick your teeth together with glazed raisin dumplings that were fiendishly delicious.

Today I had no time for reading and I was in no mood for sweet-meats. I was oiled and scraped in every pore yet still uneasy with the results. I had been in filthy locations before, but something about descending into sewers to find hacked-up human remains left me shuddering. It would have been bad enough even without remembering that I myself had once dropped a man's decayed carcase through a manhole. A couple of years and plenty of heavy rainstorms should have ensured there was no chance I would stumble across unwelcome ghosts. But down there in the Cloaca Maxima I had almost been glad of Anacrites' irritating presence to prevent me dwelling on the past.

It was over. There was no need for Helena ever to find out. I was still unsure how she would react to hearing that her missing uncle Publius had been left lying dead until he was positively fermenting, then shoved in the Cloaca, and shoved there by me . . . By now I thought I was safe. I had convinced myself I would never have to face her with the truth.

Even so, I must have been brooding. Here at Glaucus' gym I was on home ground. Informers learn that home is where you should never relax. Places where you are known are where bad characters come to find you. And when I noticed the group who were waiting outside for me today, I had already walked past them and given them time to emerge from the doorway of the pastry shop so they were above me on the steps.

I heard the clatter of boots.

I didn't stop. Instead of turning to see who was behind me, I took three running skips then a giant leap down the rest of the steps to pavement level. *Then* I turned.

There was a large group. I didn't count them. About four or five from the pastry shop, followed by more streaming out of the library. I would have yelled for help, but out of the corner of my eye I noticed the pastry shop proprietor beetling off into the gymnasium.

'Stop right there!' It was worth a try. They did pause slightly.

'You Falco?'

'Certainly not.'

'He's lying.'

'Don't insult me. I'm Gambaronius Philodendronicus, a wellknown gauze-pleater of these parts.'

'It's Falco!' Spot on.

This was clearly no genteel outing of philosophy students. These were rough. Street-stroppy. Unfamiliar faces with fighters' eyes, shedding menace like dandruff. I was stuck. I could run; they would catch me. I could make a stand; that was even more stupid. No weapons were visible, but they probably had them concealed under those dark clothes. They were built like men who could do a lot of harm without any help from equipment.

'What do you want?'

'You, if you're Falco.'

'Who sent you?'

'Florius.' They were smiling. It wasn't pretty, or cheerful.

'Then you've got the wrong man; you want Petronius Longus.' Naming him was my only chance. He was bigger than me, and there was a faint hope I could somehow warn him.

'We've seen Petronius already,' they sniggered. I went cold. After his night on watch at the Circus he would have been asleep alone at the office. When Petronius was dog-tired he slept like a stone. In the army we used to joke that wild bears could eat him from the feet up and he wouldn't notice until they were tickling him behind the ears.

I knew what kind of punishment squad this was. I had once seen a man who had been beaten up on the orders of Milvia's mother. He was dead when he was discovered. He must have hoped for an end to it long before he actually passed out. These heavies worked for that family; I had no reason to think Milvia's husband was any more scrupulous than her mother. Desperately I tried not to imagine Petro enduring an assault like that.

'Did you kill him?'

'That's for next time.' The terror tactic. Make it hurt, then give the victim days or weeks to think about death coming for him.

They were co-ordinated. The pack had spread; now they were creeping down on two sides to encircle me. I edged backwards slowly. The flight of steps from the gym was steep; I wanted them away from there. I glanced quickly behind me, ready for the off.

When they rushed me, I was looking at one, but I jumped another. Springing forward into the pack, I dived low, and hit him around the knees. It brought him down. I rolled over him and threw myself up a few steps. I got an arm around the neck of a different lump of muscle and bodily dragged him with me back towards the gym, fighting to put him between me and some of the others. I clung on, using my feet to deter the rest as they weighed in. If they had had knives I would have been done for, but these lads were physical. They were stamping too. I was dodging furiously.

For a few moments I was heading for a short walk to Hades. I took some heavy blows and kicks, but then there was a racket from above us. Help at last.

I lost my man, but managed to squeeze his neck so hard I damn near killed him. As he crouched coughing at my feet I sent him down the steps with a flying kick. Someone behind me cheered raucously. Out came Glaucus, followed by a herd of his clients. Some had been weight-lifting; they were in loincloths with wristbands. Some had been at swordplay with Glaucus himself and were armed with wooden practice swords – blunt, but good for vicious whacks. A couple of generous souls had even left their baths. Naked and glistening with oil, they rushed out to help – useless for grappling opponents, but themselves impossible to catch hold of. It added wildly to the confusion as we launched ourselves into a fierce streetfight.

'I waste my time, Falco!' Glaucus snarled as we both worked over a couple of nut-headed thugs.

'Right! You haven't taught me anything useful –'

The clients at Glaucus' gym usually honed their bodies discreetly, hardly speaking to each other. We went there for exercise, cleanliness, and the fierce hands of the Cilician masseur, not chat. Now I saw a man who I happened to know was a rising barrister digging his fingers into someone's eyes as viciously as if he had been born in the Suburra slums. An engineer tried to break another thug's neck, clearly enjoying the experience. The prized masseur was keeping his hands out of trouble, but that did not prevent him from using his feet for wholly unacceptable purposes.

'How could you get trapped right on the damned doorstep?' Glaucus grunted, fielding a punch then slamming in a rapid set of four.

'They were holed up in your sweetmeat shop –' His man was out of it, so I threw him mine to hold while I battered him. 'Must have had a complaint. I keep telling you the cinnamon mice are stale –'

'Behind!' I spun, in time to knee the next bastard as he leapt at me. 'Talk less and watch your guard,' Glaucus advised.

I trapped a wrestler about to put a fatal lock on his neck. 'Take your own orders,' I grinned. Glaucus screwed the grappler's nose around until it snapped. 'Nice trick. Requires a calm temperament,' I smiled at the blood-stained victim. 'And very strong hands.'

All down the street there was action. It was a friendly commercial alley. Pausing only to remove their goods from the danger zone, the shopkeepers had come out to help Glaucus, who was a popular neighbour. Passers-by who felt left out started throwing punches; if they were hopeless at that they lobbed apples instead. Dogs barked.

Women hung out of upstairs windows, yelling a mixture of encouragement and abuse, then emptied buckets of who-knows-what on fighters' heads for the fun of it. Washing was caught on the practice swords and came down, tangling around frantically tussling figures. Weightlifters were showing off their pectorals carrying horizontal human weights. A startled donkey skidded on the road, tipping wineskins off his back so that they burst and doused his furious driver, making a slippery patch on the paving which claimed several victims who crashed to the ground and were painfully trampled.

Then some idiot fetched the vigiles.

A whistle alerted us.

As the red tunics rushed into the alley, order reimposed itself in seconds. All they saw was a normal street scene. The Florius gang, with the skill of long practice, had melted away. Two feet stuck out from behind a barrel of salt fish – evidently somebody sleeping it off. Something that looked like red tunic dye was being sluiced along with a bucket of water and swept down a drain by a girl who was loudly singing a rude song. Groups of men sized up fruit on stalls, making studied comparisons. Women leant out of windows adjusting pulleys on the drying lines above the alley. Dogs lay grinning on their backs and waggling their bodies madly as passers-by tickled their tums. I was pointing out to Glaucus how the gable on his bathhouse was capped by an excellent acroterion of truly classic design, while he thanked me for my generous praise of his fine Gorgon-featured antefix.

The sky was blue. The sun was hot. Two fellows walking up the steps of the gymnasium discussing the Senate had no clothes on for some reason, but otherwise there was nobody the guardians of the law could arrest.

XLIII

WHEN I REACHED Fountain Court, returning by a roundabout route for safety, Petronius was being carried out feet first. Lenia and some of her staff must have found him. They had seen Florius' heavies rushing off in suspicious haste. Not for the first time I wished Lenia could be as good at spotting trouble when it arrived as she was at noticing it leave.

I had run up the back lane, past the lamp-black ovens, the midden and the poultry yard. I hopped over the work in progress in the ropewalk, leapt the cesstrench and barged into the laundry through its rear entrance. In the yard wet clothes slapped me in the face and woodsmoke choked me, then indoors I nearly skidded and upended myself on the wet floor. As I was flailing a girl with a wash-paddle shoved me upright. I skated past the office and flew to a halt in the colonnade.

Petro was lying on a rough stretcher people had made from clothes rails and a customer's toga.

'Stand back; here's his heartbroken boyfriend!'

'Enough of your biting wit, Lenia – Is he dead?'

'I wouldn't be joking.' No, she had some standards. He was alive. His condition was sad, though.

If he was conscious he was in too much pain to show a reaction even when I turned up. Torn bandages covered much of his head and face, his left arm, and his right hand. His legs were badly cut and grazed. 'Petro!' There was no response.

They were dragging him to a litter. 'He's going to his auntie's.'

'What auntie?'

'Sedina, the one with the flower stall. She was fetched over, but you know how fat she is; she'd have died if we'd let her struggle all the way upstairs. Anyway, I didn't want the poor duck to see him until I'd cleaned him up a bit. She's toddled home to get the bed ready. She'll look after him.' Lenia must have patched him up and made all the arrangements.

'Good thinking. He'll be safer than here.'

'Well, he's all right, old Petro.'

'Thanks, Lenia.'

'It was a gang of street rubbish,' she told me.

'I met them myself.'

'You were luckier, then.'

'I had help.'

'Falco, why's he safer at Sedina's?'

'They promised me they'd be coming back for him.'

'Olympus! Is this about that silly little skirt of his?'

'Message from her husband, I was told. Clear, but will he listen?'

'He'll be out of it for days. Where does it leave you, Falco?'

'I'll manage.'

As the litter lurched off, I sent a runner to the vigiles begging for Scythax, their doctor, to attend Petronius at his aunt's house. I asked Lenia whether anyone had told Silvia; before he collapsed Petro had refused to have his wife involved. Well, you could see why. 'And what does he want done about dear little Milvia?' I enquired.

'I must have somehow forgotten to ask him!' Lenia grinned.

Helena Justina had been over at her parents' house and had missed the furore. When she came home shortly after me, I explained what had happened, trying to put an acceptable gloss on it. Helena could tell when I was disguising a crisis. She said nothing. I watched her tussle with her emotions, then she dumped the baby in my arms and briefly put her arms around both of us. Since I was bigger, I was the one who received the kiss.

She had bustled off, busying herself while she came to terms with the problem, when we heard a tremendous racket outside in Fountain Court. I was on my feet before I remembered not to react too sharply in case Helena noticed my nervousness; in fact she was out on the porch ahead of me. Across the road Lenia, watched by a jeering group of her staff, was giving a foully obscene mouthful to none other than the jaunty Balbina Milvia.

When the girl saw us, she scuttled straight across. I waved to Lenia to let me handle it, and curtly nodded to Milvia to come up. We wheeled her into what passed for our ornamental salon and sat her down while we stood.

'Oh, what a pretty baby!' she gurgled, immune to hostility.

'Helena Justina, take the baby to another room. I'll not have my daughter contaminated by street grime.'

'Falco, that's a terrible thing to say,' squeaked Milvia. Helena, set-faced, simply carried Julia off to her cradle. I waited for her return. Milvia stared at me, owl-eyed.

When Helena re-entered she looked even more angry than I was. 'If you came here to see Petronius Longus, don't waste your time, Milvia.' I had rarely heard Helena so contemptuous. 'He was badly beaten up this morning and has been taken to a safe house away from your family.'

'No! Is Petronius hurt? Who did it?'

'A rabble sent by your husband,' Helena explained coldly.

Milvia seemed not to take this in so I added, 'Florius, in a touchy mood. This is your fault, Milvia.'

'Florius wouldn't –'

'Florius just did. How does he know what's going on? Did you tell him?'

Milvia faltered for once. She even blushed slightly. 'I think it must have been Mother who mentioned it.'

I bit back an oath. This was why Rubella had been forced to suspend Petro; Flaccida was too dangerous, and it was her life's work to cause trouble for the vigiles. 'Well, that was a bad day's work.'

'I'm *glad* Florius knows!' cried Milvia defiantly. 'I want –'

'What I am sure you don't want,' Helena cut in, 'is to destroy Petronius Longus. He is already seriously injured. Face facts, Milvia. This can only make him consider what it is *he* wants. I can tell you the answer to that: Petronius wants his job back, and as a loving father he wants to be able to see his children again.' I noticed that she had not mentioned his wife.

Milvia looked at us. She was hoping to find out where he was; she realised we were not intending to say. Used only to handing out orders, she was stuck.

'Give Florius a message from me,' I told her. 'He made a mistake today. He had two free citizens beaten up, in my case without lasting effects but it happened in front of witnesses. So I have an aedile, a judge, and two senior centurions who will support me if I take Florius to court.' Helena looked startled. I could not afford litigation; I would resent wasting my money, too. Still, Florius was not to know that. And as an informer I often did court work; at the Basilica there were barristers who owed me a few favours. I meant it when I told Milvia, 'Your husband will come unstuck if I raise a compensation claim. Tell him if he bothers either Petronius or me again, I shall have no hesitation.'

Milvia had been brought up by gangsters. Although she pretended to know nothing about her background, she must have noticed that her relatives lived in a world that thrived on secrecy. The publicity of a court case was something her father had always shunned (at least until the case where Petronius had had him arraigned). Her husband was a novice in crime, but he lived obscurely too. He gambled, an activity based on hints and bluff, and was now involved with rack-rents; that relied on heavy threat, not open writs.

'Florius won't listen to me.'

'You'll have to make him,' snapped Helena. 'Otherwise it won't only be his name that is spread all over the *Daily Gazette*. You'll be there among the scandals too. You can kiss goodbye to the last threads of respectability attaching to your family. All Rome will know.'

'But I haven't done anything!'

'That's the whole point of the *Daily Gazette*,' smiled Helena serenely. Trust a senator's daughter to know how to crush an upstart. There is nothing more ruthless than a born patrician lady wiping out a new man's wife. 'Forget the corn supply schedules, Senate rulings, articles on the Imperial family, Games and Circuses, portents and miracles. What Romans want to read about are people who claim they never did anything wrong having their love affairs exposed!'

Milvia was still little more than twenty – not yet sufficiently hard-faced to brave it out. She would be. But with luck, Petronius had met her before she learned to be bad with courage. Helpless, but like a true flighty bit, she changed the subject petulantly. 'Anyway, I came about something else.'

'Don't annoy me,' I said.

'I wanted to beg Petronius to help.'

'Well, whatever it is, your husband has prevented that.'

'But it's important!'

'Tough. Petro's unconscious – and he's fed up with you anyway.'

'What is it?' Helena asked her, having noticed an edge of genuine hysteria. I had noticed it too, but I didn't care.

Milvia was on the verge of tears. A poignant effect. Petronius would probably have fallen for it, were he not laid up. It didn't impress me. 'Oh, Falco, I don't know what to do. I'm so worried.'

'Tell us what it is then.' Helena's eyes had a glorious glint that meant any minute she would lose her patience and dot Milvia with a dish of marinading celery hearts. I was eager to see it, yet I preferred the idea of eating them. With any luck Ma had brought these for us; if they came from our family market garden on the Campagna, they would be flavoursome specimens.

'I wanted to ask Petronius, but if he's not here, then you'll have to help me, Falco –'

'Falco is very busy,' Helena responded crisply, in the role of my able assistant.

Milvia cantered on, undeterred: 'Yes, but this might be connected with what he's helping Petronius to work on –' The celery hearts were in danger again, but I was in luck. Balbina Milvia's next words gave Helena pause. In fact she silenced both of us. 'My mother has vanished. She hasn't been home for two days and I can't find her anywhere. She went to the Games and never came home. I think she's been captured by that man who cuts up women and puts them in the aqueducts!'

Before Helena could stop me I heard myself replying cruelly that if it were true then the bastard had appalling taste.

XLIV

I WAS READY to despatch the desolate Milvia with even more harsh words, but we were interrupted by Julius Frontinus on one of his regular check-up visits. He patiently signalled that I should carry on. I explained to him briefly that the girl thought her missing mother might have been seized by our killer, and that she was begging our help. He probably deduced that I didn't believe the piteous tale, even before I muttered, 'One problem in a situation like this is that it gives people ideas. Every woman who stays out an hour longer than usual at market is liable to be put down as the next victim.'

'And the danger is that the real victims will be overlooked?' It was a long time since I had been employed by an intelligent client.

Helena tackled the girl. 'When members of families disappear, Milvia, the reasons tend to be domestic. In my experience things get touchy when a forceful widow comes to live with her in-laws. Have you had any family arguments recently?'

'Certainly not!'

'That seems rather unusual,' Frontinus commented, uninvited. I had forgotten that to reach his consulship he would first have held senior legal positions; he was used to interrupting evidence with scathing quips.

'Balbina Milvia,' I said, 'this is Julius Frontinus, the illustrious ex-Consul. I seriously advise you not to lie to him.'

She blinked. I had no doubt that her father had inveigled fairly senior members of the establishment to dine with him – drinking, gorging, accepting gifts and the attentions of dancing girls, or boys: what top-notch power-brokers call hospitality, though the spoilsport public tends to view it as bribery. A consul might be something new.

'Have there been any disagreements in your home?' repeated Frontinus coolly.

'Well – possibly.'

'Concerning what?'

Concerning Petronius Longus, I was prepared to bet. Flaccida was bound to have taken Milvia to task for canoodling with a member of a vigiles enquiry team. Then Flaccida had her fun passing on the news to Florius. Florius for his part might well blame Flaccida for the daughter's infidelity, either because he imagined she was condoning it or at least for bringing the girl up badly. There must have been a hurricane of bad feeling in that household.

Helena smiled at Frontinus. 'In case you feel you may have missed something, sir, I should explain we're dealing with a major hub of organised crime.'

'Something else that could benefit from a commission of enquiry,' I teased him.

'One thing at a time, Falco,' said the Consul, unabashed.

I gazed at Milvia. 'If you really think your mother may be dead, you don't seem very upset.'

'I am hiding my grief bravely.'

'How stoical!' Perhaps she was thinking that she would become even richer if Mama had been despatched. Perhaps that was why she was so eager to know for sure.

Frontinus banged a finger on the table, grabbing the girl's attention. 'If your mother has been taken by the villain we are chasing, we shall pursue the matter with vigour. But if she has just gone to stay with a friend as the result of a tiff, you should not impede my enquiry with a trivial complaint. Now answer me: has there been such a tiff?'

'There may have been.' Milvia squirmed and stared at the floor. I had seen naughty schoolgirls wriggle more efficiently. But Milvia had never been to school. Gangsters' children don't mix well, and their loving parents don't want them to pick up nasty habits, let alone moral standards. Education had been lavished on Milvia through a series of tutors, presumably terrified ones. There was not much to show for their efforts. No doubt they took the money, bought a few sets of Livy to leave around the schoolroom, then spent the rest of the equipment budget on pornographic scrolls for themselves.

'Was this trouble between your mother and you? Or was your husband involved?' If Petronius failed me as a partner, I could do worse than let the ex-Consul take his place. He soon got his teeth into an interrogation, and appeared to be enjoying it. What a pity he was going to govern Britain. A real waste of talent.

Milvia wrung her expensive skirts between her heavily beringed little fingers. 'Mother and Florius did have a bit of scene the other day.'

Frontinus looked down his nose. 'A scene?'

'Well, rather a terrible argument.'

'About what?'

'Oh . . . just a man I had been friendly with.'

'Well!' Frontinus sat up, like a judge who wanted to go home to lunch. 'Young woman, I have to warn you that your domestic situation is serious. If a man discovers that his wife has committed adultery, he is legally bound to divorce her.'

One thing that must have been drilled into Milvia was that, in order to hold on to her father's money, she and Florius must never part. She was no wide-eyed idealist ready to sacrifice her cash for the sake of true love with Petro. Milvia was too fond of her caskets of hard gemstones and her fine quality silver tableware. Blinking like a shy rabbit, she quavered, 'Divorce?'

Frontinus had noticed her hesitance. 'Otherwise the husband can be taken to court on a charge of acting as a pimp. Allowing a Roman matron to be dishonoured is something we don't tolerate – I assume you realise that if your husband actually catches you in bed with another man, he is entitled to draw a sword and kill you both?'

All this was true. It would ruin Florius. He was hardly going to run his wife and Petro through in the proper fit of maddened rage, and subjected to the ancient scandal laws about pimping he would become a laughing stock. 'I like the Consul's sense of humour,' I said openly to Helena.

She feigned disapproval. 'His sense of justice, you mean, Marcus Didius.'

'I prefer not to be the agent of marital disharmony,' Julius Frontinus told Milvia kindly. He was a tough old shoot. He had dealt with dim girlikins before. He could see beyond their glimmering silks and wide painted eyes, to just how dangerous they were. 'I shall overlook what I have heard today. I can see that you wish to preserve your marriage, so you will obviously end your affair with all speed. And we all say, very good luck to you!'

Milvia was stunned. Her extortionist family owned a battery of tame lawyers who were famously good at discovering outmoded statutes with which to hammer the innocent. It was something new to find herself the victim of antique legislation, let alone to be subjected to delicate blackmail by a high-ranking senator.

Frontinus seemed so sympathetic she must have wanted to squeal.

'As for your missing mother, you are clearly desolate without her. You must make every effort to discover whether she has taken refuge with a friend or relative. Falco will conduct enquiries on your behalf if time permits, but unless you produce proof that your mother has been abducted this is a private affair. There could be many other explanations. Though if a crime is thought to have been committed, surely that is a matter for the vigiles?'

'Oh, I can't go to them.'

Frontinus looked at me. 'They might not be very sympathetic, sir. They spend a great deal of time investigating crookery in which the missing woman is heavily involved. Flaccida will not be their favourite maiden in distress.'

'I need help,' Milvia wailed.

'Hire an informer then,' said Helena.

Milvia opened her rosebud mouth to wail that that was why she had come to me, then she registered the word 'hire'. A fee would not, of course, have been levied by Petronius. 'Do I have to pay you, Falco?'

'It is considered polite,' answered Helena. She did my accounts.

'Well, of course then,' pouted Milvia.

'In advance,' said Helena.

Frontinus looked amused. For our work on his formal enquiry, we were letting him pay in arrears.

XLV

H IS ILLUSTRIOUSNESS WAS not best pleased when I informed him later that he had lost half his team on sick leave. The way I told it, Petronius Longus, that selfless scourge of organised crime, had been attacked by a gang in retaliation for putting away the criminal Balbinus Pius. If, before he employed us, Frontinus had already been briefed on Petro's suspension from the vigiles, he would soon understand the connection with Milvia. I wasn't going to tell him unless he asked.

'Let us hope he recovers quickly. And how do you feel about carrying on alone, Falco?'

'I'm used to working solo, sir. Petronius should soon be back on his feet.'

'Not soon enough,' the Consul warned. 'I have just received a message brought by a very excited public slave.'

Then he came out with the real reason for his visit: there was news at last from Bolanus. Far from abandoning the case as I had been beginning to suspect, the engineer's assistant had been busy. He had stuck with his personal theory that the aqueducts which came to Rome from Tibur were the ones to investigate. He had organised systematic inspections of all their water towers and settling tanks, right out across the Campagna. Eventually his men extracted more human remains, a major find we were told – several arms and legs, in various stages of decomposition – near the inlets above Tibur.

Julius Frontinus looked at Helena apologetically. 'I am afraid I shall have to rob you of your husband for a few days. He and I need to make a site visit.'

Helena Justina smiled at him. 'That's no problem, sir. A trip to the country is just what the baby and I need.'

Frontinus tried nervously to look like a man who admired the spirit of modern women. I just smiled.

XLVI

FLACCIDA'S DISAPPEARANCE FROM home gave me a chance to show off.

There was a day's pause before we left Rome, so I used that to investigate for Milvia. Needless to say, it was not as much fun as pursuing widows can be. All the widows for whom I had previously worked were not merely provided with twinkling inheritances, but highly attractive and susceptible to a handsome grin. In fact since I met Helena I had given up that kind of client. Life was risky enough.

The pause occurred while I waited for my travel companion to clear his private affairs, which were necessarily more complex than mine. He had a few million sesterces invested in land to demand his attention, and a Senate reputation to cultivate, not to mention his imminent posting to Britain. The preparations for three years at the edge of the Empire couldn't be left to his underlings; his toga folders and secretaries might not yet appreciate how terrible the province was.

Frontinus had insisted on supervising the Tibur investigations. So long as he didn't try to supervise me I wasn't arguing. As a Roman I had little neighbourhood knowledge and no remit except as a member of his aqueduct investigation team. His presence would strengthen my hand. Given the status of the landowners who patronised that district, resistance to enquiries was quite likely. The filthy rich have more secrets to guard than the poor.

Seizing my chance, therefore, while his honour sorted out his own business, I took myself down to the Florius homestead and spied around outside. A slave trotted out to go shopping, so I collared him, slipped him a small coin, added a few more at his suggestion, and asked what the word was about the missing dame. He clearly hated Flaccida, and willingly revealed that no one in the household knew anything of her whereabouts. I did not trouble to knock and speak to Milvia.

There was definitely no vigiles presence in the street, or I would have spotted them. So I took a stroll back up the Aventine, barged in on Marcus Rubella in the Fourth Cohort's Twelfth District headquarters, and asked him outright what had happened to his surveillance team.

'The Balbinus exercise is finished, Falco. He's dead and we wouldn't want to be accused of harassment. What surveillance team?'

Rubella was an ex-chief centurion, with twenty years of legionary experience behind him and now in command of a thousand hard-bitten ex-slaves who formed his fire-fighting cohort. He had a shorn head, a stubbly chin, and still, dark eyes that had witnessed un-reasonable amounts of violence. He liked to think of himself as a dangerous spider twitching the strands of a large and perfectly formed web. I reckoned he thought too much of himself, but I made sure never to underestimate or cross the man. He was no fool. And he wielded a great deal of power in the district where I lived and worked.

I saw down in his office uninvited, leaned back in a relaxed man-ner, and placed my boots gently on the rim of his officer-quality work table, letting my heel nudge his silver inkwell as if I might deliberately knock it off.

'What team? The surveillance outfit that any intelligent tribune like yourself, Marcus Rubella, will have installed to observe the Balbinus widow, Cornella Flaccida.'

Rubella's brown eyes dawdled on his desk set. His long army career had left him with a respect for equipment; it persisted even now that he held a post where officially there was none. He always kept his inkpot full and his sand tray topped up. A jerk of my in-solent foot could make a fine mess of his office. I smiled at him like a man who had no intention of doing it. He looked uneasy.

'I cannot comment on any ongoing investigation, Falco.'

'That's all right. Stuff your comments; I'm not the clerk who edits the *Daily Gazette* searching for a sensational paragraph. I just want to know where Flaccida has parked herself. It's in your long-term interests.' I could rely on that argument to find favour here. Rubella was a born officer. He never moved unless it was in his own interests, but if it was he jumped.

'What's the score?'

I came clean. He was a professional and I respected that too much to mess him about. Anyway, offering to share a confidence always bothered him, which was pleasing enough. 'Flaccida has had a big fight with her son-in-law, dopey Florius. She's bunked off from home. Dim little Milvia thinks the aqueduct killer has nabbed her mama – nonsense of course. The aqueduct killer likes his victims juicier; that's the one thing about him we do know.'

'So how far have you got?' asked Rubella. 'Is it true a severed head washed up in the Cloaca yesterday?'

'Not quite what the excellent Etruscan engineers originally allowed for – yes, it's true. And a torso in the Tiber the same morning. To tell the truth we seem to be getting nowhere – and that's with full co-operation from all cohorts of the vigiles, and two separate investigations under way. The one for the Curator of the Aqueducts appears to have run into the ground completely; I'm not sorry to hear it, since it's being led by the Chief Spy.'

Rubella snorted quietly. 'You don't like him.'

'I just don't approve of his methods, his attitude, or the fact that he's allowed to pollute the earth . . . The team I'm on –' Tactfully, I omitted to specify that I was working with Petronius, whom Rubella himself had suspended from duty. 'My team does have a few leads. I'm just off to Tibur with the ex-Consul in charge. Frontinus; do you know him?' No; one up to me. 'Some missing sections of corpses have apparently turned up. Maybe you can tell me, Rubella – what's the set-up for law enforcement out there?'

'In Latium?' The tribune spoke of the countryside with a townsman's disgust. He was scathing about its local administration too: 'I suppose the better villages may have someone like a duovir who organises a posse if they happen to be beset by particularly virulent chicken-rustlers.'

'In foreign provinces the army does the job.'

'Not in sacred Italy, Falco. We are a nation of free men; can't have soldiers giving orders – people might ignore them, and how would the poor lads feel? There's a cohort of the Urban Guard out at Ostia, but that's an exception because of the port.'

'Protecting the newly arrived corn supply,' I added. 'There are Urbans at Puteoli too, for the same reason.'

Rubella looked annoyed at my knowing so much. 'You won't find much regular policing anywhere else.'

'It stinks.'

'They claim there's no crime in the country.'

'And all their goats have human heads, and their horses can swim under the sea!'

'The Campagna's wild – and the worst thing about it is the people who live there. That's why you and I inhabit the big city, Falco, where nice friendly fellows in red tunics ensure we can sleep safe at night.'

This was a romantic view of the vigiles and their effectiveness, but he knew that.

I could cope with Latium. Unknown to Rubella I had spent half my childhood there. I knew the right way up to plant garlic. I knew that mushrooms grow nicely in cowpats, but best not to mention it when you serve them. And he was right; I preferred Rome.

I went back to my original enquiry. 'I doubt if Flaccida has been abducted by a killer. He would have to be brave – and sharp, too. Petronius Longus would probably say we should suspect Florius of wanting her dead. He has his fingers in the gangs now, so he could try to organise it. And he has a motive a mile high. My own cynical theory is that Milvia herself would like to see her nagging parent out of the way –'

'How about Petro?' joked Rubella. 'I always thought he was big, and quiet – and deep!'

'He'd like to see the back of the old hag, but he'd rather catch her out in a felony and throw her to a judge. Milvia's story is that she wants Petronius to find out where her darling mother is. If I can tell her the old bitch is safe, it helps keep the young girl away from Petro.'

'Is it true that somebody put him on his back?' Rubella usually knew the score of any draughts game on his patch.

'Florius heard about the affair. Flaccida told him; that's why they had their bust-up. He decided to make his presence felt at last.'

'Rome can do without Florius thinking big.' The thought of Florius flexing his muscles was sufficient to worry Rubella. 'Will it affect Petro's attitude to the woman?'

'We can only hope so.'

'You don't sound optimistic.'

I had known Petro a long time. 'Well, I do believe he wants his job back.'

'Funny way of showing it. I gave him an ultimatum, which he seems to have ignored.'

'And you know that,' I pointed out gently, 'because Petronius has been seen going to Milvia's house – by your men. Ever since the Balbinus trial you have had a full-time set of peepers following every move made by Flaccida. But then presumably when she flew away, your man tightened his boot-thongs and followed her to her new roost?'

'I've had to call them off,' Rubella complained. 'She's too clever to give us any leads. It's too expensive watching her – and without Petronius Longus I'm seriously short of manpower.'

'So did you call off the surveillance before she did her flit? Or have the Fates finally smiled on me for once?'

He enjoyed keeping me waiting. Then he grinned. 'They pull out at the end of today's shift.'

I lifted my feet from his table, carefully avoiding his inkpot and sand tray. To add emphasis, I leant forwards and adjusted their positions slightly, aligning them neatly. I don't know whether the bastard felt any gratitude for my restraint. But he did give me an address for Cornella Flaccida.

She had taken herself an apartment in the Vicus Statae, below the Esquiline, near the Servian Walls. To reach it I had to walk down past the apsidal end of the Circus, through places which had featured so strongly in our hunt for the aqueduct killer: past the Temple of the Sun and Moon, through the Street of the Three Altars, around the Temple of the Divine Claudius. I detoured via the Street of Honour and Virtue and called in hoping to see Marina; she was out. Knowing Marina, I was not surprised.

Flaccida's new doss was a second-floor spread in a clean apartment block. When her husband was convicted and his wealth forfeited to the Treasury, she would have been allowed to keep any money that she could prove was her own – her dowry, for instance, or any purely personal inheritance. So although she was claiming to be destitute, she had already set herself up with slaves, beaten black and blue as her staff always were, and basic furniture. The whole show had been decorated with co-ordinating frescos and the kind of Greek-style vases that are turned out in sets in Southern Italy for householders who just want to fill up space aesthetically without the bother of hunting in flea-markets. It looked as if Flaccida had established her bolthole some time previously. I bet neither Milvia nor Florius had ever been told it was here.

She was in. I could tell that because her vigiles tail was lurking in a street food shop opposite. Pretending I didn't know his presence was supposed to be a secret, I called out and waved to him. Flaccida probably knew he was there. If the surveillance was about to be lifted, blowing his cover could do no harm in any case.

I was allowed in, if only to prevent me alarming the neighbours. It was not a home where one was offered sesame cakes and mint tea.

Just as well. I would have felt unsafe accepting anything into which poison could have been stirred.

To celebrate her freedom from the younger generation, the doughty dame must just have had her hair touched up, in not quite the same blonde as its previous shade. She lay sprawled on an ivory couch, wearing garments in clashing purple and deep crimson whose purchase must have made a large number of fullers and dyers extremely happy. When she sent this outfit to the laundry there was going to be an outcry from other customers whose clothes came back streaky after the hideous colours bled.

She made no attempt to rise and greet me. That may have been because her shoes had platform soles several inches deep which must have been crippling to stand or walk on. Or maybe she thought I wasn't worth it. Well, the feeling was mutual.

'This is a surprise! Cornella Flaccida, I'm delighted to see you alive and well. The word is you've been grabbed for dissection.'

'Who by?' Flaccida obviously supposed it was some underworld enemy. She must have plenty.

'Could be anyone, don't you think? So many people harbour a fantasy of hearing that you've been tortured and massacred –'

'Oh, you always get do-gooders!' She rasped with laughter that set my teeth on edge.

'My money would be on Florius or Milvia – though oddly enough it was your daughter who sent out the bloodhound. Her affection for you is so great, she's actually employing me. I shall have to report to her that you are flourishing – though I don't necessarily have to reveal your whereabouts.'

'How much?' she demanded wearily, assuming I wanted a bribe to keep quiet.

'Oh, I couldn't take money.'

'I thought you were an informer?'

'Let's say, I'll be perfectly happy if you join the general move in your family to lay off my good friend Lucius Petronius. I'm just relieved I don't have to add you to the women who have been hacked to pieces and dumped in the aqueducts.'

'No,' Flaccida agreed, unmoved. 'You wouldn't want to see me grinning up at you from a fountain bowl. And I don't want to come plopping out in the hot room of some men's baths, giving the bastards an excuse to make dirty cracks.'

'Oh, don't worry,' I assured her. 'This killer likes his morsels young and fresh.'

XLVII

MAKING ARRANGEMENTS AND saying goodbye took longer for a fortnight away than it did when we left Rome for six months. My choice would have been not to tell anyone, but there were dangers in that. Apart from the mood of suppressed hysteria in Rome which might cause people to report that the whole family must have been snatched by the aqueduct killer, the weather was still warm and we didn't want my mother to pop in and leave half a sea-bass for us in our best room, with no lid on the plate.

That doesn't mean I did notify Ma. Instead I asked my sister Maia to tell her, after we had gone. Ma would have loaded us down with parcels to take to Great-Auntie Phoebe on the family farm. The Campagna rolls round south and eastern Rome in a gigantic arc from Ostia to Tibur, but in Ma's mind only the dot on the Via Latina where her mad brothers lived ever counted. Telling her that we were not going anywhere near Fabius and Junius would be like banging my head on a log-chopping block. For Ma, the only reason for going into the country was to bring back choice crops extracted for free from startled relatives whom you hadn't seen in years.

I was really going for wine. There was no point at all in making a trip to the Campagna simply to chase after a maniac who killed women. Latium was where a Roman boy went when his cellar was low.

'Get some for me!' croaked Famia, Maia's husband, who was a soak. As usual he made no attempt to pay for it. I winked at my sister to let her know I had no intention of complying, though I would probably bring back some cabbages so she could make him hangover cures.

'Artichokes, please,' said Maia. 'And some baby marrows if they're still available.'

'Excuse me, I'm supposed to be going to catch a pervert.'

'According to Lollius, he has already solved that case for you.'

'Don't tell me anyone has started taking Lollius seriously.'

'Only Lollius himself.' Maia had a dry way of insulting her sisters' husbands. Her only blind spot was her own, and that was understandable. Once she let herself notice Famia's deficiencies the rest of us would be in for a lengthy diatribe. 'How's Petronius?' she asked. 'Is he going with you?'

'He's been laid up by the criminal world's society for the preservation of marriages – a smart group of lads with strict moral consciences who see themselves as the thunderbolt of Jupiter. They knocked him about so badly I'm hoping that when his black eyes clear up again he'll march straight back to Arria Silvia.'

'Don't bet on it,' scoffed Maia. 'He may bang on the door – but will she open up? Last I heard, Silvia was making the best of her loss.'

'What does that mean, sis?'

'Oh, Marcus! It means her husband did the dirty, so she dumped him, and now she's been seen going around with a new escort.'

'*Silvia?*'

Maia gave me a hug. For some reason she always regarded me as a winsome innocent. 'Why not? When I saw her, she looked as if she was having the most fun for years.'

My heart sank.

'How's your poetry?' If Maia was trying to cheer me up with this bright enquiry after my hobby (which I knew she ridiculed) the ploy failed.

'I'm thinking of holding a public recitation sometime soon.'

'Juno and Minerva! The sooner you leave for the country the better, dear brother!'

'Thanks for the support, Maia.'

'I'm always ready to save you from yourself.'

I had one minor task to complete. I could not face an hour of twittering from Milvia, so I refused to visit her house. I wrote a terse report, to which Helena attached a bill for my services, payable on receipt. I assured the girl I had seen her mother, and spoken to her personally. I said Flaccida was well and had enrolled herself for a series of speculative lectures on the natural sciences, from which she did not wish to be disturbed.

That done, my next call was to Petronius at his aunt's house, a trip I was required to make in company with our earnest supervisor, the ex-Consul. His idea of man-management was to check up personally on staff who might be malingering. Once again I had suggested Frontinus come in plain clothes, lest he cause Petro's wheezing Aunt Sedina to expire with excitement at the idea of having such an eminent man sitting on the edge of a bed in her house and examining her errant nephew. Instead, Sedina greeted me warmly, then treated my companion as if she assumed he was my shoe-changing slave. I was honoured with the visitor's bowl of almonds to munch, but I let the Consul have one or two.

When we first walked in I saw that my old friend looked even worse now the bruises and swellings had reached the glorious stage. He was covered in so many rainbows that he could have played Iris on stage. He was also conscious, and sufficiently himself to greet me with a barrage of obscenities. I let him get it out of his system, then stepped aside so he could see Frontinus lurking behind me, bearing a flagon of medicinal cordial. As consuls go, he was well brought up. I had taken grapes. That gave something for Petro to chew on as he fell gloomily silent in the presence of the great.

Small talk is difficult with an invalid who has only himself to blame. We were hardly going to humour him by discussing his symptoms. Wondering how he could ever have caught his disease was out too. Stupidity is an ailment nobody talks about openly.

Frontinus and I made the mistake of confessing we had come to say farewell before a junket to Tibur. This immediately gave Petro the idea that he would hire a litter and come along with us. He could still hardly move; he would be useless. Still, it might be good to remove him from any danger of renewed attacks from Florius – and I was quite pleased to put him out of Milvia's reach too. His aunt soon stopped being put out in case her own hospitality wasn't good enough, and came round to thinking that fresh country air was just what her big daft treasure needed. So we were stuck with him.

'All very well, but it won't help Lucius Petronius get back together with his wife,' said Helena, when I told her afterwards.

I said nothing. I had been to the Campagna with that rascal before. Grape-gathering with Petronius on various relatives' farms had taught me exactly how he intended to convalesce: Petro's idea of a nice country holiday was lying in the shade of a fig tree with a rough stone jar of Latium wine, and getting his arms around a buxom country girl.

Our final venture was to walk over to the Capena Gate to see Helena's family. Her father was out, taking his elder son on a vote-catching visit to some other senators. Her mother seized our baby with a rather public display of affection, implying that she was displeased with other members of her tribe. Claudia Rufina seemed very quiet. And Justinus only made a brief appearance looking serious, then slid off somewhere by himself. Julia Justa told Helena he was trying to reject the idea of entering the Senate, even though his papa had mortgaged himself deeply to make election funds available; the son had now been sentenced to take an improving trip abroad.

'Where to, Mama?

'Anywhere,' commented the noble Julia, rather forcefully. We had a distinct feeling we were only being favoured with half the story, but everyone was being held on a tight rein so there was no chance of a private chat.

'Well, he won't be going before Aulus and Claudia's wedding presumably,' Helena consoled herself. Justinus was her favourite, and she would miss him if he were exiled from Rome.

'Claudia's grandparents are due here in a couple of weeks,' her mother replied. 'One does one's best.' Julia Justa sounded more depressed and hard-done-by than usual. I had always thought her a shrewd woman. She was that rarity among patricians, a good wife and mother. She and I had had our differences, but only because she lived by high moral standards. If she was in difficulty with one of her sons, I sympathised. She would not want me to offer help.

Hoping to discover what was up, I tried to run the senator to earth at Glaucus' gym, which we both patronised, but Camillus Verus was not there.

A day later we were all settled at Tibur. Frontinus was staying with patrician friends in a lavishly equipped villa which had stunning views. Helena and I had rented a little farm down on the plain, just a couple of outbuildings attached to a rustic dwelling. We installed Petro in bachelor lodgings above the shack where the winepress would operate if there was one, while his aunt shared a corridor with us. Sedina had insisted on coming along to continue nursing her darling. Petronius was livid, but there was nothing he could do. So much for his romantic aspirations. He was to be pampered, fussed over – and supervised.

'This is a dump, Falco.'

'You chose to come. Still, I agree. We could probably buy this place for not much more than we're paying in rent.'

Disastrous words.

'That's a good idea,' said Helena, coming upon us unexpectedly. 'We can start your portfolio of Italian land, ready for when you decide to qualify for a higher rank. Then we can show off talking about "our summer residence at Tibur".'

I was alarmed. 'Is that what you want?'

'Oh, I want what you want, Marcus Didius.' Helena smiled wickedly. She hadn't answered the question, as she well knew.

She looked more at ease and less weary already than she had been in Rome, so I spoke less grumpily than I intended. 'Even to annoy my sister Junia with her fancy aspirations, I won't invest good money in anywhere as pitiful as this.'

'It's good land, my lad,' reported Petro's waddling aunt, coming in with a bundle of limp greenery in her shawl. 'There are wonderful nettles all over the back; I'm just going to conjure up a nice pan of soup for us all.' Like all townswomen, Auntie Sedina loved to come to the Campagna so she could demonstrate her domestic skills by producing dubious dishes from ghastly ingredients that would be shunned with shrieks of terror by the country-born.

Buying a patch of six-foot-high wild nettles in the faint hope of becoming an equestrian sounded about my level of ambition. Only an idiot would do it. Nobody lived down here on the flat. It was unhealthy and dingy. Anyone with taste and money acquired a minor palace on a plot surrounded by topiary among the picturesque crags over which the River Anio tumbled in a dramatic cascade.

The Anio was the pretty waterway into which, according to Bolanus, some local madman habitually threw dissected human body parts.

XLVIII

I HAD NOT come to enjoy the scenery.

The first task was to familiarise myself rapidly with the area. We were perched at the southern end of the Sabine Hills. We had come out on the ancient Via Tiburtina, crossing the Anio twice, first outside Rome on the Pons Mammaeus, and then later on the five-arched Pons Lucanus, dominated by the handsome tomb of the Plautii. We were already in rich man's territory, signalled by the thermal springs at Aquae Albulae, into which Sedina had made sure she dunked Petronius. Since the hot baths were supposed to cure throat and urinary infections I could not see that they had much relevance for a man who had been punched and kicked halfway to oblivion, and the unsavoury sight of his wounds certainly caused a flurry of fast-exiting invalids. The feeder lakes were pretty: an astonishing vivid blue. The smell of sulphur pervading the neighbourhood was thoroughly off-putting.

Lest we turn into tourists, the Emperor had done his best to spoil the succeeding area. It was being used to quarry the travertine stone for the huge new Flavian Amphitheatre in Rome, the process scarring the landscape and filling up the roads with carts. It must be distressing the snobs who had made their holiday homes here, but they could hardly protest about Vespasian's pet scheme.

All the way across the Campagna we had been accompanied by the high, handsome arches of the major aqueducts. Even when they veered away from the road, we could still see the great tawny arcades, dominating the plain as they strode towards Rome from the hills. They took a wide sweep, travelling miles in the process, in order to provide as gentle a gradient as possible and arrive at the city still high enough to supply its citadels, the Palatine and the Capitol.

At the point where the plain ran out and the hills started, encircled by fine olive groves and commanding unparalleled vistas, stood Tibur. There the incoming River Anio was forced to turn round three corners through a narrow gorge, producing fabulous cascades. The high ground ended abruptly in an escarpment, and the river simply fell straight over the edge, tumbling two hundred yards in its descent.

Sacred to the Sibyl Albunia, this breathtaking spot had been provided not just with the Sibyl's elegant crag-top temple but those of Hercules Victor and Vesta as well, popular subjects for artists throughout Italy when painting landscapes in roundels to adorn the walls of fashionable dining-rooms. Here statesmen created opulent country houses, inspiring yet more derivative art. Poets haunted the place like intellectual vagrants. Maecenas, the financier of Caesar and power-broker of Augustus, had his sumptuous nook here. Augustus himself came. Varus, the legendary military incompetent who lost three whole legions in Germany, owned a spread and had a road named after him. Everywhere was dripping with wealth and appropriately snobbish. The town centre was neat, clean, and prettied up with well-positioned maidenhair ferns. The populace seemed friendly. They usually do in towns where the main occupation is overcharging visitors.

We knew Bolanus was up in the hills, so a messenger was sent to announce our arrival. Meanwhile, Julius Frontinus and I shared out the job of checking the real estate. He took the sinister mansions with private racing stadia and armed guards, the ones which were supposed to be impenetrable to strangers. Most opened the gate for a consular official with six lictors. (Of course he had brought the lictors. They deserved a holiday. He was thoroughly considerate.) I took the rest of the properties, which were fewer than I had feared. Tibur was a millionaires' playground. So exclusive it was worse than the Bay of Neapolis in high summer.

Helena Justina had decided she would co-ordinate our efforts. Sedina helped look after Julia, in the periods when she had put Petronius down for a nap. That left Helena free to organise Frontinus and me, a task she set about with glee.

She drew up a map of the whole district, plotting who lived where, and whether they should go on our list of suspects. For various reasons, the list ended up shorter than it might have been.

'Since the aqueduct killer has apparently been at his grisly trade for a long time, we can omit anyone with recently acquired property,' Helena reminded us. 'Since he kills so repeatedly, we can probably ignore all the large villas which are occupied only on a very irregular basis. Their owners don't come here often enough. We are looking for something extremely specific: a family who use

Tibur not just as a relaxing resort where they may – or may not – be staying at given times of year, and from which they may – or just as easily may not – return to Rome for major festivals. Your search is for people who routinely visit *all* the Games, and who have done so assiduously for decades. If they own a house with access to the river, so much the better.'

Obtaining this information was normally not difficult. If Frontinus found any property-owners at home he asked them outright about their habits and movements. People responded well. Assisting an official tribunal is a public duty – with penalties for default. My approach was more subtle, but worked equally well; I invited folk to gossip about their neighbours. I found plenty of material.

'You both learned a lot,' Helena said, sitting us down for a conference after a day's hard work. Frontinus had been brought down to the farm; he was not at all shy of visiting a set of huts in a nettle patch. Helena grumbled at him just as much as at me: 'The trouble is, your work has not thrown up many likely suspects.'

'Are we going wrong?' Frontinus asked meekly.

'Don't let her bully you,' I grinned.

She looked upset. 'Am I being bossy, Marcus?'

'You are being yourself, dear heart.'

'I don't want to behave immodestly.'

'Cobnuts, Helena! You can see the Consul and I are listening like woolly lambs. Tell us the score.'

'Well look, this is a typical example: Julius Frontinus interviewed a family called the Luculli. They have a large house near the cascade, with a sublime aspect towards the Temple of the Sibyl –'

'They are staying here at the moment, and readily admit that they all went to Rome together for several days of the last Games,' Frontinus reported, still looking slightly nervous of Helena's enthusiasm.

'Yes, but, sir –' That 'sir' was a sop to his vanity; he took it well. 'The Luculli are a family who have been loaded with money for three or four generations. As a result, they have bought themselves villas in all the fashionable resorts. They have *two* on the Bay of Neapolis – facing each other from Cumae and Surrentum – plus their yachting base on the Alban Lake, their northern estate at Clusium, their southern one at Velia, and in this area they not only own the house in Tibur where we found them, but another at Tusculum and yet a third at Praeneste – which it turns out is really their old-fashioned favourite when seeking cooler air to escape to from the heat of summer in Rome.'

Frontinus looked thoroughly quashed.

I rubbed it in cheerfully. 'So the chances of the lucky Luculli following a regular pattern are zero.'

'Quite,' said Helena. 'They are always on the move. Even if they regularly visit Rome for festivals, half the time they aren't staying here. The person you want kidnaps his victims, then apparently always disposes of them in exactly the same way, and presumably in the same place.'

'So have we come up with anybody suitable?' I asked.

'No.' Helena looked despondent. 'Very few fit that category. I thought we had one – a Roman, living here for twenty years, goes to Rome for all the major festivals – but it's a woman: Aurelia Maesia. She has a villa near the Sanctuary of Hercules Victor.'

'I remember her.' Frontinus had done the interview. 'A widow. Decent background. Never remarried. Came home to a family estate after her husband died, but now goes into Rome to stay with her sister whenever there is a major event to patronise. She is well over fifty –' His tone hinted that that was a gallant estimate. 'She was suspicious of our enquiry, but surely incapable of murder. Besides, she stops in Rome throughout the Games. Our killer seized Asinia after the opening ceremony, then put at least one of her hands into the water supply very soon afterwards. That means if Bolanus really has found where he does it and it's up here, the man must have returned to Tibur virtually the next day.'

'That's another knot in the pattern,' I warned. 'The killer goes to Rome for festivals – yet evidently he comes back after the opening ceremony. But he doesn't stay here. He must go back to Rome a second time, because the torsos and heads are then dumped in the river and the Great Sewer. It's rather distinct behaviour.' An obvious explanation struck me. 'Aurelia Maesia must have litter-bearers, or a driver. Does her litter drop her at her sister's in Rome, return here, and then fetch her at the end of the Games?'

'She uses a driver.' Frontinus was touchingly keen to show off. 'I remembered to ask her. She travels in a carriage, but the driver stays with it at a stables just outside Rome. She likes it to be available in case she and her sister want a country drive.'

Aurelia Maesia was no good then, but at least we had found one person who came near to fitting our profile. It encouraged us to believe there could be others somewhere.

'Don't be disheartened,' I said to Frontinus. 'The more folk we rule out, the easier it will be to spot who we want.'

He agreed, yet threw in a different problem. 'If our man Bolanus is right that the dismembered body parts are entering the aqueducts at source then Tibur itself isn't the place to be.'

'Tibur is supplied from the Aqua Marcia,' said Helena, 'but that's an incoming branch which ends here. The main conduit that goes to Rome starts miles away.'

'Halfway to Sublaqueum,' I added, not to be outdone with supplying facts. 'Only another thirty miles of territory where we have to identify every house and farm, then ask the owners nicely if they happen to be murderers!'

B Y ARRANGEMENT BOLANUS reported to Frontinus the next day. I met them both at the house where Frontinus was staying. Bolanus was wearing the same ancient tunic and belt he had had on when I first met him, to which he had added a brimmed hat to guard against the weather and a knapsack for travelling. His plan was to drag Frontinus and me all the way to Sublaqueum, for reasons which I suspected had more to do with a wish to see the dam on which he had once worked than our search. But as a public servant he knew very well how to make a pleasant site visit sound like a logistical necessity.

Frontinus had sent a message to ask Petro if he wanted to be driven to the villa to help us take stock, but my partner refused quite shamelessly. 'No thanks. Tell his honour I'd rather laze about here counting geese.'

'Flirting with the neighbour's kitchen maid, you mean,' I growled.

'Certainly not!' he exclaimed, with a grin. I was right. He had spotted that she was plump in all the right places, eighteen years old, and given to looking over our boundary fence in the yearning hope that something masculine would glide up for a chat. I myself had only noticed the girl because I had had a perfectly sensible conversation with Helena Justina about the meagre amount of herb-plucking and goat-milking that the little madam was given to do. Helena took the view that she was trouble, while I feebly tried to argue that unseemly habits don't inevitably end in tragedy.

Petronius Longus was turning out to be more of a typical informer than I had ever been. He just would not take work seriously. If there was a flagon to drink or an attractive woman to moon at, he was in there. He seemed to think the freelance life was about lying in bed until he ruined his reputation, then spending the rest of the day enjoying himself. If that left me doing all the work, he just laughed at my stupidity.

It was a complete reversal of his dedicated approach in the vigiles. Even as a lad in the army he had been more conscientious. Perhaps he needed a supervisor to kick against. If so, as his friend I would never be able to issue orders, so that was out. And he knew how to dodge the Consul.

'Petronius Longus not with you?' was the first thing Frontinus asked me.

'Sorry, sir. He's feeling a little off-colour again. He wanted to come but his auntie put her veto on allowing him out.'

'Oh really?' responded Frontinus, like a cockerel who knew he was having his tail tweaked by pranksters.

'Really, sir.'

Bolanus grinned, understanding the situation, then quietly took the heat off by talking about our trip into the hills.

Frontinus was driven there in a fast, practical carriage, while Bolanus and I rode mules. We first took the Via Valeria, the great road through the Appenines. It climbed through gentle, attractively wooded slopes, accompanied by the graceful arches of the Aqua Claudia. At this point they followed the River Anio, though below Tibur they took a long sweep south-east, to avoid the escarpment and its sudden drastic drop in height.

The Sabine Hills run basically north and south. We started out heading in a north-easterly direction for most of the first day. The valley of the Anio widened and became more agricultural, with vineyards and olive groves. We bought a snack, then pressed on to where the river took a turn to the south and we had to leave the main road. This was near the by-way north which I was told led to Horace's Sabine Farm; as a part-time amateur poet I would have liked to divert and pay tribute at the Bandusian Spring, but we were seeking a killer, not culture. For informers, that's sadly routine.

We stayed the night in a small settlement before turning off the highway on to the little-used country road down the Anio valley to Nero's retreat at Sublaqueum. Once there next day, we braced ourselves to be amazed. There was a new village, grown from the workshops and huts provided to house all the builders and craftsmen who created Nero's villa. The place was discreet and tidy, much emptier than it would have been then, yet with inhabitants still clinging on.

The location was splendid. At the head of a picturesque forested valley, where the river collected its feeder streams and first became significant, had once been three small lakes. Nero dammed the waters and raised their levels to create the fabulous pleasure lakes around his magnificent marbled summer home. It was a typical Roman extravagance; given beautiful scenery in a private and peaceful spot, he added architecture of such astounding scope that now nobody came here to look at the views, only at the last villa complex built by a vulgar rich man. A remote, contemplative valley had been destroyed to make Nero's holiday playground, where he could amuse himself with every kind of luxury while pretending to be a recluse. He hardly ever came here; he died soon after it was built. Nobody else wanted it. Sublaqueum could never be the same again.

Bolanus proudly advised us that the middle dam, on which he had worked, was the largest in the world. Fifty feet high, the top was wide enough to drive ten horses abreast, if you were that kind of ostentatious maniac. It was paved with special tiles, with a dip in the middle to act as a spillway so the waters could continue on their natural route downstream.

The dam was truly enormous, a massive embankment of core rubble, covered with fitted blocks and sealed with hydraulic lime and crushed rock to form an impenetrable, waterproof plaster. Very nice. Who could blame any emperor who had access to the world's finest engineers for using them to landscape his garden in this way? It was much better than a sunken pond with a lamprey and some green weed.

A bridge high across the entire dam gave access to the villa and its glamorous amenities. Bolanus told us plenty of stories about the place's opulence, but we were in no mood to go sightseeing.

Frontinus walked us out on to the bridge. By the time we got to the middle, I for one just longed to return to land. But if the height made the Consul sway, he showed no sign of it. 'We have come along with you, Bolanus, since we trust your expertise. Now convince us this visit to the dam has a salient point.'

Bolanus paused. He gazed down the valley, a sturdy figure, unmoved by the importance of the ex-Consul grilling him. He waved an arm at the scenery: 'Isn't that marvellous?' Frontinus screwed his mouth up and nodded in silence. 'Right! I wanted another look,' said Bolanus. 'The Anio Novus aqueduct is needing a complete overhaul. It was never helped by being drawn off the river; we already knew from the bad quality of the original Anio Vetus that the channel would deliver too much mud. I reckon that could be improved dramatically if the Emperor could be persuaded to extend it right up here and draw the waters off the dam —'

Frontinus had pulled out his note-tablet and was writing this down. I foresaw him encouraging Vespasian to restore the aqueduct. For the struggling treasury to find the enormous budget for an extension might take longer. Still, Julius Frontinus was only in his mid-forties. He was the type who would mull over a suggestion like this for years. In a few decades' time, I could well find myself smiling as the *Daily Gazette* saluted an Anio Novus extension, when I would remember standing here above Nero's lake while an engineer's assistant earnestly propounded his theories . . .

This had nothing to do with the murders. I quietly mentioned that.

I sensed that the dogged Bolanus had another of his long educational talks ready. I shifted unhappily, looking at the sky. It was blue, with the slight chilly tinge of approaching autumn. Far away, buzzards or kestrels wheeled. Bolanus, who had a weak eye, had been suffering from the glare and the breeze. Even so he had removed his hat, in case the wind lifted it and spun it over the dam and down the valley.

'I've been thinking a lot about the Anio Novus.' Bolanus liked to drop in a vital point, then leave his audience tantalised.

'Oh?' I said, in the cool tone of a man who knew he was being sneakily played with.

'You asked me to consider how human hands and such could enter the water supply. From where they end up in Rome, I decided they must come via the four major systems that start above Tibur. That's the Claudia, Marcia, Anio Vetus and Anio Novus aqueducts. The Anio Vetus, the oldest of all, and the Marcia both run mainly underground. Another point: the Marca and Claudia are both fed by several springs, connected to the aqueducts by tunnels. But the Anio Vetus and Anio Novus are drawn direct from the river whose name they both bear.'

We gazed down at the damned river running far below us.

'Relevant?' prodded Frontinus.

'I think so.'

'You always believed the remains were first thrown into the river,' I said. 'You suggested that when we first talked.'

'Good memory!' He beamed.

A bad thought struck. 'You think they are thrown in *here*!'

We glanced at one another, then once more looked down over the dam. I immediately saw problems; anyone up here on the bridge tossing things off the top would be visible for miles. The dam had a vertical face on its reservoir side, but a long sloped bank on the river side. Hurling limbs far enough to ensure they landed in the Anio would be impossible, and for the killer entailed a risk of throwing himself off with them. It would be particularly dangerous if there was more wind; even today, when the valley itself was full of bird-song and wild flowers, warm, humid and still, up here constant blus-ters threatened to make us lose our step.

I explained my doubts. 'Picturesque thought – but think again!'

Bolanus shrugged. 'Then you have to look at the river between here and the Via Valeria.'

All I wanted was to walk very carefully back to the firm ground at the end of the dam.

L

M Y COMPANIONS EAGERLY consigned to me the task of surveying the relevant estates. We lodged that night at
Sublaqueum and I spent the rest of the afternoon ascertaining that
most of the cultivated land at the head of the valley and on the
lower slopes of Mount Livata now formed part of the huge Imperial
estate. Any Emperor planning a pleasure park is wise to ensure that
he will only be overlooked by the flatterers he brings along to help
him enjoy his isolation. Gossipmongers are never off duty.

Now the villa had passed to Vespasian. It lay almost deserted and
could well remain so. Our new ruler and his two sons had a distaste
for the flamboyant trappings of power which Nero revelled in.
When they wanted to visit the Sabine Hills – as they frequently did,
in fact – they went north: to Reate, Vespasian's birthplace, where
the family owned several estates and spent their summers in old-
fashioned peace and quiet, like clean-living country boys.

None of the Imperial slaves who nowadays tended Nero's spread,
or the ordinary folk in its associated village, would be able to afford
to make a habit of visits to Rome for entertainment. We still needed
to look for a private villa, owned by people with the leisure, the
money, and the social inclination to honour the major festivals year
after year.

Next day we returned as far as the Via Valeria, looking out for
that kind of estate. Frontinus and Bolanus went ahead to install us in
overnight lodgings again, while I stopped to make enquiries at one
private villa that looked sufficiently substantial.

'Over to you. I did my share at Tibur,' Frontinus cheerfully
informed me.

'Yes, sir. What about you, Bolanus? Want to help out at an interview?'

'No, Falco. I just contribute technical expertise.'

Thanks, friends.

This villa was owned by the Fulvius brothers, a jolly trio of bachelors. They were all in their forties, and happily admitted they liked going to Rome for the Games. I asked if their driver returned here after delivering them: oh no, because the Fulvii did not bother with an extra hand; they took it in turns to drive themselves. They were fat, curious, bursting with funny stories, and quite uninhibited. I quickly acquired a picture of a riotous group, merry on wine and squabbling gently, trundling up to Rome and back when the fancy took. They said they went often, though were not slavish attenders and sometimes missed a festival. Although none of them had ever married, they seemed too fun-loving (and too much in each other's pockets) for one of them to be a secret, brooding murderer of the kind I sought.

'By the way – did you happen to go to the city for the last Ludi Romani?'

'Actually, no.' Well, that absolved them from the murder of Asinia.

When I pressed them, it turned out they had probably not been to Rome since the Apolline Games, which take place in July – and they confessed rather shamefacedly they meant the July of the previous year. So much for these men of the world. The jolly bachelors were positively home-loving.

In the end I told the Fulvii the reason for my enquiries, and asked whether they knew of any of their neighbours who habitually travelled to Rome for festivals. Did they, for instance, on their own noisy journeys ever pass another local vehicle on the same errand? They said no. They glanced at one another afterwards, and looked as if they might be sharing a private joke of some kind, but I took them at their word.

That could be a mistake. The Anio flowed right through their estate. They let me look round. Their grounds were full of huts, stables, animal pens, storage barns, and even a gazebo in the form of a mock-temple on the sunny riverbank, in any of which abducted females might be held, tortured, killed and hacked to bits. I was well aware that the Fulvii might look like happy, open-natured souls, yet could well harbour dark jealousies and indulge long-held hates through vicious acts.

I was a Roman. I had a deep-seated suspicion of anyone who chose to live in the countryside.

Moving on down the valley, I reached another private entrance, not far above where water was diverted from the river into the conduit of the Anio Novus. This estate looked subtly different from the flourishing groves of the Fulvii. There were olive trees, though as on so many hillsides these looked as if nobody owned them; it rarely means they are abandoned in fact. The owner here probably turned up to harvest them. Still, the trees had a tangled, unpruned look which would have made my olive-growing friends in Baetica eye them askance. Too much vegetation grew around the trunks. Tame rabbits sat and looked at me instead of scampering for their lives.

I nearly rode on, but duty compelled me to turn off and investigate. I followed an overgrown track, buried in a tangled wood. Before I had gone any distance I met a man. He was standing by a pile of logs at the side of the track, doing nothing in particular. If he had had an axe or any other sharp tool with him I might have felt nervous, but he was just looking as if he hoped nobody would come along and ask him to do any work. Since this was private land I had to stop.

'Hello!'

His answer was a fathomless country stare. He was a slave, probably: tanned and sturdy from outdoor work. Hair unstyled, several teeth missing, coarse skin. Age indeterminate, but fifty maybe. Neither over-tall nor dwarfish. Badly dressed rather than ugly. Wearing a rough brown tunic, belt and boots. Hardly a god, yet no worse than scores of thousands of other lowborns who cluttered up the Empire, reminding the rest of us just how fortunate we were to have schooling, character, and the energy to look out for ourselves.

'I was just riding to the house. Can you tell me who lives here?'

'The old man.' A reluctant country voice came from a wide-cheeked, not-exactly-hostile face. He was answering, though. Since I had not introduced myself, that was more than I would have expected in Rome. He was probably under orders to discourage strangers who might be livestock thieves. I put aside my prejudice.

'You work for him?'

'That's my task in life.' I had met the type before. He blamed the world for all his misfortunes. A slave his age might have expected to gain his freedom one way or another. Maybe he lacked the opportunity to earn his price through fiddling, or to demonstrate the right kind of loyalty. He certainly lacked the cheek and charm of most sophisticated slaves in Rome.

'I need to know if anyone from here ever goes to Rome for the Circus Maximus Games?'

'Not the old man. He's eighty-six!'

We laughed a little. That explained the faint air of neglect on the estate. 'Does he treat you well?'

'Couldn't ask for better.' With the joke, the slave had become more approachable.

'What's his name?'

'Rosius Gratus.'

'Does he live here alone?'

'He does.'

'No relatives?'

'Up in Rome.'

'Can I go and see him?' The slave shrugged agreement. I gathered I might not gain much from the experience, but I had been wrong in my judgement earlier; there was no opposition to my request. 'Thanks – and what's *your* name?'

He gazed at me with the slight trace of arrogance some people show: as if they expect everybody to know who they are. 'Thurius.'

I nodded, and rode on.

Rosius Gratus was sitting in a long chair under a portico, lost in dreams of events sixty years ago. It was obvious that this was how he spent hours every day. He was covered with a rug, but I could see a shrunken, hook-shouldered figure, white-haired and watery-eyed. He seemed well cared for and, considering his age, pretty fit. But he was not exactly ready to take seven turns around a running stadium. He certainly was no murderer.

A housekeeper had let me in and left me to talk to him unsupervised. I asked him a few simple questions, which he answered with an air of great courtesy. He looked to me as if he were pretending to be dafter than he was, but most old men enjoy doing that for their private amusement. I was looking forward to doing it myself one day.

I told him, by way of conversation, that I had come here from Tibur.

'Did you see my daughter?'

'I thought your family were in Rome, sir?'

'Oh . . .' The poor old stick looked confused. 'Yes, that may be so. Yes, yes; I do have a daughter in Rome –'

'When did you last see your daughter, sir?' I deduced he had been abandoned out here for so long he had forgotten what family he had.

'Oh . . . I saw her not long ago,' he assured me, though somehow it sounded as if it happened a long time back. He was so vague it could just as well have been two days ago. As a witness, the old chap managed to seem wickedly unreliable. His deep-set eyes suggested that he knew it too, and didn't care if he misled me.

'You don't visit Rome a lot, nowadays?'

'Do you know, I'm eighty-six!'

'That's wonderful!' I assured him. He had already told me twice.

He seemed eager for company, though he had little of interest to say to anyone. I managed to extricate myself fairly gently. Something about Rosius Gratus suggested he could well be up to mischief, but once I knew he could not be the murderer I needed to be on my way.

I cantered back to the road, this time seeing nobody along the track.

LI

T HE PLACE WHERE we would be staying lay near the various springs which fed the Aqua Marcia. Bolanus had suggested their underground position would make access for the killer both difficult and unlikely. That was not how the dismembered hands entered the supply.

But Bolanus reckoned he could provide our answer. He and Frontinus were waiting for me as arranged, at the forty-second milestone: beside a large mud reservoir where the Anio Novus began. The valley was full of birdsong. It was a bright country afternoon, in grim contrast to the dark conversations we were about to hold.

A dam with a sluice in the bed of the river helped steer part of the current into this basin. It formed a huge settling tank which filtered out impurities before the start of the aqueduct. Now for the first time in years it had been drained and cleaned out. Banks of dredged-up mud were drying all around it. Slow-moving public slaves were unloading their breakfast from a donkey, leaving their tools in his pack: a typical scene. The donkey turned his head suddenly and grabbed a bit to eat himself; he knew how to get the better of the water board.

'With aqueducts,' Bolanus explained to us, 'it's difficult and unnecessary to design a filtration system along the whole run. We tend to make a big effort at the start, then have extra tanks at the end, just before distribution starts. But that means anything which gets past the first filter can go all the way to Rome.'

'Arriving as little as a day later,' I reminded him, remembering what he had told me in an earlier discussion.

'My star pupil! Anyway, as soon as I came up here I could see we had problems. This basin had never been cleared since Caligula inaugurated the channel. You can imagine what we found in the mud.'

'That was when you uncovered more remains?' Frontinus prompted.

Bolanus looked sick. 'I found a leg.'

'Was that all?' Frontinus and I exchanged a glance. The message that had reached us previously had implied limbs of all sorts and sizes.

'That was enough for me! It was horrendously decayed; we had to bury it.' Bolanus, who had seemed so sanguine, had become appalled now he had actually seen the gruesome relics involved. 'I can't describe what it was like clearing out the mud. There were a few loose bones we could not identify.'

A foreman produced them for us. Workmen like to keep a jar of interesting finds. All the better if it includes parts of old skeletons.

'I'll ask somebody who hunts,' suggested Frontinus, ever practical, as he fearlessly handled the pieces of knuckle and leg bone. 'But even if we decide they are human, they won't help identification.'

'No, but these might.' Bolanus himself was unpacking his knapsack.

He produced a small fold of material; it looked like a napkin from one of his excellent lunch hampers. Carefully unfolding it, he revealed a gold earring. It was of good workmanship, crescent-shaped and covered with handsome granulation, with five dangling chains, each ending in a fine gold ball. Bolanus held it up between his fingers in silence, as if to imagine it hanging gracefully on a female ear.

Accompanying the earring was a string of jewellery, probably part of a longer necklace, since there was no clasp. Bright blue glass beads – lapis, or something very similar – had metal caps which joined them to small squares of delicate patterns cut from sheet gold.

'It's very unusual to find items like this up here,' Bolanus said. 'In the sewers, yes. They could have been lost in the street or anything. Coins and all kinds of gems turn up there – one work gang even discovered half a silver dinner service once.'

'It looks as though somebody threw them into the water to get rid of them,' I said. 'What girl goes tripping along a remote river-bank in her big city finery?' My companions were silent, leaving it to me to comment on girls.

Depressed by the conversation, Frontinus walked back towards the river. 'Should I have the bed of the Anio dragged?' he asked glumly as I followed him, sharing his low mood. 'I could send my allocation of public slaves; may as well use them for something.'

'In due course, maybe. But for now we should avoid any obvious official activity. Everything should look normal. We don't want to scare off the killer. We need to lure him out – and then grab him.'

'Before he kills again,' Frontinus sighed. 'I don't like this, Falco. We must be close to him now – but it could go badly wrong.'

Bolanus had joined us. For a moment we all watched the water rushing into a diversion pipe that currently fed the aqueduct. I turned round and scanned the woods, almost as if I suspected the killer might be lurking up there watching us.

'I'll tell you what I think happens,' said Bolanus in a sombre voice. Then he paused.

He was upset. The isolated spot had worked on him; in his imagination he was sharing the last moments of the women who had been brought so far from home to a terrible fate, possibly killed, mutilated and dismembered very near to where we stood.

I helped him out. 'The killer lives somewhere locally. He abducts his victims in Rome, probably because he is not known there and he hopes he won't be traced. Then he brings them forty miles back here.'

Bolanus found his voice again. 'After he has finished whatever he does to these girls, he drives back to Rome to dispose of their heads and torsos in the river and the Cloaca – probably to minimise the chance of anything pointing to him locally. But first he cuts off their limbs and throws them into the river –'

'Why doesn't he just throw all the parts into the Anio, or else take everything to Rome?' Frontinus asked.

'I imagine,' I said slowly, 'he wants the large pieces as far away as possible because they look like identifiable human remains for longer. So he takes them back to Rome – but while he's disposing of them in the sewer or the river he's vulnerable. He wants just a couple of large parcels which will sink out of sight quickly if he's being observed. But he thinks he's safe chucking the smaller limbs away here because they will quickly deteriorate beyond being recognised. Thrown into the stream, they could be eaten by carrion birds or animals, either here in the hills or down on the Campagna. And anything that went over the cascade at Tibur would be well smashed up.'

'Right, Falco,' said Bolanus. 'I don't think he ever intends that they should turn up in the water supply in Rome. But sometimes smaller and lighter parts – hands, for instance – find their way into the Novus basin, and then on into the channel. The killer may still be unaware that this happens. If they happen to float out of the filtration system, the body parts will travel on to Rome. At the end of the run, two aqueducts join on one arcade; the Novus is carried above the Aqua Claudia, with switching shafts. And the Claudia also has an interchange with the Marcia, as I showed you both –'

Frontinus and I nodded, remembering how we saw the torrent crashing from one aqueduct to the other.

'So we can see how these small relics might move around once they reach Rome. The only puzzle,' said Bolanus slowly, 'is the first hand, the one that Falco found, which was supposed to have been pulled out on the Aventine, in a castellum of the Aqua Appia.'

It seemed a long time ago that Petro and I had shared a drink in Tailors' Lane. 'Are there no links between the Aqua Appia and any of the Tibur channels?' I asked.

'There are possibilities. The Appia source isn't underground; it starts at a reservoir in some ancient quarries on the Via Collatina.'

'So anyone could have driven past one day and thrown in a package?'

Bolanus didn't like it. 'More likely your public fountain has two jets, drawn from different aqueducts. It enables us to maintain a supply by a swap if needs be. It's true the Appia serves the Aventine; the terminus is by the Temple of Luna. But there could be a second feed from the Aqua Claudia –'

'So it all fits,' Frontinus interrupted. 'And it all starts here.'

'But who is this bastard?' fretted Bolanus, for whom the hunt was starting to be personal.

'All I found back along the road,' I reported, 'was a trio of cheerful brothers who – apparently – have not been to Rome for ages, with a few slaves, plus an old man who looks too feeble to go anywhere.'

'So what do you suggest?' asked the Consul. 'We know what the bastard does, and we know he does some of it here. Unless we act, at the next festival he will be here doing it again.'

'If we were very cold-blooded,' I answered him slowly, 'when the Augustan Games start' – they were only a week away – 'we would station your public slaves behind trees all the way up this valley from here to Sublaqueum, telling them to make themselves look like twigs until they spot someone chucking something suspicious out into the Anio.'

'But to do that and catch him in the act –'

'– a woman has to die first.'

Frontinus took a deep breath. 'We shall do it if we have to.' Pragmatic to the end, it seemed.

237

I smiled. 'But if we can, I want to catch him earlier.'

'Good, Falco!'

'We have a few leads. Before the Augustales begin, I want us to be set up for trapping him in Rome. We haven't much time. I'll stay at Tibur for one more day, and give our suspects list a final look-over. I want to be quite sure we haven't missed anything. We know the killer is prepared to travel long distances. Maybe he actually lives at Tibur but comes up into the hills when he starts butchering the bodies.'

So it was back to Tibur. As we moved away from the sunny riverbank a startled kingfisher swooped away in a brilliant flash of colour. Behind us a dragonfly hovered in stunning livery above the sparkling and seemingly clear waters of the contaminated Anio.

LII

<hr>

FOR DISCOVERING OUR festival-visitor, Tibur itself still seemed the best base. Back along the Via Valeria we saw little to interest us. There were one or two grand country homes, their porticos bearing the names of famous men, although most lay deserted and some of the names were so illustrious that even the high-ranking Frontinus blenched at the thought of politely suggesting that the current generation might be involved in a long and extremely sordid series of murders. In between, the farm-owners geared their trips to Rome to markets rather than festivals. The absentee landlords, of whom there were plenty, ruled themselves out by their very absence as they do from most responsibilities.

Back in Tibur my own reception was mixed. Julia Junilla was crying when I arrived at the nettle patch farm. 'Dear, dear – come to Father!' As I picked her up, mere tears turned to lusty, red-in-the-face screams.

'She is wondering who this stranger is,' Helena suggested mildly, above the row.

I could take a hint. 'And what are you thinking, my darling?'

'Oh I remember all too well.'

The baby must have remembered too, because she suddenly welcomed me with a very squelchy burp.

Lucius Petronius, my beaten-up partner, was looking better. His bruises were fading. By lamplight he just looked as if he hadn't washed his face for a week. He could now move about more freely too, when he bothered to exert himself. 'So how was seeking suspects in Sublaqueum?'

'Oh, just how I like it – all gazing at idyllic scenery and thinking poetic thoughts.'

'Find anything?'

'Charming people who never go anywhere. Clean-living country types who lead blameless lives and who tell me oh, no, they entertain no suspicions that any of their pleasant neighbours may be cutting up female flesh in some grim little hut in the woods.'

He stretched his big frame. I could tell that our convalescent boy was started to feel bored. 'So what now?'

'Back to Rome, fairly urgently. But I'm quickly going to double-check some of the fancy villas Julius Frontinus went to earlier.'

'I thought you sent him to the ones that would refuse you access?'

'I'm going disguised as an itinerant handyman – the type I know every one of them will welcome with open arms.'

He raised an eyebrow sceptically. 'Does that type exist?'

'Every fine home in the Empire has at least one fountain that won't work. I shall offer to fix it for them –' I grinned at him. 'And you can come along as my terrible apprentice if you want.' Petronius accepted readily, though he did try to convince me his natural position was as the fountain-fixer's manager instead. I said since he looked like a roughneck fresh from a tavern fight he had to play the tool-carrying role. 'Next door's kitchen maid not up to much then?'

'Too young,' he smirked. 'Too bloody dangerous. Besides,' he admitted, 'she smells of garlic and she's dafter than a painter's brush.'

Every investigation should include an interlude where the trusty informer puts on a dirty one-sleeved tunic, slicks his hair back with salad oil, and sets off to knock on doors. I had done it before. Petronius, used to imposing his requests for information by means of a cudgel and a threat of imprisonment, had to learn a few tricks – mainly how to keep quiet. Still, his Auntie Sedina assured him he was perfect at looking gormless (the first requirement in a trades-man). Helena put us through a rehearsal, at which she made various sound suggestions, such as 'Pick your nose with more conviction!' and 'Don't forget to suck your teeth and murmur, *"Ooh! This looks like a tricky one; I think you've got a problem here . . ."'*

The way it worked was this: dressed in scruffy togs and carrying a large bag which contained various heavy chunks of equipment we had collected from the farm outbuildings, Petro and I sauntered past the elegant gates of the opulent homesteads we wanted to investi-gate. We were always eating a melon. As the fierce guards came out to glare at us walking by, we greeted them cheerfully and offered them a slice of fruit. After passing the time of day for a few moments we usually persuaded our new friends, with melon juice still running down their chins, to let us in. We heaved our bag up the drive, and very respectfully informed the suspicious house steward that this was his big chance to surprise the owner by renovating the fountain that had failed to work for years. Most let us try, since they had nothing to lose. While we applied our ingenuity they naturally stayed there watching, just in case we were burglars after the drinking cups. That gave us the chance to engage them in chat, and once we had the fountain flowing again (which we usually achieved, I'm proud to say) they were so grateful they were ready to tell us anything.

Well, all right; some of them told us to get lost.

There was one particular house which Petro and I both viewed with suspicion. While I was away he had been examining Helena's lists and formulating theories (the kitchen maid must have been an absolute disaster close to). He shared my feeling that we ought to re-investigate the villa owned by Aurelia Maesia. Though female, her pattern of travelling to Rome most resembled what we were look-ing for.

She lived in Tibur itself. Her house was on the western side, near the Hercules Victor complex. This noteworthy sanctuary was the most important in Tibur, set on the steep hill above the lower reaches of the Anio as it travelled past the town. Massive stonework supported old arcades whereupon sat a large piazza, surrounded by double-height colonnades which had been left open on one side to give a dramatic view down the valley. In the centre of the temenos the temple to the demigod was approached by a high flight of steps; immediately below it lay a small theatre. A market filled the colon-nades, so the area hummed. They had an oracle too.

'Why don't we just consult the oracle?' Petro growled. 'Why waste effort dressing up as layabouts and getting drenched to the armpits when we can just pay a fee and be told the answer?'

'Oracles can only deal with simple stuff. "What is the Meaning of Life?" And "How can I get the better of my mother-in-law?" You aren't expected to tax them with technical complexities such as "Please name this bastard who kidnaps and kills for fun". That calls for sophisticated powers of deduction.'

'And idiots like you and me who don't know when to turn a bad job down.'

'That's right. Oracles are whimsical. They tease and mislead. You and I stick in there with jaws like sheep tics and produce an un-rebuttable result.'

'Well then,' chaffed Petro. 'Let's go and make ourselves a pest.'

Like most women's houses which ought to be impossible for dubious men to enter, Aurelia Maesia's well-trimmed grounds were simplicity itself to penetrate. There may have been a porter and steward at the house but we were admitted by a female cook who took us straight to the lady herself.

She must have been sixty. She was dressed in a stately manner, with gold pendant earrings set with amber and dangling pearls. She had a fleshy face, about to droop and go more gaunt; her skin was meshed with a web of fine lines. I put her down as pleasant but dull. The moment we met her I knew she was not our murderer, but that did not preclude her driver or anyone else with whom she habitually shared her carriage on her trips to Rome.

She had been writing a letter, with difficulty since she was not using a scribe and her eyesight was clearly very poor. As we shuffled in, she looked up rather nervously. We went through the routine and, our cover accepted, were led to a dry fountain in a licheny courtyard. It was ancient, but elegant. Sparrows hopped hopefully in the two tiered bowls, watching our approach with cheeping curiosity. A lad had been put in charge of us.

'I'm Gaius.' I set our bag down carefully, to avoid revealing that most of its supposedly technical contents were just farmyard junk. Extracting a blunt stick, I began scratching off lichen boldly. Petro stood in the background, staring at the sky in an aimless manner.

'Who's he?' asked the lad, still checking our credentials.

'He's Gaius too.'

'Oh! How do I tell which is which?'

'I'm the clever one.'

When Petro took a turn at the introductions, he always called us 'Titus', saying 'like the Emperor's son'; it gave him a childish pleasure to assume Imperial trapping when we were playing at louts.

'And you are?'

'Titus,' said the lad.

Petronius gave him a lazy grin. 'Like the Emperor's son!'

Young Titus had apparently heard that one before.

'Seems a nice lady, Aurelia what's-her-name,' I offered, after some time cleaning the weathered stone. 'Lives here, does she? I only ask because a lot of our clients in this area only come down on holiday.'

'Lived here for years,' said Titus.

'Still, I expect she goes to Rome sometimes?'

'Quite often really.'

Petronius had a finger up his nose. Titus almost copied him, then fell shy of it. I looked up and addressed Petronius: 'Listen, our Gaius

– look around and see if you can find me a little stone or a bit of chipped tile from somewhere –'

'Why do I always have to go?'

'You're the fetcher, that's why.'

Petro managed to look as if he had no idea what I wanted, wandering off aimlessly while I kept Titus trapped in tedious chat.

'Bit of a trip for your mistress, Rome? I don't mean to be rude, but she doesn't look in her prime.' To the lad she must have seemed a real antique. 'Still, she obviously has the money to be comfortable. Now you and I, if we went, we'd be banging about on some old cart – but a lady now –'

'She goes in her own carriage.'

'Some charioteer takes her?'

'Damon.'

'That's a nice Greek name.'

'He drives her up and brings her back again. She stays with her sister; they make a family party up at festivals. It's regular.'

'That's nice.'

'Wonderful!' he chortled; obviously his idea of entertainment involved far more thrills than two sixty-year-old women were expected to devise. He was about fourteen, and yearning to make a disgrace of himself. 'They go to the Games and natter all through it, and never have any idea who won the fights or the races. They just want to see who else is there in the audience.'

'Still –' I was poking at the jets with my wire. 'The ladies like to go shopping. Plenty of that in Rome.'

'Oh, she brings stuff back. The coach is always full of it.'

'This Damon who does the driving, he has a nice job. I bet you'd like to take over from him.'

'No chance, mate! Damon would never let anybody else do that.'

'Keen is he?'

'He lives with the cook. He grabs every chance to get away from her.'

Petronius came strolling back, having apparently forgotten what I sent him for.

In the course of pretending to hack dirt and vegetation off the fountain, I had discovered what I was looking for. Aurelia Maesia's villa had a domestic water pipe from the Tibur aqueduct and her fountain was supplied by a secondary pipe, though its water could be cut off with a tap. (This was a rarity since most people want spare water to sluice out the latrine.) I guessed someone had turned off the tap and forgotten they had done so. The tap was the usual big cast bronze affair, with a square loop on top which would be worked by a special removable key.

'Do me a favour, Titus: run and ask whoever keeps it to give us a lend of the key. Then I'll show you something.'

While the lad scampered off, Petro said quietly, 'There's a stable containing the carriage. It's a raeda. Damned great four-wheeled effort, covered in bronze flashings. The fellow who must be the driver was lying asleep on a bale: ginger hair, filthy beard, twisted leg – and he's only half my height.'

'Easy to spot.'

'Proverbial.'

'Damon's his name,' I said.

'Sounds like a bloody Greek shepherd.'

'A real Arcadian. I wonder if he owns a dirty great sheep-shearing knife?'

Young Titus rushed back to us, to say nobody had the key for the tap. I shrugged. In our bag was a length of iron bar I could use, taking care not to bend it. I hate to have to leave an iron bar behind. Apart from the fact you can use them to break heads, what do you do the next time you want to operate some inept householder's tap for them?

The tap was stiff and hard to turn, as I knew it would be. I could feel the water-hammer setting up immediately. It was banging all the way back through the house; that was probably why they had turned off the tap in the first place. A pity, because just as soon as it was turned back on the fountain glugged into life. It was attractive and musical, though not very level.

'Coo!' said Titus. 'That's it then!'

'Give us a chance, boy . . .'

'Perfectionist,' Petro told the lad, nodding sagely.

'See, it's all slopping to one side. Give us that stone you found, our Gaius –'I was wedging the upper tier, so the water flowed more evenly. 'Now young Titus, this is our Gaius and me: we use a stone to set you right. Other people poke in a bit of stick, and that's deliberate. Eventually it rots away, so they have to be called in again. But Gaius and me, when we mend a fountain, that's the last you ever see of us.'

Titus nodded, easily impressed by trade secrets. He was a bright lad. I could see him thinking he could make use of this expertise himself.

244

I was packing up our toolbag. 'So why's this Damon so fond of going up to Rome then?'

The lad looked round in all directions to make sure he wasn't overheard.

'After the women, isn't he?' replied Titus, showing off with special knowledge of his own.

LIII

B UT WE KNEW we were probably not looking for a ladies' man. Especially not a married one, or the rural slave equivalent. Petronius Longus agreed with me: Damon wanted to get away from the cook because she knew he couldn't drive a straight marital course, so she nagged him. I gave Petro a look. This was a situation he knew all about. He accepted the look with a filthy scowl, and we gave up mending fountains for the day.

We gave up in Tibur altogether, in fact, since time was against us. The next morning we packed up and started back to Rome. It seemed as if we had made no progress, though I felt sure we had improved on our background information to the point where if the killer made a move he would be lucky not to give himself away. And, although Damon was not an ideal suspect, he might just fit the bill. I had acquired a farm too. It would be the bane of my life, but now I could call myself a man of property.

The first person we saw when we struggled home to the Aventine was my nephew, the real Gaius. He was in a fine bate. 'Well, you've really let me down!' he raged. Gaius could lather himself up like a dying horse. I had no idea what he was on about. 'You're a fine friend, Uncle Marcus –'

Helena had gone indoors to feed the baby while I was still unpacking the donkey that had brought our luggage. 'Calm down and stop yelling. Hold this –'

'I'm not doing your dirty work!'

'Suit yourself.'

He calmed down, seeing me unmoved. He had the family trait of never wasting effort, so subsided into a typical dark, Didius sulk. He looked like my father; I hardened my heart. 'I've got a lot to do here, Gaius: if you shut up and help, I'll hear your complaint afterwards. If not, trot off and annoy someone else.'

Reluctantly Gaius stood still while I loaded him up with baggage until he could hardly stagger up the steps to our apartment.

Under the strut and bluster lurked a good little worker. Not for the first time I realised I would have to do something about him, and soon. Thinking about my Tibur nettle patch suggested a possible answer. What he needed was to be plucked from the wild streetlife he led. Maybe I could send him to the family farm. Great-Auntie Phoebe had a long history of mollifying daft young boys, and I could trust Gaius to stand up staunchly to the vagaries of my peculiar uncles, Fabius and Junius. I said nothing at this stage. His mother, my ridiculous sister Galla, would have to be allowed to vent her disgust at any sensible plan I put up. Then there was Lollius, of course; well, I looked forward to running rings around Lollius . . .

As I followed Gaius into the house I sighed. I had only been home five minutes, yet the burdens of domesticity already had me feeling cornered.

'Will you give me some money to take your donkey back to the stable, Uncle Marcus?'

'No, I won't.'

'Yes, he will,' said Helena. 'What's upsetting you, Gaius?'

'I was *promised* a job here,' stated my nephew indignantly. 'I was going to earn some money looking after the baby. I'll be sent back to school soon.'

'Don't worry,' I told him glumly. 'The school holidays have another two weeks to run yet.' Gaius never had any real idea of time.

'Anyway, I'm not going any more when I'm fourteen.'

'Fine. Tell your grandma not to waste any more money on the fees.'

'I'm leaving on my birthday.'

'Whatever you say, Gaius.'

'Why aren't you arguing?'

'I'm tired. Now listen, the Augustales are about to start and I have a lot of hard night-observation coming up. Helena will be glad to have your help with the baby. I dare say she would welcome company during the day too, but you'll have to be quiet if I've come home to sleep.'

'Are you going to explain to your baby that she's not to cry?' As a prospective nursemaid, Gaius had a nice sarcastic attitude. 'What's the observations for?'

'To catch this maniac who's putting bits of women in the water supply.'

247

'How will you do that, then?' Like all my relatives Gaius viewed my work with incredulity, astounded that anyone was crazy enough to employ me, or that the tasks I undertook could ever furnish real results.

'I have to stand outside the Circus Max until he comes along and nabs one.' Put like that, my family's mockery seemed reasonable. How could I ever expect this to work?

'Then what?'

'Then I'll nab him.'

'I'd like to see that! Can I help?'

'No, it's far too dangerous,' said Helena firmly.

'Oh, Uncle Marcus!'

'If you want to earn some pocket money, you'll do what Helena tells you. She holds the keys here, and she does the accounts.'

'She's a woman.'

'She can add up.' I grinned at her.

'In more ways than one,' she commented. 'Come and eat, you pair of rascals.'

Grudgingly, Gaius agreed to sit down at the table and tuck in. Seduced by the unusual experience of a family dinner, something Galla and Lollius had never been known to provide for their children, he finally remembered he had a message to deliver to Helena: 'Your brother came to see you yesterday.'

'Quintus? The tall friendly one? Camillus Justinus?'

'Probably. He said to tell you he's been sent away for his health.' Helena looked alarmed. 'What does that mean? Is he ill?'

Gaius shrugged his thin shoulders under his dirty tunic. 'I think it was a kind of joke. I was kipping on your porch, waiting for you to come home again.'

At the thought of the unloved scallywag hanging around our house pathetically, Helena winced. 'Did you talk to my brother?'

'He sat down with me on the steps and we had a nice chat. He's not bad. But he was very depressed.'

Tired after the journey, Helena rubbed her eyes and then gazed at my nephew with her chin in both hands. 'What made him depressed, Gaius?'

'He was talking to me in private –' Catching Helena's eye, my nephew writhed uncomfortably. But he owned up, looking embarrassed. 'Well, love, and all that stuff.'

I laughed. 'Well there's a lesson for you. That's what happens to young men who foolishly dally with actresses.'

Helena Justina filled a new food bowl for my nephew, looking thoughtful. Then, since she knew how to prevent squabbling, she filled another bowl for me.

The Games in honour of the late Emperor Augustus begin on the third day in October. Two days later is a mythical date for the opening of the gates to Hades; I was hoping that by then we would have a villain caught and ready to send down there. Immediately before the Games came a black day in the calendar, the traditional bad luck day following the Kalends, the first of the month. We had reasoned that the superstitious would avoid travelling on a black day so they would come to Rome for the festival on the Kalends instead. To be absolutely sure we were in place in time, we actually set up our watch the day before.

We were observing the city gates. Hoping our theories were correct, we concentrated on the eastern side. Petro and I took turns on the Tiburtine and Praenestine gates, where we stationed ourselves every evening just as the vehicle ban was lifted and the carts came into Rome; we remained until the traffic dispersed at dawn. Thanks to Julius Frontinus, the Prefect of Vigiles had given us help from his local men; for additional cover they were also on watch at the two gates to the north of the Praetorian Camp and two more further south.

'I hope you're prepared to be the one,' said Petro, 'who tells the vigiles they have to look for a ginger-haired midget with a beard and a wonky leg.'

'They'll think it's a big joke.'

'Falco, I've come to the conclusion anything you're involved in is a joke!' he retorted, rather bitterly I thought.

The Porta Tiburtina was where we expected the killer to drive in, whether he was our gingery suspect Damon, or somebody else. Both the Via Tiburtina and the Via Collatina enter Rome that way. There, and also at the Porta Praenestina where a road came in from the same general area of the Campagna, the vigiles were stopping and listing every vehicle.

It caused a stir, to put it mildly. We called it a traffic census, ordered by the Emperor. Each driver was asked where he had come from and 'to assist with forward planning' where he was travelling to in Rome. Quite a few hated telling us, and some probably lied on principle. When they were asked the reason for their journey, and how often they came up for festivals, some of the middle- and upper-class occupants of carriages said they would rush straight home to write complaining petitions to Vespasian. Naturally we fell back on 'Sorry, sir; it's orders from the top' and 'Don't blame me, tribune; I'm just doing my job' – and naturally that enraged them more. When they screeched off with sparks flying from their wheels, at least they were too busy fuming to stop and consider what our real motive might have been.

The fat-bodied, four-wheeled, bronze-embellished raeda lurched through the Porta Tiburtina on the Kalends. At the time I was on duty there. I had arrived in position as soon as the first vehicles were permitted to enter that night. The grand carriage was drawn by four horses but was being driven at the pace of a funeral bier. Its slow drag had already caused a traffic tail a mile long. It was easy to spot. Not just because of the irritated yells from the frustrated drivers behind it, but because up on the front was the ginger-haired small man all of us were looking for.

I stepped back and let one of the vigiles raise a baton to stop the carriage. I could see the elderly Aurelia Maesia peering out short-sightedly. She was the only passenger. Damon, the driver, was in his late forties, freckled, fair-skinned and red-haired all over, right down to ginger eyebrows and lashes. As a ladies' man he looked nothing. For some strange reason that's often the case.

As the vigiles approached with their list of questions, I watched from the shadow of the inner gate, close enough to listen in. Details were taken of Aurelia Maesia's plans to stay in Rome with her sister, whose name she gave as Aurelia Grata, at an address on the Via Lata. She stated that she was visiting for the length of the Augustales and gave her reason as a family reunion. Damon provided the name of a stable outside the Porta Metrovia where he said he would be staying with the horses and carriage, then he drove off into the regular traffic jam that was Rome at night. A member of the vigiles who had been primed in advance set off to follow on foot. He was to stick with Damon all the way to the stable, then lean on a broom there for the duration of the Games, tailing the man if he went anywhere.

Damon did not meet our criteria for the killer. If he really did stay at these stables throughout the Games, he failed to match our pattern of a man who went to Tibur to carry out each murder and returned later to dispose of his victim's torso and head. Still, if there did turn out to be some connection with Damon, I could feel a sense of quiet satisfaction: the Porta Metrovia was at the end of Cyclops Street. It was only minutes from the area where Asinia for one had disappeared, being the nearest city gate to the Circus Maximus.

LIV

THERE WERE TWO Roman festivals named for Augustus. Eight days before October had been his birthday, on which formal Games were celebrated in the Circus; we had managed to miss that during our jaunt to Tibur. Now the main ten-day series was inaugurated, working up to splendid shows for the anniversary of the old Emperor's return from abroad after pacifying the foreign provinces. Still regularly bankrupting towns throughout the Empire, this was the kind of junket I tried to avoid. I didn't flatter Emperors when they were alive, so I certainly wanted no part in their deification once Rome was rid of them.

On the day of the opening ceremony, Petro and I were as keyed up as Brutus and Cassius having bad dreams the night before the Battle of Philippi. If he stayed true to form, come the evening our killer would be out looking for his next victim. Julius Frontinus had held long consultations with the tribunes of the Fifth and Sixth Cohorts of vigiles, who patrolled the Circus area; they were to have men out in force, with particular orders to protect the safety of unaccompanied women. Every time I thought about the amount of ground to be covered and the number of people who would be flocking to and fro, I went cold. It was an enormous task.

We had toyed with the idea of putting up notices warning people to beware. Frontinus forbade it. It cost us all some heart-searching but he took the final responsibility. We had to be hard. Everything had to appear normal. We wanted the killer to strike – though to strike when we were watching and could intervene.

My sister Maia came round that first afternoon. She was a bright, curly-haired spirit, smartly turned out, ready for anything, and quite uncontrollable. 'We should go, Helena!' she cried. 'You and I are the sort who can keep our eyes open; I bet if he's there we could spot him.'

'Please don't go anywhere near the Circus.' I was terrified. I was Maia's older brother and Helena's chosen partner. According to the ancient laws of Rome, my word should be law: fat chance. These were women of character, and I was just the poor duffer who tried to do his best for them. I had no jurisdiction over either.

They were close friends, and both argumentative. 'Maia's right.' Helena knew how wound up I was, but was turning against me over this. 'Maia and I could walk about near the Circus acting as decoys.'

'Dear gods!'

'We'd be brilliant. You've got to try something,' cajoled Maia. From what she knew about the investigation, I could tell they had already been conspiring while I was out. 'You missed him at the Ludi Romani, and you're going to miss him again.'

'Oh, don't be so encouraging. You might build up my confidence.'

'You don't even really know how this piece of scum operates.'

True. We had no evidence, apart from one sighting by Pia and her ghastly boyfriend Mundus, of Asinia being spoken to by someone on foot. The man they saw might be totally unconnected with the murders. Asinia could have been picked up later, by a cart, chariot, carriage, a man with a donkey – or for all I knew Perseus swooping down on his winged horse. 'The nearest we have to a suspect is a driver.'

Maia tossed her head. 'Some hunch you and Lucius Petronius dreamed up!'

'Trust us.'

'Pardon me, Marcus. How can I do that? I *know* you and Petro!'

'Then you know we have had our successes.' I was trying to keep my temper. Faced with girls with wild theories, always appear open to suggestion.

'What I know is you're a pair of loons.'

I appealed to Helena Justina. She had been listening with the downcast air of a woman who knows it will be her task to be sensible, whatever her heart says. 'Ours is a good idea, Marcus, but I can see why you're nervous –'

'It's far too dangerous.'

'You would be there to protect us.'

'I appreciate the offer. You both mean too much to me, and I don't want you to do it. I can't lock you in –'

'You'd better not try!' interrupted Maia.

All I could do was to ask them to assure me they would listen to my warning and not try anything stupid after I was gone. They heard me with pitying expressions, then gave promises of good behaviour so solemnly that it was obvious they would do whatever they liked.

It was time to sharpen my knife and attune my mind to danger. I had no time to deal with these two when they were trying to annoy me.

There are men who would let the women they love take a risk in a desperate cause. Helena and Maia were courageous and clever; if we ever did use decoys they would be an excellent choice. But using decoys was far too dangerous. Something unexpected was bound to happen. A mistake or a trick would leave them exposed. It takes only a second for a man to grab a girl, then cut her throat and silence her for ever.

'Stay at home, please,' I begged them as I went off on my watch that night. Maybe they had been holding further discussions while I was preparing myself for action, because they both kissed me quietly, like well-behaved sweethearts. My heart sank.

They seemed far too amenable. Were they planning to try out their crazy scheme without telling me? Dear gods, I was in enough trouble.

LV

W̶E WATCHED OUTSIDE the Circus all night. Once again I was
patrolling the Street of the Three Altars; Petro set up camp at
the Temple of the Sun and Moon. It was mild, clear-skied and
humid. Not too hot, yet enough to generate an exciting atmosphere. Girls were floating about the streets in flimsy dresses, their
shoulder brooches half unpinned and their sideseams agape while
they burrowed happily in their packets of nuts and sweetmeats,
hardly looking around to see who might be ogling and following
them. Bare-armed, bare-necked, bare-headed: open invitations to
lust. I had never seen so many carefree and confident Roman
women, all apparently oblivious of their physical insecurity.

I was losing heart. There were far too many people, far too few
of us on duty, far too many exits from the Circus, far too many
streets where unwary home-goers might be picked up in the dark.

We stayed there until we were dropping. Our concentration was
stretched unendurably, not least because we were so unsure who we
were looking for amongst the throng. The Games had ended, the
litters and chairs had come and gone, the prostitutes and drunks had
taken over the district, and then even they went home. As first light
began to show, I walked along to the Temple. Petro and I stood
together for a few minutes, looking around.

The streets and temple steps were strewn with litter. Stray dogs
and huddled vagrants rooted among the debris. A few lamps
dwindled. There was silence at last, broken only by occasional disturbing noises from dark alleyways.

'If he was here, then we missed him,' said Petronius in a low
voice. 'He may have got someone.'

'What do you think?'

'I hope not.'

'But what do you *think*, partner?'

'Don't ask, Falco.'

We walked home together wearily to Fountain Court.

LVI

HELENA WOKE ME around midday. She brought me a drink, put the baby in my arms, then snuggled up on the bed at my side while I slowly came to.

I freed a strand of her hair which had become trapped under my elbow. 'Thanks for being here when I came in.' I was pretending to joke about the threats she and Maia had made. 'Did I wake you?'

'I never really went to sleep. I just dozed, worrying about you out there.'

'Nothing happened.'

'No,' said Helena quietly. 'But if you had seen him, you would have gone after him. I was worried about that.'

'I can take care of myself.'

She nestled closer, saying nothing. I lay silent myself, worrying about leaving her every night, knowing that when she thought I was doing something dangerous she stayed awake for hours, opening her eyes at every sound and sometimes even jumping up to look out down the street for my return.

With me home in her arms, Helena slipped into a doze. The baby was awake, briefly clean, charming, kicking her feet contentedly, hardly a dribble in sight. I caught her looking up at me as if she was deliberately testing her audience. She had Helena's eyes. If we could bring her safely through the dangerous childhood years, when so many lost their hold on life, then one day she would have Helena's spirit too. She would be off out there, freeborn in her own city, probably half the time without telling us where she had gone.

Women should take care. The sensible ones knew that. But Rome had to allow them to forget sometimes. Being truly free meant enjoying life without the risk of coming to harm.

Sometimes I hated my work. Not today.

Julius Frontinus came for a conference that afternoon. I loved him for his blunt approach, but the constant fear that his honour would walk in did cramp my style. Still, he had had the courtesy to let his night-patrol take their rest first.

I stepped out to the porch and whistled across to Petronius. There was no response, but almost immediately he came loping up the street. I signalled; he joined us. We all sat together, accompanied by the quiet sound of Julia Junilla's cradle as Helena gently worked the rocker with her foot.

We spoke in subdued voices. Petro and I reported on our negative results last night.

'I have seen the Prefect of Vigiles this morning.' Frontinus could be relied on to chivvy and chase. 'He had a round-up from his officers. They caught various minor offenders who might have got away with it if we had not had the Circus surrounded and the city gates watched, but nobody who seems implicated in our quest.'

'Have any women been reported missing this morning?' I asked. I sounded hoarse, not wanting to hear the answer.

'Not so far.' Frontinus was subdued too. 'We should be glad.' We were, of course, although having nothing further to go on gave us no material help.

'At least we didn't miss someone being snatched.'

'You have nothing to reproach yourselves with,' said Helena. Seated in her round-backed wicker chair she seemed slightly apart from the conference, but it was understood she was listening in. In my household debates were full-family affairs.

Helena knew what I was thinking. I had once cursed myself bitterly when a young girl was murdered and I had felt I could have prevented it. That was in the past, but I still sometimes tortured myself turning over whether I should have acted differently. I still hated the killer for leaving me with his crime on my own conscience.

I had been brooding too much recently about Helena's dead uncle, the man whose corpse Vespasian had had me dispose of in the Great Sewer. It was his daughter, Helena's young cousin, who had been killed. Sosia. She had been sixteen: bright, beautiful, inquisitive, blameless and fearless – and I had been half in love with her. Ever since then, I had never quite trusted my ability to protect women.

'I had a message from the man we sent to the Porta Metrovia stables,' said Petro, interrupting my thoughts. 'Apparently Damon, the driver we're suspicious about, has been staying there full time. It's exactly what he is supposed to do. He goes to the chop-house next door, buys himself a drink, and makes it last for hours. He does try to chat up the waitress, but she isn't having it.'

'And he was there all last night?' asked Frontinus, yearning to hear something which would implicate the driver.

'All night,' Petro gloomily confirmed.

'So that exonerates Damon?'

'Only for last night.'

'Damon should not be your killer,' Helena reminded us quietly. 'Damon is said to remain at the Porta Metrovia in case his mistress requires her carriage. Whoever killed Asinia abducted her in Rome yet threw her hand into the Anio within a matter of days – and then he drove back here to dispose of her head and torso at the end of the Games. If he follows the same pattern during these Games, maybe the vigiles can catch him among the traffic through the Tiburtina Gate – though at a fatal price for some poor woman, I'm afraid.'

'Only commercial traffic left last night,' Frontinus assured her. He must have really dragged details out of the Prefect of Vigiles.

'Can't the killer be a commercial driver of some sort – one who just happens to come from Tibur?'

'He's a private driver. He is delivering somebody for the festivals, then fetching them home again afterwards,' I said, convinced of it. 'That's why he makes two trips.'

'But not Aurelia Maesia, apparently,' Petro added with a grunt.

'No. Helena's right. We're letting ourselves be distracted by Aurelia and Damon. We're too desperate; if we aren't careful we'll miss something.'

'This morning when I was waiting for you to wake up,' Helena said, 'I had a thought. I knew from the quiet way you came in that nothing could have happened last night. Yet it was the opening of the Games, and you had been certain that that would be when he struck.'

'So, my love?'

'I wondered what was different. I was thinking about the black day. Some people might, as you say, travel to Rome early for these Games, to avoid a bad luck day. Last month the Ludi Romani started three days after the Kalends not two, so it didn't arise. That time the killer struck on the opening day of the Games, and you're assuming that's significant. But suppose whoever he brings is not particularly bothered about the grand parade? If they didn't want to travel on a bad luck day, they might just come up a day *later*.'

'You mean, he's not here yet!'

'Well, it's a thought. While you were all outside the Circus waiting for an attack last night, he might just have been arriving in
Rome.'

I glanced at Petronius, who nodded glumly. 'It's all to do again
tonight, Petro.'

'I wasn't intending to relax.'

I meant to say we ought to look through the lists of vehicles that
came in last night from Tibur, but the conversation sheered off in a
slightly different direction. 'We need a strategy in case the killer does
strike,' Julius Frontinus put in. 'Of course we all hope he will be
observed just before or during an abduction. But let's be realistic;
that would take a great deal of luck. If we miss it, and if he sets off
with his victim, there may have to be a pursuit.'

'If he leaves the city boundary, the vigiles have no jurisdiction.'

Frontinus gave me a look. 'It's up to you two then. You won't
lack support. I have made some arrangements. The crimes are being
committed in Rome, so if a pursuit is needed men can be allocated
from the Urban Cohorts –' Petronius, who loathed the Urbans,
muffled a groan. 'I have a whole cohort on the alert at the
Praetorian Camp, with a fleet of horses saddled up. The magistrate
who will hear the case if it comes to court will have to provide a
chit for the Urban Prefect. It's all set up, but we need a name for the
arrest warrant –'

'Which magistrate?' asked Petro.

'One called Marponius. Have you come across him?'

'We know Marponius.' Petro loathed him too. He glanced at me.
If we had a chance to apprehend the killer, we would do it ourselves, in Rome or out of the city – then politely request a warrant
afterwards.

'I want this all carried out correctly,' Frontinus warned, sensing
our rebellion.

'Of course,' we assured him.

Helena Justina bent over the cradle so the ex-Consul could not
see her smile.

After Frontinus had gone, Petronius told me where he had been
earlier. 'Up the Via Lata – halfway to the Altar of Peace. Very smart.
Very select. Big houses with big money living in them, all the way
out along the Via Flaminia.'

'What took you out there?'

'Checking that Aurelia Maesia really was there with her sister.'

'I thought we were now regarding the Damon line of enquiry as defunct?'

'Nobody had told me then! Dear gods, working in the vigiles has its problems, but nothing like the frustrations of working outside them. Look!' He chopped the side of his hand on the table. 'Lying low isn't working —'

'So you wanted to put pressure on?'

'Pressure's what I believe in, Falco.'

I knew he did. But I believed in lying low.

'Well, was old Aurelia there?'

'Both sisters were. Grata is even more short-sighted and decrepit than Maesia, but apparently that doesn't stop them both wobbling off to their seats at the Games every day. In the evening they have friends in to dinner. They can't go out; there's a father who also comes for the family party and he's too feeble to take elsewhere. Jupiter knows how old *he* is!'

'Did you see him?'

'No, the poor duck was asleep.'

'Lucky him!' I was feeling rough. And there were nine days of the Augustales to go yet.

In the early evening I pulled on my best working boots. I wore wrist straps, which I rarely bothered with, and two thick tunics. I had a cloak, my knife in one boot, a purse for bribes. I bathed and lightly exercised, then had a shave to fill in an hour and warm me up cursing the barber's clumsiness.

Petronius would be wasting time in tedious confabulations with his colleagues in the vigiles. I let him go on ahead to get it over with. With nothing better to do myself, I walked over by way of the Via Appia to the Porta Metrovia. I wanted to meet Damon. The indications were that he was *not* our killer, but he might know something useful about his fellow drivers from the Tibur area. I had decided it was time to question Damon directly.

The stables where Aurelia Maesia kept her carriage while she visited her sister were the usual crowded hovels with large rats sitting up and grinning in the mangers while thin cats ran away in fear. Donkeys, mules and horses risked hoof rot while dowdy grooms committed sodomy on unturned straw. There were conveyances for hire at inflated prices, and relays of better-quality horses acquired at public expense for use by the Imperial post. Graffiti advertised a farrier-cum-blacksmith, but his anvil looked cold and his booth lay empty. Next door stood an off-putting tavern with rooms for rent, waitresses who could probably be hired to complete your suite, and a drinks list that proved price regulation was an ancient myth.

I could find neither Damon the gingery driver nor the member of the vigiles who had been assigned to watch and tail him. A waitress whose scowl declared she had reason to remember told me they had both gone out.

LVII

Had all been normal, I was originally intending to call on Marina; I still had a question I wanted to ask her. Now there was no time to stop off at the Street of Honour and Virtue, not even to play the good uncle and visit my niece. Instead I strode quickly to the Temple of the Sun and Moon. There, as arranged, I met Petro and apprised him of the new development. Frontinus had given us use of the public slaves attached to the enquiry; in a trice we had them scampering in all directions, passing on the word to the vigiles that everyone should watch out for the red-haired Celtic-looking man with the gammy leg. It sounded like a joke; we knew it could be deadly serious.

'Has he taken the carriage?'

'No, but that's an eye-catching number. It's so big and so flash that he would risk being identified if it were seen near where a woman disappeared. He may go out on foot to grab the girls, then take them back to the stable.'

'If it's him,' Petro dutifully reminded me. But once someone under surveillance does something he isn't supposed to, it's easy to allocate to him the role of the villain you're searching for. Petro was forcing himself not to grow too excited. 'Let's not be led astray on this.'

'No. At least it looks as if the tail has stuck with him.'

'He'll get a bonus!' Petro should know that was doubtful in public service. But the man would do a good job. 'Damon doesn't fit!' Petro muttered, but he had a dark look as if he were wondering whether we had somehow missed something vital and Damon was, after all, the man we sought.

All we could do was wait and continue as normal. We were still swapping venues to keep us alert on watch. It was Petro's turn for the Street of the Three Altars, while tonight I took the Temple of the Sun and Moon. He thumped his shoulder in the old legionary salute, then walked off and left me.

It soon grew dark. Above the Circus I could see a faint glow from the thousands of lamps and torches that were lighting the evening spectacles. This time of year the shows could be even more magical than in summer.

It was quieter, much less raucous than the long September evenings of the Roman Games. The Augustales, being closely linked to the Imperial court, tended to be subdued in periods when the court was acting respectably as it was under Vespasian. The applause from the stadium was polite. The musicians were playing at a measured, almost boring pace, allowing them time to slide up to the right pitch when they squeezed out their notes. I almost preferred them playing flat.

'Uncle Marcus!'

A muffled cry made me start. A long, tightly wrapped cloak did its best to hide my most disreputable nephew, although beneath the hem of the sinister disguise his dirty big feet in their outsize boots were unmistakable to associates.

'Jupiter! It's Gaius –' He was slinking along the dark Temple portico, pressing himself against the pillars and adopting a low crouch, with only his eyes showing.

'Is this where you're watching for that man?'

'Come away from there, Gaius. Don't think you look invisible; you're just attracting attention to yourself.'

'I want to help you.'

Since there seemed no harm in it, I described Damon and said if Gaius saw him he was to run for me or one of the vigiles. He should be safe. As far as we knew the aqueduct killer had no taste for lads. Anyway, if he smelt our unwashed Gaius he would soon have second thoughts.

I begged my nephew when he grew tired of surveillance to go home and look after Helena for me. She would keep him out of trouble. After a few whines about unfairness he crept off, still stalking shadows. Groaning, I watched him start to walk with an exaggerated stride, practising giant steps. A child at heart, he was now playing the old game of stepping on cracks in the pavement in case a bear ate him. I could have told him, it was avoiding the cracks that mattered.

It was to be a night of irritations, apparently. I had hardly freed myself from Gaius when a new scourge sidled out of the shadows. 'What's this, Falco?'

'Anacrites! In the name of the gods, will you lose yourself, please?'

'On observation?'

'Shut up!'

He squatted down on the temple steps, like a layabout watching the crowds. He was too old and too swankily styled to pass muster for an off-duty altar boy. But he had the gall to say, 'You really stand out up here on your own, Falco.'

'If idiots like you would just leave me alone I could lounge against a pillar with a fistful of cold rissole looking like a lad's who's waiting for a friend.'

'You're in the wrong gear,' he pointed out. 'I could spot you as a plant from half a street away. You look ready for action. So what's moving tonight?'

'If you're staying at this temple, then *I'm* moving!'

He stood up slowly. 'I could help, you know.'

If we lost the killer because I turned down his offer, nobody in officialdom would accept the simple plea that I considered him an idiot. Anacrites was the Chief Spy. He was on sick leave, reallocated to light duties at the water board, but ultimately he worked for the establishment, just like me.

All the same, if Anacrites caught the killer because I passed him a clue, then Petronius Longus would strangle me. I could cope with that, but not the other things Petro would do to me first.

'We're still on general watch: any man who looks at women suspiciously. Especially if he has transport.'

'I'll keep my eyes open.'

'Thanks, Anacrites.' I managed to say it without bile rising.

To my relief he moved off, though he was heading on a course that would bring him to the Street of the Three Altars and Petro. Well, Petro could handle Anacrites.

At least I thought he could. However, unknown to me, my stalwart partner was no longer there.

It was a dreary night. It seemed more tedious than usual. At regular intervals the applause rippled skywards from the Circus. Bursts of ear-splitting music from the *cornu* bands disturbed my weary reverie. A slow trickle of exiting ticket-holders began early.

The crowds started to disperse more quickly than they had after the Ludi Romani, as if people sensed the approaching chill of autumn evenings, though in fact a warm and sunny day was ending in a perfect late summer night. I served my watch beneath swarms of bats, and then under the stars.

Enjoying the night too, the crowds slowed up again. Men suddenly discovered a need for one more drink in a bar. Women lingered, chatting, though eventually they flung their bright stoles around them — for effect rather than necessity on this balmy night — shook out the creases from their clinging skirts and strolled off amid plenty of chaperons. The Augustales were very restrained Games. Too respectable for the hardcore rabble. Too staid for the keenest race-goers. Lacking the pagan edge of longer-established series whose histories of spilt blood went back for centuries. Honouring a man-made, *self*-made gód lacked the gut attraction of the old Games that had been inaugurated under more ancient, more mysterious deities.

Strange rites had been enacted, however, for instance a visit to the second-day events by five pistachio-chewing, mulsum-swigging, parasol-wielding, late-staying, man-baiting members of the Braidmakers' Old Girls. Their leader was the loudest, crudest, brightest, boldest wench that I had seen all night. She was, of course, Marina: the fast, fickle mother of my favourite niece.

'Oh, Juno — it's Falco, girls!' How could anyone so beautiful in repose become so raucous when she spoke? Easily, in Marina's case. Just as well, perhaps. Armed with breeding and refinement too, she would have been desperately dangerous. 'Let's chase him around the Temple and see who can rip his tunic off!'

'Hello, Marina.' I sounded pompous already.

'Hello, you bastard. Can you lend me some money?'

'Not tonight.' Lending to Marina could only be viewed as a form of civic charity, though nobody put up a statue to you in return for doing it. 'Where are you off to?' At least she seemed sober. I was wondering how to get rid of her.

'Home, dearie. Where else? Marcia likes me to sing her a lullaby.'

'No, she doesn't.'

'That's right — she hates it. I just like to remind the little madam who's in charge.'

I refrained from saying that her mother had stopped out so late, little Marcia would be getting up for a new day soon.

The other retired braid-knotters were bobbing around my brother's girlfriend like a flock of vibrant, slightly uncoordinated birds. They went in for giggles and whispered bad language. They were worse than the marauding schoolgirls who normally patrolled in packs looking for boys to harass. These women had learned how to wield their power, and in the long process had gained nothing but contempt for men. No shred of romance was allowed to besmirch their brashness. They wanted to terrify me. The gods only knew what they would do if they achieved it.

'I've been looking for you –' I said.

'*Oooh!*' Marina's escort set up a round of mock-shocked twittering. I groaned.

'You dirty dog!'

'Settle down; this is business –'

'*Ooh-hoo!*' They were off again.

'Rome's finest,' I commented. 'As highly commendable as Cornelia, the mother of the Gracchi!'

'Oh, don't go on –' Marina had a short attention span, even for making life a misery for a man. 'What do you want, Falco?'

'A question. That night we met in the Forum –'

'When that weird girl threw up over the Vestals?'

'I thought she was a friend of yours?'

'Never met her before. Never seen her since. No idea who she was. She was feeling a bit demoralised so I thought I ought to see her home.' Ah well. Clearly the Braidmakers were a loving sisterhood.

'Well, never mind her – it's not the girl I'm curious about. Who was the man in the carriage that went by, the man you were shouting at?'

'What carriage?' asked Marina, totally unaware she had done anything of the sort. Her current friends reduced their bad behaviour to shuffling about impatiently. Bored with me, they were already looking around for somebody different to tyrannise. 'I never shout at men in the Forum; don't insult me, Marcus Didius.'

I described how the vehicle had appeared out of the darkness, and how I had overheard what sounded like a ribald exchange with somebody Marina thought she knew.

Marina thought about it.

I stood quietly, allowing her to pilot her thoughts woozily around the very small piece of human tissue that served her as a brain. I had learned from experience that this process could take time. I also knew it would probably not be worth it, but I was the kind of dumb professional who always had to try.

'What do you mean by a carriage?' she demanded.

'Things on wheels; horse in front; person or persons can travel long distances in huge discomfort at unbearable expense –'

'Gods, you do like to mess around, Marcus! I must have thought it was the one I see sometimes.'

'Don't you remember? Are you guessing now?'

'Oh, I'm sure I will remember if I think about it long enough – to tell you the truth, I was somewhat incapable of noticing much that night.'

'Well, that's frank.'

Marina was still slowly pondering. A neat frown creased her alabaster forehead; some men might have wanted to smooth away the creases, but I was on the verge of imprinting them there with a clenched fist. 'It can't have been him, or he would have stopped; we have a chat if I pass him.'

'Who are we talking about?'

'A fellow who parks in our street. We all have a great laugh over it. You'll love this. He brings his master to visit – respectable people, very prim family – but what they don't know is: the night before he arrives looking pious at their house, the master drops off to visit some old girl. She used to be a professional, and he's her last loyal client. He looks about a hundred; heaven knows what they can get up to. We never see her; she can hardly totter to the window to wave him off next day.'

'What's his name?'

'The master or the driver? Don't ask me. I don't inspect people's birth certificates just to pass the time of day.'

'Where do they come from? Is it outside Rome? Could it be somewhere like Tibur?'

'I shouldn't think so,' murmured Marina. 'You said it was a carriage, but it's not what I would call one. I'm talking about one of those sit-up-and-suffer carts like a box on two big wheels.'

'No covering, but they nip along? Get away! The old fellow can't sit up on front?'

'Oh, he clings on manfully.'

'Have they been in your street this week?'

'I haven't noticed.' Marina had a slightly shifty look; I guessed she wanted to avoid telling me she had been out a lot, dumping Marcia somewhere else. There was no point in trying to pursue that.

'This driver isn't a small red-haired man with a limp?'

'Oh, gods, where do you think them up? No; he's a man, so he's ugly – but ordinary.' Once again I reluctantly acknowledged that this was not our convenient suspect Damon.

'Does he flirt?'

'How would I know?' scoffed Marina, drawing herself up indignantly. 'What's this about?'

I spoke gently: 'Oh, I just wondered if the vehicle we saw in the Forum belonged to the man who must have been there that night throwing the head of a murdered woman down the Cloaca Maxima.'

She went pale. Her fluttery friends grew still. 'You're trying to frighten me.'

'Yes, I am. All of you, take care tonight. Marina, if you see this sit-up-and-suffer cart, try to find me or Petronius.'

'Is it him? The bastard you're looking for?'

'It doesn't sound quite right, but I need to check. If it's not him, the real bastard is still likely to be out and about.'

I told her I would be coming to see her tomorrow and would want her to point out the house of the ancient prostitute, who would have to be interviewed. So much for the Street of Honour and Virtue. As usual, it was living up flagrantly to its charming name.

I stayed at the Temple until nearly dawn. I saw nothing relevant.

What Marina had said was niggling me. While I waited far longer than usual for Petro, I realised I badly wanted to consult with him. He must be clinging on until the very last minute, reluctant to admit we had wasted another night.

I walked down the temple steps, taking care not to step on any cracks in case I alerted the pavement bears. I began to pace round the Circus in search of Petro. If he was there, I never found him. Instead, by the now closed grand exit gate under its arch in the centre of the apse, I saw something that caught my attention. Torches. They were bright, and apparently newly lit, whereas the few lamps left in the streets had all faded to a dim flicker.

I had run into a group of slaves, led by a young man in patrician whites whom I recognised immediately. From his anxious behaviour I knew before I even called his name that he was in some kind of trouble.

'Aelianus!'

Helena's least favourite brother had been rushing to and fro out-side the Circus gate. When he saw me, pride made him slow and straighten up. 'Falco!' It came out with too much urgency. He knew that I knew he was desperate. 'Marcus Didius – perhaps you can help me.'

'What's wrong?' I had a bad feeling.

'Nothing, I hope – but I seem to have lost Claudia.'

The feeling was correct then: and a nightmare had begun.

LVIII

'How long has she been missing?'
    'Oh, gods! Hours!'
'*Hours?*'
'Since this evening –'
I gave the dawn sky a meaningful glance. 'Last night.'
'You don't have to tell me! This is terrible – and we're expecting her grandparents any day now –'
He pulled himself up, shaking his head at himself for clinging to such trivialities. I had wanted to see Aelianus in misery, but not like this. He was arrogant, crass and snobbish, and had hurt Helena very much by criticising us. Now he stood in the street, a hot, bothered, stocky young figure trying to bluff it out. I knew, and he must appreciate, that he was staring at a tragedy.
'Keep calm.' Relief at having somebody to share his grief nearly made him useless. I gripped his shoulders to stop him panicking. The smart white cloth of his handsomely napped tunic was soaked with sweat.
'Claudia wanted to go to the Games and I didn't. I dropped her off –'
'By herself? I'm no social prude, but she's a young girl, and a stranger to Rome!'
'Justinus used to go with her, but –' Justinus had gone abroad. This was not the time to ask his brother why.
'So you left her. Do your parents know that?'
'They know now! When I came to pick her up as we had arranged, Claudia failed to meet me. Then I made a lot of mistakes.'
'Tell me.'
'I looked everywhere. I was annoyed with her at first – I nearly went off in disgust for a drink –' I said nothing. 'I assumed she was tired of waiting. Claudia does not have a high opinion of my organising powers.' It sounded as though there might be more to this than

268

a lovers' tiff. 'I thought she must have given up on me and walked home.'

I bit back an angry exclamation of *Alone?*

It was not far. Up to the start of the Street of the Three Altars, and turn right down the Via Appia. You could see the Capena Gate from the first crossroads, behind the Aqua Appia and Aqua Claudia. To reach the Camillus house would take only a few minutes for Aelianus, frantically hurrying, and not much longer even for Claudia. She would know the way. She would feel safe.

'So you rushed back home?'

'No luck.'

'Did you confess to your father?'

'Another mistake! I was ashamed. I tried to put things right myself – I quietly grabbed all the slaves I could find and came back to search. It was no good, of course. I went into the Circus but everyone near her seat had left. Of course the aediles in charge just laughed at me. I went home; told Papa; he is informing the vigiles while I keep searching –'

'You're too late.' There was nothing to gain by sparing him the truth. Claudia Rufina was a sensible, thoughtful girl. Far too considerate to be merely playing up. 'Aulus –' I rarely called him by his private name. 'This is very serious.'

'I understand.' No excuses. No wild self-reproach either, though I could see he blamed himself. Well, I knew how that felt. 'Will you help me, Falco?'

I shrugged. This was my job. The Camilli were in part my family anyway.

'You don't know the worst.' Aelianus was gritting his teeth to confess. 'Earlier I spoke to an itinerant food-seller. The man said he had seen a girl who matched my description of Claudia waiting alone by the gate. A little while later she was talking to the driver of a vehicle – a cart, he said, but he was unsure exactly. He thought she got in, then she was driven off at speed.'

'Which direction?'

He had no idea, of course. Nor had he demanded a description of whoever was driving her. And the food-seller was long gone.

We sent the slaves home.

I walked Aelianus briskly to the Street of the Three Altars. That was when I found a member of the vigiles on Petro's usual spot, and he told me Petronius had gone off somewhere.

'Where in Hades is he?'

'Following a suspect, sir.'

'What suspect?'

'Ginger, with the bad leg.'

'Here? Damon? He had a vigiles tail on him!' Besides, we had all agreed: Damon was not our suspect.

'Petro went along to share the job. He said things here had gone dead. He was following his nose.'

'When was this?'

'Way back. He ordered me to wait here, but everyone's gone home now. I was just coming to tell you to give up expecting him.'

I swore under my breath. 'Was Damon alone?'

'Had a woman with him.'

'Smart girl in a white dress, rather big nose?'

'No. Filthy piece in a red skirt, showing her legs.' He could have switched later. Girls who show their legs can often sense trouble. Red skirt might have ditched him. Claudia would have appeared a much easier target – but Damon could still be with the red skirt, while somebody else had Claudia. If so, we had no idea who.

'Find where they got to. Find Petro. Tell him – no; first get a message to your commander: a respectable girl has been abducted this evening while we all stood around like bloody wall paintings. Whoever took her has transport. In case he hasn't left the city yet, we need every vehicle that's on the road tonight searched – and we need to start now. Concentrate in the eastern districts; he will be heading for Tibur.'

The stand-in watcher looked worried: 'There won't be much moving; most vehicles have been and gone.'

'Oh, I know that!'

I grabbed Aelianus. He was white-faced, his straight hair flopping anyhow, his heart about to burst.

'Aulus, I'll do all I can. If she's still alive, I'll get her back for you. But I can't promise anything, so prepare yourself.'

He took it well. 'What shall I do?'

I scrutinised him briefly. He had controlled his panic. He was one of a bright family. I didn't like him, but I could trust his tenacity. 'I need an arrest warrant, but we don't yet know a name. Do your best for me. The man who arranged everything is the ex-Consul Frontinus; he knows your father. The magistrate who has to issue the document is called Marponius.' Quickly I gave him addresses for both. 'They don't look like stop-outs, so you ought to be able to find them. Get Marponius to issue the chit for "the abductor of Claudia Rufina". That should be specific enough. Rush it to the Praetorian Camp. The Urban Cohorts can then ride after this villain if he has left Rome.'

'What about you, Falco?'

'I'll go straight to the camp now and try to persuade them to mount up. If I can't shift them without the warrant, I'll go ahead alone.'

'I'll come with you –'

'No! I need you to organise some back-up for me, Aulus!' I could not take him, knowing what I might eventually find. For a lad of twenty-three to lose his future wife like this would be terrible enough. He must be spared seeing what was done to her. 'The warrant is vital. Then you can do something else for me: Helena will be expecting me home. She'll grow frantic if I don't arrive. Please go and tell her what's happening.' Helena would understand that he must not be allowed to follow me.

He was her brother so he could take another message too: 'Give her my love – and if you really want to be a hero, force yourself to kiss my child for me.'

Well, that should keep reluctant young Uncle Aulus occupied.

LIX

E VERYTHING WAS STILL against me.
   As I set off, all the battered wine wagons and marble carts in
Rome were struggling to leave the city before dawn. After the
Games ended the private hire transport had taken off the audience
and then dispersed. I had to walk. From the Circus to the Praetorian
Camp is a damned long way.

By the Gardens of Maecenas I shoved a drunk off a donkey, com-
mandeering it for the Empire. The drunk didn't care. He was out of
it. The donkey put up a fight, but I was in a hard mood. I kicked
him into action and cajoled him the rest of the way to the Porta
Tiburtina with a stick I found; there I fell off just as the vigiles were
preparing to disperse.

'Hold it! Urgent – have any private vehicles left this way tonight?'

'Oh, shit, Falco. It's been a heavy night; there's been hundreds.'

'Got the list?'

'We thought we were finished; we've already sent it off to the
Prefect.'

'Help me out, lads – a big four-horse carriage, or a sit-up-and-
beg?'

'Could well have been, but don't ask us!'

'Jupiter – you're a disgrace to public office! Is this why I paid my
census tax?'

'Give over – who coughs up the tax?'

'Not enough people to pay for an efficient watch, apparently.
Stop here. Don't argue – the creep has snatched a young girl who
was to marry a senator. We've got to find her. Search *everything* that
comes this way and try to get word to the other city gates –'

I hauled my stolen donkey back into service. We went under the
arcade of the Anio Vetus, then rode parallel to the huge triple mass
of the Aqua Marcia, carrying both the Tepula and the Julia above it.
Unplanned originally, the newer channels were not even centred;
the arches had had to be reinforced, but even so the top cover of the

Marcia was cracking due to the uneven distribution of weight . . . Thanks to Bolanus, I knew these details intimately. I also knew what might be floating down in their waters soon.

I forced the donkey to the Praetorian Camp. As always it was a bad experience. The camp itself is a monstrous spread in the shadow of the Servian Walls, mirrored by an even more gigantic parade ground that takes up most of the space between the Viminal and Colline gates; the troops inside are bastards to a man.

It was fairly quiet for once. So quiet I had the odd experience of hearing the beasts roaring in the Imperial menagerie just outside the city. From a clubroom nearby my ears were assailed by the distinctive noise of Guardsmen finishing off their routine fifteen flagons a night. The set of bullies on the gate must have been halfway there too, but they carried it well. The wine made them slow to respond to an emergency, but infused them with a certain wild flair once they got the hang of things. A kind soul patted my donkey, who responded by biting him. The burly Guardsman was so tough – or so tipsy – he never felt a thing.

The centurion of the Urbans who had been instructed to stay on alert to help us was a neat, mild soul who had turned in for an early night. Nice to think of the hard-baked and notorious city guardians having a quiet read in their tidy bunks then blowing out their lamps while the city rampaged, untroubled by their attentions. After an agonising wait, he turned up in a long Greek nightshirt just to tell me that without a judge's warrant he was going back to bed. I advised him to check how much pension he had collected in the regimental savings bank, because for exile in further Armenia it might not be enough. He sniffed, and left.

In despair, I heard myself pouring out my troubles to the Praetorian duty watch. These big lads in shiny breastplates were a soft touch for a heartbreaking tale. Ever keen to put one over on the Urbans, whom they regarded as inferior barrack companions, they led me to the prepared horses, and wittily suggested that they should look the other way while I snuck off with one. I thanked them, pointed out that the horses were in fact mules, then chose the best.

First light was blossoming above the Seven Hills as I spent half an hour kick-starting my stubborn mount, then galloped out of Rome on the Via Tiburtina, chasing after a killer who might not even have come this way.

LX

IT WAS TWENTY miles, and probably more than that, from Rome to Tibur. As I rode out in the cold, grey early morning there was ample time for thinking. Most of my thoughts were bad. The easiest to bear was that I had totally misjudged events, and was making a pointless journey. Claudia would turn up; she might be safely at home already. If she had actually been abducted, Petronius Longus or somebody else might have seen it and arrested the man; while I was looking for Petro on the streets he could have been sequestered in some patrol house, applying hooks to the killer's anatomy. Or the vehicle searches that I had ordered might discover the girl before she came to harm. Her abductor might be arrested at the city gates. My last hope was that even if she was now on her way to Tibur, helpless and terrified – assuming she was still alive – I might manage to overtake her kidnapper . . .

I would find her. Nothing would stop me. But she was probably already dead. In view of what she might have had to endure first, I almost prayed that by now she was.

For the first few hours I saw nobody. I travelled out on the empty Campagna, the only traveller on the road. It was far too early even for the farmers to have woken. Now the mule had settled into his rhythm, the music of his galloping hooves soothed my panic. I tried not to think directly about Claudia, so instead I remembered Sosia.

Hers was another death I could have and should have prevented. She had grown up with Helena's family, another young girl they cherished, for whose terrible loss they would always blame me. We never spoke of it, but none of us would ever forget. Sosia and Helena had been very close. At first Helena had blamed me bitterly for her young cousin's death, though she had allowed herself to forgive me. How could I expect her to overlook the same fault a second time? Aelianus would by now have told her that Claudia had gone missing: every moment that passed on my solitary journey was a moment Helena would spend at home fretting over the dark fate of her young friend, losing faith in me and worrying about me at the same time. I had lost faith in myself before I left the Tiburtina Gate.

It grew light. I was riding into the sun. It shone low over the Sabine Hills, somewhere perhaps lighting a hovel where scores of poor women had been tortured, killed, and cut up. The tricky light made me more weary than I was already. Squinting into the glare sapped my fading concentration. It made me irritable and heartsick. I had spent too many hours riding against time on filthy quests to free the world of villains. Worse villains only arose to take their places. Fouler in their habits, more vindictive in their attitudes.

People in the farmhouses were beginning to stir. I began to meet country carts. Most were coming the wrong way, towards Rome. Those I passed heading east delayed me frustratingly while I searched them. Angry at these hold-ups, which I dared not omit, I grew sick of cabbage nets and turnips, damson punnets and leaky skins of wine. Toothless old men who smelled of garlic held me up as they slowly pulled coverings aside. Excited youths with untrustworthy eyes stared ghoulishly. I asked them all if they had been passed by another vehicle; those who denied it sounded as if they were lying, those who thought they might have been were only saying what I obviously wanted to hear.

I hated the Campagna. I hated the dreamers and dawdlers who lived on it. I hated myself. Why did I do this? I wanted to be a poet, working in some peaceful library, cut off from the midden of humanity, absorbed in my own unreal world of the mind. (Supported financially by a millionaire patron in love with the arts. Falco? No chance!)

Midday found me well on, in fact already at Aquae Albulae. There my initial spurt ended. The mule was tiring rapidly. I too was stiff and half dead. I had been up all night. I desperately needed rest, and just had to hope the killer would pause on the road too. He couldn't know I was following.

I stabled the beast and plunged into the warm sulphur baths. I went to sleep. Someone pulled me out before I drowned; I snatched a couple of hours dead to the world on the masseur's slab, face down under a towel, with flies dancing themselves silly all over my exposed parts. Badly bitten and groggy, I came to, bought food and drink, and tried to swap my mule at a tiny mansio where they kept a relay for the official couriers.

'My journey's vital – for the state – but I came away too fast to collect a pass. I've found this in my purse, though –' The man in charge took the token I offered without curiosity. Aquae Albulae was a relaxed hole. 'Afraid it's time-expired.'

He shrugged, tossing it into a bowl. 'Oh dear, I'll have to say to the auditors "Which of the evil blighters slipped me that, then?" and look thick.'

'Also, it's made out to the Governor of Baetica,' I confessed.

'Nice fellow, I'm sure. That grey's a good horse.'

'Thanks! I hope my reinforcements will come through here soon. Tell them Falco says gee up, will you?'

I ate on the hoof.

Seven fast Roman miles later I was entering Tibur on the grey.

Now I was in the kind of quandary only I could impose on myself: I had come to catch a man I didn't know, who lived I knew not where, and who at that very moment might be doing the gods knew what to Claudia. In the absence of other bright ideas, I followed my only hunch. Even though all the latest evidence said it was the wrong tack, I turned past the sanctuary of Hercules Victor and took myself to Aurelia Maesia's house.

Time was running out. It must be mid-afternoon. Neither a horseman nor a driver could travel any distance in the dark. If I had to stop later, so would he. And he had a victim for company. Alive or dead. Perhaps alive *now* – but not for much longer once he stopped travelling.

Would he feed her? Would she be able to attend to her other needs? How could it happen, without his risking discovery? He must have her trussed up, silenced and out of sight. She had been with him for a night and almost a day now. Even if I managed to rescue her, she would never be the same again.

As I approached Aurelia Maesia's villa, I could only hope this would be where I found him. But by then, I was resigned to the fact that I had probably come to the wrong place.

LXI

IT WAS PERFECTLY clear that Aurelia Maesia was not expected home for days. The slaves were all out on a terrace, sunning themselves. Garden tools leant neatly against a statue. No work was being done. They had borrowed the best lounging chairs and were sprawled in them, so lethargic they could not bring themselves to scramble to their feet even when I appeared. Anyway, if they moved too fast they might have knocked their drinks over.

'Where's Damon?'

'Enjoying himself in Rome.'

'The bastard!' snarled the cook (his official ladyfriend).

'When he goes up to Rome, does he ever drive back in the carriage on his own?'

'Is it likely?' cackled the cook, adding routinely, 'That bastard.'

I was perfectly happy to abuse Damon, but I needed fast answers. Spotting the lad, Titus, I signalled that I would like a word with him and we two moved off.

'Aren't you Gaius the fountain-mender?'

I winked. 'I was working under cover; I expect you realised.' He said nothing. If he felt too betrayed by the deception he would refuse to co-operate. I gave him no time to start feeling annoyed: 'Now's your chance to help in a desperate situation. Listen, Titus: bad things have been going on and I'm trying to catch the villain.'

His eyes were wide. 'Are you talking about Damon?'

'I thought I might be. But I'm starting to get a new idea – tell me: Aurelia Maesia visits her sister. Her name is Aurelia Grata, yes?' Titus nodded. Aurelia *Grata* . . . Somewhere in the murk of the Falco consciousness a memory had stirred. 'And at the sister's house their old father joins them?'

'Yes.'

A bell was now ringing loudly in my tired brain. Echoes then sounded from several directions: 'His name wouldn't be Rosius Gratus?'

'That's right.'

'Lives up on the road to Sublaqueum?'

'Yes.'

I breathed gently. No point rushing this. 'And he travels to Rome too, when his daughter from Tibur is going up for festivals – so does your mistress take him with her?'

'No. The old girl can't stand being penned up with him in the carriage. They get on, but it's best if they don't see too much of each other. That's why he continues to live on his own estate. He likes his drive to Rome in any case. He's a bit of a racer, actually.'

'What's his conveyance?'

'A cisium.'

'What – an old man in a topless two-wheeler, out in all weathers?'

'It's what he's always used.' I could hear Marina saying *Oh, he clings on manfully.*

'Does he go to the Circus with the women?'

'No, he sleeps all day and only wakes up for his dinner.'

'But is Rosius Gratus still a man of the world in other ways?'

Titus blushed. 'Afraid so.'

I raised my eyebrows and grinned. 'He sees a woman?'

'Always has done. It's supposed to be his big secret but we all have a laugh over it. How did you know?'

'Somebody who lives in the same street mentioned it. Well, that's another reason for not travelling with his daughter. Old Rosius surely doesn't drive himself?'

'Someone takes him.'

'And this someone brings home the cisium while the old fellow stays with his daughters, then drives back to fetch the old fellow at the end of the festival?'

'Probably. The old fellow wouldn't need the cisium; I told you, he just nods off on a couch all day. Am I helping?' asked the boy earnestly.

'Very much, Titus. You've told me what I should have worked out for myself days ago. The problem was, I listened to someone I shouldn't have.'

'What do you mean?'

'Somebody told me Rosius Gratus never goes to Rome.'

'That's ridiculous.'

'People tell lies, Titus.' As I turned to find my horse I gazed at him gently. 'You'll learn to look out for it. Take my advice: be especially careful of men who are standing around doing nothing, by the side of a track in a wood.' I swung into the saddle. It was an effort. 'This driver of the cisium – would his name be Thurius?'

'That's him.'

I should have known.

Titus wanted to give me directions, but there was no need: I had to ride up the Via Valeria to the point where the aqueducts were taken from the River Anio, then turn off along the road to Sublaqueum. I had to do it, moreover, not in the whole day it would normally take for such a journey but in the few hours before dark.

I left a message with young Titus in case helpers ever followed me. I had no hope of support now. There was no time for them to get here. I was in this alone.

The Imperial post couriers can ride fifty miles in a day if they change horses, and so could I. Being already in possession of a cursus publicus mount helped me bluff. I managed to swap the grey for a stocky chestnut with a blaze at a relay station just before the road to Horace's Farm. Another lost opportunity to visit the Bandusian Spring. I didn't care now. I had gone right off water.

The light was growing murky. I passed the aqueduct sources at the thirty-fifth and thirty-eighth milestones. On I galloped down the Sublaqueum road for four more miles until I came to the large mud reservoir. I stopped, looking for Bolanus. One of his public slaves soon appeared.

'Bolanus saw a cart drive by earlier. He went after it on a donkey.'

'Alone?'

'We've finished cleaning the basin. There was only him and me and a dragnet. He told me to wait here and warn you if you came.'

'I know where he's gone. Stay here in case help follows me; give them directions to the Rosius Gratus estate, will you?'

Upstream of the sluice that directed water into the basin, I could see the dragnet they had roped up across the river. Chilled, I prayed they had not caught anything today. I rode on, spurred by desperation. Now Bolanus had put himself in danger too. With his stiff back and his dim eye he would be no match for a vicious killer.

At the Rosius Gratus estate I slowed my mare to a canter. On the track to the house I saw nobody. The villa buildings lay silent; no slaves making their own entertainment here. My previous visit had given me the impression there was only a small staff. The housekeeper was here, anyway, because she had heard the horse and came out to investigate.

279

'Name's Falco. I was here the other day. I need a word with Thurius – is he back from Rome?' She nodded. 'What's he doing?'

'No idea. I don't keep track of that one.' She sounded disapproving. It all fitted.

'Where shall I look for him?'

'He should be in the stable, but if not you'll be hard put to find him. He goes off into the woods somewhere.' She looked curious, but was preoccupied with her work and let me go by myself.

'Thanks. If you see him first, don't mention me; I want to give him a surprise.'

'All right.' Obviously they left Thurius to his own devices. That was probably because they found him awkward to deal with. It was all as I expected: a loner; odd habits; unpopular. 'You look all in, Falco.'

'Long day.' And I knew it was not finished yet.

I tried the stable first.

I failed to find the driver, or Bolanus, but I did come across the cisium. Its two horses, still steaming, had been watered and fed. I stabled my own alongside them.

I walked around the elderly vehicle. As everyone had said, it was a high-based simple spin-along. Two big iron-bound wheels and a seat with space for two passengers. Under the seat was built a box, fastened by a strong padlock so that if the cisium was parked its luggage could be safely left. It was locked now.

I banged gently on the box. Nothing. With relief I noticed that what looked like crude air holes had been driven through the planks. I looked around for the key. No luck. Naturally. I had not expected this to be easy.

This was a stable; there had to be tools. I wasted a few seconds doing one of the pointless things you do; trying to pick the lock with a nail. Ridiculous. I was too tired to think straight. A lock that could be undone that way would be useless. I needed something stronger. Keeping an eye out for Thurius, I went and searched the outbuildings until I found a store. As at most remote villas, it was well-equipped. A crowbar partially bent the hooks of the lock, weakening the metal, then I struck it off with one furious blow of a hammer. Sweat poured off me: not from exertion but from sheer anxiety.

I stood still, listening. Nothing moved here or at the house. I braced myself and flung open the box.

There were several filthy smells, human in origin. But apart from some sacking, the source of these odours, there was nothing inside.

LXII

I WOULD HAVE to search the woods.

I wanted to shout her name: *Claudia!* If she could hear my voice it might give her strength to hang on.

It had grown too dark. I went to the house, begging a lantern. I knew I needed help. I asked the housekeeper to summon the other slaves who worked there. There were not enough of them, yet quite quickly – as though they had been waiting for something to happen – a motley crew of short-legged, shambling, shifty labourers assembled and stared at me.

'Look, you don't know me but my name is Falco and I am working for the government. I have to find Thurius. I believe he has kidnapped a young girl, and he intends to kill her –'

I noticed a few exchanged glances. Nobody had ever voiced suspicions, presumably, yet they were none of them surprised. I fought down my anger. They could have saved who could say how many women and girls. Well, at least they could help me try to rescue Claudia now.

'If you think you see him, don't approach. Just yell loudly for the rest of us.'

They did not need telling twice.

We patrolled the woods from dusk until it grew too dark to carry on even with torches. We called. We searched cattle byres and woodstacks. We thwacked bushes with branches, startling wildlife who had lived in the coppices undisturbed for years. We set up flares along the track and in clearings. A loose donkey did wander out of a thicket to greet us; it must be the one that Bolanus had used, though there was no sign of him. Thurius never showed himself and we never flushed him out, but he must have been there, and he must have realised we were after him.

My lack of stealth was deliberate. It was my last hope of deterring him from touching the girl.

I kept them at it all night. Wherever he was sheltering, I had to pin him down as long as it was dark. We kept the racket up, moving from place to place until eventually the first rays of light began to slide across the placidly running waters of the Anio. Then I passed the word that everyone was to sit tight, stop calling out, and keep absolutely still while we watched for Thurius to emerge from his hiding place.

I had spent much of the night near the river. Something drew me there and held me. I had snatched some rest, crouching down on my heels with my back to a tree bole, while my brain raced and continued listening. Now I was awake, as much as a man can be who has not seen a bed for two nights.

As the first light crept over the hills, I walked to the riverbank quietly and washed my face. The water was cold. So was the air, much chillier up in these hills than back in Rome. It was so early that sound carried a vast distance. I let the water from my cupped hands ripple back into the river as gently as possible, making no more noise than the splashing of a mountain trout.

Against a stone in the water something bright just showed in the early light. I bent down and stared. It was an earring. Not a pair to the one Bolanus had shown me; that would be too great a coincidence. This was a simple hoop, probably not even gold. There was a socket for a pendant bead, but that was missing. I dipped my fist into the cold river for it, then turned back to land, pausing to shake off the water and shove the jewellery into my purse. Standing there in the Anio I suddenly felt exposed. The killer must be very close. If he knew I was here, he could even be watching me.

I clambered up the bank, making more noise than I intended. Then I noticed something. Under some low-growing trees stood a small shack. In last night's darkness I had missed it. There was nothing much to it, just sagging walls and a hump-shouldered roof. Rank, flowerless vegetation snuggled up to its lichen-covered boards, but in the briars round about there were glistening blackberries among huge, rampaging spiders' webs.

All around me was silence, apart from the gentle lapping of the river at my back. I felt like a mythical hero who had finally reached the Oracle, though what was likely to greet me would be neither a hag-born hermit nor a golden sphinx. There was a well-trodden path along the riverbank, but I approached through the undergrowth directly from where I stood. One great web blocked my way. I pushed it aside with a stick, courteously allowing the fat spider time to scuttle off into the weeds. All the time my eyes were on the closed door of the shack.

When I reached it the door seemed to be jammed. It opened inwards. There was no lock, but although the top edge gaped a few inches when I leant on it, the bottom stuck. I was trying to be quiet but in the end I forced it open a crack with a mighty shove. Inside something must be lying right up against the door; it was still too dark to make out much, though as I leaned close I was struck by old and disturbing smells. This place must be a fishing hut. It smelt as if pigs had been kept in it but on the Rosius Gratus estate there were no pigs. Just as well, or disposing of bodies would have been easy, and there would have been no long trail of evidence to bring me here from Rome.

Whatever was impeding my progress would have to be moved bodily before I could enter. It felt like the dead weight of a filled wheatsack – or a body. But it was heavier than the body of a young girl. I looked around to see if I could break into the hut some other way. Then I heard a twig snap.

I spun round. A man was standing fifty strides away.

I had only a glimpse before he plunged back into the thicket from which he must have emerged seconds earlier, clearly not knowing I was there. If it was anyone but Thurius he had no need to flee. I yelled and forced my tired limbs to race after him.

He must be better rested than me, but he might not be as fit. I hoped the slaves from the house would help to cut off his escape, but I was disappointed; they must all have sneaked home for their breakfast, ignoring my orders to sit tight. No one answered my cry, and as we crashed through the wood no one rose in our path to intercept.

Everything went quiet. I had lost him somewhere.

'Thurius! The game's up. Show yourself and make an end to this!'

No answer. I could hardly blame him. I was a stranger and he knew every inch of ground. He must be sure he could get away.

He had set off ahead of me working his way towards the track that led off the estate. I thought I heard hoofbeats. I was stricken with visions of Thurius fleeing on horseback all the way to Sublaqueum . . .

There was no hope of shelter at the house. He would realise his fellow slaves would want to establish their own innocence and pay him back for fooling them. Those who had let themselves ignore his strange behaviour over the years would be quick to denounce him now – and if they turned to violence, it wouldn't be the first time a newly discovered killer was bludgeoned to death by the people he had lived among.

I crept through the bushes, aiming for the track. I was watching a pile of long logs, which could hide a prone man behind them. As I edged nearer, Thurius exploded from the undergrowth almost on top of me.

I jumped up, giving him a mighty shock. He had just made a break for freedom, not realising I had worked so near. Before I could throw myself at him, I saw it would be too dangerous: he was now carrying a long axe.

He looked as surprised as me for a moment, but then he recovered angrily. Pulling up short, he growled and swung his weapon.

'Give up, Thurius –'

The blade sliced low, threatening my knees. I moved towards a tree, hoping to trap him into embedding the axeblade in its trunk. He snorted and made another wide, controlled sweep, this time at head level. The little knife I kept in my boot would be no match for this. I didn't even reach for it.

He looked as I remembered: nothing special. Unkempt, badly dressed, missing teeth: a typical rural slave. No more crazed than most passers-by on the streets of Rome. You would avoid knocking into him by accident, but you wouldn't look at him twice. If I was out late at night, and he made the offer casually, I might even accept a lift from him.

'I'm not alone. The Urban Cohorts are riding hard behind. Give yourself up.'

His only reply was another aggressive swipe of the axe, cutting off fine branches above my head. Immediately he followed up with a lower stroke the other way. In the army I had been taught to take on Celts wielding long broadswords this way – but as a soldier I had been armoured, with weapons of my own, not to mention ranks of snarling colleagues forming impenetrable blocks on either side.

I stepped towards him. Light flashed; he whirled the axe again. I leapt like a Cretan dancer, heels to buttocks, saving my legs. Grabbing at a branch, I landed safe then put a tree between us. I managed to crack off the branch partially, but a long green strand of bark peeled back and caught fast. Useless.

Dear gods, this was a town boy's nightmare: I wanted to be walking decent pavements where the criminals followed proper rules of misconduct and where I could drop into a winebar when the pace grew hot. Here I was, facing a desperate axeman in a misty wood, starved, exhausted, deserted by my only helpers, and now risking amputation of my lower limbs. As a way of earning a salary it stank.

I dragged at the branch and this time it broke free. The stem was thick enough to make the axe bite if he hit it. Better still, the far end divided into a mass of twiggy branches, which were still in leaf. As Thurius made his next swing, I dodged the glinting blade. Then I jumped at him, thrusting the great bunch of long twigs full in his face. He started back, stumbled, lost ground. I pressed on, dashing my branch again at his eyes. He turned and ran. I followed but the branch caught in the undergrowth and I lost hold of it. I let it go and kept running.

Thurius was pounding hard, still towards the track. I veered off to one side, putting myself between him and escape from the estate. Smashing down bushes, we struggled on. A fox broke cover suddenly and scampered away. A jay lumbered off with its strange laboured flight and a harsh cry. Once again I fancied I heard hoofbeats, this time much closer. Breathing hurt. Sweat was pouring off me. My aching legs could hardly keep going. Even so, as Thurius reached the track I was gaining; then my foot skidded on a clump of fungi and dropped into a hole, making me pull up with a cry of anguish. I managed to stay upright, but my boot turned over under me. I hopped free of the squashed and slimy toadstool stems, slipped again, then stepped wincingly after Thurius. He stopped and glanced back, then set off down the track.

Ignoring the pain in my ankle I began to hop with what had to be one final sprint. A twisted ankle rights itself, though it prefers time to settle. I had no time. My strength would give out at any moment. But I would catch him first if I could.

I heard a horse whinny. My heart sank, imagining he had a tethered mount somewhere. Then Thurius threw out his arms. Horse and rider had crashed out of the wood on the far side, and were galloping straight at him.

He couldn't stop. He stumbled and lost the axe. The horse reared over him, but was reined back. Thurius staggered, still keeping upright, still determined to escape. He feinted with one arm at the horse, ducked its hooves, and hurled himself down the track again. I had kept running. I crashed past the horse, glimpsing a familiar rider, who dragged it sideways to give me space. Then I caught up and launched myself on to Thurius.

I flung him down, face first in the leafmould. I was so angry that once I made contact he stood no chance. I fell on his back, making sure I landed heavily. I pinioned his arms and clung on, commanding him to give up. He wrenched sideways, still thrashing. I pulled him up bodily and smashed him face down again. By then the horseman had dismounted and come rushing up. Next minute, my furious helper was booting Thurius in the ribs as if he meant to finish him.

'Steady!' I yelled, leaning out of the way of the flying boots. It stopped both of them. Thurius finally capsized with his face in the ruts of the track.

Still astride my captive, I started controlling my breathing. 'Nice action,' I gasped, looking up at the other man.

'Basic training,' he answered.

'Oh, you never lose it.' I managed to grin, though extra exertion was a trial. 'I don't suppose you would consider throwing up the governorship of Britain and entering into a formal partnership with me?'

Julius Frontinus – soldier, magistrate, administrator, author and future expert on the water supply – smiled modestly. A look of genuine yearning crossed his face. 'That might be one of history's great "What if?" questions, Falco.'

Then I accepted a hand up, while the ex-Consul held down our captive by planting one of his feet on the villain's neck.

That was fine. We felt like heroes. But we now had to try to find Claudia.

LXIII

THURIUS WAS REFUSING to talk. I had a feeling that he always would. Some want to boast; some go to their fate still denying everything. Thurius was plainly the silent type.

Unwilling to let him out of sight, I lashed his hands behind him with my belt before we threw him across the Consul's horse. I explained about finding the hut by the river. We took Thurius with us while we trekked back to it. This time I thought I knew what we were going to find.

To my surprise, as we approached the shack I saw the door was standing open. Outside, crouching on the ground, was Bolanus, with bruises all over him, shaking his head. Hearing our approach he staggered upright. I rushed to support him.

'In there —' He was swaying and woozy. 'I followed him — saw him take her in — I yelled: he ran out and set on me — then we heard you in the woods. I drove him off, but I was passing out. I could still hear you away in the woods. I got inside and collapsed against the door. I knew I just had to keep him out —'

'You were there all night? Dear gods, sit down —'

Bolanus only gestured despairingly towards the hut. Frontinus and I glanced at each other, then at the shack.

The three of us approached the battered doorway. Fresh air had not dispersed the musty smell. In the light of day the full horror of the place hit us: the dark floor, clearly stained with old congealed blood. The cleaver hung up on a nail: sharp, clean, its handle ebonised with age and use. The row of butcher's knives. The discoloured bucket. The sacks piled neatly, ready for the next gruesome adventure. The coiled ropes. And the latest victim.

When I saw the low bench where he had dumped her, a despairing cry strangled itself in my throat. Trussed up there lay a shape, human in size and form, covered with cloth and motionless. We had found her at last. I had to turn away.

Frontinus pushed past me and went in.

'I know her.' I was rooted to the spot. Bolanus gave me a horrified look, then touched my arm and followed the Consul.

They brought the body out. Gently they laid the woman on the
damp ground, turning her away from us to give them access to her
arms, which had been bound behind her back. Frontinus asked for a
knife, and I passed him mine. Careful and meticulous, he edged the
point under the cords and worked the blade up until the bindings
sheared through. He freed her arms, legs and body. I bestirred myself
and helped him as he turned her carefully on to her back and set
about removing the gag from around her face.

We lifted away part of the filthy cloth that covered her mouth.
Exposing her to the fresh breezes of the Sabine Hills, I forced myself
to look.

My stomach lurched. Harsh blonde locks, besmirched face paint
clogged on sagging skin, a trashily expensive necklace with thick
ropes of gold and monstrous gobbets of polished bloodstone – my
brain could hardly take it in. I realised this was not Claudia.

'She's alive!' exclaimed Frontinus, checking her haggard neck for
a pulse.

Then she opened her eyes and groaned. As she blinked in pain at
the daylight, I accepted the amazing truth: we had rescued Cornella
Flaccida.

It took us a long time to bring her round properly, but once she
could see us she looked set to harangue us and she wanted to be up
and flying at Thurius. He was fortunate that after her two-day ordeal
locked in the cisium she could only lie helpless, crying out in agony
while we tried to massage the blood back into her limbs. The cisium
was wide enough for her to have been stretched out straight, and the
ropes had not cut off her circulation completely, or she could never
have survived. As feeling returned she was racked with pain. It
would be a day or so before she could stand or walk. It seemed as if
nothing sexual had been done to her, but she had been expecting it.
That must have been terrible enough.

Before she really knew where she was, she was croaking angrily.
In view of what I had been afraid of finding, any noise from her was
welcome. And after being tied up for two days, bounced along for
forty miles in a dark confined space, dehydrated and starved, motion
sick and forced to soil herself, while all the time expecting the fate
of the women who had previously been dismembered by Thurius,
even Flaccida was entitled to be furious. She must have thought she

would never be missed, and if missed never traced: she was sharp enough to have noticed that Rubella had called off his surveillance. Her family had no idea where she had gone to live. Her beaten-up slaves could hardly be expected to report her disappearance; they would be glad to find themselves left in peace. Like so many others before her she would have vanished from Rome without trace. Once the narrowness of her escape hit home, she fell silent and subsided into deep shock.

Discovering Flaccida here did not solve the mystery of what had happened to Aelianus' betrothed, but it left some hope that young Claudia's fate that night might have been less dreadful.

'What now?' asked Frontinus. He had told me briefly how Aelianus had found him, dressed for action and with a fierce horse ready saddled at his house. He had sent Aelianus to sort out the warrant with the judge Marponius, while he himself, ever practical, hurtled after me on the Tiburtina road. 'The Urban Cohorts and my own staff should be here very soon. A conveyance can be found for the woman once she has had a chance to recover somewhat – but I'd like to get this bastard on his way to the judge in double quick time.'

It suited me. I wanted to go home.

As for Thurius, I had already thought up a way to take him back. A way that was secure for us, unpleasant for him, and highly appropriate. I took very great care not to kill him: I wrapped him in the most disgusting old cloths I could find, head and all. I tied him up just enough to make him suffer, but not enough to cut off his circulation and finish him. Then I locked him in the box of his master's cisium. Frontinus and I drove it back to Rome. We took two days to do it and throughout the journey we left Thurius incarcerated in the box.

LXIV

H OME.
  Helena Justina had not heard me come in. When the baby started crying and the dog started whining, she tried to rouse herself, lifting her head from her arms where she sat dismally at the table. I could tell her condition was desperate. She had been reading my poetry.

'Don't move,' I said. 'I've got Julia and Nux has got me.' The dog had attached herself to my leg, gripping my knee with both paws even while I crossed the room. It was presumably affectionate, though a burglar might have checked in his stride.

'Giving you the hero's welcome!'

I winced, as Julia really put her heart into it. Nux began to bound up and down in crazy circles all around me. 'This never happened to Odysseus.'

Then I was holding the pair of them, one arm round each, while they both cried all over my disgustingly filthy tunic. I should have washed first, but I had an urgent need to hold these two very tightly. 'I ought to get clean – but I wanted to come home first.' Now I was here, it would be hard to get out again. I was too tired in any case.

Helena murmured something incoherent and clung to me for a considerable period given just how badly I stank; then she leaned back a little, courteously disguising her relief at putting a space between herself and the stubbly dark-eyed wreck she was in love with.

For a long time she simply gazed at me. I could endure that.

'Some women think heroes are wonderful,' Helena mused. 'Rather a trial around the house, if you ask me. I find the worst thing is how often they go missing. You can never tell when you need to ask for their laundry back, or whether this would be the day to start buying their favourite fruit again.'

I smiled inanely at her, while peace crept over me like insidious wine. Nux, who had galloped from the room, now scrabbled back,

290

tail end first, towing her much-chewed basket as a welcome home gift.

In fairness to Helena, I had to tell her what had happened, in a brief form at least. Helena Justina spared me the effort of finding the words and worked it out for herself. 'You caught the killer. You had to fight him –' She was fingering a bruise on my cheekbone. A nerve flinched under her touch, but despite the pain I leaned against her hand. 'You're exhausted. Had he taken another woman?'

'Yes.'

'It wasn't Claudia.'

'I know. So has Claudia turned up?'

'No, but someone is here who knows what happened to her.'

'Your brother?'

'No, Aulus went home in disgust. Gaius!'

Some moments after she called him, my rascallion nephew shuffled in looking strangely shy. For once he was cleaner than me. In fact he looked as if Helena must have kept him here, feeding him up and encouraging unfamiliar habits of hygiene, for most of the time I had been away.

She spoke to him quietly. 'Tell Uncle Marcus everything you said to me and my brother Aelianus about that night at the Circus Maximus.'

Gaius appeared to think he was in for a clouting. Helena had taken the baby, so I lolled limply, letting him see that nothing on earth would drag me from my stool. Nux was sprawled all over my feet, for one thing.

'Helena's brother –'

'Aelianus?'

'No, the other one.'

'Justinus? He's abroad.'

'He is now,' cried Helena, with unusual force.

Gaius braced himself and rushed through his tale. 'Justinus drove up in a little cart when I was there helping you. I saw a girl run out from the Circus. He seemed to be expecting her. They had a chat, then he gave her a big kiss, lifted her into the cart, and whizzed off.'

'Was the girl –'

'Claudia Rufina,' confirmed Helena. 'The bad boy! Quintus has eloped with his brother's wealthy bride. And you know what, Marcus –'

I could guess: 'Your noble family all blame me?'

I was too tired even to laugh.

Gaius complained that we were squashing the baby, so he carefully took charge and carried her off to play with her in another room. Responding to his gruff authority, Julia stopped crying immediately.

I sat for a moment, staring round the simple apartment that I called home. It looked unusually clean and neat. On the table, as well as the battered scroll of my over-written odes which Helena had been reading to console herself, lay my favourite cup and bowl, set very precisely opposite my habitual stool as if their readiness would ensure my return. Near them was a document which I could see was the deed of sale for the farm at Tibur which I had promised to buy; she had been organising the purchase. Flipping off the top of the inkwell I seized the pen, dipped it quickly and scrawled my signature.

'You haven't read that,' Helena remonstrated quietly.

'No, but you have.'

'Falco, you trust people too easily.'

'Is that right?'

'I'll make you read it tomorrow.'

'That's why I trust you,' I smiled.

Another disaster was about to make itself manifest. Helena went across to the laundry for a pail of water so I could wash before I fell into bed. She must have spoken to Petronius. When he galloped across to see me he already knew I had solved the case, and had come home in glory with Thurius. This was going to be difficult.

'Well, where were you when you were needed?' I chaffed him, tackling the issue before he could take the initiative.

'Trailing through half the low winebars in the Suburra while a useless fool called Damon tried unsuccessfully to pull a sharp bird in a red dress who ran bloody rings around him. She kept him out drinking till all hours, then when Damon went for his tenth leak of the night, she skipped. Then I had to follow the besotted idiot while he went back to all the bars they had visited earlier, trying to find where he had dropped his purse – though of course, really the girl had made off with it –'

'Useless.' I was in no mood for elaborate inquests.

Petro gave me a long stare.

I knew what this was. I held up my hand wearily. 'Lucius Petronius, you have something you are burning to tell me.'

'When you're fit.'

'I'm fit now. Your life needs a new turn. You are itching for your real job – lured no doubt by the thrill of dull routine and time-consuming reports for superiors, the complaining hatred of the public and the pitiful, though regular, salary –'

'Something like that.'

'There's more? Oh, I think I can guess. You are planning a joyful return to your wife.' If I had been less tired, I would have been more careful. 'Now steady, old friend.'

'You've been nagging me to do it, so I'm telling you first.'

'I deduce you haven't told Silvia?'

'Not yet, no.'

'So I'm supposed to be honoured – Have you even seen Silvia recently?'

A suspicious expression appeared on his face. 'You're telling me something.'

I should have lied. In fact I should never have started this. He was my friend, and I knew just how short his temper could be. But I was too exhausted to be subtle or careful. 'I did hear that Arria Silvia had been seen out with another man.'

Petronius Longus said nothing immediately.

'Forget it,' I mumbled.

His voice was low: his temper high. 'Who told you this?'

'Maia. It's probably gossip –'

'How long have you known about this, Falco?'

'No time –'

He was on his feet.

I had been friends with Petronius Longus for many years. We had shared tragedy, wine, and bad behaviour in almost equal measure. He knew things about me nobody else was ever likely to discover, and I realised exactly what he wanted to say. 'Petro, you helped me with my stinking work, you endured my slapdash methods and my lousy old apartment, you put up with being criticised over breakfast, and now you've watched me collar Thurius and take the credit for the job. To cap all that I've just told you your wife's slumming, at the very moment when you humbled your pride and decided you were going back to her. Well, there you are: you want to end our partnership, and I've just handed you an excuse for a major quarrel.'

I was too tired to find the energy to argue. Petro gazed at me for a moment, then I heard him breathe in and out quietly. Half a smile creased his face, though he said nothing.

He walked out of our apartment at his normal steady pace, and I heard him thump down the outer steps with scornful finality.

★

After a moment there were sounds of Helena returning. The pail crashed against the outdoor banister as it always did when she lugged it home full, and she muttered to herself. Then her voice called out sharply as if warning a visitor not to come up, apparently without effect, because feet pattered eagerly up our steps and a head I knew thrust itself round the door. Slick hair, pale eyes, and an insufferable sympathetic air. The familiar unwelcome body followed. It was my old antagonist: Anacrites.

He wore a neutral-coloured tunic with faintly rakish styling, close-fitting boots, and a hard leather belt. Hung on the belt were a small purse, a large note tablet, and a set of nail files to keep him occupied if he ever needed to lean against an Ionic column for hours observing a suspect. Somebody must have been giving him lessons. He had the classic informer's look: tough, slightly truculent, perhaps amiable if you got to know him, a curious and faintly unreliable sort of character.

'Welcome home, and congratulations! I hear that Petronius Longus is unwinding your partnership?' I covered my eyes and shuddered quietly. I was so exhausted I was helpless, and Anacrites could see that. He did the dirty work very gently, like a tooth-puller assuring you it's not going to hurt just at the moment when he makes you scream. 'Mother was right, Falco. Aren't you glad there's someone else available? It looks as if it's you and me now after all!'